# Rex Stout

REX STOUT, the creator of Nero Wolfe, was born in Noblesville, Indiana, in 1886, the sixth of nine children of John and Lucetta Todhunter Stout, both Quakers. Shortly after his birth, the family moved to Wakarusa, Kansas. He was educated in a country school, but by the age of nine he was recognized throughout the state as a prodigy in arithmetic. Mr. Stout briefly attended the University of Kansas, but left to enlist in the Navy, and spent the next two years as a warrant officer on board President Theodore Roosevelt's yacht. When he left the Navy in 1908, Rex Stout began to write free-lance articles and worked as a sightseeing guide and as an itinerant bookkeeper. Later he devised and implemented a school banking system which was installed in four hundred cities and towns throughout the country. In 1927 Mr. Stout retired from the world of finance and, with the proceeds of his banking scheme, left for Paris to write serious fiction. He wrote three novels that received favorable reviews before turning to detective fiction. His first Nero Wolfe novel, *Fer-de-Lance*, appeared in 1934. It was followed by many others, among them *Too Many Cooks, The Silent Speaker, If Death Ever Slept, The Doorbell Rang* and *Please Pass the Guilt*, which established Nero Wolfe as a leading character on a par with Erle Stanley Gardner's famous protagonist, Perry Mason. During World War II, Rex Stout waged a personal campaign against Nazism as chairman of the War Writers' Board, master of ceremonies of the radio program "Speaking of Liberty," a member of several national committees. After the war he turned his attention to mobilizing public opinion against the wartime use of thermonuclear devices, was an active leader in the Authors' Guild, and resumed writing his Nero Wolfe novels. Rex Stout died in 1975 at the age of eighty-eight. A month before his death, he published his seventy-second Nero Wolfe mystery, *A Family Affair*. Ten years later, a seventy-third Nero Wolfe mystery was discovered and published in *Death Times Three*.

W9-DGU-102

# The Rex Stout Library

# REX STOUT

# The League of Frightened Men

*Introduction
by Robert Goldsborough*

**BANTAM BOOKS**
NEW YORK · TORONTO · LONDON · SYDNEY · AUCKLAND

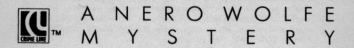

A NERO WOLFE
MYSTERY

*This edition contains the complete text
of the original hardcover edition.*
NOT ONE WORD HAS BEEN OMITTED.

THE LEAGUE OF FRIGHTENED MEN

*A Bantam Crime Line Book / published by arrangement with
the estate of the author*

*PRINTING HISTORY*
*Farrar & Rinehart edition published 1935*
*Bantam edition / August 1982*
*Bantam reissue / February 1992*

CRIME LINE *and the portrayal of a boxed "cl" are trademarks of
Bantam Books, a division of Bantam Doubleday Dell Publishing
Group, Inc.*

*All rights reserved.*
*Copyright 1935 by Rex Stout.*
*Copyright renewed © 1963 by Rex Stout.*
*Introduction copyright © 1992 by Robert Goldsborough.*
*Cover art copyright © 1992 by Tom Hallman.*
*No part of this book may be reproduced or transmitted in any
form or by any means, electronic or mechanical, including
photocopying, recording, or by any information storage and
retrieval system, without permission in writing from
the publisher.*
*For information address: Bantam Books.*

*If you purchased this book without a cover you should be
aware that this book is stolen property. It was reported as
"unsold and destroyed" to the publisher and neither the author
nor the publisher has received any payment for this "stripped
book."*

ISBN 0-553-25933-4

*Published simultaneously in the United States and Canada*

Bantam Books are published by Bantam Books, a division of
Bantam Doubleday Dell Publishing Group, Inc. Its trademark,
consisting of the words "Bantam Books" and the portrayal of a
rooster, is Registered in U.S. Patent and Trademark Office and
in other countries. Marca Registrada. Bantam Books, 666 Fifth
Avenue, New York, New York 10103.

PRINTED IN THE UNITED STATES OF AMERICA

OPM     0 9 8 7 6 5 4 3 2

# Introduction

The League of Frightened Men, published both by the *Saturday Evening Post* (in serialization) and by Farrar & Rinehart in 1935, was Rex Stout's second Nero Wolfe novel, appearing the year after *Fer-de-Lance*. It ranks as a personal favorite, for several reasons.

First, the story's pivotal figure, the quirky, brilliant, and depraved Paul Chapin, supplies Wolfe with his most complex adversary, a far more intriguing character, for instance, than the megalomaniacal underworld kingpin Arnold Zeck, who makes his appearance several books deeper into the series.

Chapin, author of "obscene" novels probing the dark side of the human spirit, was badly crippled as the result of a college hazing incident at Harvard. Chagrined classmates formed a "League of Atonement," which paid his hospital bills and through the years tried in other, less tangible ways to make amends. Although accepting the group's money and sympathy, Chapin remained bitter, sardonically reacting to their efforts.

Now, at a class reunion, one member of the league falls to his death from a seaside cliff, and the others receive copies of a poem apparently authored by Chapin in which he claims credit for the act. Then another of the group dies violently, followed by another poem suggesting that more deaths will occur. And when a third member of the league disappears, Nero Wolfe is hired by remaining members to "stop Chapin."

Although famed clinician Karl Menninger praised the Wolfe stories because the detective "never dives into the realm of psychiatry" or "pretends to believe that murderers are mostly sick," John McAleer wrote in his biography of Stout that in the early Wolfe stories, the author "still was close to his own interlude as a psychological novelist." McAleer went on to suggest that "possibly such characterizations [as Paul Chapin] were intended to counterpoint Rex's unannounced probing of his own psyche." Whatever Stout's motivation, Chapin remains the most interesting psychological study in the series, and one whom Wolfe comes to know primarily through reading his novels.

In addition to the compelling characterization of Chapin, the book is a treasure trove for lovers of the corpus. In no other volume, for instance, do we find such a rich variety of Wolfean aphorisms:

—"It takes a fillip on the flank for my mare to dance."
—"To assert dignity is to lose it."
—"All genius is distorted. Including my own."
—"To be broke is not a disgrace, it is only a catastrophe."
—"If you eat the apple before it's ripe, your only reward is a bellyache."
—"I love to make a mistake, it is the only assur-

ance that I cannot reasonably be expected to
assume the burden of omniscience."
—"I have all the simplicities, including that of
brusqueness."

The Archie Goodwin in this book, as in other early
Stout works, is markedly more rough edged and
unsophisticated than the smoother version who
evolved in the postwar years. His grammar is defi-
cient (". . . the obscenity don't matter" and "Where's
the other club members?"), but that is as integral to
his street-smart persona as his colorful phrasing. For
example, he complains of inactivity to Wolfe: "If you
keep a keg of dynamite around the house you've got to
expect some noise sooner or later. That's what I am, a
keg of dynamite." Or his threat to a would-be tough
guy: "Don't try to scare me with your bad manners. I
might decide to remove your right ear and put it
where the left one is, and hang the left one on your
belt for a spare."

Inspector Cramer shows an uncharacteristically
self-effacing side in *League*, when he tells Archie that
"I arrested a man once and he turned out to be guilty,
that's why I was made an inspector." And in what
other Wolfe book does the cigar-chomping Cramer
actually *light* one of his stogies? And smoke a pipe,
too? You can look it up.

Cramer's match-lighting moments are only two of
several singular occurrences in *League*. A sampling of
others:

—The "client" is actually a committee, the members of which Wolfe assesses varying rates,
depending on their financial condition.

—Wolfe is "kidnapped" from the brownstone in a car driven by a *woman*.

—Archie gets drugged and Wolfe is forced to rescue him.

—Wolfe claims he once was married.

—Name brands, which Rex Stout normally avoided in his writing, are extolled by Archie, specifically Underwood typewriters and the Cadillac in which Cramer is chauffeured.

Back to the psychopathic genius Paul Chapin, who makes Archie nervous ("for once Wolfe might be underrating a guy") and Wolfe cautious ("He is possessed of a demon, but he is also, within certain limits, an extraordinarily astute man"). Chapin refers to one of Wolfe's ploys as "vulgar and obvious cunning," and later he tells the detective that he, Wolfe, will be a character in an upcoming Chapin novel. "You will die, sir, in the most abhorrent manner conceivable to an appalling infantile imagination. I promise you."

We are never to learn whether Paul Chapin indeed dispatched the detective in print, but the suggestion was enough for Archie to "permit myself a grin at the thought of the awful fate in store for Nero Wolfe."

# —Robert Goldsborough

# The League
## of Frightened Men

# Chapter 1

Wolfe and I sat in the office Friday afternoon. As it turned out, the name of Paul Chapin, and his slick and thrifty notions about getting vengeance at wholesale without paying for it, would have come to our notice pretty soon in any event; but that Friday afternoon the combination of an early November rain and a lack of profitable business that had lasted so long it was beginning to be painful, brought us an opening scene—a prologue, not a part of the main action—of the show that was about ready to begin.

Wolfe was drinking beer and looking at pictures of snowflakes in a book someone had sent him from Czechoslovakia. I was reading the morning paper, off and on. I had read it at breakfast, and glanced through it again for half an hour after checking accounts with Hortsmann at eleven o'clock, and here I was with it once more in the middle of the rainy afternoon, thinking halfheartedly to find an item or two that would tickle the brain which seemed about ready to dry up on me. I do read books, but I never yet got any real satisfaction out of one; I always have a feeling there's nothing alive about it, it's all dead and gone, what's the use, you might as well try to enjoy yourself on a picnic in a graveyard. Wolfe asked me once why the devil I ever pretended to read a book, and I told him for cultural reasons, and he said I might as well forgo the pains, that culture was like money, it comes easiest to those who need it least. Anyway, since it was a morning paper and this was the middle of the afternoon, and I had already gone through it twice, it wasn't much better than a book and I was only hanging onto it as an excuse to keep my eyes open.

Wolfe seemed absorbed in the pictures. Looking at him, I said to myself, "He's in a battle with the elements. He's fighting his way through a raging blizzard, just sitting there comfortably looking at pictures of snowflakes. That's the advantage of being an artist, of having imagination." I said aloud, "You mustn't go to sleep, sir, it's fatal. You freeze to death."

Wolfe turned a page, paying no attention to me. I said, "The shipment from Caracas, from Richardt, was twelve bulbs short. I never knew him to make good a shortage."

Still no result. I said, "Fritz tells me that the turkey they sent is too old to broil and will be tough unless it is roasted two hours, which according to you will attenuate the flavor. So the turkey at forty-one cents a pound will be a mess."

Wolfe turned another page. I stared at him a while and then said, "Did you see the piece in the paper about the woman who has a pet monkey which sleeps at the head of her bed and wraps its tail around her wrist? And keeps it there all night? Did you see the one about the man who found a necklace on the street and returned it to its owner and she claimed he stole two pearls from it and had him arrested? Did you see the one about the man on the witness-stand in a case about an obscene book, and the lawyer asked him what was his purpose in writing the book, and he said because he had committed a murder and all murderers had to talk about their crimes and that was his way of talking about it? Not that I get the idea, about the author's purpose. If a book's dirty it's dirty, and what's the difference how it got that way? The lawyer says if the author's purpose was a worthy literary purpose the obscenity don't matter. You might as well say that if my purpose is to throw a rock at a tin can it don't matter if I hit you in the eye with it. You might as well say that if my purpose is to buy my poor old grandmother a silk dress it don't matter if I grabbed the jack from a Salvation Army kettle. You might as well say—"

I stopped. I had him. He did not lift his eyes from the page, his head did not move, there was no stirring of his massive frame in the specially constructed enormous chair behind his desk; but I saw his right forefinger wiggle faintly—his minatory wand, as he once called it—and I knew I had him. He said:

"Archie. Shut up."

I grinned. "Not a chance, sir. Great God, am I just going to sit here until I die? Shall I phone Pinkertons and ask if they want a hotel room watched or something? If you keep a keg of dynamite around the house you've got to expect some noise sooner or later. That's what I am, a keg of dynamite. Shall I go to a movie?"

Wolfe's huge head tipped forward a sixteenth of an inch, for him an emphatic nod. "By all means: At once."

I got up from my chair, tossed the newspaper halfway across the room to my desk, turned around, and sat down again. "What was wrong with my analogies?" I demanded.

Wolfe turned another page. "Let us say," he murmured patiently, "that as an analogist you are supreme. Let us say that."

"All right. Say we do. I'm not trying to pick a quarrel, sir. Hell no. I'm just breaking under the strain of trying to figure out a third way of crossing my legs. I've been at it over a week now." It flashed into my mind that Wolfe could never be annoyed by that problem, since his legs were so fat that there was no possibility of them ever getting crossed by any tactics whatever, but I decided not to mention that. I swerved. "I stick to it, if a book's dirty it's dirty, no matter if the author had a string of purposes as long as a rainy day. That guy on the witness-stand yesterday was a nut. Wasn't he? You tell me. Or else he wanted some big headlines no matter what it cost him. It cost him fifty berries for contempt of court. At that it was cheap advertising for his book; for half a century he could buy about four inches on the literary page of the *Times*, and that's not even a chirp. But I guess the guy was a nut. He said he had done a murder, and all murderers have to confess, so he wrote the book, changing the characters and circumstances, as a means of confessing without putting himself in jeopardy. The judge was witty and sarcastic. He said that even if the guy was an inventor of stories and was in a court, he needn't try for the job of court jester. I'll bet the lawyers had a good hearty laugh at that one. Huh? But the author said it was no joke, that was why he wrote the book and any obscenity in it was only incidental, he really had croaked a guy. So the judge soaked him fifty bucks for contempt of court and chased him off the stand. I guess he's a nut? You tell me."

Wolfe's great chest went up and out in a sigh; he

put a marker in the book and closed it and laid it on the desk, and leaned himself back, gently ponderous, in his chair.

He blinked twice. "Well?"

I went across to my desk and got the paper and opened it out to the page. "Nothing maybe. I guess he's a nut. His name is Paul Chapin and he's written several books. The title of this one is *Devil Take the Hindmost*. He graduated from Harvard in 1912. He's a lop; it mentions here about his getting up to the stand with his crippled leg but it doesn't say which one."

Wolfe compressed his lips. "Is it possible," he demanded, "that lop is an abbreviation of lopsided, and that you use it as a metaphor for cripple?"

"I wouldn't know about the metaphor, but lop means cripple in my circle."

Wolfe sighed again, and set about the process of rising from his chair. "Thank God," he said, "the hour saves me from further analogies and colloquialisms." The clock on the wall said one minute till four—time for him to go up to the plant-rooms. He made it to his feet, pulled the points of his vest down but failed as usual to cover with it the fold of bright yellow shirt that had puffed out, and moved across to the door.

At the threshold he paused. "Archie."

"Yes, sir."

"Phone Murger's to send over at once a copy of *Devil Take the Hindmost*, by Paul Chapin."

"Maybe they won't. It's suppressed pending the court decision."

"Nonsense. Speak to Murger or Ballard. What good is an obscenity trial except to popularize literature?"

He went on towards the elevator, and I sat down at my desk and reached for the telephone.

# Chapter 2

After breakfast the next morning, Saturday, I fooled with the plant records a while and then went to the kitchen to annoy Fritz.

Wolfe, of course, wouldn't be down until eleven o'clock. The roof of the old brownstone house on West Thirty-fifth Street where he had lived for twenty years, and me with him for the last seven of them, was glassed in and partitioned into rooms where varying conditions of temperature and humidity were maintained—by the vigilance of Theodore Horstmann—for the ten thousand orchids that lined the benches and shelves. Wolfe had once remarked to me that the orchids were his concubines; insipid, expensive, parasitic and temperamental. He brought them, in their diverse forms and colors, to the limits of their perfection, and then gave them away; he had never sold one. His patience and ingenuity, supported by Horstmann's fidelity, had produced remarkable results and gained for the roof a reputation in quite different circles from those whose interest centered in the downstairs office. In all weathers and under any circumstances whatever, his four hours a day on the roof with Horstmann—from nine to eleven in the morning and from four to six in the afternoon—were inviolable.

This Saturday morning I finally had to admit that Fritz's good humor was too much for me. By eleven o'clock I was back in the office trying to pretend there might be something to do if I looked for it, but I'm not much good at pretending. I was thinking, ladies and gentlemen, my friends and customers, I won't hold out for a real case with worry and action and profit in it, just give us any old kind of a break. I'll even tail a chorus-girl for you, or hide in the bathroom for the guy that's stealing the toothpaste, anything this side of industrial espionage. Anything . . .

Wolfe came in and said good morning. The mail didn't take long. He signed a couple of checks I had made out for bills he had gone over the day before, and asked me with a sigh what the bank balance was, and gave me a few short letters. I tapped them off and went out with them to the mailbox. When I got back Wolfe was starting on a second bottle of beer, leaning back in his chair, and I thought I saw a look in his half-closed eyes. At least, I thought, he's not back on the pretty snowflakes again. I sat at my desk and let the typewriter down.

Wolfe said, "Archie. One would know everything in the world there is to know, if one waited long enough. The one fault in the passivity of Buddha as a technique for the acquisition of knowledge and wisdom is the miserably brief span of human life. He sat through the first stanza of the first canto of the *preamble*, and then left for an appointment with . . . let us say, with a certain chemist."

"Yes, sir. You mean, we just go on sitting here and we learn a lot."

"Not a lot. But more, a little more each century."

"You maybe. Not me. If I sit here about two more days I'll be so damn goofy I won't know anything."

Wolfe's eyes flickered faintly. "I would not care to seem mystic, but might not that, in your case, mean an increase?"

"Sure." I grunted. "If you had not once instructed me never again to tell you to go to hell, I would tell you to go to hell."

"Good." Wolfe gulped beer and wiped his lips. "You are offended. So, probably, awake. My opening remark was in the nature of a comment on a recent fact. You will remember that last month you were away for ten days on a mission that proved to be highly unremunerative, and that during your absence two young men were here to perform your duties."

I nodded. I grinned. One of the men had been from the Metropolitan Agency as Wolfe's bodyguard, and the other had been a stenographer from Miller's. "Sure. Two could handle it on a sprint."

"Just so. On one of those days a man came here and asked me to intercept his destiny. He didn't put it that way, but that was the substance of it. It proved not feasible to accept his commission . . . "

I had opened a drawer of my desk and taken out a loose-leaf binder, and I flipped through the sheets in it to the page I wanted. "Yes, sir. I've got it. I've read it twice. It's a bit spotty, the stenographer from Miller's wasn't so hot. He couldn't spell—"

"The name was Hibbard."

I nodded, glancing over the typewritten pages. "Andrew Hibbard. Instructor in psychology at Columbia. It was on October twentieth, a Saturday, that's two weeks ago today."

"Suppose you read it."

"*Viva voce?*"

"Archie." Wolfe looked at me. "Where did you pick

that up, where did you learn to pronounce it, and what
do you think it means?"

"Do you want me to read this stuff out loud, sir?"

"It doesn't mean out loud. Confound you." Wolfe
emptied his glass, leaned back in his chair, got his
fingers to meet in front of his belly and laced them.
"Proceed."

"Okay. First there's a description of Mr. Hibbard.
*Small gentleman, around fifty, pointed nose, dark
eyes—*"

"Enough. For that I can plunder my memory."

"Yes, sir. Mr. Hibbard seems to have started out
by saying, *How do you do, sir, my name is—*"

"Pass the amenities."

I glanced down the page. "How will this do? *Mr.
Hibbard said, I was advised to come to you by a friend
whose name need not be mentioned, but the motivat-
ing force was plain funk. I was driven here by fear.*"

Wolfe nodded. I read from the typewritten sheets:

Mr. Wolfe: *Yes. Tell me about it.*

Mr. Hibbard: *My card has told you, I am in the
psychology department at Columbia. Since you are
an expert, you probably observe on my face and in my
bearing the stigmata of fright bordering on panic.*

Mr. Wolfe: *I observe that you are upset. I have no
means of knowing whether it is chronic or acute.*

Mr. Hibbard: *It is chronic. At least it is becoming
so. That is why I have resorted to . . . to you. I am
under an intolerable strain. My life is in danger . . .
no, not that, worse than that, my life has been forfeited.
I admit it.*

Mr. Wolfe: *Of course. Mine too, sir. All of us.*

Mr. Hibbard: *Rubbish. Excuse me. I am not
discussing original sin. Mr. Wolfe, I am going to be
killed. A man is going to kill me.*

Mr. Wolfe: *Indeed. When? How?*

Wolfe put in, "Archie. You may delete the Misters."

"Okay. This Miller boy was brought up right, he didn't miss one. Somebody told him, always regard your employer with respect forty-four hours a week, more or less, as the case may be. Well. Next we have:

Hibbard: *That I can't tell you, since I don't know. There are things about this I do know, also, which I must keep to myself. I can tell you . . . well . . . many years ago I inflicted an injury, a lasting injury, on a man. I was not alone, there were others in it, but chance made me chiefly responsible. At least I have so regarded it. It was a boyish prank . . . with a tragic outcome. I have never forgiven myself. Neither have the others who were concerned in it, at least most of them haven't. Not that I have ever been morbid about it—it was twenty-five years ago—I am a psychologist and therefore too involved in the morbidities of others to have room for any of my own. Well, we injured that boy. We ruined him. In effect. Certainly we felt the responsibility, and all through these twenty-five years some of us have had the idea of making up for it. We have acted on the idea—sometimes. You know how it is; we are busy men, most of us. But we have never denied the burden, and now and then some of us have tried to carry it. That was difficult, for pawn—that is, as the boy advanced into manhood he became increasingly peculiar. I learned that in the lower schools he had given evidence of talent, and certainly in college—that is to say, of my own knowledge, after the injury, he possessed brilliance. Later the brilliance perhaps remained, but became distorted. At a certain point—*

Wolfe interrupted me. "A moment. Go back a few

sentences. Beginning *that was difficult, for pawn*—
did you saw *pawn*?"

I found it. "That's it. *Pawn*. I don't get it."

"Neither did the stenographer. Proceed."

*At a certain point, some five years ago, I decided
definitely he was psychopathic.*

Wolfe: *You continued to know him then?*

Hibbard: *Oh yes. Many of us did. Some of us saw
him frequently; one or two associated with him
closely. Around that time his latent brilliance seemed
to find itself in maturity. He . . . well . . . he did
things which aroused admiration and interest. Convinced as I was that he was psychopathic, I nevertheless felt less concern for him than I had for a long
time, for he appeared to be genuinely involved in
satisfactory—at least compensatory—achievement.
The awakening came in a startling manner. There
was a reunion—a gathering—of a group of us, and one
of us was killed—died—obviously, we unanimously
thought, by an accident. But he—that is, the man we had
injured—was there; and a few days later each of us
received through the mail a communication from him
saying that he had killed one of us and that the rest
would follow; that he had embarked on a ship of vengeance.*

Wolfe: *Indeed. Psychopathic must have begun to
seem almost an euphemism.*

Hibbard: *Yes. But there was nothing we could do.*

Wolfe: *Since you were equipped with evidence, it
might not have proven hazardous to inform the police.*

Hibbard: *We had no evidence.*

Wolfe: *The communication?*

Hibbard: *They were typewritten, unsigned, and
were expressed in ambiguous terms which rendered
them worthless for practical purposes such as evi-*

*dence. He had even disguised his style, very cleverly; it was not his style at all. But it was plain enough to us. Each of us got one; not only those who had been present at the gathering, but all of us, all members of the league. Of* course—

Wolfe: *The league?*

Hibbard: *That was a slip. It doesn't matter. Many years ago, when a few of us were together discussing this, one—maudlin, of course—suggested that we should call ourselves the League of Atonement. The phrase hung on, in a way. Latterly it was never heard except in jest. Now I fancy the jokes are ended. I was going to say, of course all of us do not live in New York, only about half. One got his warning, just the same, in San Francisco. In New York a few of us got together and discussed it. We made a sort of an investigation, and we saw—him, and had a talk with him. He denied sending the warnings. He seemed amused, in his dark soul, and unconcerned.*

Wolfe: *Dark soul is an odd phrase for a psychologist?*

Hibbard: *I read poetry week-ends.*

Wolfe: *Just so. And?*

Hibbard: *Nothing happened for some time. Three months. Then another of us was killed. Found dead. The police said suicide, and it seemed that all indications pointed in that direction. But two days later a second warning was mailed to each of us, with the same purport and obviously from the same source. It was worded with great cleverness, with brilliance.*

Wolfe: *This time, naturally, you went to the police.*

Hibbard: *Why naturally? We were still without evidence.*

Wolfe: *Only that you would. One or some of you would.*

Hibbard: *They did. I was against it, but they did go—*

Wolfe: *Why were you against it?*

Hibbard: *I felt it was useless. Also . . . well . . . I could not bring myself to join in a demand for retribution, his life perhaps, from the man we had injured . . . you understand . . .*

Wolfe: *Quite. First, the police could find no proof. Second, they might.*

Hibbard: *Very well. I was not engaged in an essay on logic. A man may debar nonsense from his library of reason, but not from the arena of his impulses.*

Wolfe: *Good. Neat. And the police?*

Hibbard: *They got nowhere. He made total asses of them. He described to me their questioning and his replies—*

Wolfe: *You still saw him?*

Hibbard: *Of course. We were friends. Oh yes. The police went into it, questioned him, questioned all of us, investigated all they could, and came out empty-handed. Some of them, some of the group, got private detectives. That was two weeks, twelve days ago. The detectives are having the same success as the police. I'm sure of it.*

Wolfe: *Indeed. What agency?*

Hibbard: *That is irrelevant. The point is that something happened. I could speak of apprehensions and precautions and so forth, I know plenty of words of that nature, I could even frame the situation in technical psychological terms, but the plain fact is that I'm too scared to go on. I want you to save me from death. I want to hire you to protect my life.*

Wolfe: *Yes. What happened?*

Hibbard: *Nothing. Nothing of any significance except to me. He came to me and said something, that's all. It would be of no advantage to repeat it. My shameful admission is that I am at length completely frightened. I'm afraid to go to bed and I'm afraid to get up. I'm afraid to eat. I want whatever measure of security you can sell me. I am accustomed to the arrangement of words, and the necessity of talking intelligently to you has enforced a semblance of order and urbanity in a section of my brain, but around and beneath that order there is a veritable panic. After all my exploration, scientific and pseudo-scientific, of that extraordinary phenomenon, the human psyche, devil-possessed and heaven-soaring, I am all reduced to this single simple primitive concern: I am terribly afraid of being killed. The friend who suggested my coming here said that you possess a remarkable combination of talents and that you have only one weakness. She did not call it cupidity; I forget her phrasing. I am not a millionaire, but I have ample private means besides my salary, and I am in no state of mind for haggling.*

Wolfe: *I always need money. That is of course my affair. I will undertake to disembark this gentleman from his ship of vengeance, in advance of any injury to you, for the sum of ten thousand dollars.*

Hibbard: *Disembark him? You can't. You don't know him.*

Wolfe: *Nor does he know me. A meeting can be arranged.*

Hibbard: *I didn't mean—hah. It would take more than a meeting. It would take more, I think, than all your talents. But that is beside the point. I have failed to make myself clear. I would not pay ten thousand dollars, or any other sum, for you to bring this man to—justice? Ha! Call it justice. A word that reeks with maggots. Anyhow, I would not be a party to that, even*

*in the face of death. I have not told you his name. I
shall not. Already perhaps I have disclosed too much.
I wish your services as a safeguard for myself, not as
an agency for his destruction.*

Wolfe: *If the one demands the other?*

Hibbard: *I hope not. I pray not . . . could I
pray? No. Prayer has been washed from my strain of
blood. Certainly I would not expect you to give me a
warrant of security. But your experience and
ingenuity—I am sure they would be worth whatever
you might ask—*

Wolfe: *Nonsense. My ingenuity would be worth
less than nothing, Mr. Hibbard. Do I understand that
you wish to engage me to protect your life against the
unfriendly designs of this man without taking any
steps whatever to expose and restrain him?*

Hibbard: *Yes, sir. Precisely. And I have been told
that once your talents are committed to an enterprise,
any attempt to circumvent you will be futile.*

Wolfe: *I have no talents. I have genius or nothing.
In this case, nothing. No, Mr. Hibbard; and I do need
money. What you need, should you persist in your
quixotism, is first, if you have dependents, generous
life insurance; and second, a patient acceptance of the
fact that your death is only a matter of time. That of
course is true of all of us; we all share that disease
with you, only yours seems to have reached a rather
acute stage. My advice would be, waste neither time
nor money on efforts at precaution. If he has decided
to kill you, and if he possesses ordinary intelligence—
let alone the brilliance you grant him—you will die.
There are so many methods available for killing a
fellow-being! Many more than there are for most of
our usual activities, like pruning a tree or threshing
wheat or making a bed or swimming. I have been often*

*impressed, in my experience, by the ease and lack of
bother with which the average murder is executed.
Consider: with the quarry within reach, the purpose
fixed, and the weapon in hand, it will often require up
to eight or ten minutes to kill a fly, whereas the
average murder, I would guess, consumes ten or
fifteen seconds at the outside. In cases of slow poison
and similar ingenuities death of course is lingering,
but the act of murder itself is commonly quite brief.
Consider again: there are certainly not more than two
or three methods of killing a pig, but there are
hundreds of ways to kill a man. If your friend is half
as brilliant as you think him, and doesn't get in a rut
as the ordinary criminal does, he may be expected to
evolve a varied and interesting repertory before your
league is half disposed of. He may even invent something new. One more point: it seems to me there is a
fair chance for you. You may not, after all, be the
next, or even the next or the next; and it is quite
possible that somewhere along the line he may mis-
calculate or run into bad luck; or one of your league
members, less quixotic than you, may engage my
services. That would save* you.

I took my eyes from the sheet to look at Wolfe.
"Pretty good, sir. Pretty nice. I'm surprised it didn't
get him, he must have been tough. Maybe you didn't
go far enough. You only mentioned poison really, you
could have brought in strangling and bleeding and
crushed skulls and convulsions—"

"Proceed."

Hibbard: *I will pay you five hundred dollars a
week.*

Wolfe: *I am sorry. To now my casuistry has
managed a satisfactory persuasion that the money I*

*have put in my bank has been earned. I dare not put this strain upon it.*

Hibbard: *But . . . you wouldn't refuse. You can't refuse a thing like this. My God. You are my only hope. I didn't realize it, but you are.*

Wolfe: *I do refuse. I can undertake to render this man harmless, to remove the threat—*

Hibbard: *No. No!*

Wolfe: *Very well. One little suggestion: if you take out substantial life insurance, which would be innocent of fraud from the legal standpoint, you should if possible manage so that when the event comes it cannot plausibly be given the appearance of suicide; and since you will not be aware of the event much beforehand you will have to keep your wit sharpened. That is merely a practical suggestion, that the insurance may not be voided, to the loss of your beneficiary.*

Hibbard: *But . . . Mr. Wolfe . . . look here . . . you can't do this. I came here . . . I tell you it isn't reasonable—*

Wolfe stopped me. "That will do, Archie."

I looked up. "There's only a little more."

"I know. I find it painful. I refused that five hundred dollars—thousands perhaps—once; I maintained my position; your reading it causes me useless discomfort. Do not finish it. There is nothing further except Mr. Hibbard's confused protestations and my admirable steadfastness."

"Yes, sir. I've read it." I glanced over the remaining lines. "I'm surprised you let him go. After all—"

Wolfe reached to the desk to ring for Fritz, shifted a little in his chair, and settled back again. "To tell you the truth, Archie, I entertained a notion."

"Yeah. I thought so."

"But nothing came of it. As you know, it takes a

fillip on the flank for my mare to dance, and the fillip was not forthcoming. You were away at the time, and since your return the incident has not been discussed. It is odd that you should have innocently been the cause, by mere chance, of its revival."

"I don't get you."

Fritz came with beer. Wolfe took the opener from the drawer, poured a glass, gulped, and leaned back again. He resumed, "By annoying me about the man on the witness-stand. I resigned myself to your tantrum because it was nearly four o'clock. As you know, the book came. I read it last night."

"Why did you read it?"

"Don't badger me. I read it because it was a book. I had finished *The Native's Return*, by Louis Adamic, and *Outline of Human Nature*, by Alfred Rossiter, and I read books."

"Yeah. And?"

"This will amuse you. Paul Chapin, the man on the witness-stand, the author of *Devil Take the Hindmost*, is the villain of Andrew Hibbard's tale. He is the psychopathic avenger of an old and tragic injury."

"The hell he is." I gave Wolfe a look; I had known him to invent for practice. "Why is he?"

Wolfe's eyelids went up a shade. "Do you expect me to explain the universe?"

"No, sir. Retake. How do you know he is?"

"By no flight. Pedestrian mental processes. Must you have them?"

"I'd greatly appreciate it."

"I suppose so. A few details will do. Mr. Hibbard employed the unusual phrase, *embark on a ship of vengeance*, and that phrase occurs twice in *Devil Take the Hindmost*. Mr. Hibbard did not say, as the stenographer has it, *that was difficult, for pawn*, which is of course meaningless; he said, *that was difficult, for Paul*, and caught himself up pronouncing the name, which he did not intend to disclose. Mr. Hibbard said things indicating that the man was a writer, for instance speaking of his disguising his style in the warnings. Mr. Hibbard said that five years ago the man began to be involved in compensatory achievement. I telephoned two or three people this morning. In 1929 Paul Chapin's first successful book was published, and in 1930 his second. Also, Chapin is a cripple through an injury which he suffered twenty-five years ago in a hazing accident at Harvard. If more is needed . . . "

"No. Thank you very much. I see. All right. Now that you know who the guy is, everything is cozy. Why is it? Who are you going to send a bill to?"

Two of the folds in Wolfe's cheeks opened out a little, so I knew he thought he was smiling. I said, "But you may just be pleased because you know it's corn fritters with anchovy sauce for lunch and it's only ten minutes to the bell."

"No, Archie." The folds were gently closing. "I mentioned that I entertained a notion. It may or may not be fertile. As usual, you have furnished the fillip. Luckily our stake will be negligible. There are several possible channels of approach, but I believe . . . yes. Get Mr. Andrew Hibbard on the phone. At Columbia, or at his home."

"Yes, sir. Will you speak?"

"Yes. Keep your wire and take it down as usual."

I got the number from the book and called it. First the university. I didn't get Hibbard. I monkeyed around with two or three extensions and four or five people, and it finally leaked out that he wasn't anywhere around, but no one seemed to know where he was. I tried his home, an Academy number, up in the same neighborhood. There a dumb female nearly riled me. She insisted on knowing who I was and she sounded doubtful about everything. She finally seemed to decide Mr. Hibbard probably wasn't home. Through the last of it Wolfe was listening in on his wire.

I turned to him. "I can try again and maybe with luck get a human being."

He shook his head. "After lunch. It is two minutes to one."

I got up and stretched, thinking I would be able to do a lot of destructive criticism on a corn fritter myself, especially with Fritz's sauce. It was at that moment that Wolfe's notion decided to come to him instead of waiting longer for him to go to it. It was a coincidence, too, though that was of no importance; she must have been trying to get our number while I was talking.

The telephone rang. I sat down again and got it. It was a woman's voice, and she asked to speak to Nero Wolfe. I asked if I might have her name, and when she said "Evelyn Hibbard" I told her to hold the line and put my hand over the transmitter.

I grinned at Wolfe. "It's a Hibbard."

His brows lifted.

"A female Hibbard named Evelyn. Voice young, maybe a daughter. Take it."

He took his receiver off and I put mine back to my ear and got my pad and pencil ready. As Wolfe asked her what she wanted I was deciding again that he was the only man I had ever met who used absolutely the same tone to a woman as to a man. He had plenty of changes in his voice, but they weren't based on sex. I scribbled on the pad my quick symbols, mostly private, for the sounds in the receiver:

"I have a note of introduction to you from a friend, Miss Sarah Barstow. You will remember her, Mr. Wolfe, you . . . you investigated the death of her father.* Could I see you at once? If possible. I'm talking from the Bidwell, Fifty-second Street. I could be there in fifteen minutes."

"I'm sorry, Miss Hibbard, I am engaged. Could you come at a quarter past two?"

"Oh." A little gasp floated after that. "I had hopes . . . I just decided ten minutes ago. Mr. Wolfe, it is very urgent. If you could possibly . . . "

"If you would describe the urgency."

"I'd rather not, on the telephone—but that's silly. It's my uncle, Andrew Hibbard, he went to see you two weeks ago, you may remember. He has disappeared."

"Indeed. When?"

"Tuesday evening. Four days ago."

"You have had no word of him?"

"Nothing." The female Hibbard's voice caught. "Nothing at all."

"Indeed." I saw Wolfe's eyes shift to take in the clock—it was four minutes past one—and shift again towards the door to the hall, where Fritz stood on the threshold, straight for announcing. "Since ninety hours have passed, another one may be risked. At a quarter past two? Will that be convenient?"

"If you can't . . . all right. I'll be there."

Two receivers were returned simultaneously to their racks. Fritz spoke as usual:

"Luncheon, sir."

---

*See *Fer-de-Lance*, by Rex Stout.

# Chapter 3

I'm funny about women. I've seen dozens of them I wouldn't mind marrying, but I've never been pulled so hard I lost my balance. I don't know whether any of them would have married me or not, that's the truth, since I never gave one a chance to collect enough data to form an intelligent opinion. When I meet a new one there's no doubt that I'm interested and I'm fully alive to all the possibilities, and I've never dodged the issue as far as I can tell, but I never seem to get infatuated. For instance, take the women I meet in my line of business—that is, Nero Wolfe's business. I never run into one, provided she's not just an item for the cleaners, without letting my eyes do the best they can for my judgment, and more than that, it puts a tickle in my blood. I can feel the nudge on the accelerator. But then of course the business gets started, whatever it may happen to be, and I guess the trouble is I'm too conscientious. I love to do a good job more than anything else I can think of, and I suppose that's what shorts the line.

This Evelyn Hibbard was little and dark and smart. Her nose was too pointed and she took too much advantage of her eyelashes, but nobody that knew merchandise would have put her on a bargain counter. She had on a slick gray twill suit, with a fur piece, and a little red hat with a narrow brim on the side of her head. She sat straight without crossing her legs, and her ankles and halfway to her knees was well trimmed but without promise of any plumpness.

I was at my desk of course with my pad, and after the first couple of minutes got only glances at her in between. If worry about her uncle was eating her, and I suppose it was, she was following what Wolfe called the Anglo-Saxon theory of the treatment of emotions and desserts: freeze them and hide them in your belly. She sat straight in the chair I had shoved up for her, keeping her handsome dark eyes level on Wolfe but once in a while flapping her lashes in my direction. She had brought with her a package wrapped in brown paper and held it on her lap. Wolfe leaned back in his seat with his chin down and his forearms laid out on the arms of the chair; it was his custom to make no effort to join his fingers at the high point of his middle mound sooner than a full hour after a meal.

She said that she and her younger sister lived with their uncle in an apartment on One Hundred Thirteenth Street. Their mother had died when they were young. Their father was remarried and lived in California. Their uncle was single. He, Uncle Andrew, had gone out Tuesday evening around nine o'clock, and had not returned. There had been no word from him. He had gone out alone, remarking casually to Ruth, the younger sister, that he would get some air.

Wolfe asked, "This has no precedent?"

"Precedent?"

"He has never done this before? You have no idea where he may be?"

"No. But I have an idea . . . I think . . . he has been killed."

"I suppose so." Wolfe opened his eyes a little. "That would naturally occur to you. On the telephone you mentioned his visit to me. Do you know what its purpose was?"

"I know all about it. It was through my friend Sarah Barstow that I heard of you. I persuaded my uncle to come to see you. I know what he told you and what you said to him. I told my uncle he was a sentimental romantic. He was." She stopped, and kept her lips closed a moment to get them firm again; I looked up to see it. "I'm not. I'm hard-boiled. I think my uncle has been murdered, and the man who killed him is Paul Chapin, the writer. I came here to tell you that."

So here was the notion Wolfe had entertained, coming right to his office and sitting on a chair. But too late? The five hundred a week had gone out to get some air.

Wolfe said, "Quite likely. Thank you for coming. But it might be possible, and more to the point, to engage the attention of the police and the District Attorney."

She nodded. "You are like Sarah Barstow described you. The police have been engaged since Wednesday noon. They have been willing so far, at the request of the president of the university, to keep the matter quiet. There has been no publicity. But the police—you might as well match me at chess against Capablanca. Mr. Wolfe . . ." The fingers of her clasped hands, resting on the package on her lap, twisted a closer knot, and her voice tightened. "You don't know. Paul Chapin has the cunning and subtlety of all the things he mentioned in his first warning, the

one he sent after he killed Judge Harrison. He is
genuinely evil . . . all evil, all dangerous . . . you
know he is not a man . . ."

"There, Miss Hibbard. There now." Wolfe sighed.
"Surely he is a man, by definition. Did he indeed kill a
judge? In that instance the presumption is of course in
his favor. But you mentioned the first warning. Do
you by any chance have a copy of it?"

She nodded. "I have." She indicated the package.
"I have all the warnings, including . . ." She swallowed. ". . . the last one. Dr. Burton gave me his."

"The one after the apparent suicide."

"No. The one . . . another one came this morning
to them. I suppose to all of them; after Dr. Burton told
me I telephoned two or three. You see, my uncle has
disappeared . . . you see . . ."

"I see. Indeed. Dangerous. For Mr. Chapin, I
mean. Any kind of a rut is dangerous in his sort of
enterprise. So you have all the warnings. With you? In
that package?"

"Yes. Also I have bundles of letters which Paul
Chapin has at various times written to my uncle, and
a sort of diary which my uncle kept, and a book of
records showing sums advanced to Paul Chapin from
1919 to 1928 by my uncle and others, and a list of the
names and addresses of the members—that is, of the
men who were present in 1909 when it happened. A
few other things."

"Preposterous. You have all that? Why not the
police?"

Evelyn Hibbard shook her head. "I decided not.
These things were in a very private file of my uncle's.
They were precious to him, and they are now precious
to me . . . in a different way. The police would get no

help from them, but you might. And you would not abuse them. Would you?"

At the pause I glanced up, and saw Wolfe's lips pushing out a little . . . then in, then out again . . . That excited me. It always did, even when I had no idea what it was all about. I watched him. He said, "Miss Hibbard. You mean you removed this file from the notice of the police, and kept it, and have now brought it to me? Containing the names and addresses of the members of the League of Atonement? Remarkable."

She stared at him. "Why not? It has no information that they cannot easily obtain elsewhere—from Mr. Farrell or Dr. Burton or Mr. Drummond—any of them—"

"All the same, remarkable." Wolfe reached to his desk and pushed a button. "Will you have a glass of beer? I drink beer, but would not impose my preferences. There is available a fair port, Solera, Dublin stout, Maderia, and more especially a Hungarian *vin du pays* which comes to me from the cellar of the vineyard. Your choice . . ."

She shook her head. "Thank you."

"I may have beer?"

"Please do."

Wolfe did not lean back again. He said, "If the package could perhaps be opened? I am especially interested in that first warning."

She began to untie the string. I got up to help. She handed me the package and I put it on Wolfe's desk and got the paper off. It was a large cardboard letter-file, old and faded but intact. I passed it to Wolfe, and he opened it with the deliberate and friendly exactness which his hands displayed towards all inanimate things.

Evelyn Hibbard said, "Under *I*. My uncle did not call them warnings. He called them intimations."

Wolfe nodded. "Of destiny, I suppose." He removed papers from the file. "Your uncle is indeed a romantic. Oh yes, I say *is*. It is wise to reject all suppositions, even painful ones, until surmise can stand on the legs of fact. Here it is. Ah! *Ye should have killed me, watched the last mean sigh.* Is Mr. Chapin in malevolence a poet? May I read it?"

She nodded. He read:

*Ye should have killed me, watched the last mean
   sigh*
*Sneak through my nostril like a fugitive slave*
*Slinking from bondage.*
*Ye should have killed me.*
*Ye killed the man,*
*Ye should have killed me!*

*Ye killed the man, but not*
*The snake, the fox, the mouse that nibbles his hole,*
*The patient cat, the hawk, the ape that grins,*
*The wolf, the crocodile, the worm that works his
   way*
*Up through the slime and down again to hide.*
*Ah! All these ye left in me,*
*And killed the man.*
*Ye should have killed me!*

*Long ago I said, trust time.*
*Banal I said, time will take its toll.*
*I said to the snake, the ape, the cat, the worm:*
*Trust time, for all your aptitudes together*
*Are not as sure and deadly. But now they said:*
*Time is too slow; let us, Master.*

*Master, count for us!*
*I said no.*
*Master, let us. Master, count for us!*
*I felt them in me. I saw the night, the sea,*
*The rocks, the neutral stars, the ready cliff.*
*I heard ye all about, and I heard them:*
*Master, let us. Master, count for us!*
*I saw one there, secure at the edge of death;*
*I counted: One!*
*I shall count two I know, and three and four . . .*
*Not waiting for time's toll.*
*Ye should have killed me.*

Wolfe sat with the paper in his hand, glancing from it to Miss Hibbard. "It would seem likely that Mr. Chapin pushed the judge over the edge of a cliff. Presumably impromptu. I presume also, totally unobserved, since no suspicions were aroused. There was a cliff around handy?"

"Yes. It was in Massachusetts, up near Marblehead. Last June. A crowd was there at Fillmore Collard's place. Judge Harrison had come east, from Indiana, for commencement, for his son's graduation. They missed him that night, and the next morning they found his body at the foot of the cliff, beaten among the rocks by the surf."

"Mr. Chapin was among them?"

She nodded. "He was there."

"But don't tell me the gathering was for purposes of atonement. It was not a meeting of this incredible league?"

"Oh no. Anyway, Mr. Wolfe, no one ever quite seriously called it a league. Even Uncle Andrew was not—" she stopped short, shut her lips, stuck her chin up, and then went on, "as romantic as that. The crowd was just a crowd, mostly from the class of 1912, that Fillmore Collard had taken up from Cambridge. Seven or eight of the—well, league—were there."

Wolfe nodded and regarded her for a moment, then got at the file again and began pulling things out of its compartments. He flipped through the sheets of a loose-leaf binder, glanced inside a record book, and shuffled through a lot of papers. Finally he looked at Miss Hibbard again:

"And this quasi-poetic warning came to each of them after they had returned to their homes, and astonished them?"

"Yes, a few days later."

"I see. You know, of course, that Mr. Chapin's little effort was sound traditionally. Many of the most effective warnings in history, particularly the ancient ones, were in verse. As for the merits of Mr. Chapin's execution, granted the soundness of the tradition, it seems to me verbose, bombastic, and decidedly spotty. I cannot qualify as an expert in prosody, but I am not without an ear."

It wasn't like Wolfe to babble when business was on hand, and I glanced up wondering where he thought he was headed for. She was just looking at him. I had to cut my glance short, for he was going on:

"Further, I suspect him specifically, in his second stanza—I suppose he would call it stanza—of plagiarism. It has been many years since I have read Spenser, but in a crack of my memory not quite closed up there is a catalogue of beasts—Archie. If you wouldn't mind, bring me that Spenser? The third shelf, at the right of the door. No, farther over—more yet—dark blue, tooled. That's it."

I took the book over and handed it to him, and he opened it and began skimming.

"*The Shepheardes Calender*, I am certain, and I think *September*. Not that it matters; even if I find it, a petty triumph scarcely worth the minutes I waste. You will forgive me, Miss Hibbard? *Bulls that bene bate . . . Cocke on his dunghill. . . . This wolvish sheepe would catchen his pray . . .* no, certainly not that. Beasts here and there, but not the catalogue in my memory. I shall forgo the triumph; it isn't here. Anyway, it was pleasant to meet Spenser again, even for so brief a nod." He slid forward in his chair, to a perilous extreme, to hand the book to Miss Hibbard. "A fine example of bookmaking, worth a glance of friendship from you. Printed of course in London, but bound in this city by a Swedish boy who will probably starve to death during the coming winter."

She summoned enough politeness to look at it, turn it over in her hand, glance inside, and look at the backbone again. Wolfe was back at the papers he had taken from the file. She was obviously through with the book, so I got up and took it and returned it to the shelf.

Wolfe was saying, "Miss Hibbard. I know that what you want is action, and doubtless I have tried your patience. I am sorry. If I might ask you a few questions?"

"Certainly. It seems to me—"

"Of course. Pardon me. Only two questions, I think. First, do you know whether your uncle recently took out any life insurance?"

She nodded impatiently. "But, Mr. Wolfe, that has nothing to do with—"

He broke in to finish for her, "With the totalitarian evil of Paul Chapin. I know. Possibly not. Was it a large amount of insurance?"

"I think so. Yes. Very large."

"Were you the beneficiary?"

"I don't know. I suppose so. He told me you spoke to him of insurance. Then, about a week ago, he told me he had rushed it through and they had distributed it among four companies. I didn't pay much attention because my mind was on something else. I was angry with him and was trying to persuade him . . . I suppose my sister Ruth and I were the beneficiaries."

"Not Paul Chapin?"

She looked at him, and opened her mouth and closed it again. She said, "That hadn't occurred to me. Perhaps he would. I don't know."

Wolfe nodded. "Yes, a sentimental romantic might do that. Now, the second question. Why did you come to see me? What do you want me to do?"

She gave him her eyes straight. "I want you to find proof of Paul Chapin's guilt, and see that he pays the penalty. I can pay you for it. You told my uncle ten thousand dollars. I can pay that."

"Do you have a personal hostility for Mr. Chapin?"

"Personal?" She frowned. "Is there any other kind of hostility except personal? I don't know. I hate Paul Chapin, and have hated him for years, because I loved my uncle and my sister Ruth loved him and he was a fine sensitive generous man, and Paul Chapin was ruining his life. Ruined his life . . . oh . . . now . . ."

"There, Miss Hibbard. Please. You did not intend to engage me to find your uncle? You had no hope of that?"

"I think not. Oh, if you do! If you do that . . . I think I have no hope, I think I dare not. But then— even if you find him, there will still be Paul Chapin."

"Just so." Wolfe sighed, and turned his eyes to me. "Archie. Please wrap up Miss Hibbard's file for her. If I have not placed the contents in their proper compartments, she will forgive me. The paper and string are intact? Good."

She was protesting, "But you will need that—I'll leave it—"

"No, Miss Hibbard. I'm sorry. I can't undertake your commission."

She stared at him. He said, "The affair is in the hands of the police and the District Attorney. I would be hopelessly handicapped. I shall have to bid you good day."

She found her tongue. "Nonsense. You don't mean it." She exploded, forward in her chair. "Mr. Wolfe, it's outrageous! I've told you all about it . . . you've asked me and I've told you . . . the reason you give is no reason at all . . . why—"

He stopped her, with his finger wiggling and the quality in his voice, without raising it, that always got me a little sore because I never understood how he did it. "Please, Miss Hibbard. I have said no, and I have given you my reason. That is sufficient. If you will just take the package from Mr. Goodwin. Of course I am being rude to you, and on such occasions I always regret that I do not know the art of being rude elegantly. I have all the simplicities, including that of brusqueness."

But he got up from his chair, which, though she didn't know it, was an extraordinary concession. She, on her feet too, had taken the package from me and was mad as hell. Before turning to go, though, she realized that she was more helpless than she was mad. She appealed to him:

"But don't you see, this leaves me . . . what can I do?"

"I can make only one suggestion. If you have made no other arrangements and still wish my services, and the police have made no progress, come to see me next Wednesday."

"But that's four whole days—"

"I'm sorry. Good day, Miss Hibbard."

I went to open the door for her, and she certainly had completely forgotten about her eyelashes.

When I got back to the office Wolfe was seated again, with what I supposed Andrew Hibbard would have called the stigmata of pleasure. His chin was up, and he was making little circles with the tip of his finger on the arm of his chair. I came to a stop by his desk, across from him, and said:

"That girl's mad. I would say, on a guess, she's about one-fifth as mad as I am."

He murmured, "Archie. For a moment, don't disturb me."

"No, sir. I wouldn't for anything. A trick is okay, and a deep trick is the staff of life for some people, but where you've got us to at present is wallowing in the unplumbed depths of—wait a minute, I'll look it up, I think it's in Spenser."

"Archie, I warn you, some day your are going to become dispensable." He stirred a little. "If you were a woman and I were married to you, which God forbid, no amount of space available on this globe, to separate us, would put me at ease. I regret the necessity for my rudeness to Miss Hibbard. It was desirable to get rid of her without delay, for there is a great deal to be done."

"Good. If I can help any—"

"You can. Your notebook, please. Take a telegram."

I sat down. I wasn't within a hundred miles of it, and that always irritated me. Wolfe dictated:

"Regarding recent developments and third Chapin warning you are requested to attend meeting this address nine o'clock Monday evening November fifth without fail. Sign it Nero Wolfe and address."

"Sure." I had it down. "Just send it to anybody I happen to think of?"

Wolfe had lifted up the edge of his desk blotter and taken a sheet of paper from underneath and was pushing it at me. He said, "Here are the names. Include those in Boston, Philadelphia, and Washington; those farther away can be informed later by letter. Also, make a copy of the list; two—one for the safe. Also—"

I had taken the paper from him and a glance showed what it was. I stared at him, and I suppose something in my face stopped him. He interrupted himself, "Reserve your disapproval, Archie. Save your fake moralities for your solitude."

I said, "So that's why you had me get the Spenser, so she would have something to look at. Why did you steal it?"

"I borrowed it."

"You say. I've looked in the dictionary. That's what I mean, why didn't you borrow it? She would have let you have it."

"Probably not." Wolfe sighed. "I didn't care to risk it. In view of your familiarity with the finer ethical points, you must realize that I couldn't very well accept her as a client and then propose to others, especially to a group—"

"Sure, I see that all right. Now that the notion you entertained has drifted in on me, I'd have my hat off if I had one on. But she'd have let you have it. Or you could have got the dope—"

"That will do, Archie." He got a faint tone on. "We shall at any rate be acting in her interest. It appears likely that this will be a complicated and expensive business, and there is no reason why Miss Hibbard should bear the burden alone. In a few minutes I shall be going upstairs, and you will be fairly busy. First,

send the telegrams and copy the list. Then—take this, a
letter to Miss Hibbard, sign my name and mail it this
evening by special delivery: *I find that the enclosed
paper did not get back into your file this afternoon, but
remained on my desk. I trust that its absence has not
caused you any inconvenience. If you are still of a mind
to see me next Wednesday, do not hesitate to call upon
me.*"

"Yes, sir. Send her the list."

"Naturally. Be sure your copies are correct. Make
three copies. I believe you know the home address of
Mr. Higgam of the Metropolitan Trust Company?"

I nodded. "Up at Sutton—"

"Find him tomorrow and give him a copy of the list.
Ask him to procure first thing Monday morning a
financial report on the men listed. No history is
required; their present standing is the point. For
those in other cities, telegraph. We want the information by six o'clock Monday."

"Hibbard's name is here. Maybe the other dead ones."

"The bank's ingenuity may discover them, and not
disturb their souls. Get in touch with Saul Panzer and
tell him to report here Monday evening at eight-
thirty. Durkin likewise. Find out if Gore and Cather
and two others—your selection—will be available for
Tuesday morning."

I grinned. "How about the Sixty-first Regiment?"

"They will be our reserve. As soon as you have
sent the telegrams, phone Miss Hibbard at her home.
Try until you get her. Employ your charm. Make an
appointment to call on her this evening. If you get to
see her, tell her that you regret that I refused her
commission, and that you have my leave to offer her
your assistance if she wishes it. It will save time. It
will afford you an opportunity to amass a collection of

facts from her, and possibly even a glance through the papers and effects of Mr. Hibbard. Chiefly for any indication of an awareness on his part that he would not soon return. We are of course in agreement with some of the tendencies of the law; for instance, its reluctance to believe a man dead merely because he is not visible on the spot he is accustomed to occupy."

"Yes, sir. Take my own line with her?"

"Any that suggests itself."

"If I go up there I could take the list along."

"No, mail it." Wolfe was getting up from his chair. I watched him; it was always something to see. Before he got started for the door, I asked:

"Maybe I should know this, I didn't get it. What was the idea asking her about the life insurance?"

"That? Merely the possibility that we were encountering a degree of vindictive finesse never before reached in our experience. Chapin's hatred, diluted of course, extended from the uncle to the niece. He learned of the large sum she would receive in insurance, and in planning Hibbard's murder planned also that the body would not be discovered; and the insurance money would not be paid her."

"It would some day."

"But even a delay in an enemy's good fortune is at least a minor pleasure. Worth such a finesse if you have it in you. That was the possibility. And another one: let us say Chapin himself was the beneficiary. Miss Hibbard was sure he would kill her uncle, would evade discovery, and would collect a huge fortune for his pains. The thought was intolerable. So she killed her uncle herself—he was about to die in any event—and disposed of the body so that it could not be found. You might go into that with her this evening."

I said, "You think I won't? I'll get her alibi."

# Chapter 4

There was plenty doing Saturday evening and Sunday. I saw Evelyn Hibbard and had three hours with her, and got Saul and Fred and the other boys lined up, and had a lot of fun on the telephone, and finally got hold of Higgam the bank guy late Sunday evening after he returned from a Long Island week-end. The phone calls were from members of the league who had got the telegrams. There were five or six that phoned, various kinds; some scared, some sore, and one that was apparently just curious. I had made several copies of the list, and as the phone calls came I checked them off on one and made notes. The original, Hibbard's, had a date at the top, February 16, 1931, and was typewritten. Some of the addresses had been changed later with a pen, so evidently it had been kept up-to-date. Four of the names had no addresses at all, and of course I didn't know which ones were dead. The list was like this, leaving out the addresses and putting in the business or profession as we got it Monday from the bank:

Andrew Hibbard, psychologist
Ferdinand Bowen, stockbroker

Loring A. Burton, doctor
Eugene Dreyer, art dealer
Alexander Drummond, florist
George R. Pratt, politician
Nicholas Cabot, lawyer
Augustus Farrell, architect
Wm. R. Harrison, judge
Fillmore Collard, textile-mill owner
Edwin Robert Byron, magazine editor
L. M. Irving, social worker
Lewis Palmer, Federal Housing Administration
Julius Adler, lawyer
Theodore Gaines, banker
Pitney Scott, taxi-driver
Michael Ayers, newspaperman
Arthur Kommers, sales manager
Wallace McKenna, congressman from Illinois
Sidney Lang, real estate
Roland Erskine, actor
Leopold Elkus, surgeon
F. L. Ingalls, travel bureau
Archibald Mollison, professor
Richard M. Tuttle, boys' school
T. R. Donovan
Phillip Leonard
Allan W. Gardner
Hans Weber

For the last four there were no addresses, and I couldn't find them in the New York or suburban phone books, so I couldn't ask the bank for a report. Offhand, I thought, reading the names and considering that they were all Harvard men, which meant starting better than scratch on the average, offhand it looked pretty juicy; but the bank reports would settle that. It was fun stalling them on the phone.

But the real fun Sunday came in the middle of the afternoon. Someone had leaked on Hibbard's disappearance and the Sunday papers had it, though they didn't give it a heavy play. When the doorbell rang around three o'clock and I answered it because I happened to be handy and Fritz was busy out back, and I saw two huskies standing there shoulder to shoulder, I surmised at first glance it was a couple of bureau dicks and someone had got curious about me up at Hibbard's the night before. Then I recognized one of them and threw the door wide with a grin.

"Hello, hello. You late from church?"

The one on the right spoke, the one with a scar on his cheek I had recognized. "Nero Wolfe in?"

I nodded. "You want to see him? Leap the doorsill, gentlemen."

While I was closing the door and putting the chain on they were taking off their hats and coats and hanging them on the rack. Then they were running their hands over their hair and pulling their vests down and clearing their throats. They were as nervous as greenhorns on their first tail. I was impressed. I was so used to Wolfe myself and so familiar with his prowess that I was apt to forget the dents some of his strokes had made on some tough professional skulls. I asked them to wait in the hall and went to the office and told Wolfe that Del Bascom of the Bascom Detective Agency was there with one of his men and wanted to see him.

"Did you ask them what they wanted?"

"No."

Wolfe nodded, and I went out and brought them in. Bascom went across to the desk to shake hands; the other gentleman got his big rumpus onto a chair I shoved up, but nearly missed it on the way down on account of staring at Wolfe. I suspected he wasn't overwhelmed by prestige as much as he was by avoirdupois, having never seen Wolfe before.

Bascom was saying, "It's been nearly two years since I've seen you, Mr. Wolfe. Remember? The hay fever case. That's what I called it. Remember the clerk that didn't see the guy lifting the emeralds because he was sneezing?"

"I do indeed, Mr. Bascom. That young man had invention, to employ so common an affliction for so unusual a purpose."

"Yeah. Lots of 'em are smart, but very few of them is quite smart enough. That was quite a case. I'd have been left scratching my ear for a bite if it hadn't been for you. I'll never forget that. Is business pretty good with you, Mr. Wolfe?"

"No. Abominable."

"I suppose so. We've got to expect it. Some of the agencies are doing pretty well on industrial work, but I never got into that. I used to be a workingman myself. Hell, I still am." Bascom crossed his legs and cleared his throat. "You taken on anything new lately?"

"No."

"You haven't?"

"No."

I nearly jumped at the squeak, it was so unexpected. It came from the other dick, his chair between Bascom and me. He squeaked all of a sudden:

"I heard different."

"Well, who opened your valve?" Bascom glared at him, disgusted. "Did I request you to clamp your trap when we came in here?" He turned to Wolfe. "Do you

know what's eating him? You'll enjoy this, Mr. Wolfe.
He's heard a lot of talk about the great Nero Wolfe,
and he wanted to show you haven't got him buffaloed."
He shifted and turned on the glare again. "You sap."

Wolfe nodded. "Yes, I enjoy that. I like bravado.
You were saying, Mr. Bascom?"

"Yeah. I might as well come to the point. It's like
this. I'm on a case. I've got five men on it. I'm pulling
down close to a thousand dollars a week, four weeks
now. When I wind it up I'll get a fee that will keep me
off of relief all winter. I'm getting it sewed up. About
all I need now is some wrapping paper and a piece of
string."

"That's fine."

"All of that. And what I'm here for is to ask you to
lay off."

Wolfe's brows went up a shade. "To ask me?"

"To lay off." Bascom slid forward in his chair and
got earnest. "Look here, Mr. Wolfe. It's the Chapin
case. I've been on it for four weeks. Pratt and Cabot
and Dr. Burton are paying me—that's no secret, or if
it was, it wouldn't be for you after Monday. Pratt's a
sort of a friend of mine, I've done him a good turn or
two. He phoned me last night and said if I wanted to
hang my own price tag on Paul Chapin I'd better get
a move on because Nero Wolfe was about to begin.
That was how I found out about the telegrams you
sent. I dusted around and saw Burton and Cabot and
one or two others. Burton had never heard of you
before and asked me to get a report on you, but he
phoned me this morning and told me not to bother. I
suppose he had inquired and got an earful."

Wolfe murmured, "I am gratified at the interest
they displayed."

"I don't doubt it." Bascom laid a fist on the desk for

emphasis and got more earnest still. "Mr. Wolfe. I want to speak to you as one professional man to another. You would be the first to agree that ours is a dignified profession."

"Not explicitly. To assert dignity is to lose it."

"Huh? Maybe. Anyway, it's a profession, like the law. As you know, it is improper for a lawyer to solicit a client away from another lawyer. He would be disbarred. No lawyer with any decency would ever try it. And don't you think our profession is as dignified as the law? That's the only question. See?"

Bascom waited for an answer, his eyes on Wolfe's face, and probably supposed that the slow unfolding on Wolfe's cheeks was merely a natural phenomenon, like the ground swell on an ocean. Wolfe finally said, "Mr. Bascom. If you would abandon the subtleties of innuendo? If you have a request to make, state it plainly."

"Hell, didn't I? I asked you to lay off."

"You mean, keep out of what you call the Chapin case? I am sorry to have to refuse your request."

"You won't?"

"Certainly not."

"And you think it is absolutely okay to solicit another man's clients away from him?"

"I have no idea. I shall not enter into a defense of my conduct with you; what if it turned out to be indefensible? I merely say, I refuse your request."

"Yeah. I thought you would." Bascom took his fist off the desk and relaxed a little. "My brother claimed you regarded yourself as a gentleman and you'd fall for it. I said you might be a gentleman but you wasn't a sap."

"Neither, I fear."

"Well and good. Now that that's out of the way,

maybe we can talk business. If you're going to take on the Chapin case, that lets us out."

"Probably. Not necessarily."

"Oh yes, it does. You'll soak them until they'll have to begin buying the cheaper cuts. I know when I'm done, I can take it. I couldn't hang onto it much longer anyhow. God help you. I'd love to drop in here once a week and ask you how's tricks. I'm telling you, this cripple Chapin is the deepest and slickest that's ever run around loose. I said I had it about sewed up. Listen. There's not the faintest chance. Not the faintest. I had really given that up, and had three men tailing him to catch him on the next one—and by God there goes Hibbard and we can't even find what's left of him, and do you know what? My three men don't know where Chapin was Tuesday night! Can you beat it? It sounds dumb, but they're not dumb, they're damn good men. So as I say, I'd love to drop in here—"

Wolfe put in, "You spoke of talking business."

"So I did. I'm ready to offer you a bargain. Of course you've got your own methods, we all have, but in these four weeks we've dug up a lot of dope, and it's cost us a lot of money to get it. It's confidential naturally, but if your clients are the same as mine that don't matter. It would save you a lot of time and expense and circling around. You can have all the dope and I'll confer with you on it any time, as often as you want." Bascom hesitated a moment, wet his lips, and concluded, "For one thousand dollars."

Wolfe shook his head gently. "But, Mr. Bascom. All of your reports will be available to me."

"Sure, but you know what reports are. You know, they're all right, but oh hell. You would really get some dope if I let you question any of my men you wanted to. I'd throw that in."

"I question its value."

"Oh, be reasonable."

"I often try. I will pay one hundred dollars for what you offer.—Please! I will not haggle. And do not think me discourteous if I say that I am busy and need all the time the clock affords me. I thank you for your visit, but I am busy." Wolfe's fingers moved to indicate the books before him on the desk, one of them with a marker in it. "There are the five novels written by Paul Chapin; I managed to procure the four earlier ones yesterday evening. I am reading them. I agree with you that this is a difficult case. It is possible, though extremely unlikely, that I shall have it solved by midnight."

I swallowed a grin. Wolfe liked bravado all right; for his reputation it was one of his best tricks.

Bascom stared at him. After a moment he pushed his chair back and got up, and the dick next to me lifted himself with a grunt. Bascom said, "Don't let me keep you. I believe I mentioned we all have our own methods, and all I've got to say is thank God for that."

"Yes. Do you wish the hundred dollars?"

Bascom, turning, nodded. "I'll take it. It looks to me like you're throwing the money away, since you've already bought the novels, but hell I'll take it."

I went across to open the door, and they followed.

# Chapter 5

By dinner time Monday we were all set, so we enjoyed the meal in leisure. Fritz was always happy and put on a little extra effort when he knew things were moving in the office. That night I passed him a wink when I saw how full the soup was of mushrooms, and when I tasted the tarragon in the salad dressing I threw him a kiss. He blushed. Wolfe frequently had compliments for his dishes and expressed them appropriately, and Fritz always blushed; and whenever I found occasion to toss him a tribute he blushed likewise, I'd swear to heaven, just to please me, not to let me down. I often wondered if Wolfe noticed it. His attention to food was so alert and comprehensive that I would have said off hand he didn't, but in making any kind of a guess about Wolfe off hand wasn't good enough.

As soon as dinner was over Wolfe went up to his room, as he had explained he would do; he was staging it. I conferred with Fritz in the kitchen a few minutes and then went upstairs and changed my clothes. I put on the gray suit with pin checks, one of the best fits I ever had, and a light blue shirt and a dark blue tie. On my way back down I stopped in at Wolfe's room, on the same floor, to ask him a question. He was in the tapestry chair by the reading lamp with one of Paul Chapin's novels, and I stood waiting while he marked a paragraph in it with a lead pencil.

I said, "What if one of them brings along some foreign object, like a lawyer for instance? Shall I let it in?"

Without looking up, he nodded. I went down to the office.

The first one was early. I hadn't looked for the line to start forming until around nine, but it lacked twenty minutes of that when I heard Fritz going down the hall and the front door opening. Then the knob of the office door turned, and Fritz ushered in the first victim. He almost needed a shave, his pants were baggy, and his hair wasn't combed. His pale blue eyes darted around and landed on me.

"Hell," he said, "you ain't Nero Wolfe."

I admitted it. I exposed my identity. He didn't offer to shake hands. He said:

"I know I'm early for the party. I'm Mike Ayers, I'm in the city room at the *Tribune*. I told Oggie Reid I had to have the evening off to get my life saved. I stopped off somewhere to get a pair of drinks, and after a while it occurred to me I was a damn fool, there was no reason why there shouldn't be a drink here. I am not referring to beer."

I said, "Gin or gin?"

He grinned. "Good for you. Scotch. Don't bother to dilute it."

I went over to the table Fritz and I had fixed up in the alcove, and poured it. I was thinking, hurrah for Harvard and bright college days and so on. I was also thinking, if he gets too loud he'll be a nuisance but if I refuse to pander to his vile habit he'll beat it. And having learned the bank reports practically by heart,

I knew he had been on the *Post* four years and the *Tribune* three, and was pulling down ninety bucks a week. Newspapermen are one of my weak spots anyhow; I've never been able to get rid of a feeling that they know things I don't know.

I poured him another drink and he sat down and held onto it and crossed his legs. "Tell me," he said, "is it true that Nero Wolfe was a eunuch in a Cairo harem and got his start in life by collecting testimonials from the girls for Pyramid Dental Cream?"

Like an ass, for half a second I was sore. "Listen," I said, "Nero Wolfe is exactly—" Then I stopped and laughed. "Sure," I said. "Except that he wasn't a eunuch, he was a camel."

Mike Ayers nodded. "That explains it. I mean it explains why it's hard for a camel to go through a needle's eye. I've never seen Nero Wolfe, but I've heard about him, and I've seen a needle. You got any other facts?"

I had to pour him another drink before the next customer arrived. This time it was a pair, Ferdinand Bowen, the stockbroker, and Dr. Loring A. Burton. I went to the hall for them to get away from Mike Ayers. Burton was a big fine-looking guy, straight but not stiff, well-dressed and not needing any favors, with dark hair and black eyes and a tired mouth. Bowen was medium-sized, and he was tired all over. He was trim in black and white, and if I'd wanted to see him any evening, which I felt I wouldn't, I'd have gone to the theater where there was a first night and waited in the lobby. He had little feet in neat pumps, and neat little lady-hands in neat little gray gloves. When he was taking his coat off I had to stand back so as not to get socked in the eye with his arms swinging around, and I don't cotton to a guy with that sort of an attitude towards his fellowmen in confined spaces.

Particularly I think they ought to be kept out of elevators, but I'm not fond of them anywhere.

I took Burton and Bowen to the office and explained that Wolfe would be down soon and showed them Mike Ayers. He called Bowen Ferdie and offered him a drink, and he called Burton Lorelei. Fritz brought in another one, Alexander Drummond the florist, a neat little duck with a thin mustache. He was the only one on the list who had ever been to Wolfe's house before, he having come a couple of years back with a bunch from an association meeting to look at the plants. I remembered him. After that they came more or less all together: Pratt the Tammany assemblyman, Adler and Cabot, lawyers, Kommers, sales manager from Philadelphia, Edwin Robert Byron, all of that, magazine editor, Augustus Farrell, architect, and a bird named Lee Mitchell, from Boston, who said he represented both Collard and Gaines the banker. He had a letter from Gaines.

That made twelve accounted for, figuring both Collard and Gaines in, at ten minutes past nine. Of course they all knew each other, but it couldn't be said they were getting much gaiety out of it, not even Mike Ayers, who was going around with an empty glass in his hand, scowling. The others were mostly sitting with their funeral manners on. I went to Wolfe's desk and gave Fritz's button three short pokes. In a couple of minutes I heard the faint hum of the elevator.

The door of the office opened and everybody turned their heads. Wolfe came in; Fritz pulled the door to behind him. He waddled halfway to his desk, stopped, turned, and said, "Good evening, gentlemen." He went to his chair, got the edge of the seat up against the back of his knees and his grip on the arms, and lowered himself.

Mike Ayers demanded my attention by waving his glass at me and calling, "Hey! A eunuch *and* a camel!"

Wolfe raised his head a little and said in one of his best tones, "Are you suggesting those additions to Mr. Chapin's catalogue of his internal menagerie?"

"Huh? Oh. I'm suggesting—"

George Pratt said, "Shut up, Mike," and Farrell the architect grabbed him and pulled him into a chair.

I had handed Wolfe a list showing those who were present, and he had glanced over it. He looked up and spoke. "I am glad to see that Mr. Cabot and Mr. Adler are here. Both, I believe, attorneys. Their knowledge and their trained minds will restrain us from vulgar errors. I note also the presence of Mr. Michael Ayers, a journalist. He is one of your number, so I merely remark that the risk of publicity, should you wish to avoid it—"

Mike Ayers growled, "I'm not a journalist, I'm a newshound. I interviewed Einstein—"

"How drunk are you?"

"Hell, how do I know?"

Wolfe's brow lifted. "Gentlemen?"

Farrell said, "Mike's all right. Forget him. He's all right."

Julius Adler the lawyer, about the build of a lead-pencil stub, looking like a necktie clerk except for his eyes and the way he was dressed, put in, "I would say yes. We realize that this is your house, Mr. Wolfe, and that Mr. Ayers is lit, but after all we don't suppose that you invited us here to censor our private habits. You have something to say to us?"

"Oh, yes . . ."

"My name is Adler."

"Yes, Mr. Adler. Your remark illustrates what I knew would be the chief hindrance in my conversation with you gentlemen. I was aware that you would be antagonistic at the outset. You are all badly frightened, and a frightened man is hostile almost by reflex, as a defense. He suspects everything and everyone. I knew that you would regard me with suspicion."

"Nonsense." It was Cabot, the other lawyer. "We are not frightened, and there is nothing to suspect you of. If you have anything to say to us, say it."

I said, "Mr. Nicholas Cabot."

Wolfe nodded. "If you aren't frightened, Mr. Cabot, there is nothing to discuss. I mean that. You might as well go home." Wolfe opened his eyes and let them move slowly across the eleven faces. "You see, gentlemen, I invited you here this evening only after making a number of assumptions. If any one of them is wrong, this meeting is a waste of time, yours and mine. The first assumption is that you are convinced that Mr. Paul Chapin has murdered two, possibly three, of your friends. The second, that you are apprehensive that unless something is done about it he will murder you. The third, that my abilities are equal to the task of removing your apprehension; and the fourth, that you will be willing to pay well for that service. Well?"

They glanced at one another. Mike Ayers started to get up from his chair and Farrell pulled him back. Pratt muttered loud enough to reach Wolfe, "Good here." Cabot said:

"We are convinced that Paul Chapin is a dangerous enemy of society. That naturally concerns us. As to your abilities . . ."

Wolfe wiggled a finger at him. "Mr. Cabot. If it amuses you to maintain the fiction that you came here this evening to protect society, I would not dampen the diversion. The question is, how much is it worth to you?"

Mike Ayers startled all of us with a sudden shout, "Slick old Nick!" and followed it immediately with a falsetto whine, "Nicky darling . . ." Farrell poked him in the ribs. Someone grumbled, "Gag him." But the glances of two or three others in the direction of Cabot showed that Wolfe was right; the only way to handle that bird was to rub it in.

A new voice broke in, smooth and easy. "What's the difference whether we're scared or not?" It was Edwin Robert Byron, the magazine editor. "I'd just as soon say I'm scared, what's the difference? It seems to me the point is, what does Mr. Wolfe propose to do about it? Grant him his premise—"

"Grant hell." Mike Ayers got up, flinging his arm free of Farrell's grasp, and started for the table in the alcove. Halfway there he turned and blurted at them, "You're damned tootin' we're scared. We jump at noises and we look behind us and we drop things, you know damn well we do. All of you that didn't lay awake last night wondering how he got Andy and what he did with him, raise your hands. You've heard of our little organization, Wolfe you old faker? The League of Atonement? We're changing it to the Craven Club, or maybe the League of the White Feather." He filled his glass and lifted it; I didn't bother to call to him that he had got hold of the sherry decanter by mistake. "Fellow members! To the League of the White Feather!" He negotiated the drink with one heroic swallow. "You can make mine an ostrich plume." He scowled, and made a terrific grimace of disgust and indignation. "Who the hell put horse manure in that whiskey?"

Farrell let out a big handsome guffaw, and Pratt seconded him. Drummond the florist was giggling. Bowen the stockbroker, either bored or looking successfully like it, took out a cigar and cut off the end and lit it. I was over finding the right bottle for Mike Ayers, for I knew he'd have to wash the taste out of his mouth. Lee Mitchell of Boston got to his feet:

"If I may remark, gentlemen." He coughed. "Of

course I am not one of you, but I am authorized to say
that both Mr. Collard and Mr. Gaines are in fact apprehensive, they have satisfied themselves of the standing
of Mr. Wolfe, and they are ready to entertain his
suggestions."

"Good." Wolfe's tone cut short the buzz of comment. He turned his eyes to me. "Archie. If you will
just pass out those slips."

I had them in the top drawer of my desk, twenty
copies just in case, and I took them and handed them
around. Wolfe had rung for beer and was filling his
glass. After he had half emptied it he said:

"That, as you see, is merely a list of your names
with a sum of money noted after each. I can explain it
most easily by reading to you a memorandum which I
have here . . . or have I? Archie?"

"Here it is, sir."

"Thank you.—I have dictated it thus; it may be put
into formal legal phrasing or not, as you prefer. I would
be content to have it an initialed memorandum. For the
sake of brevity I have referred to you, those whose
names are on the list you have—those absent as well as
those present—as *the league.* The memorandum provides:

> 1. *I undertake to remove from the league all*
>    *apprehension and expectation of injury from*
>    *(a) Paul Chapin.*
>    *(b) The person or persons who sent the met-*
>        *rical typewritten warnings.*
>    *(c) The person or persons responsible for the*
>        *deaths of Wm. R. Harrison and Eugene*
>        *Dreyer, and for the disappearance of*
>        *Andrew Hibbard.*
> 2. *Decision as to the satisfactory performance of*

> the undertaking shall be made by a majority
> vote of the members of the league.
> 3. The expenses of the undertaking shall be borne
> by me, and in the event of my failure to per-
> form it satisfactorily the league shall be under
> no obligation to pay them, nor any other obli-
> gation.
> 4. Upon decision that the undertaking has been
> satisfactorily performed, the members of the
> league will pay me, each the amount set after
> his name on the attached list; provided, that the
> members will be severally and jointly respon-
> sible for the payment of the total amount.

"I believe that covers it. Of course, should you
wish to make it terminable after a stated period—"

Nicholas Cabot cut in, "It's preposterous. I won't
even discuss it." Julius Adler said with a smile, "I
think we should thank Mr. Wolfe's secretary for
adding it up and saving us the shock. Fifty-six thousand, nine hundred and fifteen dollars. Well!" His
brows went up and stayed up. Kommers, who had
spent at least ten bucks coming from Philadelphia,
made his maiden speech, "I don't know much about
your abilities, Mr. Wolfe, but I've learned something
new about nerve." Others began to join in the chorus;
they were just going to crowd us right in the ditch.

Wolfe waited, and in about a minute put up his
hand, palm out, which was a pretty violent gesture for
him. "Please, gentlemen. There is really no ground for
controversy. It is a simple matter: I offer to sell you
something for a stated price on delivery. If you think
the price exorbitant you are under no compulsion to
buy. However, I may observe in that connection that
on Saturday Miss Evelyn Hibbard offered to pay me

ten thousand dollars for the service proposed. There is no single item on that list as high as ten thousand dollars; and Miss Hibbard is not herself in jeopardy."

George Pratt said, "Yeah, and you turned her down so you could soak us. You're just out to do all the good you can, huh?"

"Anyhow, the memorandum is preposterous throughout." Nicholas Cabot had gone to Wolfe's desk and reached for the memorandum, and was standing there looking at it. "What we want is Paul Chapin put where he belongs. This attempt at evasion—"

"I'm surprised at you, Mr. Cabot." Wolfe sighed. "I phrased it that way chiefly because I knew two shrewd lawyers would be here and I wished to forestall their objections. Circumstances have got the idea of Paul Chapin's guilt so firmly fixed in your mind that you are a little off balance. I could not undertake specifically to remove your apprehension by getting Mr. Chapin convicted of murder, because if I did so and investigation proved him innocent two difficulties would present themselves. First, I would have to frame him in order to collect my money, which would be not only unfair to him but also a great bother to me, and second, the real perpetrator of these indiscretions would remain free to continue his career, and you gentlemen would still be scared—or dead. I wished to cover—"

"Rubbish." Cabot pushed the memorandum impatiently away. "We are convinced it is Chapin. We know it is."

"So am I." Wolfe nodded, down, and up, and at rest again. "Yes, I am convinced that it is Chapin you should fear. But in preparing this memorandum I thought it well to cover all contingencies, and you as a lawyer must agree with me. After all, what is really known? Very little. For instance, what if Andrew Hibbard, tormented by remorse, was driven to undertake vengeance on behalf of the man you all had injured? *Ye should have killed me.* What if, after killing two of you, he found he couldn't stomach it, and went off somewhere and ended his own life? That would contradict nothing we now know. Or what if another of you, or even an outsider, proceeded to balance some personal accounts, and took advantage of the exudations of the Chapin stew to lay a false scent? That might be you, Mr. Cabot, or Dr. Burton, or Mr. Michael Ayers . . . anyone. You say rubbish, and really I do too, but why not cover the contingencies?"

Cabot pulled the memorandum back beneath his eyes. Julius Adler got up and went to the desk and joined in the inspection. There was some murmuring among the others. Mike Ayers was sprawled in his chair with his hands deep in his pockets and his eyes shut tight. Julius Adler said:

"This last provision is out of the question. This joint responsibility for the total amount. We wouldn't consider it."

Wolfe's cheeks unfolded a little. "I agree with you, Mr. Adler. I shall not insist upon it. As a matter of fact, I inserted it purposely, so there would be something for you to take out."

Adler grunted. Drummond the florist, who had gone to join them, as had Pratt and Arthur Kommers, giggled again. Cabot looked at Wolfe with a frown and said, "You aren't at all nimble, are you?"

"Moderately. I'm really not much good at negotiation, I am too blunt. It is a shortcoming of temperament not to be overcome. For instance, my proposal to you. I can only present it and say, take it or leave it. I compensate for the handicap by making the proposal so attractive that it cannot very well be refused."

I was surprised, all of a sudden, to see the shadow of a smile on Cabot's face, and for a second I damn near liked him. He said, "Of course. I sympathize with your disability."

"Thank you." Wolfe moved his eyes to take in the others. "Well, gentlemen? I will mention two little points. First, I did not include in the memorandum a stipulation that you should co-operate with me, but I shall of course expect it. I can do little without your help. I would like to feel free to have Mr. Goodwin and another of my men call upon you at any reasonable time, and I would like to talk with a few of you myself. I may?"

Three or four heads nodded. George Pratt, with the group at the desk, said, "Good here." Cabot smiled openly and murmured, "Don't forget your disability."

"Good. The second point, about the money. In my opinion, the sums I have listed are adequate but not extortionate. If I fail to satisfy you I get nothing, so it comes to this: would Mr. Gaines be willing at this moment to pay me eight thousand dollars, and Dr. Burton seven thousand, and Mr. Michael Ayers one hundred and eighty, in return for a guarantee of freedom from the fear which has fastened itself upon them? I take it that you agree that it is proper to have the amounts graded in accordance with ability to pay."

Again heads nodded. He was easing them into it; he was sewing them up. I grinned to myself, "Boss, you're cute, that's all, you're just cute." Lee Mitchell from Boston spoke again:

"Of course I can't speak definitely for Mr. Collard and Mr. Gaines. I think I may say—you can probably count them in. I'll go back to Boston tonight and they'll wire you tomorrow."

Cabot said, "You can cross Elkus out. He wouldn't pay you a cent."

"No?"

"No. He's as sentimental as Andy Hibbard was. He'd sooner see us all killed than help catch Paul Chapin."

"Indeed. It is disastrous to permit the vagaries of the heart to infect the mind. We shall see—Gentlemen. I would like to satisfy myself now on one point. Frankly, I do not wish it to be possible for any of you to say, at any time in the future, that I have acted with a ruthlessness or vindictiveness which you did not contemplate or desire. My understanding is that you are all convinced that Paul Chapin is a murderer, that he has threatened you with murder, and that he should be caught, discovered, convicted and executed. I am going to ask Mr. Goodwin to call off your names. If my understanding is correct, you will please respond with *yes*."

He nodded at me. I took up the list on which I had checked those present. Before I could call one, Lee Mitchell said, "On that I can answer for Mr. Collard and Mr. Gaines. Unqualifiedly. Their response if *yes*."

There was a stir, but no one spoke. I said, "Ferdinand Bowen."

The broker said, husky but firm, "Yes."

"Dr. Loring A. Burton."

For a moment there was no reply, then Burton murmured in a tone so low it was barely heard, "No." Everyone looked at him. He looked around, swallowed, and said suddenly and explosively, "Nonsense! Yes, of course! Romantic nonsense. Yes!"

Farrell said to him, "I should hope so. The wonder is you weren't first."

I went on, "Augustus Farrell."

"Yes."

I called the others, Drummond, Cabot, Pratt, Byron, Adler, Kommers; they all said *yes*. I called, "Michael Ayers." He was still sprawled in his chair. I said his name again. Farrell, next to him, dug him in the ribs: "Mike! Hey! Say yes." Mike Ayers stirred a little, opened his eyes into slits, bawled out, "Yes!" and shut his eyes again.

I turned to Wolfe, "That's all, sir."

I usually heard Fritz when he went down the front hall to answer the doorbell, but that time I didn't; I suppose because I was too interested in the roll I was calling. So I was surprised when I saw the door of the office opening. The others saw me look and they looked too. Fritz came in three steps and waited until Wolfe nodded at him. "A gentleman to see you, sir. He had no card. He told me to say, Mr. Paul Chapin."

"Indeed." Wolfe didn't move. "Indeed. Show him in."

# Chapter 6

Fritz went back to the hall to get the visitor. I missed a bet, but Wolfe probably didn't—I don't know; I should have been taking notice of the expressions on the faces of our guests, but I wasn't; my eyes were glued on the door. I imagine all the others' were too, except Wolfe's. I heard the thud of Paul Chapin's walking-stick on the rubber tile of the hall.

He limped in and stopped a few paces from the door. From where he was he couldn't see Wolfe, on account of the group gathered at the desk. He looked at the group, and at those around on chairs, and tossed his head up twice, his chin out, like a nervous horse trying to shake the rein. He said, "Hello, fellows," and limped forward again, far enough into the room so he could see Wolfe, first sending a quick sharp glance at me. He was standing less than eight feet from me. He was dressed for evening, a dinner coat. He wasn't a big guy at all, rather under medium size than over; you couldn't call him skinny, but you could see the bone structure of his face—flat cheeks, an ordinary nose, and light-colored eyes. When he turned his back to me so as to face Wolfe I saw that his coat didn't hang straight down over his right hip pocket, and I un-crossed my legs and brought my feet back to position, just in case.

There had been no audible replies to his salutation. He looked around again, back again at Wolfe, and smiled at him. "You are Mr. Wolfe?"

"Yes." Wolfe had his fingers intertwined on his belly. "You are Mr. Chapin."

Paul Chapin nodded. "I was at the theater. They've done a book of mine into a play. Then I thought I'd drop in here."

"Which book? I've read all of them."

"You have? Really. I wouldn't suppose . . . *The Iron Heel.*"

"Oh yes. That one. Accept my congratulations."

"Thank you. I hope you don't mind my dropping in. I knew of this gathering, of course. I learned of it from three of my friends, Leo Elkus and Lorry Burton and Alex Drummond. You mustn't hold it against them, except possibly Leo. He meant well, I think, but the others were trying to frighten me. They were trying it with a bogy, but for a bogy to be effective its terrors must be known to the victim. Unfortunately you were unknown to me. You have terrors, I suppose?"

Since Chapin's first word he had kept his eyes on Wolfe, ignoring the others. They were regarding him with varying reactions on their faces: Mitchell of Boston with curiosity, Bowen with a sour poker face, Cabot with uncomfortable indignation, Mike Ayers with scowling disgust . . . I was looking them over. Of a sudden Dr. Burton left his chair, strode to the desk, and grabbed Chapin by the arm. He said to him:

"Paul, for God's sake. Get out of here! This is terrible. Get out!"

Drummond the florist put in, his cultured tenor

transformed by intensity into a ferocious squeal, "This is the limit, Paul! After what we—after what I—you dirty murdering rat!"

Others, breaking their tension, found their tongues. Wolfe stopped them. He said sharply, "Gentlemen! Mr. Chapin is my guest!" He looked at Chapin, leaning on his stick. "You should sit down. Take a chair.—Archie."

"No, thanks. I'll be going in a moment." Chapin sent a smile around; it would have been merely a pleasant smile but for his light-colored eyes where there was no smile at all. "I've been standing on one foot for twenty-five years. Of course all of you know that; I don't need to tell you. I'm sorry if I've annoyed you by coming here; really, I wouldn't disconcert you fellows for anything. You've all been too kind to me, you know very well you have. If I may get a little literary and sentimental about it—you have lightened life's burden for me. I'll never forget it, I've told you that a thousand times. Of course, now that I seem to have found my métier, now that I am standing on my own feet—that is, my own foot—" he smiled around again—"I shall be able to find my way the rest of the journey without you. But I shall always be grateful." He turned to Wolfe. "That's how it is, you see. But I didn't come here to say that, I came to see you. I was thinking that possibly you are a reasonable and intelligent man. Are you?"

Wolfe was looking at him. I was saying to myself, look out, Paul Chapin, look out for those half-closed eyes, and if you take my advice you'll shut up and beat it quick. Wolfe said:

"I reach that pinnacle occasionally, Mr. Chapin."

"I'll try to believe you. There are few who do. I just wanted to say this to you: my friends have wasted a lot of time and money pursuing a mirage which someone has cleverly projected for them. I tell you straight, Mr. Wolfe, it's been a shock to me. That they should suspect *me*, knowing as they do how grateful I am for all their kindness! Really, incredible. I wanted to put this before you and save you from the loss of your time and money too. You would not be so fatuous as to chase a mirage?"

"I assure you, sir, I am far too immobile to chase anything whatever. But perhaps—since you are by your own admission definitely out of it—perhaps you have a theory regarding the incidents that have disturbed your friends? It might help us."

"I'm afraid not." Chapin shook his head regretfully. "Of course, it appears more than likely that it's a practical joke, but I have no idea—"

"Murder isn't a joke, Mr. Chapin. Death is not a joke."

"Oh, no? Really, no? Are you so sure? Take a good case. Take me, Paul Chapin. Would you dare to assert that my death would not be a joke?"

"Why, would it?"

"Of course. A howling anticlimax. Death's pretensions to horror, considering what in my case has preceded it, would be indescribably ludicrous. That is why I have so greatly appreciated my friends, their thoughtfulness, their solicitude—"

A cry from behind interrupted him; a cry, deeply anguished, in the voice of Dr. Burton: "Paul! Paul, for God's sake!"

Chapin wheeled about on his good leg. "Yes?" Without raising his voice a particle he got into it a concentrated scorn that would have withered the love of God. "Yes, Lorry?"

Burton looked at him, said nothing, shook his head,

and turned his eyes away. Chapin turned back to Wolfe. Wolfe said:

"So you adhere to the joke theory."

"Not adhere precisely. It seems likely. So far as I am concerned, Mr. Wolfe, the only point is this: I suffer from the delusion of my friends that I am a source of peril to them. Actually, they are afraid of me. Of *me*! I suffer considerably, I really do. The fact is that it would be difficult to conceive of a more harmless creature than I am. I am myself afraid! Constitutionally afraid of all sorts of things. For instance, on account of my pathetic physical inadequacy, I go in constant fear of this or that sort of violent attack, and I habitually am armed. See—"

Paul Chapin had us going all right. As his right hand came around behind him and his fingers started under the edge of his dinner coat, there were two or three cries of warning from the group, and I took it on the jump. With my momentum and him balanced against his walking-stick, I damn near toppled him over, but I had my grip on his right wrist and saved him from a tumble. With my left hand I jerked the gat from his hip pocket.

"Archie!" Wolfe snapped at me. "Release Mr. Chapin."

I let go his wrist. Wolfe was still snapping: "Give him back his—article."

I looked at the gat. It was a thirty-two, an old veteran, and a glance showed me it wasn't loaded. Paul Chapin, his light-colored eyes having no look in them at all, held out his hand. I put the gun in it and he let it sit there on his palm as if it was a dish of applesauce.

Wolfe said, "Confound you, Archie. You have deprived Mr. Chapin of the opportunity for a dramatic and effective gesture. I know, Mr. Chapin. I am sorry. May I see the gun?"

Chapin handed it to him and he looked it over. He threw the cylinder out and back, cocked it, snapped the trigger, and looked it over again. He said, "An ugly weapon. It terrifies me. Guns always do. May I show it to Mr. Goodwin?"

Chapin shrugged his shoulders, and Wolfe handed the gat to me. I took it under my light and gave it a few warm glances; cocked it, saw what Wolfe had seen, and grinned. Then I looked up and saw Paul Chapin's eyes on me and stopped grinning. You could still have said there was no look in them, but behind them was something I wouldn't have cared to bring into plain sight. I handed him the gun, and he stuck it back into his hip pocket. He said, half to me and half to Wolfe, in an easy tone:

"That's it, you see. The effect is psychological. I learned a good deal about psychology from my friend Andy Hibbard."

There were ejaculations. George Pratt stepped to Chapin and glared at him. Pratt's hands were working at his sides as he stammered, "You—you snake! If you weren't a goddam cripple I'd knock you so far I'll say you'd be harmless—"

Chapin showed no alarm. "Yes, George. And what made me a goddam cripple?"

Pratt didn't retreat. "I helped to, once. Sure I did. That was an accident, we all have 'em, maybe not as bad as yours. Christ, can't you ever forget it? Is there no man in you at all? Has your brain got twisted—"

"No. Man? No." Chapin cut him off, and smiled at him with his mouth. He looked around at the others. "You fellows are all men though. Aren't you? Every one. God bless you. That's an idea, depend on God's blessing. Try it. I tried it once. Now I must ask you to excuse me." He turned to Wolfe. "Good evening, sir. I'll go. Thank you for your courtesy. I trust I haven't put too great a strain on your intelligence."

He inclined his head to Wolfe and to me, turned and made off. His stick had thumped three times on the rug when he was halted by Wolfe's voice:

"Mr. Chapin. I almost forgot. May I ask you for a very few minutes more? Just a small—"

Nicholas Cabot's voice broke in, "For God's sake, Wolfe, let him go—"

"Please, Mr. Cabot. May I, gentlemen? Just a small favor, Mr. Chapin. Since you are innocent of any ill intent, and as anxious as we are to see your friends' difficulties removed, I trust you will help me in a little test. I know it will seem nonsensical to you, quite meaningless, but I should like to try it. Would you help me out?"

Chapin had turned. I thought he looked careful. He said, "Perhaps. What is it?"

"Quite simple. You use a typewriter, I suppose?"

"Of course. I type all my manuscripts myself."

"We have a typewriter here. Would you be good enough to sit at Mr. Goodwin's desk and type something at my dictation?"

"Why should I?" He hesitated, and was certainly being careful now. He looked around and saw twelve pairs of eyes at him; then he smiled and said easily, "But for that matter, why shouldn't I?" He limped back towards me.

I pulled the machine up into position, inserted a sheet of paper, got up, and held my chair for him. He shook his head and I moved away, and he leaned his stick up against the desk and got himself into the chair, shoving his bum leg under with his hand.

Nobody was saying a word. He looked around at Wolfe and said, "I'm not very fast. Shall I double-space it?"

"I would say, single-space. In that way it will most nearly resemble the original. Are you ready?" Wolfe suddenly and unexpectedly put volume and depth into his voice: "*Ye should have killed me*—comma—*watched the last mean sigh*—"

There was complete silence. It lasted ten seconds. Then Chapin's fingers moved and the typewriter clicked, firm and fast. I followed the words on it. It got through the first three, but at the fourth it faltered. It stopped at the second *l* in *killed*, stopped completely. There was silence again. You could have heard a feather falling. The sounds that broke it came from Paul Chapin. He moved with no haste but with a good deal of finality. He pushed back, got himself onto his feet, took his stick, and thumped off. He brushed past me, and Arthur Kommers had to move out of his way. Before he got to the door he stopped and turned. He did not seem especially perturbed, and his light-colored eyes had nothing new in them as far as I could see from where I was.

He said, "I would have been glad to help in any authentic test, Mr. Wolfe, but I wouldn't care to be the victim of a trick. I was referring, by the way, to intelligence, not to a vulgar and obvious cunning."

He turned. Wolfe murmured, "Archie," and I went out to help him on with his coat and open the door for him.

# Chapter 7

When I got back to the office everybody was talking. Mike Ayers had gone to the table to get a drink, and three or four others had joined him. Dr. Burton stood with his hands dug into his pockets, frowning, listening to Farrell and Pratt. Wolfe had untwined his fingers and was showing his inner tumult by rubbing his nose with one of them. When I got to his desk Cabot the lawyer was saying to him:

"I have an idea you'll collect your fees, Mr. Wolfe. I begin to understand your repute."

"I shall make no discount for flummery, sir." Wolfe sighed. "For my part, I have an idea that if I collect my fees I shall have earned them. Your friend Mr. Chapin is a man of quality."

Cabot nodded. "Paul Chapin is a distorted genius."

"All genius is distorted. Including my own. But so for that matter is all life; a mad and futile ferment of substances meant originally to occupy space without disturbing it. But alas, here we are in the thick of the disturbance, and the only way that has occurred to us to make it tolerable is to join in and raise all the hell our ingenuity may suggest.—How did Paul Chapin acquire his special distortion? I mean the famous accident. Tell me about it. I understand it was at college, a hazing affair."

"Yes. It was pretty terrible." Cabot sat on the edge of the desk. "No doubt of that, but good God, other men, the war, for instance . . . oh well. I suppose Paul was distorted from the beginning. He was a freshman, the rest of us were sophomores and on up. Do you know the Yard?"

"The Yard?"

"At Harvard."

"I have never been there."

"Well. There were dormitories—Thayer Hall. This was at Thayer Middle Entry—Hell Bend. We were having a beer night downstairs, and there were some there from outside—that's how fellows like Gaines and Collard happened to be present. We were having a good time around ten o'clock when a fellow came in and said he couldn't get in his room; he had left his key inside and the doors had snap locks. Of course we all began to clap."

"That was a masterpiece, to forget one's key?"

"Oh no. We were clapping the opportunity. By getting out a hall window, or another room, you could make your way along a narrow ledge to the window of any locked room and get in that way. It was quite a trick—I wouldn't try it now for my hope of the Supreme Court—but I had done it in my freshman year and so had many others. Whenever an upperclassman forgot his key it was the native custom to conscript a freshman for that service. There was nothing extraordinary about it, for the agility of youth. Well, when this fellow—it was Andy Hibbard—when he announced he had locked himself out, of course we welcomed the opportunity for a little discipline. We looked around for a victim. Somebody heard a noise in the hall and looked out and saw one going by, and called to him to come in. He came in. It was Chapin."

"He was a freshman."

Cabot nodded. "Paul had a personality, a force in him, already at that age. Maybe he was already distorted. I'm not a psychiatrist. Andy Hibbard has told me . . . but that wouldn't help you any. Anyway, we had been inclined to let him alone. Now, here he was delivered to us by chance. Somebody told him what was expected of him. He was quite cool about it. He asked what floor Andy's room was on, and we told him the fourth, three flights up. He said he was sorry, in that case he couldn't do it. Ferd Bowen said to him, 'What's the matter, you're not a cripple, are you?' He said he was perfectly sound. Bill Harrison, who was serious-minded in his cradle, asked him if he had vertigo. He said no. We marched him upstairs. Ordinarily not more than a dozen or so would probably have gone up to see the fun, but on account of the way he was taking it thirty-five of us herded him up. We didn't touch him. He went, because he knew what would happen if he didn't."

"What would happen?"

"Oh, things. Whatever might occur to us. You know college kids."

"As few as possible."

"Yes. Well, he went. I'll never forget his face as he was getting out of the hall window, backwards. It was white as a sheet, but it was something else too, I don't know what. It got me. It got Andy Hibbard too, for he jumped forward and called to Chapin to come back in, he would do it himself. Others grabbed Andy and told him not to be a damn fool. All who could crowded up and looked out of the window. It was moonlight. Others ran to one of the rooms and looked out of the windows there. Chapin got onto the ledge all right, and got straightened up and moved along a little, his hand stretched out as far as he could, trying to reach the next window. I didn't see it, I wasn't looking, but they said that all of a sudden he began to tremble, and down he went."

Cabot stopped. He reached in his pocket for his case and lit a cigarette. He didn't hold the match to it as steady as he might have. He took a couple of puffs and said, "That's all. That's what happened."

Wolfe grunted. "You say there were thirty-five of you?"

"Yes. So it turned out." Cabot pulled at his cigarette. "We chipped in, of course, and did all we could. He was in the hospital two months and had three operations. I don't know where he got a list of our names; I suppose from Andy. Andy took it hard. Anyway, the day he left the hospital he sent all of us copies of a poem he had written. Thanking us. It was clever. There was only one of us smart enough to see what kind of thanks it was. Pitney Scott."

"Pitney Scott is a taxi-driver."

Cabot raised his brows. "You should write our class history, Mr. Wolfe. Pit took to drink in 1930, one of the depression casualties. Not, like Mike Ayers, for the annoyance of other people. For his own destruction. I see you have him down for five dollars. I'll pay it."

"Indeed. That would indicate that you are prepared to accept my proposal."

"Of course I am. We all are. But you know that. What else can we do? We are menaced with death, there's no question about it. I have no idea why, if Paul had this in him, he waited so long to get it out— possibly his recent success gave him a touch of confidence that he needed, or money to finance his plans—I don't know. Of course we accept your proposal. Did you know that a month ago Adler and Pratt and Bowen seriously discussed the notion of hiring a gangster to kill him? They invited me in, but I wouldn't—everyone's squeamishness begins somewhere, and I suppose that was the starting point for mine—and they abandoned the idea. What else can we do? The police are helpless, which is understandable and nothing against them; they are equipped to frustrate many kinds of men, but not Paul Chapin—I grant him his quality. Three of us hired detectives a month ago, and we might as well have engaged a troop of Boy Scouts. They spent days looking for the typewriter on which the warnings were written, and never even found it; and if they had found it they would not have been able to fasten it on Paul Chapin."

"Yes." Wolfe reached out and pressed the button for Fritz. "Your detectives called on me and offered to place their findings at my disposal—with your consent." Fritz appeared, and Wolfe nodded for beer. "Mr. Cabot. What does Mr. Chapin mean when he says that you killed the man in him?"

"Well . . . that's poetry, isn't it?"

"It might be called that. Is it merely poetry, or is it also technical information?"

"I don't know." Cabot's eyes fell. I watched him and thought to myself, he's actually embarrassed; so there's kinks in your love-life too, huh, smoothie? He went on, "I couldn't say; I doubt if any of us could. You'd have to ask his doctor."

A new voice cut in. Julius Adler and Alex Drummond had come over a few minutes before and stood listening; Adler, I suppose, because he was a lawyer and therefore didn't trust lawyers, and Drummond since he was a tenor. I never saw a tenor that wasn't inquisitive. At this point Drummond horned in with a giggle:

"Or his wife."

Wolfe snapped at him, "Whose wife?"

"Why, Paul's."

If I had seen Wolfe astonished only three times in seven years, which is what I would guess, this was the fourth. He even moved in his chair. He looked at Cabot, not at Drummond, and demanded, "What is this nonsense?"

Cabot nodded. "Sure, Paul has a wife."

Wolfe poured a glass of beer, gulped half of it, let it settle a second, and swallowed the rest. He looked around for his handkerchief, but it had dropped to the floor. I got him one out of the drawer where I kept them, and he wiped his lips.

He said, "Tell me about her."

"Well . . ." Cabot looked for words. "Paul Chapin is full of distortions, let us say, and his wife is one of them. Her name was Dora Ritter. He married her three years ago, and they live in an apartment on Perry Street."

"What is she like and who was she?"

Cabot hesitated again, differently. This time he didn't seem to be looking for words, he was looking for a way out. He finally said, "I don't see—I really don't see that this is going to help you any, but I suppose you'll want to know it. But I'd rather not—you'd better get it from Burton himself." He turned and called, "Lorry! Come over here a minute."

Dr. Burton was with the group at the table, talking and working on a highball. He looked around, made some remark to Farrell the architect, and crossed to Wolfe's desk. Cabot said to him:

"Mr. Wolfe has just asked me who Paul's wife was. Maybe I'm being more delicate than the circumstances require, but I'd rather you'd tell him."

Burton looked at Wolfe and frowned. He looked at Cabot, and his voice sounded irritated: "Why not you, or anybody? Everybody knows it."

Cabot smiled. "I said maybe I was overdelicate."

"I think you were." Burton turned to Wolfe. "Dora Ritter was a maid in my employ. She is around fifty, extremely homely, disconcertingly competent, and stubborn as a wet boot. Paul Chapin married her in 1931."

"What did he marry her for?"

"I am as likely to tell you as he is. Chapin is a psychopath."

"So Mr. Hibbard informed me. What sort of maid was she?"

"What sort?"

"Was she in your office, for instance?"

Burton was frowning. "No. She was my wife's maid."

"How long have you known her and how long has Chapin known her?—Wait." Wolfe wiggled a finger. "I must ask you to bear with me, Dr. Burton. I have just received a shock and am floundering in confusion. I have read all of Paul Chapin's novels, and so naturally supposed myself to be in possession of a fairly complete understanding of his character, his temperament, his processes of thought and his modes of action. I thought him incapable of following any of the traditional channels leading to matrimony, either emotional or practical. Learning that he has a wife, I am greatly shocked; I am even desperate. I need to have disclosed everything about her that is discoverable."

"Oh. You do." Burton looked at him, sizing him up, with sour steadiness. "Then I might as well disclose it myself. It was common gossip." He glanced at the others. "I knew that, though naturally it didn't reach my ears. If I show reluctance, it is only because it was . . . unpleasant."

"Yes."

"Yes, it was. I presume you don't know that of all of us, this group, I was the only one who knew Paul Chapin before the college days. We came from the same town—I more or less grew up with him. He was in love with a girl. I knew her—one of the girls I knew, that was all. He was infatuated with her, and he finally, through persistence, reached an understanding with her before he went away to college. Then the accident occurred, and he was crippled, and it was all off. In my opinion it would have been off anyway, sooner or later, without the intervention of an accident. I didn't go home for my vacations; I spent my summers working. It wasn't until after I was through with medical school that I went back for a visit, and discovered that this girl had become . . . that is . . . I married her."

He glanced aside at Cabot's cigarette case thrust at him by the lawyer, shook his head, turned back to Wolfe and went on, "We came to New York. I was lucky in my profession; I have a good bedside manner and a knack with people's insides, especially women. I made a lot of money. I think it was in 1923 that my wife engaged Dora Ritter—yes, she was with us eight years. Her competence was a jewel in a nigger's ear—"

"Ethiope."

"Well, that's a nigger. One day Paul came to me and said he was going to marry my wife's maid. That was what was unpleasant. He made a nasty scene out of it."

Wolfe inclined his head. "I can imagine him explaining that the action contemplated was by way of a paraphrase on the old institution of whipping-boy."

Dr. Burton jerked his head up, startled, and stared at him. "How the devil did you know that?"

"He said that?"

"Those words. He said paraphrase."

"I suspected he would have lit on that." Wolfe scratched his ear, and I knew he was pleased. "Having read his novels, I am not unacquainted with his style of thought and his taste in allusion.—So he married her. She, of course, having but one jewel and the rest all slag, would not be finicky. Do they make a happy pair? Do you ever see her?"

"Not frequently." Burton hesitated, then went on, "I see her very seldom. She comes once or twice a week to dress my wife's hair, and occasionally to sew. I am usually not at home."

Wolfe murmured, "It is a temptation to cling to competence when we find it."

Burton nodded. "I suppose so. My wife finds it impossible to forgo the indulgence. Dora is an expert hag."

"Well." Wolfe took some beer. "Thank you, doctor. It has often been said, you will find romance in the most unlikely spots. Mr. Chapin's no longer upsets me, since it fits my presumptions. By the way, this probably clears up another little point. Permit me.— Archie, would you ask Mr. Farrell to join us?"

I went and got Farrell and brought him over. He was brisk; the Scotch was putting some spring into him. He gave Wolfe an amiable look.

"Mr. Farrell. Earlier this evening you remarked to Dr. Burton that it was a wonder he was not the first. I suppose that you meant, the first victim of Mr.

Chapin's campaign. Did that remark mean anything in particular?"

Farrell looked uncomfortable. "Did I say that?"

"You did."

"I don't remember it. I suppose I thought I was cracking a joke, I don't know."

Wolfe said patiently, "Dr. Burton has just been telling me the exegesis of Chapin's marriage and the former occupation of his wife. I thought perhaps—"

"Oh, he has." Farrell shot a glance at Burton. "Then what are you asking me for?"

"Don't be testy, Mr. Farrell; let me save your life in amity. That was the basis of your remark?"

"Of course. But what the devil have Lorrie Burton's private affairs got to do with it? Or mine or anybody's? I thought what we are going to pay you for is to stop—"

He broke off. He looked around at the others and his face got red. He finished to Wolfe in a completely different tone, "Forgive me. I forgot for a moment."

"Forgot what?"

"Nothing of any importance. Only that I'm out of it. In your total of fifty-odd thousand, you've got me down for ten dollars. Your sources of information are up-to-date. Have you any idea what architects have been up against the past four years? Even good ones. I did the new city hall at Baltimore in 1928. Now I couldn't get—you're not thinking of doing any building, Mr. Wolfe? A telephone stand or a dog kennel or anything? I'd be glad to submit designs—Oh, the devil. Anyway, I forgot I'm just here ex-officio, I'm not paying my way.—Come on, Lorrie, come and finish your drink. You ought to be home in bed, you're sagging worse than I am." He took Burton's arm.

Moving off, they halted for Wolfe: "Mr. Farrell. I

am under the same necessity of earning your ten dollars as Mr. Collard's nine thousand. If you have comments—"

"Hell no. I haven't even got a comment. Nor am I even contributing ten bucks to the pot of retribution, I'm taking it out in Scotch."

George Pratt said to Cabot, "Come on, Nick, have a little refreshment," and they followed the other two. Alex Drummond was left alone at the corner of Wolfe's desk; he jerked to join the procession, then jerked back. He looked at Wolfe with his bright little eyes, stepped closer to him, and made his voice low:

"Uh—Mr. Wolfe. I imagine your sources of information are pretty good."

Wolfe said without looking at him, "They are superlative."

"I imagine so. Gus Farrell hasn't really been up against it for more than a couple of months, but I notice you are aware of it. Uh—I wonder if you would be willing to enlighten me regarding another item on your list. Just curiosity."

"I haven't engaged to satisfy your curiosity."

"No. But I was wondering. Why have you got Gaines down for eight thousand and Burton for seven thousand and so on, and Ferd Bowen for only twelve hundred? He's something in Wall Street—I mean really something. Isn't he? The firm of Galbraith and Bowen . . ." Drummond made his voice a little lower. "Frankly, it's more than curiosity . . . he handles a few little investments for me . . ."

Wolfe looked at him and looked away again. I thought for a minute he wasn't going to reply at all, but he did, with his eyes shut. "Don't bother to disparage your investments. It can have no effect on the amount of your payment to me, for that has already been calculated and recorded. As for your question, my sources of information may be superlative, but they are not infallible. If Mr. Bowen ventures to object that I have belittled him, I shall consider his protest with an open mind."

"Of course," Drummond agreed. "But if you could just tell me in confidence—"

"If you will excuse me." Wolfe opened his eyes, got his chin up, and raised his voice a little. "Gentlemen. Gentlemen? Could I have a word with you?"

They approached his desk, three or four from the corner the bookshelves made, and the wet contingent from the alcove table. Two or three still in chairs stayed there. Drummond, his hide too thick to show any red from Wolfe's sandpapering, trotted around to the far side. Mike Ayers flopped into a chair again, stretching out his legs; his mouth gaped wide in a free-for-all yawn, then suddenly he clamped his lips tight with a look of indignant and wary surprise. I had a notion to go and move him off the rug, but decided he was going to hold it. Wolfe was handing it to them in his handsome manner:

"The hour is getting late, and I would not wish to detain you beyond necessity. I take it that we are in agreement—"

Arthur Kommers interrupted, "I ought to leave in a minute to catch the midnight back to Philadelphia. Do you want my initials on that thing?"

"Thank you, sir. Not at present. There is a phrase to be deleted. I shall ask Mr. Cabot to prepare copies in his office tomorrow morning and send them to me for distribution." He sent a glance at the lawyer, and Cabot nodded. "Thank you.—In that connection, Mr. Farrell, I wish to make a proposal to you. You are broke, but you have a fairly intelligent face. To be broke is not a disgrace, it is only a catastrophe. You can help me. For instance, you can take, or send, copies of the memorandum to those members of the league not present this evening, and arrange for their co-operation. I will pay you twenty dollars a day. There will be other little jobs for you."

The architect was staring at him. "You're quite a guy, Mr. Wolfe. By God if you're not. But I'm not a detective."

"I shall keep my demands modest, and expect no intrepidity."

"All right." Farrell laughed. "I can use twenty dollars."

"Good. Report here tomorrow at eleven.—Now, Dr. Burton. Your lifelong acquaintance with Paul Chapin places you in a special position, for my purpose. Could you dine with me tomorrow evening?"

Without hesitation, Burton shook his head. "I'm sorry, I shall be engaged."

"Could you call on me after dinner? Forgive me for not asking permission to call on you instead. My disinclination to leave my home has a ponderable basis."

But Burton shook his head again. "I'm sorry, Mr. Wolfe, I can't come." He hesitated, and went on, "More frankly, I won't. It's softness in me. I'm not as soft about it as Andy Hibbard and Leo Elkus. I answered yes to the question you put this evening, though you made it as raw as possible. Of course you did that purposely. I answered yes, and I'll pay my share, but that's as far as I'll go. I will not confer on ways and means of exposing Paul Chapin's guilt and getting him convicted and electrocuted.—Oh, don't misunderstand me. I don't pretend to be standing on a principle, I'm perfectly aware it's only a temperamental prejudice. I wouldn't move a finger to protect Paul or save him from the consequences of his crimes. In fact, in so far as the thing may be considered a personal issue between him and myself, I am ready to defeat him by a violence equal to his own."

"You are ready?" Wolfe had opened his eyes on him. "You mean you are prepared?"

"Not specially." Burton looked irritated. "It is of no importance whatever. I always seem to talk too much when Paul Chapin is concerned; I wish to the Lord I'd never heard of him. As far as that goes, of course we all do. I only meant . . . well, for years I've kept an automatic pistol in the drawer of my study-table. One evening last week Paul came to see me. For years, of course, he was welcome at my house, though he seldom came. On this occasion, on account of recent events, I told the butler to keep him in the reception hall; and before I went to the reception hall I took the pistol from the drawer and stuck it in my pocket.— That was all I meant; I would be perfectly willing to use personal violence if the circumstances required it."

Wolfe sighed. "I regret your soft spot, Dr. Burton. But for that you might, for instance, tell us which evening Mr. Chapin went to see you and what it was he wanted."

"That wouldn't help you." Burton was brusque. "It was personal—that is, it was only neurotic nonsense."

"So, they say, was Napoleon's dream of empire. Very well, sir. By all means cling to the tattered shreds of humanity that are left you; there are enough of us in that respect quite unclothed. I must somehow manage my enterprise without stripping you. I would like as ask, gentlemen: which of you were most intimate with Mr. Hibbard?"

They looked at each other. George Pratt said, "We all saw Andy off and on." Julius Adler put in, "I would say that among us Roland Erskine was his closest friend. I would boast that I was next."

"Erskine the actor?" Wolfe glanced at the clock. "I was thinking he might join us after the theater, but scarcely at this hour. He is working, I believe."

Drummond said, "He's in *The Iron Heel*, he has the lead."

"Then he couldn't dine. Not at a civilized hour." Wolfe looked at Julius Adler. "Could you come here at two o'clock tomorrow afternoon and bring Erskine with you?"

"Perhaps." The lawyer looked annoyed. "I suppose I could manage it. Couldn't you come to my office?"

"I'm sorry, sir. Believe me, I am; but knowing my habits as I do, it seems extravagantly improbable. If you could arrange to bring Mr. Erskine—"

"All right. I'll see what I can do."

"Thank you.—You had better run, Mr. Kommers, or you'll miss your train. Another reason, and one of the best, for staying at home.—Gentlemen, so far as our business is concerned I need not further detain you. But in connection with my remark to Mr. Kommers it occurs to me that no publication either before or since the invention of printing, no theological treatise and no political or scientific creed, has ever been as narrowly dogmatic or as offensively arbitrary in its prejudices as a railway timetable. If any of you should care to remain half an hour or so to help me enlarge upon that . . ."

Byron the magazine editor, who had stuck in his shell all evening, suddenly woke up. He got up from his chair and slipped his head in between a couple of shoulders to see Wolfe. "You know, that idea could be developed into a first-rate little article. Six hundred to seven hundred words, about. The Tyranny of the Wheel, you could call it, with a colored margin of trains and airplanes and ocean liners at top speed—of course liners don't have wheels, but you could do something about that—if I could persuade you, Mr. Wolfe—"

"I'm afraid you could only bewilder me, Mr. Byron."

Cabot the lawyer smiled. "I never saw a man less likely to be bewildered, even by Eddie Byron. Good night, Mr. Wolfe." He picked up the memorandum and folded it and put it in his pocket. "I'll send you these in the morning."

They got moving. Pratt and Farrell went and got Mike Ayers to his feet and slapped him around a little. Byron started trying to persuade Wolfe again and was pulled off by Adler. Kommers had gone. The others drifted to the hall, and I went out and stood around while they got their hats and coats on. Bowen and Burton went off together, as they had come. I held the door for Pratt and Farrell to get Mike Ayers through; they were the last out.

After I had shut the door and bolted it I went to the kitchen for a pitcher of milk. Fritz was sitting there reading that newspaper printed in French, with his butler shoes still on, in spite of how he loved to put on his slippers after dinner on account of things left on his toes and feet by the war to remember it by. We said what we always said under those circumstances. He said, "I could bring your milk, Archie, if you would just tell me," and I said, "If I can drink it I can carry it."

In the office, Wolfe sat back with his eyes closed. I took the milk to my desk and poured a glass and sat down and sipped at it. The room was full of smoke and the smell of different drinks and chairs were scattered around and cigar and cigarette ashes were all over the rugs. It annoyed me, and I got up and opened a window. Wolfe said, "Close it," and I got up and closed it again. I poured another glass of milk.

I said, "This bird Chapin is a lunatic, and it's long past midnight. I'm damn good and sleepy."

Wolfe kept his eyes shut, and also ignored me in other ways. I said, "Do you realize we could earn all that jack and save a lot of trouble just by having a simple little accident happen to Paul Chapin? Depression prices on accidents like that run from fifty bucks up. It's smart to be thrifty."

Wolfe murmured, "Thank you, Archie. When I exhaust my own expedients I shall know where to turn.—A page in your notebook."

I opened a drawer and took out a book and pencil.

"Phone Mr. Cabot's office at nine o'clock and make sure that the memorandums will be here by eleven, ready for Mr. Farrell. Ask where the reports from the Bascom Agency are and arrange to get them. The men will be here at eight?"

"Yes, sir."

"Send one of them to get the reports. Put three of them on Paul Chapin, first thing. We want a complete record of his movements, and phone anything of significance."

"Durkin and Keems and Gore?"

"That is your affair. But Saul Panzer is to get his nose onto Andrew Hibbard's last discoverable footstep. Tell him to phone me at eleven-thirty."

"Yes, sir."

"Put Cather onto Chapin's past, outside the circle of our clients, especially the past two years. As complete as possible. He might succeed in striking an harmonious chord with Dora Chapin."

"Maybe I could do that myself. She's probably a lulu."

"I suspect that of being a vulgarization of the word *allure*. If she is alluring, resist the temptation for the moment. Your special province will be the deaths of

Harrison and Dreyer. First read the Bascom reports, then proceed. Wherever original investigation is indicated and seems still feasible after the lapse of time, undertake it. Use men as necessary, but avoid extravagance. Do not call upon any of our clients until Mr. Farrell has seen them.—That's all. It's late."

Wolfe opened his eyes, blinked, and closed them again. But I noticed that the tip of his finger was doing a little circle on the arm of the chair. I grinned:

"Maybe we've got this and that for tomorrow and next day, but maybe right now you're troubled by the same thing I am. Why is this Mr. Chapin giving hip room to a Civil War gat with the hammer nose filed off so that it's about as murderous as a beanshooter?"

"I'm not troubled, Archie." But his finger didn't stop. "I'm wondering whether another bottle of beer before going to bed would be judicious."

"You've had six since dinner."

"Seven. One upstairs."

"Then for God's sake call it a day. Speaking of Chapin's cannon, do you remember the lady dope-fiend who carried a box of pellets made out of flour in her sock, the usual cache, and when they took that and thought she was frisked, she still had the real thing in the hem of her skirt? Of course I don't mean that Chapin had another gun necessarily, I just mean, psychologically . . ."

"Good heavens." Wolfe pushed back his chair, not of course with violence, but with determination. "Archie. Understand this. As a man of action you are tolerable, you are even competent. But I will not for one moment put up with you as a psychologist. I am going to bed."

# Chapter 8

I had heard Wolfe, at various times, make quite a few cracks about murder. He had said once that no man could commit so complicated a deed as a premeditated murder and leave no opening. He had also said that the only way to commit a murder and remain safe from detection, despite any ingenuity in pursuit and trusting to no luck, was to do it impromptu; await your opportunity, keep your wits about you, and strike when the instant offered; and he added that the luxury of the impromptu murder could be afforded only by those who happened to be in no great hurry about it.

By Tuesday evening I was convinced of one thing about the death of Wm. R. Harrison, Federal judge from Indianapolis: that if it had been murder at all it had been impromptu. I would like to say another thing right here, that I know when I'm out of my class. I've got my limitations, and I never yet have tried to give them the ritz. Paul Chapin hadn't been in Nero Wolfe's office more than three minutes Monday night when I saw he was all Greek to me; if it was left to me to take him apart he was sitting pretty. When people begin to get deep and complicated they mix me up. But pictures never do. With pictures, no matter how many pieces they've got that don't seem to fit at first, I'm there forty ways from Sunday. I spent six hours Tuesday with the picture of Judge Harrison's death—reading the Bascom reports, talking with six people including thirty minutes on long distance with Fillmore Collard, and chewing it along with two meals—and I decided three things about it: first, that if it was murder it was impromptu; second, that if anybody killed him it was Paul Chapin; and third, that there was as much chance of proving it as there was of proving that honesty was the best policy.

It had happened nearly five months back, but the things that had happened since, starting with the typewritten poems they had got in the mail, had kept their memories active. Paul Chapin had driven up to Harvard with Leopold Elkus, the surgeon, who had gone because he had a son graduating. Judge Harrison had come on from Indianapolis for the same reason. Drummond had been there, Elkus told me, because each year the doubt whether he had really graduated from a big university became overwhelming and he went back every June to make sure. Elkus was very fond of Drummond, the way a taxi-driver is of a cop. Cabot and Sidney Lang had been in Boston on business, and Bowen had been a house-guest at the home of Theodore Gaines; presumably they were hatching some sort of a financial deal. Anyway, Fillmore Collard had got in touch with his old classmates and invited them for the week-end to his place near Marblehead. There had been quite a party, more than a dozen altogether.

Saturday evening after dinner they had strolled through the grounds, as darkness fell, to the edge of a hundred-foot cliff at the base of which the surf roared among jagged rocks. Four, among them Cabot and

Elkus, had stayed in the house playing bridge. Paul
Chapin had hobbled along with the strollers. They had
separated, some going to the stables with Collard to see
a sick horse, some back to the house, one or two staying
behind. It was an hour or so later that they missed
Harrison, and not until midnight did they become really
concerned. Daylight came before the tide was out
enough for them to find his cut and bruised body at the
foot of the cliff, wedged among the rocks.

A tragic accident and a ruined party. It had had no
significance beyond that until the Wednesday following, when the typewritten poem came to each of them.
It said a good deal for Paul Chapin's character and
quality, the fact that none of them for a moment
doubted the poem's implications. Cabot said that what
closed their minds to any doubt was the similarity in the
manner of Harrison's death to the accident Chapin had
suffered from many years before. He had fallen from a
height. They got together, and considered, and tried to
remember. After the interval of four days there was a
good deal of disagreement. A man named Meyer, who
lived in Boston, had stated Saturday night that he had
gone off leaving Harrison seated on the edge of the cliff
and had jokingly warned him to be ready to pull his
parachute cord, and that no one else had been around.
Now they tried to remember about Chapin. Two were
positive that he had limped along after the group stroll-
ing to the house, that he had come up to them on the
veranda, and had entered with them. Bowen thought he
remembered seeing him at the stables. Sidney Lang had
seen him reading a book soon after the group returned,
and was of the opinion that he had not stirred from his
seat for an hour or more.

All the league was in on it now, for they had all got
warnings. They got nowhere. Two or three were

inclined to laugh it off. Leopold Elkus thought Chapin guiltless, even of the warnings, and advised looking elsewhere for the culprit. Some, quite a few at first, were in favor of turning it over to the police, but they were talked down, chiefly by Hibbard and Burton and Elkus. Collard and Gaines came down from Boston, and they tried to reconstruct the evening and definitely outline Chapin's movements, but failed through disagreements. In the end they delegated Burton, Cabot and Lang to call on Chapin.

Chapin had smiled at them. At their insistence he described his Saturday evening movements, recollecting them clearly and in detail; he had caught up with them at the cliff and sat there on a bench, and had left with the group that returned to the house; he had not noticed Harrison sitting on the cliff's edge. At the house, not being a card-player, he had got into a chair with a book and had stayed there with it until aroused by the hubbub over Harrison's absence—approaching midnight. That was his smiling story. He had been not angry, but delicately hurt, that his best friends could think him capable of wishing injury to one of them, knowing as they did that the only struggle in his breast was between affection and gratitude, for the lead. Smiling, but hurt. As for the warnings they had received, that was another matter. Regarding that, he said, his sorrow that they should suspect him not only of violence but threats of additional violence, was lost in his indignation that he should be accused of so miserable a piece of versifying. He criticized it in detail and with force. As a threat it might be thought effective, he couldn't say as to that, but as poetry it was rotten, and he had certainly never supposed that his best friends could accuse him of such an offense. But then, he had ended, he realized that he would have to forgive them and he did so, fully and without reservation, since it was obvious that they were having quite a scare and so should not be held to account.

Who had sent the warnings, if he hadn't? He had no idea. Of course it could have been done by anyone knowing of that ancient accident who had also learned of this recent one. One guess was as good as another, unless they could uncover something to point their suspicion. The postmark might furnish a hint, or the envelopes and paper, or the typewriting itself. Maybe they had better see if they couldn't find the typewriter.

The committee of three had called on him at his apartment in Perry Street, and were sitting with him in the little room that he used for a study. As he had offered his helpful suggestion he had got up and limped over to his typewriter, patted it, and smiled at them:

"I'm sure that discreditable stuff wasn't written on this, unless one of you fellows sneaked in here and used it when I wasn't looking."

Nicholas Cabot had been tough enough to go over and stick in a sheet of paper and type a few lines on it, and put the sheet in his pocket and take it away with him, but a later examination had shown that Chapin was quite correct. The committee had made its report, and subsequent discussions had taken place, but weeks had gone by and the thing petered out. Most of them, becoming a little ashamed of themselves and convinced that someone had tried a practical joke, made a point of continuing their friendly relations with Chapin. So far as was known by the six men I talked to, it hadn't been mentioned to him again.

I reported all this, in brief outline, to Wolfe Tuesday evening. His comment was, "Then the death of this Judge Harrison, this man who in his conceit permitted himself the awful pretensions of a reader of chaos—whether designed by Providence or by Paul Chapin, his death was extempore. Let us forget it; it might clutter up our minds, but it cannot crowd oblivion. If Mr. Chapin had been content with that man's death and had restrained his impulse to rodomontade, he might have considered himself safely avenged—in that instance. But his vanity undid him; he wrote that threat and sent it broadcast. That was dangerous."

"How sure are you?"

"Sure—"

"That he sent the threat."

"Did I not say he did?"

"Yeah. Excuse me for living."

"I would not take that responsibility; I have all I can do to excuse myself.—But so much for Judge Harrison; whatever chaos he inhabits now, let us hope he contemplates it with a wiser modesty. I would tell you about Mr. Hibbard. That is, I would tell you nothing, for there is nothing to tell. His niece, Miss Evelyn Hibbard, called on me this morning."

"Oh, she did. I thought she was coming Wednesday."

"She anticipated it, having received a report of last evening's gathering."

"Did she spill anything new?"

"She could add nothing to what she told you Saturday evening. She has made another thorough search of the apartment, helped by her sister, and can find nothing whatever missing. Either Mr. Hibbard's absence was unforeseen by him, or he was a remarkably intelligent and strong-willed man. He was devoted to two pipes, which he smoked alternately. One of them is there in its usual place. He made no uncommon withdrawal from his bank, but he always carried a good deal of cash."

"Didn't I tell you about the pipe?"

"You may have. Saul Panzer, after a full day, had to offer one little morsel. A news vendor at One Hundred Sixteenth Street and Broadway, who has known Mr. Hibbard by sight for several years, saw him enter the subway between nine and ten o'clock last Tuesday evening."

"That was the only bite Saul got?"

Wolfe nodded, on his way slanting forward to reach the button on his desk. "The police had got that too, and no more, though it has been a full week since Mr. Hibbard disappeared. I telephoned Inspector Cramer this morning, and Mr. Morley at the District Attorney's office. As you know, they lend information only at usurious rates, but I gathered that they have exhausted even conjecture."

"Morley would deal you an extra card any time."

"Perhaps, but not when he has none to deal. Saul Panzer is following a suggestion I offered him, but its promise is negligible. There is no point in his attempting a solitary fishing expedition; if Mr. Chapin went for a walk with Mr. Hibbard and pushed him off a bridge into the East River, we cannot expect Saul to dive for the corpse. The routine facilities of the police and Bascom's men have covered, and are covering, possibilities of that nature. As for Mr. Chapin, it would be useless to question him. He has told both Bascom and the police that he spent last Tuesday evening in his apartment, and his wife sustains him. No one in the neighborhood remembers seeing him venture forth."

"You suggested something to Saul?"

"Merely to occupy him." Wolfe poured a glass of beer. "But on the most critical front, at the moment, we have met success. Mr. Farrell has gained the adherence of twenty individuals to the memorandum—all but Dr. Elkus in the city, and all but one without, over the telephone. Mr. Pitney Scott, the taxi-driver, is excluded from these statistics; there would be no profit in hounding him, but you might find occasion to give him a glance; he arouses my curiosity, faintly, in another direction. Copies of the memorandum have been distributed, for return. Mr. Farrell is also collecting the warnings, all copies except those in the possession of the police. It will be well to have—"

The telephone rang. I nearly knocked my glass of milk over getting it. I'm always like that when we're on a case, and I suppose I'll never get over it; if I had just landed ten famous murderers and had them salted down, and was at the moment engaged in trying to run down a guy who had put a slug in a subway turnstile, Fritz going to answer the doorbell would put a quiver in me.

I heard a few words, and nodded at Wolfe. "Here's Farrell now." Wolfe pulled his phone over, and I kept my receiver to my ear. They talked only a minute or two.

After we had hung up, I said, "What what? Farrell taking Mr. Somebody to lunch at the Harvard Club? You're spending money like a drunken sailor."

Wolfe rubbed his nose. "I am not spending it. Mr. Farrell is. Decency will of course require me to furnish it. I requested Mr. Farrell to arrange for an interview with Mr. Oglethorpe; I did not contemplate feeding him. It is now beyond remedy. Mr. Oglethorpe is a member of the firm which publishes Mr. Chapin's books, and Mr. Farrell is slightly acquainted with him."

I grinned. "Well, you're stuck. I suppose you want him to publish your essay on The Tyranny of the Wheel. How's it coming on?"

Wolfe ignored my wit. He said, "Upstairs this morning I spent twenty minutes considering where Paul Chapin might elect to type something which he would not wish to be traced to him. The suggestion in one of Bascom's reports, that Chapin has a duplicate set of type-bars for his machine which he substitutes on occasion, I regard as infantile. Not only would the changing of the bars be a difficult, laborious and uninspired proceeding; there is also the fact that the duplicate set would have to be concealed in some available spot, and that would be hazardous. No. Not that. Then there is the old trick of going to a type-writer agency and using one of their machines exposed for sale. But a visit from Paul Chapin, with his infirmity, would be remembered; also, that is excluded by the fact that all three of the warnings were executed on the same typewriter. I considered other possibilities, including some of those explored by Bascom, and one seemed to offer at least a faint promise. Mr. Chapin might call at the office of his publisher and, wishing to alter a manuscript, or even merely to write a letter, request the use of a type-writer. I am counting on Mr. Farrell to discover that; having discovered it, he may be able to get Mr. Oglethorpe's permission to take a sample of the work of the machine that Chapin used—or if that is not known, of each machine in their office."

I nodded. "That's not very dumb. I'm surprised that Farrell can still pay his dues at the Harvard Club."

"When a man of a certain type is forced into drastic financial retrenchment, he first deserts his family, then goes naked, and then gives up his club. Which reminds me, I gave Mr. Farrell twenty dollars this afternoon. Please record it. You may also note on your list those who have initialed the memorandum, and file the various copies. Also, note that we have an additional contributor, Miss Evelyn Hibbard. I arranged it with her this morning. The amount is three thousand dollars." He sighed. "I made a large reduction from the ten thousand she offered Saturday on account of the altered circumstances."

I had been waiting for that, or something like it. I made the Farrell entry in the cashbook, but didn't get out the list. I felt like clearing my throat, but I knew that wouldn't do, so I swallowed instead. I put the cashbook back and turned to Wolfe:

"You understand, sir, I wouldn't accuse you of trying to put anything over. I know you just forgot about it."

His eyes opened at me. "Archie. You are trying the cryptic approach again. To what this time?"

"No, sir. This is on the level. You just forgot that Miss Evelyn Hibbard is *my* client. I went to see her Saturday at your suggestion; you couldn't take her on because you had other plans in mind. Remember, sir? So of course any arrangement she might make in this connection could only be with my advice and consent."

Wolfe was keeping his eyes open. He murmured, "Preposterous. Puerile trickery. You would not attempt to maintain that position."

I sighed, as much like one of his sighs as I could make it. "I hate to, sir. I really do. But it's the only honest thing I can do, protect my client. Of course you understand the ethics of it, I don't have to explain—"

He cut me off. "No. I would suggest that you refrain from explaining. How much would you advise your client to pay?"

"One thousand bucks."

"Absurd. In view of her original offer—"

"All right. I won't haggle. I'll split the difference with you. Two thousand. I stick there. I'm glued."

Wolfe shut his eyes. "Done, confound you. Enter it.—Now take your notebook. Tomorrow morning . . ."

# Chapter 9

Wednesday morning pretty early I was sitting in the kitchen, with the *Times* propped up in front of me but not really seeing it because I was busy in my mind mapping out the day, getting on towards the bottom of my second cup of coffee, when Fritz returned from a trip to the front door to say that Fred Durkin wanted to see me. One thing I hate to be disturbed at is my last two healthy swallows of morning coffee, so I nodded and took my time. When I got to the office Fred was sitting there scowling at his hat on the floor, where it had landed when he had tried to toss it so it would hook on the back of my chair. He always missed. I picked it up and handed it to him and said:

"A dollar even you can't do it once out of ten tries."

He shook his big Irish bean. "No time. I'm a workingman. I was just waiting for you to pick your teeth. Can I see Wolfe?"

"You know damn well you can't. Up to eleven o'clock Mr. Nero Wolfe is a horticulturist."

"Uh-huh. This is special."

"Not special enough for that. Spill it to the Chief of Staff. Has the lop put dust in your eyes? Why aren't you on his tail?"

"I don't relieve Johnny until nine. I'll be there." Durkin grabbed his hat by the brim, squinted for an aim, tossed it at the back of my chair again, and missed it by a mile. He grunted with disgust. "Listen here, Archie. It's a washout."

"What's the matter with it?"

"Well, you put three of us on this to cover him twenty-four hours a day. When Wolfe spends money like that, that shows it's important. He really wants this bird's program. Also, you told us to use taxis all we needed to, and so on. Well, it's a washout. Chapin lives in an apartment house at 203 Perry Street with six floors and an elevator. He's on the fifth. The house has a big court in the back, with a couple of trees and some shrubs, and in the spring it's full of tulips. The elevator boy told me three thousand tulips. But the idea is that there's another house on the court, facing on Eleventh Street, built by the same landlord, and so what? Anybody that wants to can go out of the Perry Street house the back way instead of the front. They can cross the court and go through a passage and come out on Eleventh Street. Of course they could get back in the same way if they felt like it. So parked in a cigar store the other side of Perry Street with my eye fastened on 203, I feel about as useful as if I was watching one of the tunnel exits at the Yankee Stadium for a woman in a dark hat. Not that I've got any kick coming, my only trouble is my honest streak. I just wanted to see Wolfe and tell him what he's paying me money for."

"You could have phoned him last night."

"I could not. I got lit last night. This is the first job I've had in a month."

"Got any expense money left?"

"Enough for a couple of days. I've learned self-control."

"Okay." I picked his hat up and put it on my desk. "That's a nice picture you've got down there. It's no good. It looks to me like there's no way out of it but three more men for Eleventh Street. That would be buying it, six tails for one cripple and—"

"Wait a minute." Fred waved a hand at me. "That's not all of it. The other trouble is that the traffic cop at the corner is going to run us in. For blocking the street. There's too many of us, all after that cripple. There's a city feller there, I guess from the Homicide Squad, I don't recognize him, and a little guy with a brown cap and a pink necktie that must be one of Bascom's men. I don't recognize him either. But get this, for example. Yesterday afternoon a taxi drives up and stops in front of 203, and in a minute Chapin hobbles out of the building on his stick, and gets in the taxi. You should have seen the hustle around there. It was like Fifth Avenue in front of St. Patrick's at one o'clock Sunday, only Perry Street is narrow. There was another taxi coming along and I beat the town dick to it by a jump and he had to run half a block to find one. Bascom's pet got into one that apparently he had waiting. I had a notion to yell to Chapin to wait a minute till we got lined up, but it wasn't necessary. It was all right, his driver went slow and none of us lost him. He went to the Harvard Club and stayed there a couple of hours and then stopped off at 248 Madison Avenue and then went back home and we all followed him. Honest to God, Archie. Three of us, but I was in front."

"Yeah. It sounds swell."

"Sure it was. I kept looking around to see if they was all right. My idea was this, it came to me while I was riding along. Why couldn't we pal up? You get one more man and him and Bascom and the town dick could cover Eleventh Street and let us on Perry Street have a little peace. I suppose they're on twelve hours now, maybe they've got reliefs, I don't know. How's that for an idea?"

"Rotten." I got up and handed him his hat. "No good at all, Fred. Out. Wolfe's not using any second-hand tailing. I'll get three men from the Metropolitan and we'll cover Eleventh Street. It's a damn shame, because as I told you, Wolfe wants Chapin covered as tight as a drum. Get back on the job and don't lose him. It sounds sad, the way you describe that traffic jam, but do the best you can. I'll get in touch with Bascom and maybe he'll call his dog off, I didn't know he had any more money to spend. Run along now, I've got some errands you wouldn't understand."

"I'm not due till nine o'clock."

"Run along anyway.—Oh, all right. One shot, just one. A quarter to a dime."

He nodded, shifted in his seat to get good position, and let her go. It was a close call; the hat hung there on its edge for a tenth of a second, then toppled off. Durkin fished a dime out of his pocket and handed it to me, and beat it.

I thought at first I'd run up to Wolfe's room and get his okay on covering Eleventh Street, but it was only eight-twenty and it always made me half-sick to see him in bed with that black silk cover drinking chocolate, not to mention that he would be sure to raise hell, so I got the Metropolitan Agency on the telephone and gave them the dope. I only ordered six-dollar men because it was nothing but a check anyway; I couldn't see why Chapin should be trying to pull anything foxy like rear exits. Then I sat for a minute and wondered who was keeping Bascom on the job, and I thought I'd phone him on the chance of his spilling it, but nobody answered. All this had made me a little late on my own schedule, so I grabbed my hat and coat and went to the garage for the roadster.

I had collected a few facts about the Dreyer business in my wanderings the day before. Eugene Dreyer, art dealer, had been found dead, on the morning of Thursday, September 20, in the office of his gallery on Madison Avenue near Fifty-sixth Street. His body had been found by three cops, one a lieutenant, who had broken in the door on orders. He had been dead about twelve hours, and the cause had been nitroglycerin poisoning. After an investigation the police had pronounced it suicide, and the inquest had verified it. But on the Monday following, the second warnings arrived; everybody got one. We had several copies in Wolfe's office, and they read like this:

> Two.
> Ye should have killed me.
> Two;
> And with no ready cliff, rocks waiting below
> To rub the soul out; no ready waves
> To lick it off and clean it of old crimes,
> I let the snake and fox collaborate.
> They found the deadly oil, sweet-burning, cunningly
> Devised in tablets easily dissolved.
> And I, their Master, I,
> I found the time, the safe way to his throat,
> And counted: two.
> One, and two, and eighty long days between.
> But wait in patience; I am unhurried but sure.
> Three and four and five and six and seven. . . .
> Ye should have killed me.

Wolfe said it was better than the first one, because it was shorter and there were two good lines in it. I took his word for it.

Hell had popped right off. They forgot all about practical jokes and yelled to the cops and the D.A.'s office to come on back and nab him; suicide was out. When I got a description of the run-around that little poem had started, I was inclined to agree with Mike Ayers and cross out League of Atonement and make it the League of the White Feather. The only ones that hadn't seemed to develop an acute case of knee-tremor were Dr. Burton and Leopold Elkus the surgeon. Hibbard had been as much scared as anyone, more if anything, but had still been against the police. Apparently he had been ready to go to bed with the willies, but also ready for the sacrifice. Elkus, of course, had been in on it, but I'm coming to that.

My date with Elkus that Wednesday morning was for nine-thirty, but I made an early start because I wanted to stop off at Fifty-sixth Street for a look at the Dreyer gallery where it had happened. I got there before nine. It wasn't a gallery any more, but a bookstore. A middle-aged woman with a wart in front of her ear was nice to me and said of course I could look around, but there wasn't much to be made of it because everything had been changed. The little room on the right, where the conference had taken place on a Wednesday evening and the body had been found the following morning, was still an office, with a desk and a typewriter and so on, but a lot of shelves had been put in that were obviously new. I called the woman over and she came in the office. I pointed at a door in the back wall and said:

"I wonder if you could tell me. Is that the closet

where Mr. Eugene Dreyer kept the materials for mixing his drinks?"

She looked hazy. "Mr. Dreyer . . . oh . . . that's the man . . ."

"The man that committed suicide in this room, yes, ma'am. I suppose you wouldn't know."

"Well, really . . ." She seemed startled. "I hadn't realized it was right in this little room . . . of course I've heard about it . . ."

I said, "Thank you, ma'am," and went back to the street and got in the roadster. People who quit living a year ago Christmas and haven't found out about it yet give me a pain, and all I've got for them is politeness and damn little of that.

Leopold Elkus hadn't quit living, I discovered when I got to him in his private room, but he was a sad guy. He was medium-sized, with a big head and big hands, and strong black eyes that kept floating away from you, not sideways or up or down but back into his head. He invited me to sit down and said in a friendly soft voice:

"Understand, Mr. Goodwin, I am seeing you only as a courtesy to my friends who have requested it. I have explained to Mr. Farrell that I will not support the enterprise of your employer. Nor will I lend any assistance."

"Okay." I grinned at him. "I didn't come to pick a scrap, Dr. Elkus. I just want to ask some questions about September nineteenth, when Eugene Dreyer died. Questions of fact."

"I have already answered any question you could possibly put. To the police several times, and to that incredibly ignorant detective . . ."

"Right. So far we agree. Just as a matter of courtesy to your friends, there's no reason why you shouldn't answer them once more, is there? To converse with the cops and Del Bascom and then draw the line at Nero Wolfe and me . . . well, that would be like . . ."

He smiled a sad smile. "Swallow a camel and strain at a gnat?" God that guy was sad.

"Yeah, I guess so. Only if you saw Nero Wolfe you wouldn't call him a gnat.—It's like this, Dr. Elkus. I know you won't lend a hand to get the goods on Paul Chapin. But in this Dreyer business you're my only source of firsthand information and so I had to get at you. I understand the other man, the art expert, has gone back to Italy."

He nodded. "Mr. Santini sailed some time ago."

"Then there's only you. There's no sense in my trying to ask you a lot of trick questions. Why don't you just tell me about it?"

He smiled sad again. "I presume you know that two or three of my friends suspect me of lying to shield Paul Chapin?"

"Yeah. Are you?"

"No. I would neither shield him nor injure him, beyond the truth.—Here is the story, Mr. Goodwin. You know, of course, that Eugene Dreyer was an old friend of mine, a classmate in college. He was pretty successful with his art gallery before the depression. I bought things from him occasionally. I have never been under the necessity of pursuing success, since I inherited wealth. My reputation as a surgeon is a by-product of my conviction that there is something wrong with all human beings, beneath the surface. By chance I have a sure and skillful hand."

I looked at his big hands folded on his lap, and nodded at his black eyes floating back into his head. He went on:

"Six years ago I gave Eugene Dreyer a tentative order for three Mantegnas—two small ones and a larger one. The price was one hundred and sixty thousand dollars. The paintings were in France. Paul Chapin happened to be in Europe at that time, and I wrote to ask him to look at them. After I received his report I ordered them. You know, I suppose, that for ten years Paul Chapin tried to be a painter. His work showed great sensitiveness, but his line was erratic and he had no feeling for form. It was interesting, but not good. I am told that he is finding himself in literature—I do not read novels.

"The paintings arrived at a time when I was overworked and had no leisure for a proper examination. I accepted them and paid for them. I was never happy with them; the friendly overtures which I made to those pictures from time to time, and there were many, were always repelled by them with an indelicacy, a faint harshness, which embarrassed and irritated me. I did not at first suspect them of imposture, I simply could not get along with them. But a few remarks made by expert persons finally aroused my suspicion. In September, nearly two months ago now, Enrico Santini, who knows Mantegna as I know the human viscera, visited this country. I asked him to look at my Mantegnas, and he pronounced them frauds. He further said that he knew their source, a certain talented swindler in Paris, and that it was not possible that any reputable dealer had handled them in good faith.

"I imagine it was the uncomfortable five years those pictures had given me, more than anything else, that caused me to act as I did with Dreyer. Ordinarily I am far too weak in my convictions to display any sort of ruthlessness, but on this occasion there was no hesitation in me at all. I told Eugene that I wished to return the pictures and receive my money back without delay. He said he had not the money, and I knew he hadn't, since I had within a year lent him considerable sums to tide him over. Nevertheless, I insisted that he must find it or suffer the consequences. I suspect that in the end I would have weakened as usual, and agreed to any sort of compromise, but unfortunately it is a trick of my temperament now and then to show the greatest determination of purpose when the resolution is most likely to falter. Unfortunately also, Mr. Santini was about to return to Italy. Eugene demanded an interview with him; that, of course, was a bluff.

"It was arranged that I should call at five o'clock Wednesday afternoon with Mr. Santini and Paul Chapin. Paul was included on account of the inspection he had given the pictures in France. I surmised that Eugene had arranged for his support, but as it turned out that was probably incorrect. We arrived. Eugene's suavity—"

I interrupted, "Just a minute, doctor. Did Paul Chapin get to the gallery before you did?"

"No. We arrived together. I was in my car, and called for him at the Harvard Club."

"Had he been there earlier that afternoon?"

"My dear sir." Elkus looked sad at me.

"Okay. You wouldn't know that. Anyway, the girl there says he hadn't."

"So I understand. I was saying, Eugene's suavity was painful, because of the nervousness it failed to hide. He mixed highballs for us, jerkily, not himself. I was embarrassed and therefore brusque. I asked Mr. Santini to make a statement and he did so; he had written it down. Eugene contradicted him. They argued; Eugene was somewhat excited but Mr. Santini remained cool. Finally Eugene called on Paul for his views, in obvious expectation of support. Paul smiled around at us, the smile that comes from his Malpighian capsules, and made a calm brief statement. He said that three months after his inspection of the pictures—a month after they had been shipped to New York—he had learned definitely that they had been painted by Vasseult, the greatest forger of the century, in 1924. That was the man Mr. Santini had named. Paul also said that he had kept silent about it because his affection for both Eugene and myself was so great that he could take no step that would injure either of us.

"I feared Eugene would collapse. He was plainly as astonished as he was hurt. I was of course embarrassed into silence. I do not know whether Eugene had in desperation swindled me, or whether he had himself been imposed upon. Mr. Santini rose. I did likewise, and we left. Paul Chapin came with us. It was noon the following day when I learned that Eugene had committed suicide by drinking nitroglycerin— apparently within a few minutes, at the most an hour, after we left. I learned it when the police arrived at my office to question me."

I nodded, and sat and looked at him a while. Then all of a sudden I straightened up in my chair and shot at him, "What made *you* think it was suicide?"

"Now, Mr. Goodwin." He smiled at me, sadder than ever. "Are all detectives alike? You know perfectly well why I thought it was suicide. The police thought so, and the circumstances indicated it."

"My mistake." I grinned. "I said no trick questions, didn't I? If you're willing to grant that a detective can have an idea in his mind, you know what mine is. Did Paul Chapin have any opportunity to put the nitroglycerin tablets in Dreyer's highball? That ignorant detective, and all the bright cops, seem to have the impression that you think he didn't."

Dr. Elkus nodded. "I labored to produce that impression. You know of course that Mr. Santini agreed with me. We are perfectly certain that Paul had no such opportunity. He went to the gallery with us, and we all entered the office together. Paul sat at my left, near the door, at least six feet away from Eugene. He touched no glass but his own. Eugene prepared the drinks and handed them around; we had only one. Departing, Paul preceded me through the door. Mr. Santini was ahead."

"Yeah. That's on the record. But in a fracas like that, so much excitement, there must have been some moving around, getting up and sitting down, walking back and forth . . ."

"Not at all. We were not excited, except possibly Eugene. He was the only one who left his chair."

"Did he change his coat, or put it on or anything, after you got there?"

"No. He wore a morning coat. He did not remove it."

"The bottle with what was left of the nitroglycerin was found in the pocket of his coat."

"So I understand."

I sat back and looked at him again. I would have given the roadster and a couple of extra tires to know if he was lying. He was as much out of my class as Paul Chapin was. There was no way for me to get at him that I could see. I said:

"Will you have lunch with Mr. Nero Wolfe tomorrow at one o'clock?"

"I'm sorry. I shall be engaged."

"Friday?"

He shook his head. "No. Not any day. You are in error regarding me, Mr. Goodwin. I am not a knot to be untangled or a nut to be cracked. Give up your hope that I am deceptive, as most men are; I am really as simple as I seem. Give up your hope, too, to demonstrate the guilt of Paul Chapin in the death of Eugene Dreyer. It is not feasible. I know it isn't; I was there."

"Could you make it Saturday?"

He shook his head and smiled, still sad. I got up from my chair and picked up my hat, and thanked him. But before I started for the door I said:

"By the way, you know that second warning Paul Chapin wrote—anyhow, somebody else wrote it. Is nitroglycerin oily and sweet-burning?"

"I am a surgeon, not a pharmacologist."

"Well, try one guess."

He smiled. "Nitroglycerin is unquestionably oily. It is said to have a sweet, burning taste. I have never tried it."

I thanked him again and went out, and down to the street, and got in the roadster and stepped on the starter. As I rolled off downtown I was thinking that Dr. Leopold Elkus was exactly the kind of man that so often makes life a damn nuisance. I never yet have had any serious trouble with an out-and-out liar, but a man that might be telling the truth is an unqualified pain in the rumpus. And what with the Harrison line-up, and now this, I suspected that I began to perceive dimly that the memorandum Wolfe had concocted was going to turn out to be just a sheet of paper to be used for any purpose that might occur to you, unless we managed somehow to bust Elkus's story wide open.

I had intended to stop off again at Fifty-sixth Street for another look at the Dreyer gallery, but after listening to Elkus I decided it would be a waste of time, considering how the place had been done over. I kept on downtown, headed for home. The best bet I could think of at the moment was a try at Santini. The police had only questioned him once on account of his sailing for Italy that Thursday night, and of course the warnings hadn't been received yet and they had no particular suspicions. Wolfe had connections in several cities in Europe, and there was a smart guy in Rome who had turned in a good one on the Whittemore bonds. We could cable him and set him on Santini and maybe get a wedge started. I'd have to persuade Wolfe it was worth about ninety-nine dollars in transatlantic words.

It was a quarter to eleven when I got there. In the office the phone was ringing, so I went on in with my hat and coat on. I knew Wolfe would eventually answer it from upstairs, but I thought I might as well get it. It was Saul Panzer. I asked him what he wanted and he said he wanted to report. I asked him what, and he said, nothing, just report. I was sore at everything anyway, so I got sarcastic. I said if he couldn't find Hibbard alive or dead, maybe he could rig up a dummy that would do. I said I had just got a smack in the eye on another angle of the case, and if he was no better than I was he'd better come on down to the office with a pinochle deck, and I hung up on him, which alone is enough to aggravate a nun.

It took me five minutes to dig the address of the Roman snoop out of the file. Wolfe came down on time, right at eleven. He said good morning, sniffed at the air, and got seated at his desk. I was impatient, but I knew I'd have to wait until he had glanced through the mail, fixed the orchids in the vase, tried his pen to see if it was working, and rung for beer. After that was all over he murmured at me:

"Had you thought of venturing forth?"

"I tiptoed out at eight-thirty and just got back. Saul just telephoned. Another nickel wasted. If you want to get puckered up, here's a nice pickle to chew on."

Fritz brought his beer and he poured a glass. I told him all about Elkus, every word of it, even that nitroglycerin was oily and sweet-burning. I thought if I gave him all of Elkus I could, he might get a notion. Then I handed him my own notion about the Roman. Right away, as I expected, he got restive. He blinked, and drank some more beer. He said:

"You can cable four thousand miles for a fact or an object, but not for a subtlety like this. As a last resort you or Saul Panzer might go to call on Mr. Santini in Florence; it might in the end be worth that chance."

I tried an argument on him, for I couldn't see any other move. I didn't seem to be making much impression, but I kept on anyway, getting stubborn, because my main point was that it was only a matter of a hundred bucks. I was forgetting that I still had to tell him about the three Metropolitan men I had ordered for Eleventh Street. I got good and stubborn.

I was stopped in the middle of my stride by the sound of Fritz going down the hall to answer the doorbell. I didn't try to pick it up again, but waited to see who it was.

Fritz stepped in and closed the door behind him. He said there was a lady there to see Wolfe. No card.

"Her name?"

Fritz shook his head; usually he was more correct. He looked uncertain.

"Show her in, Fritz."

I felt uncertain too, when I saw her. They don't come any uglier. She came in and stood looking straight at Wolfe, as if she was deciding how to do him over. At that she wasn't really ugly, I mean she wasn't hideous. Wolfe said it right the next day: it was more subtle than plain ugliness, to look at her made you despair of ever seeing a pretty woman again. Her eyes were rather small, gray, and looked as if they'd never move again when they got fixed. She had on a dark gray woolen coat with a hat to match, and an enormous gray furpiece was fastened around her neck. She sat down on the chair I pulled up for her and said in a strong voice:

"I had a hard time getting here. I think I'm going to faint."

Wolfe said, "I hope not. A little brandy."

"No." She gave a little gasp. "No, thank you." She put her hand up to the furpiece and seemed to be trying to reach under it, behind. "I've been wounded. Back there. I think you'd better look at it."

Wolfe shot me a glance, and I went. She got the thing unfastened in front, and I pulled it around and lifted it off. I gave a gasp then myself. Not that I haven't seen a little blood here and there, but not often that much, and it was so unexpected. The back of the furpiece, inside, was soaked. The collar of her coat was soaked too. She was a sight. It was still oozing out, plenty, from gashes across the back of her neck; I couldn't tell how deep they were. She moved and it came out in a little spurt. I dropped the furpiece on the floor and said to her:

"For God's sake keep still. Don't move your head." I looked at Wolfe and said, "Somebody's tried to cut her head off. I can't tell how far they got."

She spoke to Wolfe: "My husband wanted to kill me."

Wolfe's eyes on her were half closed. "Then you're Dora Ritter."

She shook her head, and the blood started, and I told her to quit. She said, "I am Dora Chapin. I have been married three years."

# Chapter 10

Wolfe didn't say anything. I stood behind her and waited, ready to catch her if she started to faint and fall forward, because I didn't know how much it might open up. Wolfe hadn't moved. He sat looking at her with his eyes nearly shut and his lips pushing out, and in, and out and in again.

She said, "He got into a fit. One of his cold fits."

Wolfe said politely, "I didn't know Mr. Chapin had fits. Feel her pulse."

I reached out and got her wrist and placed my fingers. While I was counting she began to talk:

"He doesn't have fits exactly. It's a look that comes into his eyes. I am always afraid of him, but when I see that look I am terrified. He has never done anything to me before. This morning when I saw him look like that I said something I shouldn't have said . . . look here."

She jerked her hand away from me to use it for getting into her handbag, a big leather one. Out of it she pulled something wrapped in newspaper. She unrolled the newspaper and held up a kitchen knife that had blood on it still wet and red.

"He had this and I didn't know it. He must have

been getting ready for me when he was out in the kitchen."

I took the knife from her and laid it on the desk, on top of the newspaper, and said to Wolfe:

"Her pulse is on a little sprint, but it's okay."

Wolfe put his hands on the arms of the chair, braced himself, and got to his feet. He said, "Please do not move, Mrs. Chapin," and walked around behind her and took a look at her neck. He bent down with his eyes close to her; I hadn't seen him so active for a month or more. Peering at the gashes, he said, "Please tilt your head forward, just a little, and back again." She did so, and the blood came out again; in one spot it nearly spurted at him.

Wolfe straightened up. "Indeed. Get a doctor, Archie."

She started to turn around at him, and I stopped her. She protested, "I don't need a doctor. I got here, I can get home again. I just wanted to show you, and ask you—"

"Yes, madam. For the moment my judgment must prevail . . . if you please . . ."

I was at the phone, giving a number. Someone answered, and I asked for Dr. Vollmer. She said he wasn't there, he was just leaving, if it was urgent she might be able to catch him out in front. I started to ask her to do that, then it occurred to me that I might be quicker at it myself, and I hung up and took it on the trot. Fritz was in the hall dusting and I told him to stick around. As I hopped down the stoop I noticed a taxi there at the curb: our visitor's of course. A couple of hundred feet east Dr. Vollmer's blue coupé was standing, and he was just getting in. I sprinted for him and let out a yell. He heard me and by the time I got there he was out on the sidewalk again. I told

him about the casualty that had dropped in on us, and
he got his bag out of the coupé and came along.

In my business I've seen it proved a hundred times
that one thing you never want to leave in the bureau
drawer is your curiosity. As we turned in at our stoop
I took another look at the taxi standing there. I nearly
lost my aplomb for a second when the driver looked
straight at me and tipped me a wink.

I went on in with the doc. Fritz was in the hall and
told me that Wolfe had gone to the kitchen and would
return when the doctor had finished. I told Fritz for
God's sake not to let him get started eating, and took
Vollmer into the office. Dora Chapin was still in her
chair. I introduced them, and he put his bag on the
desk and went to take a look at her. He poked around
a little and said she might have to be sewed up and he
could tell better if he could wash her off. I showed him
where the bathroom was and said there were bandages and iodine and so on, and then said:

"I'll call Fritz in to help you. I've got an errand out
front. If you need me I'll be there."

He said all right, and I went to the hall and
explained Fritz's new duties to him. Then I went out
to the sidewalk.

The taxi was still there. The driver wasn't winking
any more; he just looked at me. I said, Greetings."

He said, "I very seldom talk that much."

"How much?"

"Enough to say greetings. Any form of salutation."

"I don't blame you. May I glance inside?"

I pulled the door open and stuck my head in far
enough to get a good look at the framed card fastened
to the panel, showing the driver's picture and name.
That was only a wild guess, but I thought if it
happened to hit it would save time. I backed out again

and put a foot up on the running-board and grinned at
him:

"I understand you're a good engineer."

He looked funny for a second, then he laughed.
"That was when I was in burlesque. Now I'm just
doing straight parts. Damn it, quit grinning at me.
I've got a headache."

I rubbed the grin off. "Why did you wink at me as
I went by?"

"Why shouldn't I?"

"I don't know. Hell, don't try to be quaint. I just
asked you a friendly question. What was the idea of
the wink?"

He shook his head. "I'm a character. Didn't I say I
had a headache? Let's see if we can't think of some
place for you to go to. Is your name Nero Wolfe?"

"No. But yours is Pitney Scott. I've got you down
on a list I made up for a contribution of five dollars."

"I heard about that list."

"Yes? Who from?"

"Oh . . . people. You can cross me off. Last week
I made eighteen dollars and twenty cents."

"You know what it's for."

He nodded. "I know that too. You want to save my
life. Listen, my dear fellow. To charge five dollars for
saving my life would be outrageous. Believe me,
exorbitant. Rank profiteering." He laughed. "These
things have a bottom, I suppose. There is no such
thing as a minus quantity except in mathematics. You
have no idea what a feeling of solidity and assurance
that reflection can gave a man. Have you got a drink
in your house?"

"How about two dollars? Make it two."

"You're still way high."

"One even buck."

"Still you flatter me. Listen." Though it was cold for November, with a raw wind, he had no gloves and his hands were red and rough. He got his stiff fingers into a pocket, came out with some chicken feed, picked a nickel and pushed it at me. "I'll pay up now and get it off my mind. Now that I don't owe you anything, have you got a drink?"

"What flavor do you want?"

"I . . . if it were good rye . . ." He leaned toward me and a look came into his eyes. Then he jerked back. His voice got harsh and not friendly at all. "Can't you take a joke? I don't drink when I'm driving. Is that woman hurt much?"

"I don't think so, her head's still on. The doctor'll fix her up. Do you take her places often? Or her husband?"

He was still harsh. "I take her when she calls me, her husband too. I'm a taxi-driver. Mr. Paul Chapin. They give me their trade when they can, for old time's sake. Once or twice they've let me get drunk at their place, Paul likes to see me drunk and he furnishes the liquor." He laughed, and the harshness went. "You know, you take this situation in all its aspects, and you couldn't ask for anything more hilarious. I'm going to have to stay sober so as not to miss any of it. I winked at you because you're in on it now, and you're going to be just as funny as all the rest."

"That won't worry me any, I always have been pretty ludicrous. Does Chapin get drunk with you?"

"He doesn't drink. He says it makes his leg hurt."

"Did you know that there's a reward of five thousand dollars for finding Andrew Hibbard?"

"No."

"Alive or dead."

It looked to me as if, just stabbing around, I had hit something. His face had changed; he looked surprised, as if confronted with an idea that hadn't occurred to him. He said, "Well, he's a valuable man, that's not too much to offer for him. At that, Andy's not a bad guy. Who offered the reward?"

"His niece. It'll be in the papers tomorrow."

"Good for her. God bless her." He laughed. "It is an incontrovertible fact that five thousand dollars is a hell of a lot of more money than a nickel. How do you account for that? I want a cigarette."

I got a packet out and lit us both up. His fingers weren't steady at all, and I began to feel sorry for him. So I said, "Just figure it out. Hibbard's home is up at University Heights. If you drove downtown somewhere—say around the Perry Street neighborhood, I don't know just where—and from there to One Hundred Sixteenth Street, ordinarily what would you get for it? Let's see—two, eight miles—that'd be around a dollar and a half. But if going uptown you happened to have your old classmate Andrew Hibbard with you—or just his corpse, maybe even only a piece of it, say, his head and a couple of arms—instead of a dollar-fifty you'd get five grand. As you see, it all depends on your cargo." So as not to take my eyes off him, I blew cigarette smoke out of the corner of my mouth. Of course, riding a guy who needed a drink bad and wouldn't take it was like knocking a cripple's crutch from under him, but I didn't need to remind myself that all's fair in love and business. Basic truths like that are either born right in a man or they're not.

At that he had enough grip on himself to keep his mouth shut. He looked at his fingers trembling holding the cigarette, so long that I finally looked at them too. Finally he let his hand fall to his knee, and looked at me and began to laugh. He demanded, "Didn't I say you were going to be funny?" His voice went harsh again. "Listen, you. Beat it. Come on, now, beat it. Go back in the house or you'll catch cold."

I said, "All right, how about that drink?"

But he was through. I prodded at him a little, but he had gone completely dumb and unfriendly. I thought of bringing out some rye and letting him smell it, but decided that would just screw him down tighter. I said to myself, anon, and passed him up.

Before going in the house I went around back of the taxi and got the license number.

I went to the kitchen. Wolfe was still there, in the wooden chair with arms where he always sat to direct Fritz and to eat when he was on a relapse.

I said, "Pitney Scott's out front. The taxi-driver. He brought her. He paid me a nickel for his share, and he says that's all it's worth. He knows something about Andrew Hibbard."

"What?"

"You mean what does he know? Search me. I told him about the reward Miss Hibbard, my client, is offering, and he looked like get thee behind me, Satan. He's shy, he wants to be coaxed. My surmise is that he may not exactly know where Hibbard or his remains has been cached, but he thinks he might guess. He's got about seven months to go to pink snakes and crocodiles. I tried to get him to come in for a drink, but he fought that off too. He won't come in. He may not be workable at the present moment, but I was thinking of suggesting that you go out and look at him."

"Out?" Wolfe raised his head at me. "Out and down the stoop?"

"Yeah, just on the sidewalk, you wouldn't have to step off the curb. He's right there."

Wolfe shut his eyes. "I don't know, Archie. I don't know why you persist in trying to badger me into frantic sorties. Dismiss the notion entirely. It is not feasible. You say he actually gave you a nickel?"

"Yes, and where's it going to get you to act eccentric with a dipsomaniac taxi-driver even if he did go to Harvard? Honest to God, sir, sometimes you run it in the ground."

"That will do. Definitely. Go and see if Mrs. Chapin has been made presentable."

I went. I found that Dr. Vollmer had finished with his patient in the bathroom and had her back in a chair in the office, with her neck bandaged so that she had to hold it stiff whether she wanted to or not. He was giving her instructions how to conduct herself, and Fritz was taking away basins and rags and things. I waited till the doc was through, then took him to the kitchen. Wolfe opened his eyes at him. Vollmer said:

"Quite a novel method of attack, Mr. Wolfe. Quite original, hacking at her from behind like that. He got into one of the posterior externals; I had to shave off some of her hair."

"He?"

The doctor nodded. "She explained that her husband, to whom she has been married three years, did the carving. With a little caution, which I urged upon her, she should be all right in a few days. I took fourteen stitches. Her husband must be a remarkable and unconventional man. She is remarkable too, in her way: the Spartan type. She didn't even clench her hands while I was sewing her; the fingers were positively relaxed."

"Indeed. You will want her name and address for your record."

"I have it, thanks. She wrote it down for me."

"Thank you, doctor."

Vollmer went. Wolfe got to his feet, pulled at his vest in one of his vain attempts to cover the strip of canary yellow shirt which encircled his magnificent middle, and preceded me to the office. I stopped to ask Fritz to clean off the inside of the furpiece as well as he could.

By the time I joined them Wolfe was back in his chair and she was sitting facing him. He was saying to her:

"I am glad it was no worse, Mrs. Chapin. The doctor has told you, you must be careful not to jerk the stitches loose for a few days. By the way, his fee—did you pay him?"

"Yes. Five dollars."

"Good. Reasonable, I should say. Mr. Goodwin tells me your cab is waiting. Tell the driver to go slowly; jolting is always abominable, in your present condition even dangerous. We need not detain you longer."

She had her eyes fixed on him again. Getting washed off and wrapped up hadn't made her any handsomer. She took a breath through her nose and let it out again so you could hear it.

She said, finally, "Don't you want me to tell you about it? I want to tell you what he did."

Wolfe's head went left and right. "It isn't necessary, Mrs. Chapin. You should go home and rest. I undertake to notify the police of the affair; I can understand your reluctant delicacy; after all, one's own husband to whom one has been married three years . . . I'll attend to that for you."

"I don't want the police." That woman could certainly pin her eyes. "Do you think I want my husband arrested? With his standing and position . . . all the publicity . . . do you think I want that? That's why I came to you . . . to tell you about it."

"But, Mrs. Chapin." Wolfe wiggled a finger at her. "You see, you came to the wrong place. Unfortunately for you, you came to the one man in New York, the one man in the world, who would at once understand what really happened at your home this morning. It was unavoidable, I suppose, since it was precisely that man, myself, whom you wished to delude. The devil of it is; from your standpoint, that I have a deep aversion to being deluded. Let's just call it quits. You really do need rest and quiet, after your nervous tension and your loss of blood. Go on home."

Of course, as had happened a few times before, I had missed the boat; I was swimming along behind trying to keep up. For a minute I thought she was going to get up and go. She started to. Then she was back again, looking at him. She said:

"I'm an educated woman, Mr. Wolfe. I've been in service, and I'm not ashamed of that, but I'm educated. You're trying to talk so I won't understand you, but I do."

"Good. Then there is no need—"

She snapped at him suddenly and violently. "You're a fat fool!"

Wolfe shook his head. "Fat visibly, though I prefer Gargantuan. A fool only in the broader sense, as a common characteristic of the race. It was not magnanimous of you, Mrs. Chapin, to blurt my corpulence at me, since I had spoken of your fatuity only in general terms and had refrained from demonstrating it. I'll do that now." He moved a finger to indicate the knife which still lay on the newspaper on the desk. "Archie, will you please clean that homely weapon."

I didn't know, I thought maybe he was bluffing her. I picked up the knife and stood there with it, looking from her to him. "Wash off the evidence?"

"If you please."

I took the knife to the bathroom and turned on the faucet, rubbed the blood off with a piece of gauze, and wiped it. Through the open door I couldn't hear any talking. I went back.

"Now," Wolfe instructed me, "grip the handle firmly in your right hand. Come towards the desk, so Mrs. Chapin can see you better; turn your back. So. Elevate your arm and pull the knife across your neck; kindly be sure to use the back of the blade, not to carry the demonstration too far. You noted the length and the position of the cuts on Mrs. Chapin? Duplicate them on yourself.—Yes. Yes, quite good. A little higher for that one. Another, somewhat lower. Confound you, be careful. That will do.—You see, Mrs. Chapin? He did it quite neatly, don't you think? I am not insulting your intelligence by hinting that you expected us to think the wounds could not have been self-inflicted in the position you chose for them. More likely, you selected it purely as a matter of precaution, knowing that the front, the neighborhood of the anterior jugular . . ."

He stopped, because he had no one to talk to except me. When I turned around after my demonstration she was already getting up from her chair, holding her head stiff and a clamp on her mouth. Without a word, without bothering to make any passes at him with her little gray glass eyes, she just got up and went; and he paid no attention, he went on with his speech until she had opened the office door and was through it. I noticed she was leaving her knife, but thought we might as well have it in our collection of odds and ends. Then all of a sudden I jumped for the hall.

"Hey, lady, wait a minute! Your fur!"

I got it from Fritz and caught her at the front door and put it around her. Pitney Scott got out of his cab and came over to help her down the stoop, and I went back in.

Wolfe was glancing through a letter from Hoehn and Company that had come in the morning mail. When he had finished he put it under a paperweight—a piece of petrified wood that had once been used to bust a guy's skull—and said:

"The things a woman will think of are beyond belief. I knew a woman once in Hungary whose husband had frequent headaches. It was her custom to relieve them by the devoted application of cold compresses. It occurred to her one day to stir into the water with which she wetted the compresses a large quantity of penetrating poison which she had herself distilled from an herb. The result was gratifying to her. The man on whom she tried the experiment was myself. The woman—"

He was just trying to keep me from annoying him about business. I cut in. "Yeah. I know. The woman was a witch you had caught riding around in the curl of a pig's tail. In spite of all that, it's time for me to brush up a little on this case we've got. You can give me a shove by explaining in long words how you knew Dora Chapin did her own manicuring."

Wolfe shook his head. "That would not be a shove, Archie; it would be a laborious and sustained propulsion. I shall not undertake it. I remind you merely: I have read all of Paul Chapin's novels. In two of them Dora Chapin is a character. He of course appears in all. The woman who married Dr. Burton, Paul Chapin's unattainable, seems to be in four out of five; I cannot discover her in the latest one. Read the books, and I shall be more inclined to discuss the conclusions they have led me to. But even then, of course, I would not attempt to place plain to your eyes the sights my own have discerned. God made you and me, in certain respects, quite unequal, and it would be futile to try any interference with His arrangements."

Fritz came to the door and said lunch was ready.

# Chapter 11

Sometimes I thought it was a wonder Wolfe and I got on together at all. The differences between us, some of them, showed up plainer at the table than anywhere else. He was a taster and I was a swallower. Not that I didn't know good from bad; after seven years of education from Fritz's cooking I could even tell, usually, superlative from excellent. But the fact remained that what chiefly attracted Wolfe about food in his pharynx was the affair it was having with his taste buds, whereas with me the important point was that it was bound for my belly. To avoid any misunderstanding, I should add that Wolfe was never disconcerted by the problem of what to do with it when he was through tasting it. He could put it away. I have seen him, during a relapse, dispose completely of a ten-pound goose between eight o'clock and midnight, while I was in a corner with ham sandwiches and milk hoping he would choke. At those times he always ate in the kitchen.

It was the same in business, when we were on a case. A thousand times I've wanted to kick him, watching him progress leisurely to the elevator on his way to monkey with the plants upstairs, or read a

book tasting each phrase, or discuss with Fritz the
best storage place for dry herbs, when I was running
around barking my head off and expecting him to tell
me where the right hole was. I admit he was a
great man. When he called himself a genius he had a
right to mean it whether he did or not. I admit that he
never lost us a bet by his piddling around. But since
I'm only human, I couldn't keep myself from wanting
to kick him just because he was a genius. I came awful
close to it sometimes, when he said things like,
"Patience, Archie; if you eat the apple before it's ripe
your only reward is a bellyache."

Well, this Wednesday afternoon, after lunch, I was
sore. He went indifferent on me; he even went contrary. He wouldn't cable the guy in Rome to get into
converse with Santini; he said it was futile and expected me to take his word for it. He wouldn't help me
concoct a loop we could use to drag Leopold Elkus into
the office; according to him, that was futile too. He
kept trying to read in a book while I was after him. He
said there were only two men in the case whom he felt
any inclination to talk to: Andrew Hibbard and Paul
Chapin; and he wasn't ready yet for Chapin and he
didn't know where Hibbard was, or whether he was
alive or dead. I knew Saul Panzer was going to the
morgue every morning and afternoon to look over the
stiffs, but I didn't know what else he was doing. I also
knew that Wolfe had talked with Inspector Cramer on
the phone that morning, but that was nothing to get
excited about; Cramer had shot his bolt a week ago at
Paul Chapin and all that was keeping him awake was
the routine of breathing.

Saul had phoned around noon and Wolfe had talked
to him from the kitchen while I was out with Pitney
Scott. A little after two Fred Durkin phoned. He said

that Paul Chapin had been to the barber and a drugstore, and that the town dick and the guy in the brown
cap and pink necktie were still on deck, and he was
thinking of forming a club. Wolfe went on reading.
About a quarter to three Orrie Cather called up and
said he had got hold of something he wanted to show
us and could he come on up with it; he was at the
Fourteenth Street subway station. I told him yes.
Then, just before Orrie arrived, a call came that made
Wolfe put down his book. It was from Farrell the
architect, and Wolfe talked to him. He said he had had
a nice lunch with Mr. Oglethrope, and he had had a
tough argument but had finally persuaded him. He
was phoning from the publisher's office. Paul Chapin
had on several occasions found it convenient to make
use of a typewriter there, but there was some disagreement as to which one or ones, so he was going to
take samples from a dozen of them. Wolfe told him to
be sure that the factory number of the machine
appeared on each sample.

I said, after we hung up, "Okay, that one's turning
brown. But even if you hang the warnings on him,
you've just started. The Harrison demise is out, you'll
never tie that up. And I'm telling you that the same
goes for Dreyer, unless you get Leopold Elkus down
here and perform an operation on him. You've got to
find a hole in his story and open it up, or we've licked.
What the hell are we waiting for? It's all right for you,
you can keep occupied, you've got a book to read—
what the devil is it, anyhow?"

I got up to take a squint at it, a dark gray cover
stamped in gold: *The Chasm of the Mind*, by Andrew
Hibbard. I grunted. "Huh, maybe that's where he is,
maybe he fell in."

"Long ago." Wolfe sighed. "Poor Hibbard, he

couldn't exclude his poetic tendencies even from his title. Any more than Chapin can exclude his savagery from his plots."

I dropped back into my chair. "Listen, boss." There was nothing he hated more than being called boss. "I'm beginning to catch on. I suppose Dr. Burton has written books too, and Byron, and maybe Dreyer, and of course Mike Ayers. I'll take the roadster and drive out to Pike County for a little duck hunting, and when you get caught up with your reading just wire me care of Cleve Sturgis and I'll mosey back and we'll tackle this murder case. And take it easy, take your time; if you eat the apple after it is too ripe you'll get ptomaine poisoning or erysipelas or something, at least I hope to God you will." I was glaring at him, with no result except to make me feel like a sap, because he merely shut his eyes so as not to see me. I got up from my chair and glared anyhow. "Damn it, all I'm asking for is just a little halfway co-operation! One little lousy cablegram to that Roman wop! I ask you, should I have to work myself into turmoil—now what the hell do *you* want?"

The last was for Fritz. He had appeared in the door. He was frowning, because he never liked to hear me yell at Wolfe, and I frowned back at him. Then I saw someone standing behind him and I let the frown go and said:

"Come on in, Orrie. What's the loot?" I turned to Wolfe and smoothed my voice out and opened up the respect: "He phoned a while ago and said he had got hold of something he wanted to show us. I told you, but you were engrossed in your book."

Orrie Cather had a bundle about the size of a small suitcase, wrapped in brown paper and tied with heavy string.

I said, "I hope it's books."

He shook his head. "It's not heavy enough for books." He set it down on the desk and looked around, and I shoved up a chair for him.

"What is it?"

"Search me. I brought it here to open it. It may be just a lot of nothing at all, but I had a hunch."

I got out my pocketknife, but Wolfe shook his head. He said to Orrie, "Go on."

Orrie grinned. "Well, as I say, it may be a lot of nothing at all, but I'd got so fed up after a day and a half finding out nothing whatever about that cripple except where he buys his groceries and how often he gets his shoes shined, that when something came along that looked like it might be a little break I guess I got excited. I've just been following your instructions—"

"Yes. Let us arrive at the package."

"Right. This morning I dropped in at the Greenwich Bookshop. I got talking with the guy, and I said I supposed he had Paul Chapin's books in his circulating library, and he said sure, and I said I might like to get one, and he handed me one and I looked it over—"

I couldn't help it; I snorted and stopped him. Orrie looked surprised, and Wolfe moved his eyes at me. I sat down.

"Then I said Chapin must be an interesting guy and had he ever seen him, and he said sure, Chapin lived in that neighborhood and bought books there and came in pretty often. He showed me a photograph of Chapin, autographed, on the wall with some others. A woman with black hair was sitting at a desk in the back of the shop, and she called out to the guy that that reminded her, Mr. Chapin never had come for the package he had left there a couple of weeks ago, and with Christmas stuff coming in the package was in the way, and hadn't he better phone Mr. Chapin to send for it. The guy said maybe he would a little later, it was too early for Chapin to be up. I deposited my dollar and got my book and went down the street to a lunch counter and sat down with a cup of coffee to think."

Wolfe nodded sympathetically. Orrie looked at him suspiciously and went on: "I figured it this way. Two weeks ago was about the time the cops were warming up on Chapin. What if he got hep they would pull a search on him, and he had something in his place he didn't want them to see? There were a lot of things he might do, and one of them was to wrap it up and take it to his friends at the bookshop and ask them to keep it for him. It would be about as safe there as anywhere. Anyhow, I decided I liked Chapin well enough to do him the favor of taking a look at his package for him. I got an envelope and a piece of paper from a stationery store and went to a real estate office and bummed the use of a typewriter. I wrote a nice note to the bookshop. I had used my eyes on Chapin's signature on the autographed photograph and got it pretty good. But then I was afraid to send it, so soon after I'd been there and heard the package mentioned. I decided to wait until afternoon. So a while ago I got a boy and sent him to the bookshop with the note, and I'm telling you it worked and they gave it to him." Orrie nodded his head at the desk. "That's it."

I got up and got out my knife again. Wolfe said, "No. Untie it." I started to work at the knot, which was a lulu. Orrie wiped his hand across his forehead and said, "By God, if it's just fishing tackle or electric light bulbs or something, you'll have to give me a drink. This is the only break I've had."

I said, "Among other things, there's just a chance we might find a set of typewriter type-bars. Or love-letters from Mrs. Loring A. Burton, huh?— There's nothing doing on this knot. He didn't want me to untie it, or anybody else. Even if I do get it, I could never tie it back again the same." I picked up my knife again, and looked at Wolfe. He nodded, and I slashed the string.

I took off the paper, several thicknesses. It wasn't a suitcase, but it was leather, and not imitation. It was an oblong box made of light tan calfskin, a special job, beautifully made, with fine lines of tooling around the edges. It was a swell number. Orrie grunted:

"Jesus, I may be in for grand larceny."

Wolfe said, "Go on," but he didn't get up so he could see.

"I can't. It's locked."

"Well."

I went to the safe and got a couple of my bunches of keys, and went back and started trying. The lock was nothing remarkable; in a few minutes I had it. I laid the keys down and lifted the lid. Orrie stood up and looked in with me. We didn't say anything for a second, then we looked at each other. I never saw him look so disgusted.

Wolfe said, "Empty?"

"No, sir. We'll have to give Orrie a drink. It's not his, it's hers. I mean Dora Chapin's. It's her hand-and-foot box. Gloves and stockings and maybe other dainties."

"Indeed." To my surprise Wolfe showed interest. His lips pushed out and in. He was even going to get up. He did so, and I shoved the box across.

"Indeed. I suspect—yes, it must be. Archie. Kindly remove them and spread them on the desk.

Here, I'll help. No, Orrie, not unless you wash your
hands first.—Ha, more intimate still! But mostly stockings and gloves.—Less roughly, Archie, out of respect
for the dignity the race aspires to; what we are display-
ing on this desk-top is the soul of a man. Qualities may be
deduced—for instance, do you notice that the gloves,
varying as they do in color and material, are all of a size?
Among twenty pairs or more, not one exception? Could
you ask more of loyalty and fidelity? *O, that I were a
glove upon that hand* . . . But with Romeo it was only
rhetoric; for Paul Chapin the glove is the true treasure,
with no hope beyond either of sweet or of bitter.—
Again, let us not be carried away; it is a distortion to
regard this or that aspect of a phenomenon to the
exclusion of others. In the present case, for example, we
cannot afford to forget that these articles are of expensive materials and workmanship, that they must have
cost Dr. Burton something around three hundred dollars
and that he therefore had a right to expect that they
should get more wear. Some of them, indeed, are
practically new. To strike a balance—"

Orrie was sitting down again staring at him. It was
I who cut him off: "Where does Burton come in? I'm
asking that in English."

Wolfe fingered the gloves some more, and held up a
stocking to look through it at the light. To see him
handling female hosiery as if he understood it gave me a
new insight into the extent of his pretensions. He held
up another one, dropped it back gently to the table, and
took a handkerchief from his pocket and wiped his
hands, carefully, fingers and palms. Then he sat down.

"Read your Anglo-Saxon poets, Archie. Romeo
himself was English, in spite of geography. I am not
trying to befuddle you, I am adhering to a tradition."

"All right. Where does Burton come in?"

"I have said, he paid the bills. He paid for these articles, his wife wore them, Dora Ritter, later Chapin, appropriated them, and Paul Chapin treasured them."

"How do you know all that?"

"How could I help but know it? Here are these worn things, kept by Paul Chapin in an elegant and locked receptacle, and in a time of crisis removed by him to a place of safety against unfriendly curiosity. You saw the size of Dora Chapin's hands, you see these gloves; they are not hers. You heard Monday evening the story of Chapin's infatuation with the woman who is now Dr. Burton's wife. You know that for years Dora Chapin, then Ritter, was Mrs. Burton's personal maid, and that she still attends her, to do something to her hair, at least once a week. Knowing these things, it would seem to me that only the most desperate stupidity—"

"Yes, sir. Okay on the stupidity. But why does it have to be that Dora took them? Maybe Chapin took them himself."

"He might. But most unlikely. Surely he did not strip the stockings from her legs, and I doubt if he was familiar with her dressing-room. The faithful Dora—"

"Faithful to who? Mrs. Burton, swiping her duds?"

"But, Archie. Having seen Dora, can you not grant her rarity? Anyone can be faithful to an employer; millions are, daily, constantly; it is one of the dullest and most vulgar of loyalties. We need not, even if we could, conjecture as to the first stirring of sympathy in Dora's breast on her perceiving the bitter torment in the romantic cripple's heart. I would like to believe it was a decent and honorable bargain, that Paul Chapin offered to pay her money, and did pay her, to get him a pair of gloves his unattainable beloved had worn, but I fear not. Having seen Dora, I suspect that it was the service of romance to which she dedicated herself; and that has been her faithfulness. It may even account for her continuing to visit Mrs. Burton when her marriage freed her from the practical necessity; doubtless, fresh specimens are added from time to time. What a stroke of luck for Chapin! The beloved odor, the intimate textile from the skin of his adored, is delivered to him as it may be required; more, the fingers which an hour ago played in his lady's hair are now passing him his dinner coffee. He enjoys, daily, all the more delicate associations with the person of his passion, and escapes entirely the enforced and common-place contacts which usually render the delights of dubious profit. So much for the advantage, the peculiar thirst called emotional, of the individual; it is true that the race of man cannot be continued without it. But the biological problem is another matter."

Orrie Cather said, "I knew a guy in the army that used to take out a girl's handkerchief and kiss it before he went to sleep. One day a couple of us sneaked it out of his shirt and put something on it, and you should have heard him when he stuck his snout against it that night. He burned it up. Later he laid and cried, he was like that."

I said, "It took brains to think up one as good as that." Wolfe looked at Orrie, shut his eyes for a few seconds, and opened them again. He said:

"There are no ubiquitous handkerchiefs in this collection. Mr. Chapin is an epicure.—Archie. Repack the box, with feeling, lock it, wrap it up, and find a place for it in the cabinet.—Orrie, you may resume; you know your instructions. You have not brought us the solution of our case, but you have lifted the curtain to another room of the edifice we are exploring. Telephone at five after six as usual."

Orrie went down the hall whistling.

# Chapter 12

I had a nice piece of leather of my own, not as big as Paul Chapin's treasure box, but fancier. Sitting at my desk around five o'clock that Wednesday afternoon, killing time waiting for a visitor who had phoned, I took it out of my inside breast pocket and looked at it; I had only had it a couple of weeks. It was brown, ostrich-skin, and was tooled in gold all over the outside. On one side the tooling was fine lines about half an inch apart, with flowers stemming out from them; the flowers were orchids; the workmanship was so good that you could tell Wolfe had given the guy a Cattleya to work from. The other side was covered with Colt automatics, fifty-two perfect little gold pistols all aiming at the center. Inside was stamped in gold: *A. G. from N. W.* Wolfe had given it to me on October 23rd, at the dinner-table, and I didn't even know he knew when my birthday was. I carried my police and fire cards in it, and my operator's license. I might have traded it for New York City if you had thrown in a couple of good suburbs.

When Fritz came and said Inspector Cramer was there I put it back in my pocket.

I let Cramer get eased into a chair and then I went

upstairs to the plant-rooms. Wolfe was at the potting-bench with Horstmann, spreading out some osmundine and leaning over to smell it; a dozen or so pots of Odontoglossums, overgrown, were at his elbow. I waited until he looked around, and I felt my throat drying up.

"Well?"

I swallowed. "Cramer's downstairs. The rugged Inspector."

"What of it? You heard me speaking to him on the telephone."

"Look here," I said, "I want this distinctly understood. I came up here only for one reason, because I thought maybe you had changed your mind and would like to see him. Yes or no will do it. If you give me a bawling out it will be nothing but pure childishness. You know what I think."

Wolfe opened his eyes a little wider, winked the left one at me, twice, and turned to face the potting-bench again. All I could see was his broad back that might have been something in a Macy Thanksgiving Day parade. He said to Horstmann:

"This will do. Get the charcoal. No sphagnum, I think."

I went back down to the office and told Cramer, "Mr. Wolfe can't come down. He's too infirm."

The Inspector laughed. "I didn't expect him to. I've known Nero Wolfe longer than you have, sonny. You don't suppose I thought I was going to tear any secrets out of him? Anything he would tell me he has already told you. Can I light a pipe?"

"Shoot. Wolfe hates it. To hell with him."

"What's this, you staging on me?" Cramer packed his pipe, held a match to it, and puffed. "You don't . . . need to. Did Wolfe tell you what . . . I told him on the phone?"

"I heard it." I patted my notebook. "I've got it down."

"The hell you have. Okay. I don't want George Pratt riding me, I'm too old to enjoy it. What went on here night before last?"

I grinned. "Just what Wolfe told you. That's all. He closed a little contract."

"Is it true that he nicked Pratt for four thousand dollars?"

"He didn't nick anybody. He offered something for sale, and they gave him the order."

"Yeah." He puffed. "You know Pratt? Pratt thinks that it's funny that he has to shell out to a private dick when the city maintains such a magnificent force of brave and intelligent men to cope with such problems. He said cope. I was there. He was talking to the Deputy Commissioner."

"Indeed." I bit my lip. I always felt like a sap when I caught myself imitating Wolfe. "Maybe he was referring to the Department of Health. That never occurred to me before, a cop coping."

Cramer grunted. He sat back and looked at the vase of orchids, and pulled at his pipe. Pretty soon he said:

"I had a funny experience this afternoon. A woman called up downtown and said she wanted Nero Wolfe arrested because he had tried to cut her throat. They put her onto me because they knew I had Wolfe in mind about this case. I said I'd send a man up to get the details and she gave me her name and address. You could have flipped me cold with a rubber band when I heard it."

I said, "That's a hot one. I wonder who it could have been."

"Sure you do. I'll bet you're puzzled. Then a couple of hours later a guy came to see me. By invitation. He was a taxi-driver. He said that no matter how much diversion it offered he didn't care to take the rap for perjury, and that he saw blood on her when she got in his cab on Perry Street. That was one of the things I was wanting to mention to Wolfe on the phone, but the picture in my mind's eye of him slicing a lady's gullet was so damn remarkable that I didn't get it out." He puffed at his pipe, lit a match, and got it going again. He went on, more forceful and rugged. "Look here, Goodwin. What the hell's the idea? I've tried that Chapin woman three times, and I couldn't get her to break down enough to tell me what her name was. She put on the clamp and left it. Wolfe gets in the case late Monday night, and here already, Wednesday morning, she's chasing up to his office to show him her operation. What the hell is it about him that gets them coming like that?"

I grinned. "It's his sympathetic nature, inspector."

"Yeah. Who carved her neck?"

"Search me. She told you, Wolfe. Pull him in and give him the works."

"Was it Chapin?"

I shook my head. "If I know that secret, it's buried here." I tapped my chest.

"Much obliged. Now listen to me. I'm being serious. Am I on the level?"

"Absolutely.

"I am?"

"You know damn well you are."

"Okay. Then I'm telling you, I didn't come here to lift the silver. I've been after Chapin more than six weeks, ever since Dreyer was croaked, and what I've got on him is exactly nothing. Maybe he killed Harrisen, and I'm damn sure he killed Dreyer, and it looks like he got Hibbard, and he's got me feeling like a Staten Island flatfoot. He's as slick as a wet pavement. Right in a courtroom he confesses he committed murder, and the judge fines him fifty bucks for contempt of court! Later I find that he mentioned it beforehand to his publisher, as a publicity stunt! Covered everywhere. Is he slick?"

I nodded. "He's slick."

"Yes. Well, I've tried this and that. For one thing, I've got it figured that his wife hates him and she's afraid of him, and probably she knows enough about it to fill out a hand for us, if we could get her to spill it. So when I heard that she had dashed up here to see Wolfe, I naturally surmised that he had learned things. And I want to say this. You don't need to tell me a damn thing if you don't want to. I'm not trying to horn in. But whatever you got out of that Chapin woman, maybe you can make better use of it if you see whether it fits a few pieces I've got hold of, and you're welcome—"

"But, inspector. Wait a minute. If you think she came here friendly, to dump the can, how do you account for her calling up to get Wolfe arrested?"

"Now, sonny." Cramer's sharp eyes twinkled at me. "Didn't I say I've known Nero Wolfe longer than you have? If he wanted me to think she hadn't got confidential with him, that would be about exactly what he would tell her to do."

I laughed. While I was laughing it occurred to me that it wouldn't do any particular harm if Cramer continued to nurse that notion, so I laughed some more. I said, "He might, he sure might, but he didn't.

Why she phoned you to arrest him—wait till I get a chance to tell Wolfe about it—why she did that, she's psychopathic. So's her husband. They're both psychopathic. That's Park Avenue for batty."

Cramer nodded. "I've heard the word. We've got a department—oh, well . . ."

"And you're damn sure he killed Dreyer."

He nodded again. "I think Dreyer was murdered by Paul Chapin and Leopold Elkus."

"You don't say!" I looked at him. "That might turn out to be right. Elkus, huh?"

"Yeah. You and Wolfe won't talk. Do you want me to talk?"

"I'd love it."

He filled his pipe again. "You know about the Dreyer thing. Do you know who bought the nitroglycerin tablets? Dreyer did. Sure. A week before he died, the day after Elkus phoned him that the pictures were phony and he wanted his money back. Maybe he had ideas about suicide and maybe he didn't; I think he didn't; there's several things people take nitroglycerin for in small doses."

He took a drag at the pipe, pulled it in until I expected to see it squirt out at his belly-button, and went on leaving it to find its way by instinct. "Now, how did Chapin get the tablets out of the bottle that day? Easy. He didn't. Dreyer had had them for a week, and Chapin was in and out of the gallery pretty often. He had been there a couple of hours Monday afternoon, probably for a talk about Elkus's pictures. He could have got them then and saved them for an opening. The opening came Wednesday afternoon.— Wait a minute. I know what Elkus says. That Thursday morning a detective questioned Santini too, the Italian expert, and it checked, but of course at that

time it looked like nothing but routine. Since then I've
sent a request to Italy, and they found Santini in
Florence and had a good long talk with him. He says it
was like he told the detective in the first place, but
he forgot to mention that after they all left the office
Elkus went back for something and was in the office
alone for maybe half a minute. What if Dreyer's glass
was then maybe half full, and Elkus, having got the
tablets from Chapin, fixed it up for him?"

"What for? Just for a prank?"

"I'm not saying what for. That's one thing we're
working on now. For instance, what if the pictures
Dreyer sold Elkus were the real thing—it was six
years ago—and Elkus put them away and substituted
phonies for them, and then demanded his money back?
We're looking into that. The minute I get any evidence
what for, I'll arrange for some free board and room for
Elkus *and* Chapin."

"You haven't got any yet."

"No."

I grinned. "Anyway, you're working in a lot of nice
complications. I'll have to tell Wolfe about it; I hope to
God it don't bore him. Why don't you just decide to
believe it was suicide after all, and let it go at that?"

"Nothing doing. Especially since Hibbard disappeared. And even if I wanted to, George Pratt and
that bunch wouldn't let me. They got those warnings.
I don't blame them. Those things sound like business
to me, even if they are dolled up. I suppose you've
read them."

I nodded. He stuck his paw in his breast pocket
and pulled out some papers and began looking through
them. He said, "I'm a damn fool. I carry copies of them
around with me, because I can't get rid of a hunch that
there's a clue in them somewhere, some kind of a clue,

if I could find it. Listen to this one, the one he sent last Friday, three days after Hibbard disappeared:

*One. Two. Three.*
*Ye cannot see what I see:*
*His bloody head, his misery, his eyes*
*Dead but for terror and the wretched hope*
*That this last blow, this finis, will not fall.*

*One. Two. Three.*
*Ye cannot hear what I hear:*
*His moan for pity, now his desperate breath*
*To suck the air in through the bubbling blood.*

*And I hear, too, in me the happy rhythm,*
*The happy boastful strutting of my soul.*
*Yes! Hear! It boasts:*
*One. Two. Three.*
*Ye should have killed me.*

"I ask you, does that sound like business?" Cramer folded it up again. "Did you ever see a guy that had been beaten around the head enough so that things were busted inside? Did you ever notice one? All right, get this: *to suck the air in through the bubbling blood.* Does that describe it? I'll say it does. The man that wrote that was looking at it, I'm telling you he was looking right at it. That's why, as far as Andrew Hibbard is concerned, all I'm interested in is stiffs. Chapin got Hibbard as sure as hell, and the only question is where did he put the leavings. Also, he got Dreyer, only with that one Elkus helped him."

The Inspector stopped for a couple of pulls at his pipe. When that had been attended to he screwed his nose up at me and demanded, "Why, do *you* think it was suicide?"

"Hell no. I think Chapin killed him. And maybe Harrison, and maybe Hibbard. I'm just waiting to see you and Nero Wolfe and the Epworth League prove it on him. Also I'm annoyed about Elkus. If you get Elkus wrong you may gum it."

"Uh-huh." Cramer screwed his nose again. "You don't like me after Elkus? I wonder if Nero Wolfe will like it. I hope not to gum it, I really do. I suppose you know Elkus has got a shadow on Paul Chapin? What's he suspicious about?"

I lifted my brows a little, and hoped that was all I did. "No. I didn't know that."

"The hell you didn't."

"No. Of course you have one, and we have . . ." I remembered that I never had got hold of Del Bascom to ask him about the dick in the brown cap and pink necktie. "I thought that runt keeping the boys company down there was one of Bascom's experts."

"Sure you did. You didn't know Bascom's been off the case since yesterday morning. Try having a talk with the runt. I did, last night, for two hours. He says he's got a goddam legal right to keep his goddam mouth shut. That's the way he talks, he's genteel. Finally I just shooed him away, and I'm going to find out who he's reporting to."

"I thought you said, Elkus."

"That's my idea. Who else could it be? Do you know?"

I shook my head. "Hope to die."

"All right, if you do don't tell me, I want to guess. Of course you realize that I'm not exactly a boob. If you don't, Nero Wolfe does. I arrested a man once and he turned out to be guilty, that's why I was made an inspector. I know Wolfe expects to open up this Mr. Chapin and get well paid for it, and therefore if I expected him to pass me any cards out of his hand I *would* be a boob. But I'll be frank with you, in the past six weeks I've made so many grabs at this cripple without getting anything that I don't like him at all and in fact I'd like to rip out his guts. Also, they're giving me such a riding that I'm beginning to get saddle-sores. I would like to know two things. First, how far has Wolfe got?—Sure, I know he's a genius. Okay. But has he got enough of it to stop that cripple?"

I said, and I meant it, "He's got enough to stop any guy that ever started."

"When? I won't lose any sleep if he nicks Pratt for four grand. Can you say when, and can I help?"

I shook my head. "No twice. But he'll do it."

"All right. I'll go on poking around myself. The other thing, you might tell me this, and I swear to God you won't regret it. When Dora Chapin was here this morning did she tell Wolfe she saw nitroglycerin tablets in her husband's pocket any time between September eleventh and September nineteenth?"

I grinned at him. "There are two ways I could answer that, inspector. One way would be if she had said it, in which case I would try to answer it so you couldn't tell whether she had or not. The other way is the one you're hearing: she wasn't asked about it, and she said nothing about it. She just came here to get her throat cut."

"Uh-huh." Cramer got up from his chair. "And Wolfe started working on her from behind. He would. He's the damnedest guy at getting in the back door . . . well. So-long. I'll say much obliged some other day. Give Wolfe a Bronx cheer for me, and tell him that as far as I'm concerned he can have the money *and* the applause of the citizens in this Chapin case, and the sooner the better. I'd like to get my mind on something else."

"I'll tell him. Like to have a glass of beer?"

He said no, and went. Since he was an inspector, I went to the hall and helped him on with his coat and opened the door for him. At the curb was a police car, one of the big Cadillacs, with a chauffeur. Now, I thought, that's what I call being a detective.

I went back to the office. It looked dismal and gloomy; it was nearly six o'clock and the dark had come over half an hour ago and I had only turned on one light. Wolfe was still upstairs monkeying with the plants; he wasn't due down for seven minutes. I didn't feel like sitting watching him drink beer, and had no reason to expect anything more pertinent out of him, and I decided to go out and find a stone somewhere and turn it up to see what was under it. I opened a couple of windows to let Cramer's pipe-smoke out, got my Colt from the drawer and put it in my pocket from force of habit, went to the hall for my hat and coat, and beat it.

# Chapter 13

I didn't know Perry Street much, and was surprised when I walked up in front of number 203, across the street, having left the roadster half a block away. It was quite a joint, stucco to look like Spanish, with black iron entrance lamps and no fire escapes. On both sides were old brick houses. A few cars were parked along the block, and a couple of taxis. On my side of the street was a string of dingy stores: stationery, laundry, delicatessen, cigar store and so on. I moved along and looked in. At the delicatessen I stopped and went inside. There were two or three customers, and Fred Durkin was leaning against the end of the counter with a cheese sandwich and a bottle of beer. I turned around and went out, and walked back down to where the roadster was and got inside. In a couple of minutes Fred came along and climbed in beside me. He was still chewing and working his tongue in the corners. He asked me what was up. I said, nothing, I had just come down to gossip. I asked him:

"Where's the other club members?"

He grinned. "Oh, they're around. The city feller is probably in the laundry, I think he likes the smell. I suppose Pinkie is down at the next corner, in the

Coffee Pot. He usually deserts his post around this time to put on the nose bag."

"You call him Pinkie?"

"Oh, I can call him anything. That's for his necktie. What do you want me to call him?"

I looked at him. "You've had one or ten drinks. What's the big idea?"

"I swear to God I haven't, Archie. I'm just glad to see you. It's lonesome as hell around here."

"You chinned any with this Pinkie?"

"No. He's reticent. He hides somewhere and thinks."

"Okay. Go on back to your pickle emporium. If you see any kids scratching their initials on my car, pat 'em on the head."

Fred climbed out and went. In a minute I got out too, and walked down to the next corner, where if you was blind the smell would have told you Coffee Pot. I went in. There were three little tables along the wall, and half a dozen customers at the counter. Pinkie was there all right, along at one of the little tables, working on a bowl of soup, trying to get the spoon out of his mouth. He had his brown cap on, over one ear. I went over alongside his table and said to him, keeping my voice low:

"Oh, here you are."

He looked up. I said, "The boss wants to see you right away. I'll sit on the lid here a while. Make it snappy."

He stared at me a couple of seconds, and then squeaked so that I nearly jumped. "You're a goddam filthy liar."

The little runt! I could have reached down and jerked his gold teeth out. I slid the other chair back with my toe and sat down and put my elbows on the table and looked at him. "I said, the boss wants to see you."

"Oh, yeah?" He sneered at me with his mouth open, showing his gilded incisors. "You wouldn't string a guy, would you, mister? By God, I'll tell the goddam world you wouldn't. Who was I talking to a while ago on the goddam telephone?"

I grinned. "That was me. Listen here a minute. I can see you're tough. Do you want a good job?"

"Yeah. That's why I've got one. If you'd just move your goddam carcass away from my table . . ."

"All right, I will. Go on and eat your soup, and don't try to scare me with your bad manners. I might decide to remove your right ear and put it where the left one is, and hang the left one on your belt for a spare. Go on and eat."

He dropped his spoon in the soup-bowl and wiped his mouth with the back of his hand. "What the hell do you want, anyway?"

"Well," I said, "I was having tea with my friend, Inspector Cramer, this afternoon, and he was telling me how much he enjoyed his talk with you last night, and I thought I'd like to meet you. That's one story. Then another story might be that a certain guy whose name I needn't mention has got the idea that you're selling him out, and I'm supposed to find out, and I thought the quickest way was to ask you. How many people are you working for?"

"Of all the goddam curiosity!" He sucked something from between his teeth with his tongue. "Last night the goddam inspector, and now you. Hell, my soup's getting cold."

He got up from his chair and picked up the bowl and carried it ten feet to the table at the end. Then he came back for the bread and butter and glass of water and took them. I waited till he was through moving, then I got up and went to the end table and sat down across from him. I was sore because my nifty opening had gone wild. The counterman and the customers were watching us, but only to pass the time. I reached in my pocket and got out my roll and peeled off a pair of twenties.

"Look here," I said, "I could spot you in a day or two, but it would cost both money and time, and I'd just as soon you'd get it. Here's forty bucks. Half now if you tell me who's paying you, and the other half as soon as I check it. I'll find out, anyhow, this'll just save time."

I'll be damned if he didn't get up and pick up his soup again and start back for the first table. A couple of the customers began to laugh, and the counterman called out, "Hey, let the guy eat his soup, maybe he just don't like you." I felt myself getting sore enough to push in somebody's nose, but I knew there was no profit in that, so I swallowed it and put on a grin. I picked up the runt's bread and butter and water and took it down and set it in front of him. Then I went and tossed a dime on the counter and said, "Give him some hot soup and put poison in it." Then I left.

I walked the block back to the roadster, not in a hurry. Fred Durkin was in the cigar store as I passed by. I had a notion to see him and tell him to keep an eye on his friend Pinkie and maybe catch him on a phone call or something, but knowing how his mind worked I thought it would be better to let it stay on his main job. I got in the roadster and headed uptown.

I couldn't figure the runt at all. Was it possible that a dick that looked like that was as honest as that? Who was paying him enough to make him look at forty dollars like it was soap wrappers? Who was so particular about its not being known that he was having Paul Chapin tailed? The inspector's idea didn't seem to me to make sense, even if Leopold Elkus had helped out that day with Dreyer's highball. Why would he put a shadow on Chapin? Of course it was possible, but my practice was to let the brain off easy on an idea until it got a little better than possible. If it wasn't Elkus, who was it? It might have been any one of the bunch who was too scared for Wolfe's memorandum to quiet him down and thought he needed his own reports of the cripple's activities, but in that case why all the mystery? Driving uptown, I went over the list in my mind, without any results.

I put the roadster in the garage and walked home. It was nearly dinner time when I got there. Wolfe was in the office, at his desk. He was doing something. His beer tray had been pushed to one side, and he was leaning over a piece of paper, inspecting it with a magnifying glass, with the strong light turned on. He looked up to nod at me, and then resumed. There was a little pile of similar papers under a weight. The typewriting on the paper began, *Ye should have killed me, watched the last mean sigh*. It was the first warning.

Pretty soon he looked up again, and blinked. He put the magnifying glass on the table. I asked, "These are Farrell's samples?"

"Yes. Mr. Farrell brought them ten minutes ago. He decided to get a specimen from each machine in Mr. Oglethorpe's office. I have examined two, and discarded them—those marked with red pencil." He sighed. "You know, Archie, it is remarkable how the shortening of the days at this time of year, the early darkness, seems to lengthen the period between luncheon and dinner. I suppose I have made that comment before."

"Not very often, sir. Not more than once or twice a day."

"Indeed. It deserves more. You haven't washed."

"No, sir."

"There are two pheasants which should not be kept waiting."

I went upstairs.

After dinner we worked together at Farrell's samples; there were sixteen of them. He wasn't so good at the typewriter; he had exed out a good deal, but for our purpose that didn't matter. I brought a glass down from the plant-rooms and Wolfe went on with his. It didn't matter which of the originals we used, so long as it wasn't one of the carbons, since it had been definitely determined that they had all been written on the same machine. We did a thorough job of it, not finally eliminating one until we had both examined it. Wolfe loved that kind of work, every minute of it; when he had gone through a sample and made sure that the *a* wasn't off the line and the *n* wasn't cockeyed, he grunted with satisfaction. I liked it only when it got results. As we neared the bottom of the pile with the red pencil unanimous, I wasn't getting any gayer.

Around ten o'clock I got up and handed the last one across to him, and then went to the kitchen and got a pitcher of milk. Fritz, sitting there reading the French paper, giggled at me: "You drink milk looking like that, you curdle it." I stuck my tongue out at him and went back to the office. Wolfe had fastened the sheets together with a clip and was putting the originals back in the envelope.

I said, "Well. This has been a fine pregnant

evening. Huh?" I drank some milk and licked my lips.

Wolfe leaned back and got his fingers twined. He kept his eyes nearly open. He finally remarked, "We have sacrificed it to Mr. Chapin's adroitness, a tribute to him. And established a fact: that he did not type the warnings in his publisher's office. But he did type them, and doubtless holds himself in readiness to type another; so the machine exists and can be found. I have already another suggestion ready for Mr. Farrell—a little complicated, but worth the experiment."

"Maybe I could offer one. Tell him to get samples from the machines in Leopold Elkus's office."

Wolfe's brows went up. "Why particularly Elkus?"

"Well, for one thing Inspector Cramer got the idea of having someone in Italy get in touch with Mr. Santini. Dumb idea, of course, but he got it. Santini says that he has remembered that after they all left the office that day Elkus went back for something and was in there alone for maybe half a minute. Plenty of time to drop some tablets into a highball."

"But hardly enough to filch the bottle from Mr. Dreyer's pocket and return it again, not to mention the dexterity required."

"That's all right. Chapin did that himself some time previously, maybe the week before, and gave them to Elkus."

"Indeed. This was in the news reels?"

"It's in Cramer's bean. But it may also be in his bag one of these days. We would have to get a mirror and see how we look in it, if it turns out to be the dope and he bags it first. Another item is that Elkus has got a shadow on Chapin."

"That likewise is in Mr. Cramer's bean?"

"Yeah, likewise. But one of those dicks—"

"Archie." Wolfe wiggled a finger at me. "I think it would be as well to correct your perspective. You must not let the oddities of this case perplex you to the point of idiocy. For instance, Inspector Cramer. He is an excellent man. In nine murder cases out of ten his services would be much more valuable than mine; to mention a few points only, I need to keep regular hours, I could not function even passably where properly chilled beer was not continually available, and I cannot run fast. If I am forced to engage in extreme physical effort, such as killing a snake, I am hungry for days. But it is utterly futile, in this case or any other case in which we are interested, to give consideration to the contents of Mr. Cramer's bean. I supposed that in seven years you had learned that."

"Sure. His bean's out." I waved it out with my hand. "But what about his facts? Such as Elkus going back alone to the office?"

Wolfe shook his head. "You see, Archie? The dizzy revolutions of Mr. Chapin's cunning wheel of vengeance have hurled you off on a tangent. Consider what we have engaged to do under our memorandum: free our clients from fear of Paul Chapin's designs. Even if it were possible to prove that Dr. Elkus poisoned Mr. Dreyer's drink—which I strongly doubt—to what purpose should we attempt it? No; let us stick to the circumference of our own necessities and desires. Inspector Cramer might some day have a fact for us, as anyone might, there is no denying that, but he is welcome to this one. It is beyond our circle of endeavor."

"Still I don't see it. Look here. Say Elkus put the stuff in Dreyer's glass. Of course Chapin was in on it, look at the second warning. How are you going to

prove Chapin guilty of Dreyer's murder unless you
also prove how Elkus did his part?"

Wolfe nodded. "Your logic is impeccable. Your
premise is absurd. I haven't the slightest expectation
of proving Chapin guilty of Dreyer's murder."

"Then what the devil—"

I got that much out before I realized exactly what
he had said. I stared at him. He went on:

"It could not be expected that you should know
Paul Chapin as I know him, because you have not had
the extended and intimate association that I have
enjoyed—through his books. He is possessed of a
demon. A fine old melodramatic phrase. The same
thing can be said in modern scientific terms, but it
would mean no more and its flavor would be much
impaired. He is possessed of a demon, but he is also,
within certain limits, an extraordinarily astute man.
Emotionally he is infantile—he even prefers a vicar to
a substitute, when the original object is unattainable,
as witness his taking Dora Ritter to proxy for her
mistress. But his intellectual competence is such that
it is problematical whether factual proof could ever be
obtained of any act of his which he intended to remain
anonymous."

He stopped for some beer. I said, "If you mean you
give up, you're wasting a lot of time and money. If you
mean you're waiting for him to croak another one, and
you're tailing him to watch him do it, and he's as smart
as you say he is . . ."

I drank milk. Wolfe wiped his lips and went on: "Of
course we have our usual advantage: we are on the
offensive. And of course the place to attack the enemy
is his weak spot; those are truisms. Since Mr. Chapin
has an aversion to factual proof and has the intellectual equipment to preclude it, let us abandon the

intellectual field, and attack him where he is weak. His emotions. I am acquainting you now with this decision which was made last Sunday. We are gathering what ammunition we may. Certainly facts are not to be sneered at; I need two more of them, possibly three, before I can feel confident of persuading Mr. Chapin to confess his guilt."

Wolfe emptied his glass, I said, "Confess, huh? That cripple?"

He nodded. "It would be simple. I am sure it will be."

"What are the three facts?"

"First, to find Mr. Hibbard. His meat and bone; we can do without the vital spark if it has found another errand. That, however, is more for the satisfaction of our clients and the fulfillment of the terms of our memorandum than for the effect on Mr. Chapin. That sort of fact will not impress him. Second, to find the typewriter on which he wrote the menacing verses. That I must have, for him. Third—the possibility—to learn if he has ever kissed his wife. That may not be needed. Given the first two, I probably should not wait for it."

"And with that you can make him confess?"

"I should think so. I see no other way out for him."

"That's all you need?"

"It seems ample."

I looked at him. Sometimes I thought I could tell how much he was being fanciful; sometimes I knew I couldn't. I grunted. "Then I might as well phone Fred and Bill and Orrie and the others to come up and check out."

"By no means. Mr. Chapin himself might lead us to the typewriter or the Hibbard meat and bone."

"And I've been useful too. According to you. Why

did you buy the gasoline I burned up yesterday and today if you decided Sunday night you couldn't get the goods on him? It seems as if I'm like a piece of antique furniture or a pedigreed dog, I'm in the luxury class. You keep me on for beauty. Do you know what I think? I think that all this is just your delicate way of telling me that on the Dreyer thing you've decided I'm a washout and you think I might try something else. Okay. What?"

Wolfe's cheeks unfolded a little. "Veritably, Archie, you are overwhelming. The turbulence of a Carpathian torrent. It would be gratifying if you should discover Mr. Hibbard."

"I thought so. Forget Dreyer?"

"Let him rest in peace. At least for tomorrow."

"A thousand dicks and fifteen thousand cops have been looking for Hibbard for eight days. Where shall I bring him when I find him?"

"If alive, here. If dead, he will care as little as I. But his niece will care, I presume, to her."

"Do you tell me where to look?"

"Our little globe."

"Okay."

I went upstairs. I was riled. We had never had a case, and I suppose never will have, without Wolfe getting cryptic about it sooner or later; I was used to it and expected it, but it always riled me. In the Fairmont-Avery thing he had deliberately waited for twenty-four hours to close in on Pete Avery after he had him completely sewed up, just for the pleasure of watching me and Dick Morley of the D.A.'s office play fox-and-goose with that old fool that couldn't find his ear trumpet. I suppose his awful conceit was one of the wheels that worked the machinery that got his results, but that didn't make it any more enjoyable

when I was doing the worrying for both of us. That
Wednesday night I nearly took the enamel off of my
teeth with the brush, stabbing with it at Wolfe's
conceit.·

The next morning, Thursday, I had had my breakfast and was in the office by eight o'clock, taking
another good look at the photograph of her uncle
which Evelyn Hibbard had given to us. Saul Panzer
had phoned and I had told him to meet me in the
McAlpin lobby at eight-thirty. After I had soaked in
all I could of the photograph I made a couple of phone
calls, one to Evelyn Hibbard and one to Inspector
Cramer. Cramer was friendly. He said that on Hibbard he had spread the net pretty wide. If a body of a
man was washed up on the sand at Montauk Point,
or found in a coal mine at Scranton, or smelled in a
trunk in a Village roominghouse, or pulled out of a
turnip pit in south Jersey, he would know about it in
ten minutes, and would be asking for specifications.
That satisfied me that there was no sense in my
wasting time or shoe leather looking for a dead
Hibbard; I'd better concentrate on the possibility of a
live one.

I went to the McAlpin and talked it over with Saul
Panzer. He, with his wrinkled little mug not causing
any stranger to suspect how cute he was, and he could
be pretty damn cute—he sat on the edge of a tapestry
chair, smoking a big slick light-brown cigar that
smelled like something they scatter on lawns in the
early spring, and told me about it to date. It was
obvious from the instructions Saul had been following,
either that Wolfe had reached the same conclusion
that I had, that if Hibbard had been croaked the police
routine was the best and quickest way of finding him,

or that Wolfe thought Hibbard was still alive. Saul had been digging up every connection Hibbard had had in and around the city for the past five years, every degree of intimacy, man, woman, and child, and calling on them. Since Hibbard had been an instructor at a large university, and also a sociable man, Saul hadn't made much more than a start. I supposed that Wolfe's idea was that there was a possibility that Chapin's third warning was a fake, that Hibbard had just got too scared to breathe and had run off to hide, and that in that case he was practically certain to get in touch with someone he knew.

My heart wasn't really in it. For my part, I believed the cripple, third warning and all. In the first place, Wolfe hadn't said definitely that he didn't; and secondly, I had known Wolfe to be wrong, not often, but more than once. When the event proved that he had been wrong about something, it was a delight to see him handle it. He would wiggle his finger a little more rapidly and violently than usual, and mutter with his eyes nearly open at me, "Archie, I love to make a mistake, to assume the burden of omniscience."

But although I believed the cripple and was perfectly comfortable with the notion that Hibbard wasn't using up any more air, I couldn't see that there was anything better to be done than to smell around places where he had once been alive. I left the general list—neighbors, friends, pupils and miscellaneous—to Saul, and chose for myself the members of the League of the White Feather.

The *Tribune* office was only seven blocks away, so I called there first, but Mike Ayers wasn't in. Next I went up on Park Avenue, to Drummond's florist shop, and the little fat tenor was all ready for a talk. He

wanted to know many things, and I hope he believed
what I told him, but he had nothing to offer in
exchange that helped me any. From there I went back
down to Thirty-ninth Street to see Edwin Robert
Byron the editor, and that was also empty. For over
half an hour about all he found time for was "Excuse
me" as he was reaching for the telephone. I was
thinking, with all that practice, if he should happen to
get fired as an editor he could step right in anywhere
as a telephone girl.

When I was out working I was supposed to phone
in at eleven o'clock, at which time Wolfe got down
from the plant-rooms, to ask if there were any new
instructions. Leaving Edwin Robert Byron's office a
little before eleven, I decided I might as well roll over
to the house in person, since it was only a couple of
blocks out of my way to the next call.

Wolfe wasn't down yet. I went to the kitchen and
asked Fritz if anyone had left a corpse on the stoop for
us, and he said he didn't think so. I heard the elevator
and went to the office.

Wolfe was in one of his sighing moods. He sighed
as he said good morning and he sighed as he got into
his chair. It might have meant anything from one
measly little orchid getting bugs on it up to a major
relapse. I waited until he got his little routine chores
done before trying to pass a couple of words.

Out of one of the envelopes in the morning mail he
took some pieces of paper that looked familiar from
where I stood. I approached. Wolfe looked up at me
and back at the papers.

I asked, "What's that, Farrell's second edition?"

He handed me one of the sheets, a different size
from the others. I read it:

*Dear Mr. Wolfe:*

*Here are two more samples which I failed to deliver with the others. I found them in another pocket. I am called suddenly to Philadelphia on a chance at a commission, and am mailing them to you so you will have them first thing in the morning.*

*Sincerely,*
*Augustus Farrell*

Wolfe had already got his magnifying glass and was inspecting one of the samples. I felt my blood coming up to my head, which meant a hunch. I told myself to hang onto the aplomb, that there was no more reason to expect it of these than of the others, and there were only two chances. I stood and watched Wolfe. After a little he pushed the sheet aside and shook his head, and reached for the other one.

One more, I thought. If it's that one he's got one of his facts. I looked for an expression on his face as he examined it, but of course I might as well have saved my eyes the strain. He moved the glass along, intent, but a little too rapidly for me not to suspect that he had had a hunch too. At length he looked up at me, and sighed.

"No."

I demanded, "You mean it's not it?"

"No, I believe, is negative. No."

"Let me see the damn things."

He pushed them across and I got the glass and gave them a look. I didn't need to be very thorough, after the practice I had had the night before. I was really almost incredulous, and sore as the devil, because in the detective business nothing is more important than to find your hunches good as often as possible. If you once get off of your hunches you might as well give up and go and get a job on the Homicide Squad. Not to mention that Wolfe had said that that typewriter was one of the two things he needed.

He was saying, "It is a pity Mr. Farrell has deserted us. I am not sure that my next suggestion should await his return; and he does not, by the way, mention his return." He picked up the note from Farrell and looked at it. "I believe, Archie, that you had best abandon the Hibbard search temporarily—"

He stopped himself; and said in a different tone:

"Mr. Goodwin. Hand me the glass."

I gave it to him. His using my formal handle when we were alone meant that he was excited almost beyond control, but I had no idea what about. Then I saw what he wanted the glass for. He was looking through it at the note from Farrell! I stared at him. He kept on looking. I didn't say anything. A beautiful suspicion was getting into me that you shouldn't ever ignore a hunch.

Finally Wolfe said, "Indeed."

I held out my hand and he gave me the note and the glass. I saw it at a glance, but I kept on looking, it was so satisfactory to see that *a* off the line and a little to the left, and the *n* cockeyed, and all the other signs. I laid it on the table and grinned at Wolfe.

"Old Eagle Eye. Damn me for missing it."

He said, "Take off your coat and hat, Archie. Whom can we telephone in Philadelphia to learn where an architect there in pursuit of a commission might possibly be found?"

# Chapter 14

I started for the hall to put my coat and hat away, but before I got to the door I turned and went back.

"Listen," I said, "the roadster needs some exercise. We might fool around with the phone all afternoon and not get anywhere. Why don't we do this: you phone Farrell's friends here and see if you can get a line on him. I'll roll down to Philly and call you up as soon as I arrive. If you haven't found out anything, I'll be on the ground to look for him. I can get there by two-thirty."

"Excellent," Wolfe agreed. "But the noon train will reach Philadelphia at two o'clock."

"Yeah, I know, but—"

"Archie. Let us agree on the train."

"Okay. I thought I might get away with it."

There was plenty of time to discuss a few probabilities, since it was only a five-minute walk to the Pennsylvania Station. I caught the noon train, had lunch on the diner, and phoned Wolfe from the Broad Street Station at two minutes after two.

He had no dope, except the names of a few friends and acquaintances of Farrell's in Philadelphia. I telephoned all I could get hold of, and chased around all afternoon, the Fine Arts Club, and an architectural magazine, and the newspaper offices to see if they knew who intended to build something and so on. I was beginning to wonder if an idea that had come to me on the train could possibly have anything in it. Was Farrell himself entangled somehow in the Chapin business, and had he written that note on that typewriter for some reason maybe to be discovered, and then beat it? Was there a chance that he hadn't come to Philadelphia at all but somewhere else, even perhaps on a transatlantic liner?

But around six o'clock I got him. I had taken to phoning architects. After about three dozen I found one who told me that a Mr. Allenby who had got rich and sentimental was going to build a library for a Missouri town that had been lucky enough to give birth to him and then lose him. That was a building project I hadn't heard of before. I phoned Allenby, and was told that Mr. Farrell was expected at his home at seven o'clock for dinner.

I snatched a pair of sandwiches and went out there, and then had to wait until he had finished his meal.

He came to me in Mr. Allenby's library. Of course he couldn't understand how I got there. I allowed him ten seconds for surprise and so forth, and then I asked him: "Last night you wrote a note to Nero Wolfe. Where's the typewriter you wrote it on?"

He smiled like a gentleman being bewildered. He said, "I suppose it's where I left it. I didn't take it away."

"Well, where was it? Excuse me for taking you on the jump like this. I've been hunting you for over five hours and I'm out of breath. The machine you wrote that note on is the one Paul Chapin used for his poems. That's the little detail."

"No!" He stared at me, and laughed. "By God, that's good. You're sure? After working so hard to get all those samples, and then to write that note—I'll be damned."

"Yeah. When you get around to it . . . "

"Certainly. I used a typewriter at the Harvard Club."

"Oh. You did."

"I did indeed. I'll be damned."

"Yeah. Where do they keep this typewriter?"

"Why, it's one—it's available to any of the members. I was there last evening when the telegram came from Mr. Allenby, and I used it to write two or three notes. It's in a little room off the smoking-room, sort of an alcove. A great many of the fellows use it, off and on."

"Oh. They do." I sat down. "Well, this is nice. It's sweet enough to make you sick. It's available to anybody, and thousands of them use it."

"Hardly thousands, but quite a few—"

"Dozens is enough. Have you ever seen Paul Chapin use it?"

"I couldn't say—I believe, though—yes, in that little chair with his game leg pushed under—I'm pretty sure I have."

"Any of your other friends, this bunch?"

"I really couldn't say."

"Do many of them belong to the club?"

"Oh, yes, nearly all. Mike Ayers doesn't, and I believe Leo Elkus resigned a few years ago . . . "

"I see. Are there any other typewriters in the alcove?"

"There's one more, but it belongs to a public

stenographer. I understand this one was donated by some club member. They used to keep it in the library, but some of the one-finger experts made too much noise with it."

"All right." I got up. "You can imagine how I feel, coming all the way to Philadelphia to get a kick in the pants. Can I tell Wolfe when you're coming back, in case he wants you?"

He said probably tomorrow, he had to prepare drawings to submit to Mr. Allenby, and I thanked him for nothing and went out to seek the air and a streetcar to North Philadelphia.

The train ride back to New York, in a smoker filled with the discard from a hundred pairs of assorted lungs, was not what I needed to cheer me up. I couldn't think up anything to keep me awake, and I couldn't go to sleep. We pulled in at the Pennsylvania Station at midnight, and I walked home.

The office was dark; Wolfe had gone to bed. There was no note for me on my desk, so nothing startling had happened. I got a pitcher of milk from the refrigerator and went upstairs. Wolfe's room was on the same floor as mine; mine overlooking Thirty-fifth Street, and his in the rear. I thought possibly he was still awake and would like to hear the joyous news, so I went towards the back of the hall to see if there was light under his door—not going close, for when he went to bed there was a switch he turned on, and if anyone stepped within eight feet of his door or touched any of his windows a gong went off in my room that was enough to paralyze you. The slit under his door was dark, so I went on with my milk, and drank it while I was getting ready for bed.

Friday morning, after breakfast, I was still sitting in the office at eight-thirty. I sat there, first because I was sour on the Hibbard search anyway, and second because I was going to wait until nine o'clock and see Wolfe as soon as he got to the plant-rooms. But at eight-thirty the inside phone buzzed and I got on. It was Wolfe from his bedroom. He asked me if I had had a pleasant journey. I told him that all it would have needed to make it perfect was Dora Chapin for company. He asked if Mr. Farrell had remembered what typewriter he had used.

I told him. "A thing at the Harvard Club, in a little room off the smoking-room. It seems that the members all play tunes on it whenever the spirit moves them. The good thing about this is that it narrows it down, it rules out all Yale men and other roughnecks. You can see Chapin wanted to make it as simple as possible."

Wolfe's low murmur was in my ear: "Excellent."

"Yeah. One of the facts you wanted. Swell."

"No, Archie. I mean it. This will do nicely. I told you, proof will not be needed in this case, facts will do for us. But we must be sure beyond peradventure of the facts. Please find someone willing to favor us who is a member of the Harvard Club—not one of our present clients. Perhaps Albert Wright would do; if not him, find someone. Ask him to go to the club this morning and take you as a guest. On that typewriter make a copy—no. Not that. There must be no hole for Mr. Chapin to squirm through, should he prove more difficult than I anticipate. In spite of his infirmity, he is probably capable of carrying a typewriter. Do this: after making arrangements for a host, purchase a new typewriter—any good one, follow your fancy—and take it with you to the club. Bring away the one that is there and leave the new one; manage it as you please, by arrangement with the steward, by prestidigitation, whatever suggests itself. With, however, the knowledge of your host, for he must be qualified to furnish corroboration, at any future time, as to the identity of the machine you remove. Bring it here."

"A new typewriter costs one hundred dollars."

"I know that. It is not necessary to speak of it."

"Okay."

I hung up and reached for the telephone book.

That was how it happened that at ten o'clock that Friday morning I sat in the smoking-room of the Harvard Club with Albert Wright, a vice-president of Eastern Electric, drinking vermouth, with a type-writer under a shiny rubberized cover on the floor at my feet. Wright had been very nice, as he should have been, since about all he owed to Wolfe was his wife and family. That was one of the neatest blackmailing cases . . . but let it rest. It was true that he had paid Wolfe's bill, which hadn't been modest, but what I've seen of wives and families has convinced me that they can't be paid for in cash; either they're way above any money price that could be imagined or they're clear out of sight in the other direction. Anyway, Wright had been nice about it. I was saying:

"This is it. It's that typewriter in there that I showed you the number of and had you put a scratch under it. Mr. Wolfe wants it."

Wright raised his brows. I went on:

"Of course you don't care why, but if you do maybe he'll tell you some day. The real reason is that he's fond of culture and he don't like to see the members of a swell organization like the Harvard Club using a piece of junk like that in there. I've got a brand new Underwood." I touched it with my toe. "I just bought it, it's a new standard machine. I take it in there and leave it, and bring away the junk, that's all. If anyone sees me I am unconcerned. It's just a playful lark; the club gets what it needs and Mr. Wolfe gets what he wants."

Wright, smiling, sipped his vermouth. "I hesitate chiefly because you had me mark the junk for identification. I would do about anything for Nero Wolfe, but I would dislike getting in a mess and having the club dragged in too, perhaps. I suppose you couldn't offer any guarantees on that score?"

I shook my head. "No guarantees, but knowing how Mr. Wolfe is arranging this charade I'd take you on a thousand to one."

Wright sat a minute and looked at me, and then smiled again. "Well, I have to get back to the office. Go on with your lark. I'll wait here."

There was nothing to it. I picked up the Underwood and walked into the alcove with it and set it down on the desk. The public stenographer was there only ten feet away, brushing up his machine, but I merely got too nonchalant even to glance at him. I pulled the junk aside and transferred the shiny cover to it, put the new one in its place, and picked up the junk and walked out. Wright got up from his chair and walked beside me to the elevator.

On the sidewalk, at the street entrance, Wright shook hands with me. He wasn't smiling; I guessed from the look on his face that his mind had gone back four years to another time we shook hands. He said, "Give Nero Wolfe my warmest regards, and tell him they will still be warm even if I get kicked out of the Harvard Club for helping to steal a typewriter."

I grinned. "Steal my eye, it nearly broke my heart to leave that new Underwood there."

I carried my loot to where I had parked the roadster on Forty-fifth Street, put it on the seat beside me, and headed downtown. Having it there made me feel like we were getting somewhere. Not that I knew where, but Wolfe either did or thought he did. I didn't very often get really squeamish about Wolfe's calculations; I worried, all right, and worked myself into a stew when it seemed to me that he was overlooking a point that was apt to trip us up, but down in my heart I nearly always knew that anything he was missing would turn out in the end to be something we didn't need. In this case I wasn't so sure, and what made me not so sure was that damn cripple. There was something in the way the others spoke about him, in the way he looked and acted that Monday night, in the way those warnings sounded, that gave me an uneasy idea that for once Wolfe might be underrating a guy. That wasn't like him, for he usually had a pretty high opinion of the people whose fate he was interfering with. I was thinking that maybe the mistake he had made in this case was in reading Chapin's books. He had definite opinions about literary merit, and possibly having rated the books pretty low, he had done the same for the man who wrote them. If he was rating Chapin low, I was all ready to fall in on the other side. For instance, here beside me was the typewriter on which the warnings had been written, all three of them, no doubt about it, and it was a typewriter to which Paul Chapin had had easy and constant access, but there was no way in the world of proving that he had done it. Not only that, it was a typewriter to which most of the other persons connected with the business had had access too. No, I thought, as far as writing those warnings went, nearly anything you might say about Chapin would be underrating him.

When I got to the house it wasn't eleven o'clock

yet. I carried the typewriter to the hall and put it down on the stand while I removed my hat and coat. There was another hat and coat there; I looked at them; they weren't Farrell's; I didn't recognize them. I went to the kitchen to ask Fritz who the visitor was, but he wasn't there, upstairs probably, so I went back and got the typewriter and took it to the office. But I didn't get more than six feet inside the door before I stopped. Sitting there turning over the pages of a book, with his stick leaning against the arm of his chair, was Paul Chapin.

Something I don't often do, I went tongue-tied. I suppose it was because I had under my arm the typewriter he had written his poems on, though certainly he couldn't recognize it under the cover. But he could tell it was a typewriter. I stood and stared at him. He glanced up and informed me politely:

"I'm waiting for Mr. Wolfe."

He turned another page in the book, and I saw it was *Devil Take the Hindmost*, the one Wolfe had marked things in. I said:

"Does he know you're here?"

"Oh yes. His man told him some time ago. I've been here," he glanced at his wrist, "half an hour."

There hadn't been any sign of his noticing what I was carrying. I went over and put it down on my desk and shoved it to the back edge. I went to Wolfe's desk and glanced through the envelopes of the morning mail, the corner of my eye telling me that Chapin was enjoying his book. I brushed off Wolfe's blotter and twisted his fountain pen around. Then I got sore, because I realized that I wasn't inclined to go and sit at my desk, and the reason was that it would put me with my back to Paul Chapin. So I went there and got into my chair and got some plant records from the drawer and began looking at them. It was a damn funny experience; I don't know what it was about that cripple that got under my skin so. Maybe he was magnetic. I actually had to clamp my jaw to keep from turning around to look at him, and while I was trying to laugh it off ideas kept flashing through my mind such as whether he had a gun and if so was it the one with the hammer nose filed down. I had a good deal stronger feeling of Paul Chapin, behind me, than I've had of lots of people under my eyes and sometimes under my hands too.

I flipped the pages of the record book, and I didn't turn around until Wolfe came in.

I had many times seen Wolfe enter the office when a visitor was there waiting for him, and I watched him to see if he would vary his common habit for the sake of any effect on the cripple. He didn't. He stopped inside the door and said, "Good morning, Archie." Then he turned to Chapin and his trunk and head went forward an inch and a half from the perpendicular, in a sort of mammoth elegance. "Good morning, sir." He proceeded to his desk, fixed the orchids in the vase, sat down, and looked through the mail. He rang for Fritz, took out his pen and tried it on the scratch pad, and when Fritz came nodded for beer. He looked at me:

"You saw Mr. Wright? Your errand was success-ful?"

"Yes, sir. In the bag."

"Good. If you would please move a chair up for Mr. Chapin.—If you would be so good, sir? For either amenities or hostilities, the distance is too great. Come closer." He opened a bottle of beer.

Chapin got up, grasped his stick, and hobbled over to the desk. He paid no attention to the chair I placed for him, nor to me, but stood there leaning on his stick, his flat cheeks pale, his lips showing a faint movement like a race horse not quite steady at the barrier, his light-colored eyes betraying neither life nor death—neither the quickness of the one nor the glassy stare of the other. I got at my desk and shuffled my pad in among a pile of papers, ready to take my notes while pretending to do something else, but Wolfe shook his head at me. "Thank you, Archie, it will not be necessary.

The cripple said, "There need be neither amenities nor hostilities. I've come for my box."

"Ah! Of course. I might have known." Wolfe had turned on his gracious tone. "If you wouldn't mind, Mr. Chapin, may I ask how you knew I had it?"

"You may ask." Chapin smiled. "Any man's vanity will stand a pat on the back, won't it, Mr. Wolfe? I inquired for my package where I had left it, and was told it was not there, and learned of the ruse by which it had been stolen. I reflected, and it was obvious that the likeliest thief was you. You must believe me, this is not flattery, I really did come to you first."

"Thank you. I do thank you." Wolfe, having emptied a glass, leaned back and got comfortable. "I am considering—this shouldn't bore you, since words are the tools of your trade—I am considering the comical and tragical scantiness of all vocabularies. Take, for example, the procedure by which you acquired the contents of that box, and I got the box and all; both our actions were, by definition, stealing, and both of us are thieves; words implying condemnation and contempt, and yet neither of us would concede that he has earned them. So much for words—but of course you know that, since you are a professional."

"You said contents. You haven't opened the box."

"My dear sir! Could Pandora herself have resisted such a temptation?"

"You broke the lock."

"No. It is intact. It is simple, and surrendered easily."

"And . . . you opened it. You probably . . . " He stopped and stood silent. His voice had gone thin on him, but I couldn't see that his face displayed any feeling at all, not even resentment. He continued, "In that case . . . I don't want it. I don't want to see it.—But that's preposterous. Of course I want it. I must have it."

Wolfe, looking at him with half-closed eyes, motionless, said nothing. That lasted for seconds. All of a sudden Chapin demanded, suddenly hoarse:

"Damn you, where is it?"

Wolfe wiggled a finger at him. "Mr. Chapin. Sit down."

"No."

"Very well. You can't have the box. I intend to keep it."

Still there was no change on the cripple's face. I didn't like him, but I was admiring him. His light-colored eyes had kept straight into Wolfe's, but now they moved; he glanced aside at the chair I had placed for him, firmed his hand on the crook of his stick, and limped three steps and sat down. He looked at Wolfe again and said:

"For twenty years I lived on pity. I don't know if you are a sensitive man, I don't know if you can guess what a diet like that would do. I despised it, but I lived on it, because a hungry man takes what he can get. Then I found something else to sustain me. I got a measure of pride in achievement, I ate bread that I earned, I threw away the stick that I needed to walk

with, one that had been given me, and bought one of
my own. Mr. Wolfe, I was done with pity. I had
swallowed it to the extreme of toleration. I was sure
that, whatever gestures I might be brought, foolishly
or desperately, to accept from my fellow creatures, it
would never again be pity."

He stopped. Wolfe murmured. "Not sure. Not sure
unless you carried death ready at hand."

"Right. I learn that today. I seem to have acquired
a new and active antipathy to death."

"And as regards pity . . . "

I need it. I ask for it. I discovered an hour ago that
you had got my box, and I have been considering ways
and means. I can see no other way to get it than to
plead with you. Force"—he smiled the smile that his
eyes ignored—"is not feasible. The force of law is of
course, under the circumstances, out of the question.
Cunning—I have no cunning, except with words.
There is no way but to call upon your pity. I do so, I
plead with you. The box is mine by purchase. The
contents are mine by . . . by sacrifice. By purchase I
can say, though not with money. I ask you to give it
back to me."

"Well. What plea have you to offer?"

"The plea of my need, my very real need, and your
indifference."

"You are wrong there, Mr. Chapin. I need it too."

"No. It is you who are wrong. It is valueless to
you."

"But, my dear sir." Wolfe wiggled a finger. "If I
permit you to be the judge of your own needs you
must grant me the same privilege. What other plea?"

"None. I tell you, I will take it in pity."

"Not from me. Mr. Chapin. Let us not keep from
our tongues what is in our minds. There is one plea

you could make that would be effective.—Wait, hear me. I know that you are not prepared to make it, not yet, and I am not prepared to ask for it. Your box is being kept in a safe place, intact. I need it here in order to be sure that you will come to see me whenever I am ready for you. I am not yet ready. When the time comes, it will not be merely my possession of your box that will persuade you to give me what I want and intend to get. I am preparing for you. You said you have acquired a new and active antipathy to death. Then you should prepare for me: for the best I shall be able to offer you, the day you come for your box, will be your choice between two deaths. I shall leave that, for the moment, as cryptic as it sounds; you may understand me, but you certainly will not try to anticipate me.—Archie. In order that Mr. Chapin may not suspect us of gullery, bring the box please."

I went and unlocked the cabinet and got the box from the shelf, and took it and put it down on Wolfe's desk. I hadn't looked at it since Wednesday and had forgotten how swell it was; it certainly was a pip. I put it down with care. The cripple's eyes were on me, I thought, rather than on the box, and I had a notion of how pleased he probably was to see me handling it. For nothing but pure damn meanness I rubbed my hand back and forth along the top of it. Wolfe told me to sit down.

Chapin's hands were grasping the arms of his chair, as if to lift himself up. He said, "May I open it?"

"No."

He got to his feet, disregarding his stick, leaning on a hand on the desk. "I'll just . . . lift it."

"No. I'm sorry, Mr. Chapin. You won't touch it."

The cripple leaned there, bending forward, looking Wolfe in the eyes. His chin was stuck out. All of a sudden he began to laugh. It was a hell of a laugh, I thought it was going to choke him. He went on with it. Then it petered out and he turned around and got hold of his stick. He seemed to me about half hysterical, and I was ready to jump him if he tried any child's play like bouncing the stick on Wolfe's bean, but I had him wrong again. He got into his regular posture, leaning to the right side with his head a little to the left to even up, and from his light-colored eyes steady on Wolfe again you would never have guessed he had any sentiments at all.

Wolfe said, "The next time you come here, Mr. Chapin, you may take the box with you."

Chapin shook his head. His tone was new, sharper: "I think not. You're making a mistake. You're forgetting that I've had twenty years' practice at renunciation."

Wolfe shook his head. "Oh no. On the contrary, that's what I'm counting on. The only question will be, which of two sacrifices you will select. If I know you, and I think I do, I know where your choice will lie."

"I'll make it now. " I stared at the cripple's incredible smile; I thought to myself that in order to break him Wolfe would have to wipe that smile off, and it didn't look practical by any means I'd ever heard of. With the smile still working, fixed, Chapin put his left hand on the desk to steady himself, and with his right hand he lifted his stick up, pointing it in front of him like a rapier, and gently let its tip come to rest on the surface of the desk. He slid the tip along until it was against the side of the box, and then pushed, not in a hurry, just a steady push. The box moved, approached the edge, kept going, and tumbled to the floor. It bounced a little and rolled towards my feet.

Chapin retrieved his stick and got his weight on it

again. He didn't look at the box; he directed his smile at Wolfe. "I told you, sir, I had learned to live on pity. I am learning now to live without it."

He tossed his head up, twice, like a horse on the rein, got himself turned around, and hobbled to the door and on out. I sat and watched him; I didn't go to the hall to help him. We heard him out there, shuffling to keep his balance as he got into his coat. Then the outer door opening and closing.

Wolfe sighed. "Pick it up, Archie. Put it away. It is astonishing, the effect a little literary and financial success will produce on a spiritual ailment."

He rang for beer.

# Chapter 15

I didn't go out again that morning. Wolfe got loquacious. Leaning back with his fingers interlaced in front of his belly, with his eyes mostly shut, he favored me with one of his quiet endless orations, his subject this time being what he called bravado of the psyche. He said there were two distinct species of bravado: one having as its purpose to impress outside spectators, the other being calculated solely for an internal audience. The latter was bravado of the psyche. It was a show put on by this or that factor of the ego to make a hit with all the other factors. And so on. I did manage, before one o'clock, to make a copy of the first warning on the Harvard Club junk, and put it under the glass. It was it. Chapin had typed his poems of friendship on that machine.

After lunch I got in the roadster to hunt for Hibbard. The usual reports had come from the boys, including Saul Panzer: nothing. Fred Durkin had cackled over the phone, at a quarter to one, that he and his colleagues had made a swell procession following Paul Chapin to Nero Wolfe's house, and had retired around the corner, to Tenth Avenue, to await news of Wolfe's demise. Then they had trailed Chapin back home again.

I had about as much hope of finding Hibbard as of getting a mash note from Greta Garbo, but I went on poking around. Of course I was phoning his niece, Evelyn, twice a day, not in the expectation of getting any dope, since she would let us know if she got any kind of news, but because she was my client and you've got to keep reminding your clients you're on the job. She was beginning to sound pretty sick on the telephone, and I hardly had the heart to try to buck her up, but I made a few passes at it.

Among other weak stabs I made that Friday afternoon was a visit to the office of Ferdinand Bowen the stockbroker. Hibbard had an account with Galbraith & Bowen that had been fairly active fooling with bonds, not much margin stuff, and while I more or less took Bowen in my stride, calling on all the members of the league, there was a little more chance of a hint there than with the others. Entering the office on the twentieth floor of one of the Wall Street buildings, I told myself I'd better advise Wolfe to give a boost to Bowen's contribution to the pot, no matter what the bank report said. Surely they had the rent paid, and that alone must have been beyond the dreams of avarice. It was one of those layouts, a whole floor, that give you the feeling that a girl would have to be at least a duchess to get a job there as a stenographer.

I was taken into Bowen's own room. It was as big as a dance hall, and the rugs made you want to walk around them. Bowen sat behind a beautiful dark-brown desk with nothing on it but the *Wall Street Journal* and an ash tray. One of his little hands held a long fat cigarette with smoke curling up from it that smelled like a Turkish harlot—at least it smelled like what I would expect if I ever got close to one. I didn't like that guy. If I'd had my choice of pinning a murder on him or Paul Chapin, I'd have been compelled to toss a coin.

He thought he was being decent when he grunted to me to sit down. I can stand a real tough baby, but a bird that fancies himself for a hot mixture of John D. Rockefeller and Lord Chesterfield, being all the time innocent of both ingredients, gives me a severe pain in the sitter. I told him what I was telling all of them, that I would like to know about the last time he had seen Andrew Hibbard, and all details. He had to think. Finally he decided the last time had been more than a week before Hibbard disappeared, around the twentieth of October, at the theater. It had been a party, Hibbard with his niece and Bowen with his wife. Nothing of any significance had been said, Bowen declared, nothing with any bearing on the present situation. As he remembered it, there had been no mention of Paul Chapin, probably because Bowen had been one of the three who had hired the Bascom detectives, and Hibbard disapproved of it and didn't want to spoil the evening with an argument.

I asked him, "Hibbard had a trading account with your firm?"

He nodded. "For a long while, over ten years. It wasn't very active, mostly back and forth in bonds."

"Yeah. I gathered that from the statements among his papers. You see, one thing that might help would be any evidence that when Hibbard left his apartment that Tuesday evening he had an idea that he might not be back again. I can't find any. I'm still looking. For instance, during the few days preceding his disappearance, did he make any unusual arrangements or give any unusual orders regarding his account here?"

Bowen shook the round thing that he used to grow his hair on. "No. I would have been told . . . but I'll

make sure." From a row on the wall behind him he
pulled out a telephone, and talked into it. He waited a
while, and talked some more. He pushed the phone
back, and turned to me. "No, as I thought. There has
been no transaction on Andy's account for over two
weeks, and there were no instructions from him."

I bade him farewell.

That was a good sample of the steady progress I
made that day in the search for Andrew Hibbard. It
was a triumph. I found out as much from the other six
guys I saw as I did from Ferdinand Bowen, so I was
all elated when I breezed in home around dinner time,
not to mention the fact that with the roadster parked
on Ninetieth Street some dirty lout scraped the rear
fender while I was in seeing Dr. Burton. I didn't feel
like anything at all, not even like listening to the
charming gusto of Wolfe's dinner conversation—
during a meal he refused to remember that there was
such a thing as a murder case in the world—so I was
glad that he picked that evening to leave the radio
turned on.

After dinner we went to the office. Out of spite and
bitterness I started to tell him about all the runs I had
scored that afternoon, but he asked me to bring him
the atlas and began to look at maps. There were all
sorts of toys he was apt to begin playing with when he
should have had his mind on business, but the worst of
all was the atlas. When he got that out I gave up. I
fooled around a while with the plant records and the
expense account, then I closed my affairs for the night
and went over to his desk to look him over. He was
doing China! The atlas was a Gouchard, the finest to
be had, and did China more than justice. He had the
folded map opened out, and with his pencil in one hand
and his magnifying glass in the other, there he was

buried in the Orient. Without bothering to say good night to him, for I knew he wouldn't answer, I picked up his copy of *Devil Take the Hindmost* and went upstairs to my room, stopping in the kitchen for a pitcher of milk.

After I had got into pajamas and slippers I deposited myself in my most comfortable chair, under the reading lamp, with the milk handy on the little tile-top table, and took a crack at Paul Chapin's book. I thought it was about time I caught up with Wolfe. I flipped through it, and saw there were quite a few places he had marked—sometimes only a phrase, sometimes a whole sentence, occasionally a long passage of two or three paragraphs. I decided to concentrate on those, and I skipped around and took them at random:

*. . . not by the intensity of his desire, but merely by his inborn impulse to act; to do, disregarding all pale considerations . . .*

*For Alan there was no choice in the matter, for he knew that the fury that spends itself in words is but the mumbling of an idiot, beyond the circumference of reality.*

I read a dozen more, yawned, and drank some milk. I went on:

*She said, "That's why I admire you. . . . I don't like a man too squeamish to butcher his own meat."*

*. . . and scornful of all the whining eloquence deploring the awful brutalities of war; for the true objection to war is not the blood it soaks into the grass and the thirsty soil, not the bones it crushes, not the flesh it mangles, not the warm nutritious viscera it exposes to the hunger of the innocent birds and beasts. These things have their beauty, to compensate for the fleeting agonies of this man and that man. The trouble*

*with war is that its noble and quivering excitements
transcend the capacities of our weakling nervous
systems; we are not men enough for it; it properly
requires for its sublime sacrifices the blood and bones
and flesh of heroes, and what have we to offer? This
little coward, that fat sniveler, all these regiments of
puny cravens . . .*

There was a lot of that. I got through it, and went
on to the next. Then some more. It got monotonous,
and I skipped around. There were some places that
looked interesting, some conversations, and a long
scene with three girls in an apple orchard, but Wolfe
hadn't done any marking there. Around the middle of
the book he had marked nearly a whole chapter which
told about a guy croaking two other guys by manicuring them with an axe, with an extended explanation of
how psychology entered into it. I thought that was a
pretty good job of writing. Later I came across things
like this, for instance:

*. . . for what counted was not the worship of
violence, but the practice of it. Not the turbulent and
complex emotion, but the act. What had killed Art
Billings and Curly Stephens? Hate? No. Anger? No.
Jealousy, vengefulness, fear, enmity? No, none of
these things. They had been killed by an axe, gripped
by his fingers and wielded by the muscles of his
arm . . .*

At eleven o'clock I gave up. The milk was all gone,
and it didn't seem likely that I would catch up with
where Wolfe thought he was if I sat up all night. I
thought I detected a hint here and there that the
author of that book was reasonably bloodthirsty, but I
had some faint suspicions on that score already. I
dropped the book on the table, stretched for a good
yawn, went and opened the window and stood there

looking down on the street long enough to let the sharp cold air make me feel like blankets and hopped for the hay.

Saturday morning I started out again. It was all stale bread to me, and I suppose I did a rotten job of it; if one of those guys had had some little fact tucked away that might have helped there wasn't much chance of my prying it loose, the way I was going about it. I kept moving anyhow. I called on Elkus, Lang, Mike Ayers, Adler, Cabot and Pratt. I phoned Wolfe at eleven o'clock and he had nothing to say. I decided to tackle Pitney Scott the taxi-driver. Maybe my wild guess that day had been right; there was a chance that he did know something about Andrew Hibbard. But I couldn't find him. I called up the office of his cab company, and was told that he wasn't expected to report in until four o'clock. They told me that his usual cruising radius was from Fourteenth to Fifty-ninth streets, but that he might be anywhere. I went down and looked around Perry Street, but he wasn't there. At a quarter to one I phoned Wolfe again, expecting to be invited home to lunch, and instead he handed me a hot one. He asked me to grab a bite somewhere and run out to Mineola for him. Ditson had phoned to say that he had a dozen bulbs of a new Miltonia just arrived from England, and had offered to give Wolfe a couple if he would send for them.

The only times I ever really felt like turning Communist were the occasions when, in the middle of a case, Wolfe sent me chasing around after orchids. It made me feel too damn silly. But it wasn't as bad this time as usual, since the particular job I was on looked like a washout anyhow. It was cold and raw that Saturday afternoon, and kept trying to make out that it was going to snow, but I opened both windows of the roadster and enjoyed the air a lot and the Long Island traffic not at all.

I got back to Thirty-fifth Street around three-thirty, and took the bulbs in the office to show them to Wolfe. He felt them and looked them over carefully, and asked me to take them upstairs to Horstmann and tell him not to snip the roots. I went up, and came back down to the office, intending to stop only a minute to enter the bulbs in the record book and then beat it again to get Pitney Scott. But Wolfe, from his chair, said:

"Archie."

I knew from the tone it was the start of a speech, so I settled back. He went on:

"Now and then I receive the impression that you suspect me of neglecting this or that detail of our business. Ordinarily you are wrong, which is as it should be. In the labyrinth of any problem that confronts us, we must select the most promising paths; if we attempt to follow all at once we shall arrive nowhere. In any art—and I am an artist or nothing—one of the deepest secrets of excellence is a discerning elimination. Of course that is a truism."

"Yes, sir."

"Yes. Take the art of writing. I am, let us say, describing the actions of my hero rushing to greet his beloved, who has just entered the forest. *He sprang up from the log on which he had been sitting, with his left foot forward; as he did so, one leg of his trousers fell properly into place but the other remained hitched up at the knee. He began running towards her, first his right foot, then his left, then his right again, then left, right, left, right, left, right . . .* As you see, some of that can surely be left out—indeed, must be, if he is to accomplish his welcoming embrace in the same chapter. So the artist must leave out vastly more

than he puts in, and one of his chief cares is to leave
out nothing vital to his work."

"Yes, sir."

"You follow me. I assure you that the necessity I
have just described is my constant concern when we
are engaged in an enterprise. When you suspect me of
neglect you are in a sense justified, for I do ignore
great quantities of facts and impingements which
might seem to another intelligence—let it go without
characterization—to be of importance to our undertaking. But I should consider myself an inferior work-
man if I ignored a fact which the event proved actually
to have significance. That is why I wish to make this
apology to myself, thus publicly, in your hearing."

I nodded. "I'm still hanging on. Apology for what?"

"For bad workmanship. It may prove not to have
been disastrous, it may even turn out of no importance
whatever. But sitting here this afternoon contemplating
my glories and sifting out the sins, it occurred to me, and
I need to ask you about it. You may remember that on
Wednesday evening, sixty-five hours ago, you were
describing for me the contents of Inspector Cramer's
bean."

I grinned. "Yeah."

"You told me that it was his belief that Dr. Elkus
was having Mr. Chapin shadowed."

"Yep."

"And then you started a sentence; I think you said,
*But one of those dicks*—Something approximating
that. I was impatient, and I stopped you. I should not
have done so. My impulsive reaction to what I knew to
be nonsense betrayed me into an error. I should have
let you finish. Pray do so now."

I nodded. "Yeah, I remember. But since you've
dumped the Dreyer thing into the ash can, what does
it matter whether Elkus—"

"Archie. Confound it, I care nothing about Elkus; what I want is your sentence about a dick. What dick? Where is he?"

"Didn't I say? Tailing Paul Chapin."

"One of Mr. Cramer's men."

I shook my head. "Cramer has a man there too. And we've got Durkin and Gore and Keems, eight-hour shifts. This bird's an extra. Cramer wondered who was paying him and had him in for a conference, but he's tough, he never says anything but cuss words. I thought maybe he was Bascom's, but no."

"Have you seen him?"

"Yeah, I went down there. He was eating soup, and he's like you about meals, business is out. I waited on him a little, carried his bread and butter and so on, and came on home."

"Describe him."

"Well . . . he hasn't much to offer to the eye. He weighs a hundred and thirty-five, five feet seven. Brown cap and pink necktie. A cat scratched him on the cheek and he didn't clean it up very well. Brown eyes, pointed nose, wide thin mouth but not tight, pale healthy skin."

"Hair?"

"He kept his cap on."

Wolfe sighed. I noticed that the tip of his finger was doing a little circle on the arm of his chair. He said, "Sixty-five hours. Get him and bring him here at once."

I got up. "Yeah. Alive or dead?"

"By persuasion if possible, certainly with a minimum of violence, but bring him."

"It's five minutes to four. You'll be in the plant-rooms."

"Well? This house is comfortable. Keep him."

I got some things from a drawer of my desk and stuffed them in my pockets, and beat it.

# Chapter 16

I was not ever, in the Chapin case or any other case, quite as dumb as the prosecution would try to make you believe if I was on trial for it. For instance, as I went out and got into the roadster, in spite of all the preconceptions that had set up house-keeping in my belfry, I wasn't doing any guessing as to the nature of the fancy notion Wolfe had plucked out of his contemplation of his sins. My guessing had been completed before I left the office. On account of various considerations it was my opinion that he was cuckoo—I had told him that Cramer had had the dick in for a talk—but it was going to be diverting whether it turned out that he was or he wasn't.

I drove to Perry Street and parked fifty feet down from the Coffee Pot. I had already decided on my tactics. Considering what I had learned of Pinkie's reaction to .the diplomatic approach, it didn't seem practical to waste my time on persuasion. I walked to the Coffee Pot and glanced in. Pinkie wasn't there; of course it was nearly two hours till his soup time. I strolled back down the street, looking in at all the chances, and I went the whole long block to the next corner without a sign either of Pinkie, Fred Durkin, or anything that looked like a city detective. I went back again, clear to the Coffee Pot, with the same result. Not so good, I thought, for of course all the desertion meant that the beasts of prey were out trailing their quarry, and the quarry might stay out for a dinner and a show and get home at midnight. That would be enjoyable, with me substituting for Fred on the delicatessen sandwiches and Wolfe waiting at home to see what his notion looked like.

I drove around the block to get the roadster into a better position for surveying the scene, and sat in it and waited. It was getting dark, and it got dark, and I waited.

A little before six a taxi came along and stopped in front of 203. I tried to get a glimpse of the driver, having Pitney Scott on my mind, and made out that it wasn't him. But it was the cripple that got out. He paid, and hobbled inside the building, and the taxi moved off. I looked around, taking in the street and the sidewalk.

Pretty soon I saw Fred Durkin walking up from the corner. He was with another guy. I climbed out to the sidewalk and stood there near a street light as they went by. Then I got back in. In a couple of minutes Fred came along and I moved over to make room for him.

I said, "If you and the town dick want to cop a little expense money by pairing up on a taxi, okay. As long as nothing happens, then it might be your funeral."

Durkin grinned. "Aw, forget it. This whole layout's a joke. If I didn't need the money—"

"Yeah. You take the money and let me do the laughing. Where's Pinkie?"

"Huh? Don't tell me you're after the runt again!"

"Where is he?"

"He's around. He was behind us on the ride just now—there he goes, look, the Coffee Pot. He must have gone down Eleventh. He takes chances. It's time for his chow."

I had seen him going in. I said, "All right. Now listen. I'm going to funny up your joke for you. You and the town dick are pals."

"Well, we speak."

"Find him. Do they sell beer at that joint on the corner?—Okay. Take him there and quench his thirst. On expense. Keep him there until my car's gone from in front of the Coffee Pot. I'm going to take Pinkie for a ride."

"No! I'll be damned. Keep his necktie for me."

"All right. Let's go. Beat it."

He climbed out and went. I sat and waited. Pretty soon I saw him come out of the laundry with the snoop, and start off in the other direction. I stepped on the starter and pushed the gear lever, and rolled along. This time I stopped right in front of the Coffee Pot. I got out and went in. I saw no cop around.

Pinkie was there, at the same table as before, with what looked like the same bowl of soup. I glanced at the other customers, on the stools, and observed nothing terrifying. I walked over to Pinkie and stopped at his elbow. He looked up and said:

"Well, goddam it."

Looking at him again, I thought there was a chance Wolfe was right. I said, "Come on, Inspector Cramer wants to see you," and took bracelets out of one pocket and my automatic out of another.

There must have been something in my eyes that made him suspicious, and I'll say the little devil had nerve. He said, "I don't believe it. Show me your goddam badge."

I couldn't afford an argument. I grabbed his collar and lifted him up out of his chair and set him on his feet. Then I snapped the handcuffs on him. I kept the gat completely visible and told him, "Get going." I heard one or two mutters from the lunch counter, but didn't bother to look. Pinkie said, "My overcoat." I grabbed it off the hook and hung it on my arm, and marched him out. He went nice. Instead of trying to hide the bracelets, like most of them do, he held his hands stuck out in front.

The only danger was that a flatfoot might happen along outside and offer to help me, and the roadster wasn't a police car. But all I saw was curious citizens. I herded him to the car, opened the door and shoved him in, and climbed in after him. I had left the engine running, just in case of a hurry. I rolled off, got to Seventh Avenue, and turned north.

I said, "Now listen. I've got two pieces of information. First, to ease your mind, I'm taking you to Thirty-fifth Street to call on Mr. Nero Wolfe. Second, if you open your trap to advertise anything, you'll go there just the same, only faster and more unconscious."

"I have no desire to call—"

"Shut up." But I was grinning inside, for his voice was different; he was already jumping his character.

The evening traffic was out playing tag, and it took long enough to get to West Thirty-fifth Street. I pulled up in front of the house, told my passenger to sit still, got out and walked around and opened his door, and told him to come on. I went behind him up the steps, used my key on the portal, and nodded him in. While I was taking off my hat and coat he started reaching up for his cap, but I told him to leave it on and steered him for the office.

Wolfe was sitting there with an empty beer glass, looking at the design the dried foam had left. I shut the office door and stood there, but the runt kept going, clear to the desk. Wolfe looked at him, nodded faintly, and then looked some more. He spoke suddenly, to me:

"Archie. Take Mr. Hibbard's cap, remove the handcuffs, and place a chair for him."

I did those things. This gentleman, it appeared, represented the second fact Wolfe had demanded, and I was glad to wait on him. He held his hands out for me to take the bracelets off, but it seemed to be an effort for him, and a glance at his eyes showed me that he wasn't feeling any too prime. I eased the chair up back of his knees, and all of a sudden he slumped into it, buried his face in his hands, and stayed that way. Wolfe and I regarded him, with not as much commiseration as he might have thought he had a right to expect if he had been looking at us. To me he was the finest hunk of bacon I had lamped for several moons.

Wolfe tipped me a nod, and I went to the cabinet and poured a stiff one and brought it over. I said:

"Here, try this."

Finally he looked up. "What is it?"

"It's a goddam drink of rye whiskey."

He shook his head and reached for the drink simultaneously. I knew he had some soup in him so didn't look for any catastrophe. He downed half of it, spluttered a little, and swallowed the rest. I said to Wolfe:

"I brought him in with his cap on so you could see him that way. Anyhow, all I ever saw was a photograph. And he was supposed to be dead. And I'm here to tell you, it would have been a pleasure to plug him, and no kinds of comments will be needed now or any other time."

Wolfe, disregarding me, spoke to the runt: "Mr. Hibbard. You know of the ancient New England custom of throwing a suspected witch into the river, and if she drowned she was innocent. My personal opinion of a large drink of straight whiskey is that it provides a converse test: if you survive it you can risk anything. Mr. Goodwin did not in fact plug you?"

Hibbard looked at me and blinked, and at Wolfe and blinked again. He cleared his throat twice, and said conversationally:

"The truth of the matter is, I am not an adventurous man. I have been under a terrible strain for eleven days. And shall be—for many more."

"I hope not."

Hibbard shook his head. "And shall. God help me. And shall."

"You call on God now?"

"Rhetorically. I am further than ever from Him, as a reliance." He looked at me. "Could I have a little more whiskey?"

I got it for him. This time he started sipping it, and smacked his lips. He said, "This is a relief. The whiskey is too, of course, but I was referring particularly to this opportunity to become articulate again. No; I am further than ever from a Deity in the stratosphere, but much closer to my fellow man. I have a confession to make, Mr. Wolfe, and it might as well be to you as anyone. I have learned more in these eleven days masquerading as a roughneck than in all the previous forty-three years of my existence."

"Harun-al-Rashid—"

"No. Excuse me. He was seeking entertainment, I was seeking life. First, I thought, merely my own life, but I found much more. For instance, if you were to say to me now what you said three weeks ago, that you would undertake to remove my fear of Paul Chapin by destroying him, I would say: certainly, by all means, how much do I owe you? For I understand now that the reason for my former attitude was nothing but a greater fear than the fear of death, the fear of accepting responsibility for my own preservation.—You don't mind if I talk? God, how I want to talk!"

Wolfe murmured, "This room is hardened to it." He rang for beer.

"Thank you. In these eleven days I have learned that psychology, as a formal science, is pure hocus-pocus. All written and printed words, aside from their function of relieving boredom, are meaningless drivel. I have fed a half-starved child with my own hands. I have seen two men batter each other with their fists until the blood ran. I have watched boys picking up girls. I have heard a woman tell a man, in public and with a personal application, facts which I had dimly supposed were known, academically, only to those who have read Havelock Ellis. I had observed hungry workingmen eating in a Coffee Pot. I have seen a tough boy of the street pick up a wilted daffodil from the gutter. It is utterly amazing, I tell you, how people do things they happen to feel like doing. And I have been an instructor in psychology for seventeen years! *Merde!* Could I have a little more whiskey?"

I didn't know whether Wolfe needed him sober, but I saw no warning gesture from him, so I went and filled the glass again. This time I brought some White Rock for a chaser and he started on that first.

Wolfe said, "Mr. Hibbard. I am fascinated at the prospect of your education and I shall insist on hearing it entire, but I wonder if I could interpose a question or two. First I shall need to contradict you by observing that before your eleven days' education began you had learned enough to assume a disguise simple and effective enough to preserve your incognito, though the entire police force—and one or two other people— were looking for you. Really an achievement."

The fizz had ascended into the psychologist's nose, and he pinched it. "Oh no. That sort of thing is rule of thumb. The first rule, of course, is, nothing that looks like disguise. My best items were the necktie and the scratch on my cheek. My profanity, I fear, was not well done; I should not have undertaken it. But my great mistake was the teeth; it was the very devil to get the gold leaf cemented on, and I was forced to confine my diet almost exclusively to milk and soup. Of course, having once made my appearance, I could not abandon them. The clothing, I am proud of."

"Yes, the clothing." Wolfe looked him over. "Excellent. Where did you get it?"

"A second-hand store on Grand Street. I changed in a subway toilet, and so was properly dressed when I went to rent a room on the lower West Side."

"And you left your second pipe at home. You have estimable qualities, Mr. Hibbard."

"I was desperate."

"A desperate fool is still a fool. What, in your desperation, did you hope to accomplish? Did your venture pretend to any intelligent purpose?"

Hibbard had to consider. He swallowed some whiskey, washed it off with fizz, and coated that with another sip of whiskey. He finally said, "So help me, I don't know. I mean I don't know now. When I left home, when I started this, all that I felt moving me was fear. The whole long story of what that unlucky episode, twenty-five years ago—of what it did to me, would sound fantastic if I tried to tell it. I was too highly sensitized in spots; I suppose I still am, doubtless it will show again in the proper surroundings. I am inclining now to the environmental school—you hear that? Atavism! Anyhow, fear had me, and all I was aware of was a desire to get near Paul Chapin and keep him under my eye. I had no plans, further than that. I wanted to watch him. I knew if I told anyone, even Evelyn—my niece, there would be danger of his getting onto me, so I made a thorough job of it. But the last few days I have begun to suspect that in some gully of my mind, far below consciousness, was a desire to kill him. Of course there is no such thing as a desire without an intention, no matter how nebulous it may be. I believe I meant to kill him. I believe I have been working up to it, and I still am. I have no idea what this talk with you will do to me. I see no reason why it should have any effect one way or another."

"You will see, I think." Wolfe emptied his glass. "Naturally you do not know that Mr. Chapin has mailed verses to your friends stating explicitly that he killed you by clubbing you over the head."

"Oh yes. I know that."

"The devil you do. Who told you?"

"Pit. Pitney Scott."

I gritted my teeth and wanted to bite myself. Another chance underplayed, and all because I had believed the cripple's warning. Wolfe was saying:

"Then you did keep a bridge open."

"No. He opened it himself. The third day I was around there I met him face to face by bad luck, and of course he recognized me." Hibbard suddenly stopped, and turned a little pale. "By heaven—ha, there goes another illusion—I thought Pit . . ."

"Quite properly, Mr. Hibbard. Keep your illusion; Mr. Scott has told us nothing; it was Mr. Goodwin's acuteness of observation, and my feeling for phenomena, that uncovered you.—But to resume: if you knew that Mr. Chapin had sent those verses, falsely boasting of murdering you, it is hard to see how you could keep your respect for him as an assassin. If you knew one of his murders, the latest one, to be nothing but rodomontade . . ."

Hibbard nodded. "You make a logical point, certainly. But logic has nothing to do with it. I am not engaged in developing a scientific thesis. There are twenty-five years behind this . . . and Bill Harrison, Gene Dreyer . . . and Paul that day in the courtroom . . . I was there, to testify to the psychological value of his book . . . It was on the day that Pit Scott showed me those verses about me sucking air in through my blood that I discovered that I wanted to kill Paul, and if I wanted it I intended it, or what the devil was I doing there?"

Wolfe sighed. "It is a pity. The back-seat driving of the less charitable emotions often makes me wonder that the brain does not desert the wheel entirely, in righteous exasperation. Not to mention their violent and senseless oscillations. Mr. Hibbard. Three weeks ago you were filled with horrified aversion at the thought of engaging me to arrange that Mr. Chapin should account legally for his crimes; today you are determined to kill him yourself. You do intend to kill him?"

"I think so." The psychological runt put his whiskey glass on the desk. "That doesn't mean that I will. I don't know. I intend to."

"You are armed? You have a weapon?"

"No. I . . . no."

"You what?"

"Nothing. I should have said, he. He is physically a weakling."

"Indeed." The shadows on Wolfe's face altered; his cheeks were unfolding. "You will rip him apart with your bare hands. Into quivering bloody fragments . . ."

"I might," Hibbard snapped. "I don't know whether you taunt me through ignorance or through design. You should know that despair is still despair, even when there is an intellect to perceive it and control its hysteria. I can kill Paul Chapin and still know what I am doing. My physical build is negligible, next to contemptible, and my mental equipment has reached the decadence which sneers at the blood that feeds it, but in spite of those incongruities I can kill Paul Chapin.—I think I understand now why it was such a relief to be able to talk again in my proper person, and I thank you for it. I think I needed to put this determination into words. It does me good to hear it.—Now I would like you to let me go. I can go on, of course, only by your sufferance. You have interfered with me, and frankly I'm grateful for it, but there is no reason—"

"Mr. Hibbard." Wolfe wiggled a finger at him. "Permit me. The least offensive way of refusing a request is not to let it be made. Don't make it.—Wait, please. There are several things you either do not know or fail to consider. For instance, do you know of an arrangement I have entered into with your friends?"

"Yes. Pit Scott told me. I'm not interested—"

"But I am. In fact I know of nothing else, at the moment, that interests me in the slightest degree; certainly not your recently acquired ferocity. Further, do you know that there, on Mr. Goodwin's desk, is the typewriter on which Mr. Chapin wrote his sanguinary verses? Yes, it was at the Harvard Club; we negotiated a trade. Do you know that I am ready for a complete penetration of Mr. Chapin's defenses, in spite of his pathetic bravado? Do you know that within twenty-four hours I shall be prepared to submit to you and your friends a confession from Mr. Chapin of his guilt, and to remove satisfactorily all your apprehensions?"

Hibbard was staring at him. He emptied his whiskey glass, which he had been holding half full, and put in on the desk, and stared at Wolfe again. "I don't believe it."

"Of course you do. You merely don't want to. I'm sorry, Mr. Hibbard, you'll have to readjust yourself to a world of words and compromises and niceties of conduct. I would be glad—well?"

He stopped to look at Fritz, who had appeared on the threshold. Wolfe glanced at the clock; it was seven-twenty-five. He said, "I'm sorry, Fritz. Three of us will dine, at eight o'clock. Will that be possible?"

"Yes, sir."

"Good.—As I was saying, Mr. Hibbard, I would like to help make the readjustment as pleasant as possible for you, and at the same time serve my own convenience. The things I have just told you are the truth, but to help me in realizing the last one I shall need your co-operation. I mentioned twenty-four hours. I would like to have you remain here as my guest for that period. Will you?"

Hibbard shook his head, with emphasis. "I don't believe you. You may have the typewriter, but you don't have Paul Chapin as I do. I don't believe you'll get him to confess, ever in God's world."

"I assure you, I will. But that can be left to the

event. Will you stay here until tomorrow evening, and communicate with no one? My dear sir. I will bargain with you. You were about to make a request of me. I counter with one of my own. Though I am sure twenty-four hours will do, let us allow for contingencies; make it forty-eight. If you will agree to stay under this roof incommunicado until Monday evening, I engage that at that time, if I have not done as I said and closed the Chapin account forever, you will be free to resume your whimsical adventure without fear of any betrayal from us. Do I need to add a recommendation of our discretion and intelligence?"

As Wolfe finished speaking Hibbard unaccountably burst into laughter. For a runt he had a good laugh, deeper than his voice, which was baritone but a little thin. When he had laughed it out he said, "I was thinking that you probably have an adequate bathtub."

"We have."

"But tell me this. I am still learning. If I refused, if I got up now to walk out, what would you do?"

"Well . . . you see, Mr. Hibbard, it is important to my plans that your discovery should remain unknown until the proper moment. Certain shocks must be administered to Mr. Chapin, and they must be well timed. There are various ways of keeping a desired guest. The most amiable is to persuade him to accept an invitation; another would be to lock him up."

Hibbard nodded. "You see? What did I tell you? You see how people go ahead and do things they feel like doing? Miraculous!"

"It is indeed.—And now the bathtub, if we are to dine at eight. Archie, if you would show Mr. Hibbard the south room, the one above mine . . ."

I got up. "It'll be clammy as the devil, it hasn't been used . . . he can have mine . . ."

"No. Fritz has aired it and the heat is on; it has been properly prepared, even to Brassocattlaelias Truffautianas in the bowl."

"Oh." I grinned. "You had it prepared."

"Certainly.—Mr. Hibbard. Come down when you are ready. I warn you, I am prepared to demonstrate that the eighth and ninth chapters of *The Chasm of the Mind* are mystic nonsense. If you wish to repel my attack, bring your wits to the table."

I started out with Hibbard, but Wolfe's voice came again and we returned. "You understand the arrangement, sir; you are to communicate with no one whatever. Away from your masquerade, the desire to reassure your niece will be next to irresistible."

"I'll resist it."

Since it was two flights up, I took him to Wolfe's elevator. The door of the south room stood open, and the room was nice and warm. I looked around: the bed had been made, comb and brush and nail file were on the dresser, orchids were in the bowl on the table; fresh towels were in the bathroom. Not bad for a strictly male household. I went out, but at the door was stopped by Hibbard:

"Say. Do you happen to have a dark brown necktie?"

I grinned and went to my room and picked out a genteel solid-color, and took it up to him.

Down in the office Wolfe sat with his eyes shut. I went to my desk. I was sore as hell. I was still hearing the tone of Wolfe's voice when he said, "Sixty-five hours," and though I knew the reproach had been for himself and not for me, I didn't need a whack on the shins to inform me that I had made a bad fumble. I sat and considered the general and particular shortcomings of my conduct. Finally I said aloud, as if to myself, not looking at him:

"The one thing I won't ever do again is believe a cripple. It was all because I believed that damn warning. If it hadn't been imbedded in my nut that Andrew Hibbard was dead, I would have been receptive to a decent suspicion no matter where it showed up. I suppose that goes for Inspector Cramer too, and I suppose that means that I'm of the same general order as he is. In that case—"

"Archie." I glanced at Wolfe enough to see that he had opened his eyes. He went on, "If that is meant as a defense offered to me, none is needed. If you are merely rubbing your vanity to relieve a soreness, please defer it. There is still eighteen minutes before dinner, and we might as well make use of them. I am suffering from my habitual impatience when nothing remains but the finishing touches. Take your notebook."

I got it out, and a pencil.

"Make three copies of this, the original on the good bond. Date it tomorrow, November eleventh—ha, Armistice Day! Most appropriate. It will have a heading in caps as follows: CONFESSION OF PAUL CHAPIN REGARDING THE DEATHS OF WILLIAM R. HARRISON AND EUGENE DREYER AND THE WRITING AND DISPATCHING OF CERTAIN INFORMATIVE AND THREATENING VERSES. It is a concession to him to call them verses, but we should be magnanimous somewhere, let us select that for it. There will then be divisions, properly spaced and subheaded. The subheadings will also be in caps. The first one is DEATH OF WILLIAM R. HARRISON. Then begin . . . thus—"

I interrupted. "Listen, wouldn't it be fitting to type this on the machine from the Harvard Club? Of course it's crummy, but it would be a poetic gesture . . ."

"Poetic? Oh. Sometimes, Archie, the association of your ideas reminds me of a hummingbird. Very well, you may do that. Let us proceed." When he was giving me a document Wolfe usually began slow and speeded up as he went along. He began, "I, Paul Chapin, of 203 Perry Street, New York City, hereby confess that—"

The telephone rang.

I put my notebook down and reached for it. My practice was to answer calls by saying crisp but friendly, "Hello, this is the office of Nero Wolfe." But this time I didn't get to finish it. I got about three words out, but the rest of it was stopped by an excited voice in my ear, excited but low, nearly a whisper, fast but trying to make it plain:

"Archie, listen. Quick, get it, I may be pulled off. Get up here as fast as you can—Doc Burton's, Ninetieth Street. Burton's croaked. The lop got him with a gat, pumped him full. They got him clean, I followed him—"

There were noises, but no more words. That was enough to last a while, anyway. I hung up and turned to Wolfe. I suppose my face wasn't very placid, but the expression on his didn't change any as he looked at me. I said, "That was Fred Durkin. Paul Chapin has just shot Dr. Burton and killed him. At his apartment on Ninetieth Street. They caught him red-handed. Fred invites me up to see the show."

Wolfe sighed. He murmured, "Nonsense."

"Nonsense hell. Fred's not a genius, but I never saw him mistake a pinochle game for a murder. He's got good eyes. It looks like tailing Chapin wasn't such a bad idea after all, since it got Fred there on the spot. We've got him—"

"Archie. Shut up." Wolfe's lips were pushing out and in as fast as I had ever seen them. After ten seconds he said, "Consider this, please. Durkin's conversation was interrupted?"

"Yeah, he was pulled off."

"By the police, of course. The police take Chapin for murdering Burton; he is convicted and executed, and where are we? What of our engagements? We are lost."

I stared at him. "Good God. Damn that cripple—"

"Don't damn him. Save him. Save him for us. The roadster is in front? Good. Go there at once, fast. You know what to do, get it, the whole thing. I need the scene, the minutes and seconds, the participants—I need the facts. I need enough of them to save Paul Chapin. Go and get them."

I jumped.

# Chapter 17

I kept on the west side as far as Eighty-sixth Street and then shot crosstown and through the park. I stepped on it only up to the limit, because I didn't want to get stopped. I felt pretty good and pretty rotten, both. She had cracked wide open and I was on my way, and that was all sweetness and light, but on the other hand Fred's story of the event decorated by Wolfe's comments looked like nothing but bad weather. I swung left into Fifth Avenue, with only five blocks to go.

I pulled up short of the Burton number on Ninetieth Street, locked the ignition and jumped to the sidewalk. There were canopies and entrances to big apartment houses all around. I walked east. I was nearly to the entrance I was headed for when I saw Fred Durkin. From somewhere he came trotting toward me. I stopped, and he jerked his head back and started west, and I went along behind him. I followed him to the corner of Fifth, and around it a few feet.

I said, "Am I poison? Spill it."

He said, "I didn't want that doorman to see you with me. He saw me getting the bum's rush. They caught me phoning you and kicked me out."

"That's too bad. I'll complain at headquarters. Well?"

"Well, they've got him, that's all. We followed him up here, the town dick and me, got here at seven-thirty. It was nice and private, without Pinkie. Of course we knew who lived here, and we talked it over whether we ought to phone and decided not to. We decided to go inside the lobby, and when the hall flunky got unfriendly Murphy—that's the town dick—flashed his badge and shut him up. People were going and coming, there's two elevators. All of a sudden one of the elevator doors bangs open and a woman comes running out popeyed and yells where's Dr. Foster, catch Dr. Foster, and the hall flunky says he just saw him go out, and the woman runs for the street yelling Dr. Foster, and Murphy nabs her by the arm and asks why not try Dr. Burton, and she looks at him funny and says Dr. Burton's been shot. He turns her loose and jumps for the elevator, and on the way up to the fifth floor discovers that I'm in it with him. He says—"

"Come on, for Christ's sake."

"Okay. The door of Burton's apartment is open. The party's in the first room we go into. Two women is there, one of them whining like a sick dog and jiggling a telephone, and the other one kneeling by a guy laying on the floor. The lop is sitting in a chair looking like he's waiting his turn in a barber shop. We got busy. The guy was dead. Murphy got on the phone and I looked around. A gat, a Colt automatic, was on the floor by the leg of a chair next to a table in the middle of the room. I went over and gave Chapin a rub to see if he had any more tools. The woman that was kneeling by the meat began to heave and I went and got her up and led her away. Two men came in, a doctor and a house guy. Murphy got through on the phone and came over and slipped some irons on Chapin. I stayed with the woman, and when a couple of precinct cops came loping in I took the woman out of the room. The woman that had gone for Dr. Foster came back, she came running through the place and took the other woman away from me and took her off somewhere. I went into another room and saw books and a desk and a telephone, and called you up. One of the precinct men came snooping around and heard me, and that's when I left. He brought me downstairs and gave me the air."

"Who else has come?"

"Only a couple of radios and some more precinct guys."

"Cramer or the D.A. office?"

"Not yet. Hell, they don't need to bother. A package like that, they could just have it sent parcel post."

"Yeah. You go to Thirty-fifth Street and tell Fritz to feed you. As soon as Wolfe has finished his dinner, tell him about it. He may want you to get Saul and Orrie—he'll tell you."

"I'll have to phone my wife—"

"Well, you got a nickel? Beat it."

He went downtown, towards Eighty-ninth, and I went around the corner and east again. I approached the entrance; I didn't see any reason why I couldn't crash it, though I didn't know anyone up there. Just as I was under the canopy a big car came along and stopped quick, and two men got out. I took a look, then I got in the way of one of them. I grinned at him:

"Inspector Cramer! This is luck." I started to walk along in with him.

He stopped. "Oh! You. Nothing doing. Beat it."

I started to hand him a line, but he got sharp.

"Beat it, Goodwin. If there's anything up there that belongs to you I'll save it for you. Nothing doing."

I fell back. People were gathering, there was already quite a crowd, and a cop was there herding them. In the confusion I was pretty sure he hadn't heard the little passage between Cramer and me. I faded away, and went to where I had parked the roadster. I opened up the back and got out a black bag I kept a few things in for emergencies; it didn't look just right, but good enough. I went back to the entrance and pushed through the line while the cop was busy on the other side, and got through the door. Inside was the doorman and another cop. I stepped up to them and said, "Medical Examiner. What apartment is it?" The cop looked me over and took me to the elevator and said to the boy, "Take this gent to the fifth floor." Inside, going up, I gave the black bag a pat.

I breezed into the apartment. As Durkin had said, the party was right there, the first room you entered, a big reception hall. There was a mob there, mostly flatfeet and dicks standing around looking bored. Inspector Cramer was by the table listening to one of the latter. I walked over to him and said his name.

He looked around, and seemed surprised. "Well, in the name of—"

"Now listen, inspector. Just a second. Forget it. I'm not going to steal the prisoner or the evidence or anything else. You know damn well I've got a right to curiosity and that's all I expect to satisfy. Have a heart. My God, we've all got mothers."

"What have you got in that bag?"

"Shirts and socks. I used it to bring me up. I'd just as soon have one of your men take it down to my car for me."

He grunted. "Leave it here on the table, and if you get in the way—"

"I won't. Much obliged."

Being careful not to bump anyone, I got back against the wall. I took a look. It was a room 17 × 20, on a guess, nearly square. One end was mostly windows, curtained. At the other end was the entrance door. One long wall, the one I was standing against, had pictures and a couple of stands with vases of flowers. In the other wall, nearly to the corner, was a double door, closed, leading of course to the apartment proper. The rest of that wall, about ten feet of it, had curtains to match those at the end, but there couldn't have been windows. I figured it was closets for wraps. The light was from the ceiling, indirect, with switches at the double door and the entrance door. There was one large rug, and a good-sized table in the middle. Near where I stood was a stand with a telephone and a chair.

There were only four chairs altogether. In one of them, at the end of the table, Paul Chapin was sitting. I couldn't see his face, he was turned wrong. At the other end of the table Doc Burton was on the floor. He just looked dead and fairly comfortable; either he had landed straight when he fell or someone had stretched him out, and his arms were neatly along his sides. His head was at a funny angle, but they always are until they're propped up. Looking at him, I thought to myself that Wolfe had had him down for seven thousand bucks, and now he'd never have that to worry about again along with a lot of other things. From where I was I couldn't see much blood.

A few details had happened since I arrived. There had been phone calls. One of the dicks had gone out and come back in a couple of minutes with an Assistant Medical Examiner; apparently there had been difficulty downstairs. I hoped he wouldn't take my bag by mistake when he went. They buzzed around. Inspector Cramer had left the room by the double door, to see the women I supposed. A young woman came in from outside and made a scene, but all in all she did pretty well with it, since it appeared that it was her father that had been croaked. She had been out somewhere, and she took it hard. I've often observed that the only thing that makes it a real hardship to have dealings with stiffs is the people that are still living. This girl was the kind that makes your throat clog up because you see how she's straining to fight it back in and you know she's licked. I was glad when a dick took her away, in to her mother.

I moseyed around to get a slant at the cripple. I went around the table and got in front of him. He looked at me, but there wasn't any sign of his being aware he had ever seen me before. His stick was on the table beside him, and his hat. He had on a brown overcoat, unbuttoned, and tan gloves. He was slouched over; his hands were resting on his good knee, fastened with the bracelets. There was nothing in his face, just nothing; he looked more like a passenger in the subway than anything else. His light-colored eyes looked straight at me. I thought to myself that this was the first piece of real hundred per cent bad luck I had ever known Nero Wolfe to have. He had had his share of bad breaks all right, but this wasn't a break, it was an avalanche.

Then I remembered what I was there for, and I said to myself that I had gone around for two days pretending to hunt Andrew Hibbard knowing all the time it was hopeless, and Hibbard was at that moment eating scallops and arguing psychology with Wolfe. And until Wolfe himself said finish for that case one way or the other, hopeless was out. It was up to me to dig up a little hope.

I got against the wall again and surveyed the field. The medical guy was done. There was no telling how long Cramer would be with the women, but unless their tale was more complicated than it seemed likely to be there was no reason why it should be very long. When he returned there would probably be no delay in removing the stiff and the cripple, and then there would be nothing to keep anybody else. Cramer wouldn't be apt to go off and leave me behind, he'd want me for company. Nor could I see any reason why he would leave anyone behind, except a dick out in the hall maybe and possibly one downstairs, to keep annoyance away from the family.

That was the way it looked. I couldn't go back to Wolfe with nothing but a sob story about a poor cripple and a dead man and a grief-stricken daughter. I wandered around again to the other side of the table, to the other wall where the curtains were. I stood with my back to the curtains. Then I saw my bag on the table. That wouldn't do, so I went over and got it, casually, and went back against the curtains again. I figured the chances were about fifty to one against me, but the worst I could get was an escort to the elevator. Keeping my eyes carelessly on the array of dicks and flatfeet scattered around, I felt behind me with my foot and found that back of the curtains the floor continued flush, with no sill. If it was a closet it was built into the wall and I had no idea how deep it was or what was in there. I kept my eyes busy; I had to pick an instant when every guy there had his face turned; at least not right on me. I was waiting for something, and luck came that time; it happened. The phone rang, on the stand by the other wall. Having nothing to occupy them, they all turned involuntarily. I had my hand behind me ready to pull the curtain aside, and back I went, and let the curtain fall again, with me behind.

I had ducked going in, in case there happened to be a hat shelf at the usual height, but the shelf was further back; the closet was all of three feet deep and I had plenty of room. I held my breath for a few seconds, but heard none of the bloodhounds baying. I eased the black bag onto the floor in a corner and got behind what felt like a woman's fur coat. One thing there had been no help for: the cripple had seen me. His light-colored eyes had been right at me as I backed in. If he should decide to open his trap I hoped he would find something else to talk about.

I stood there in the dark, and after a while wished I had remembered to bring an oxygen tank. To amuse me I had the voices of the dicks outside, but they were low and I couldn't pick out many words. Somebody came in, some woman, and a little later a man. It was all of half an hour before Cramer returned. I heard the double door opening, close to my curtain, and then Cramer handing out orders. He sounded snappy and satisfied. A dick with a hoarse voice told another one, right in front of me, to carry Chapin's stick and he'd help him walk; they were taking him away. There were noises, and directions from Cramer, about removing the corpse, and in a couple of minutes heavy feet as they carried it out. I was hoping to God that Cramer or someone else hadn't happened to hang his coat in my closet, but that wasn't likely; there had been three or four piled on the table. I heard a voice telling someone to go ask for a rug to put over the soiled place where Burton had been, and Cramer and others shoving off. It sounded like there were only two left, after the guy came back with the rug; they were kidding each other about some kind of a girl. I began to be afraid Cramer had spotted them to stay for some reason or other, but pretty soon I heard them going to the door, and it opened and closed.

I'd been in the closet long enough as far as my lungs were concerned, but I thought it was just possible one was still inside the main apartment, and I waited five minutes, counting. Then I pulled the edge of the curtain a little and took a slant. I opened it up and stepped out. Empty. All gone. The double doors were closed. I went over and turned the knob and pushed, and walked through. I was in a room about five times the size of the reception hall, dimly lit, furnished up to the hilt. There was a door at the far end and a wide open arch halfway down one side. I heard voices from somewhere. I went on in a ways and called:

"Hello! Mrs. Burton!"

The voices stopped, and there were footsteps coming. A guy appeared in the arch, trying to look important. I grinned inside. He was just a kid, around twenty-two, nice and handsome and dressed up. He said, "We thought you had all gone."

"Yeah. All but me. I have to see Mrs. Burton."

"But he said . . . the Inspector said she wouldn't be bothered."

"I'm sorry, I have to see her."

"She's lying down."

"Tell her just a few questions."

He opened his moth and shut it, looked as if he thought he ought to do something, and turned and beat it. In a minute he came back and nodded me along. I followed.

We went through a room and a sort of a hall and

into another room. This was not so big, but was better lit and not so dolled up. A maid in uniform was going out another door with a tray. A woman was sitting on a couch, another woman in a chair, and the daughter I had seen in the reception hall was standing behind the couch. I walked over there.

I suppose Mrs. Loring A. Burton wasn't at her best that evening, but she could have slipped a few more notches and still have been in the money. A glance was enough to show you she was quite a person. She had a straight thin nose, a warm mouth, fine dark eyes. Her hair was piled in braids at the back, pulled back just right for you to see her temples and brow, which maybe made most of the effect; that and the way she held her head. Her neck knew some artist's trick that I've seen many a movie star try to copy without quite getting it. It had been born in her spine.

With her head up like that I could see it would take more than a murdered husband to overwhelm her into leaving decisions to daughters and so on, so I disregarded the others. I told her I had a few confidential questions to ask and I'd like to see her alone. The woman in the chair muttered something about cruel and unnecessary. The daughter stared at me with red eyes. Mrs. Burton asked:

"Confidential to whom?"

"To Paul Chapin. I'd rather not . . ." I looked around.

She looked around too. I saw that the kid wasn't the son and heir after all, it was the daughter he was interested in, probably had it signed up. Mrs. Burton said, "What does it matter? Go to my room—you don't mind, Alice?"

The woman in the chair said she didn't, and got up.

The kid took hold of the daughter's arm to steer her, by golly he wasn't going to let her fall and hurt herself. They went on out.

Mrs. Burton said, "Well?"

I said, "The confidential part is really about me. Do you know who Nero Wolfe is?"

"Nero Wolfe? Yes."

"Dr. Burton and his friends entered into an agreement—"

She interrupted me. "I know all about it. My husband . . ." She stopped. The way she suddenly clasped her fingers tight and tried to keep her lips from moving showed that a bust-up was nearer to coming through than I had supposed. But she soon got it shoved under again. "My husband told me all about it."

I nodded. "That saves time. I'm not a city detective. I'm private. I work for Nero Wolfe, my name's Goodwin. If you ask me what I'm here for there's lots of ways to answer you, but you'd have to help me pick the right one. It depends on how you feel." I had the innocence turned on, the candid eye. I was talking fast. "Of course you feel terrible, certainly, but no matter how bad it is inside of you right now, you'll go on living. I've got some questions to ask for Nero Wolfe, and I can't be polite and wait for a week until your nerves have had a chance to grow some new skin, I've got to ask them now or never. I'm here now, just tell me this and get rid of me. Did you see Paul Chapin shoot your husband?"

"No. But I've already—"

"Sure. Let's get it done. Did anybody see him?"

"No."

I took a breath. At least, then, we weren't floating with our bellies up. I said, "All right. Then it's a question of how you feel. How you feel about this, for instance, that Paul Chapin didn't shoot your husband at all."

She stared at me. "What do you mean—I saw him—"

"You didn't see him shoot. Here's what I'm getting at, Mrs. Burton. I know your husband didn't hate Paul Chapin. I know he felt sorry for him and was willing to go with the crowd because he saw no help for it. How about you, did you hate him? Disregard what happened tonight, how much did you hate him?"

For a second I thought I had carried her along; then I saw a change coming in her eyes and her lips beginning to tighten up. She was going to ritz me out. I rushed in ahead of it:

"Listen, Mrs. Burton, I'm not just a smart pup nosing around somebody's back yard seeing what I can smell. I really know all about this, maybe even some things you don't know. Right now, in a cabinet down in Nero Wolfe's office, there is a leather box. I put it there. This big. It's beautiful tan leather, with fine gold tooling on it, and it's locked, and it's full nearly to the top with your gloves and stockings. Some you've worn.—Now wait a minute, give me a chance. It belongs to Paul Chapin. Dora Ritter hooked them and gave them to him. It's his treasure. Nero Wolfe says his soul is in that box. I wouldn't know about that, I'm no expert on souls. I'm just telling you. The reason I want to know whether you hate Paul Chapin, regardless of his killing your husband, is this: what if he didn't kill him? Would you like to see them hang it on him anyway?"

She was looking at me, with the idea of ritzing me out put aside for the moment. She said, "I don't know what you're driving at. I saw him dead. I don't know what you mean."

"Neither do I. That's what I'm here to find out. I'm trying to make you understand that I'm not annoying you just for curiosity, I'm here on business, and it may turn out to be your business as well as mine. I'm interested in seeing that Paul Chapin gets no more than is coming to him. Right now I don't suppose you're interested in anything. You've had a shock that would lay most women flat. Well, you're not flat, and you might as well talk to me as sit and try not to think about it. I'd like to sit here and ask you a few things. If you look like you are going to faint I'll call the family and get up and go."

She unclasped her hands. She said, "I don't faint. You may sit down."

"Okay." I used the chair Alice had left. "Now tell me how it happened. The shooting. Who was here?"

"My husband and I, and the cook and the maid. One of the maids was out."

"No one else? What about the woman you called Alice?"

"That is my oldest friend. She came to . . . just a little while ago. There was no one else here."

"And?"

"I was in my room dressing. We were dining out, my daughter was out somewhere. My husband came to my room for a cigarette; he always . . . he never remembered to have any, and the door between our rooms is always open. The maid came and said Paul Chapin was there. My husband left to go to the foyer to see him, but he didn't go direct; he went back through his room and his study. I mention that because I stood and listened. The last time Paul had come my husband had told the maid to keep him in the foyer, and before he went there he had gone to his study and got a revolver out of the drawer. I had thought it was childish. This time I listened to see if he did it again, and he did, I heard the drawer opening. Then he called to me, called my name, and I answered what is it, and he called back, nothing, never mind, he would tell me after he had speeded his guest. That was the last . . . those were his last words I heard. I heard him walking through the apartment—I listened, I suppose, because I was wondering what Paul could want. Then I heard noises—not loud, the foyer is so far away from my room, and then shots. I ran. The maid came out of the dining-room and followed me. We ran to the foyer. It was dark, and the light in the drawing-room was dim and we couldn't see anything. I heard a noise, someone falling, and Paul's voice saying my name. I turned on the light switch, and Paul was there on his knee trying to get up. He said my name again, and said he was trying to hop to the switch. Then I saw Lorrie, on the floor at the end of the table. I ran to him, and when I saw him I called to the maid to go for Dr. Foster, who lives a floor below us. I don't know what Paul did then, I didn't pay attention to him, the first I knew some men came—"

"All right, hold it."

She stopped. I looked at her a minute, getting it. She had clasped her hands again and was doing some extra breathing, but not obtrusively. I quit worrying about her. I took out a pad and pencil, and said, "This thing, the way you tell it, needs a lot of fixing. The worst item, of course, is the light being out. That's plain silly.—Now wait a minute, I'm just talking about what Nero Wolfe calls a feeling for phenomena, I'm trying to enjoy one. Let's go back to the beginning. On his way to see Paul Chapin, your husband called to you from the study, and then said never mind. Have you any idea what he was going to say?"

"No, how could I—"

"Okay. The way you told it, he called to you after he opened the drawer. Was that the way it was?"

She nodded. "I'm sure it was after I heard the drawer open. I was listening."

"Yeah. Then you heard him walking to the foyer, and then you heard noises. What kind of noises?"

"I don't know. Just noises, movements. It is far away, and doors were closed. The noises were faint."

"Voices?"

"No. I didn't hear any."

"Did you hear your husband closing the foyer door after he got there?"

"No. I wouldn't hear that unless it banged."

"Then we'll try this. Since you were listening to his footsteps, even if you couldn't hear them any more after he got into the drawing-room, there was a moment when you figured that he had reached the foyer. You know what I mean, the feeling that he was there. When I say *Now*, that will mean that he has just reached the foyer, and you begin feeling the time, the passing of time. Feel it as near the same as you can, and when it's time for the first shot to go off, you say *Now.*—Get it? *Now.*"

I looked at the second hand of my watch; it went crawling up from the 30. She said, *"Now."*

I stared at her. "My God, that was only six seconds."

She nodded. "It was as short as that, I'm sure it was."

"In that case . . . all right. Then you ran to the foyer, and there was no light there. Of course you couldn't be wrong about that."

"No. The light was off."

"And you switched it on and saw Chapin kneeling, getting up. Did he have a gun in his hand?"

"No. He had his coat and gloves on. I didn't see a gun . . . anywhere."

"Did Inspector Cramer tell you about the gun?"

She nodded. "It was my husband's. He shot . . . it had been fired four times. They found it on the floor."

"Cramer showed it to you."

"Yes."

"And it's gone from the drawer in the study."

"Of course."

"When you turned on the light Chapin was saying something."

"He was saying my name. After the light was on he said—I can tell you exactly what he said. *Anne, a cripple in the dark, my dear Anne, I was trying to hop to the switch.* He had fallen."

"Yeah. Naturally." I finished scratching on the pad, and looked up at her. She was sitting tight. I said, "Now to go back again. Were you at home all afternoon?"

"No. I was at a gallery looking at prints, and then at a tea. I got home around six."

"Was your husband here when you got here?"

"Yes, he comes early . . . on Saturday. He was in his study with Ferdinand Bowen. I went in to say hello. We always . . . said hello, no matter who was here."

"So Mr. Bowen was here. Do you know what for?"

"No. That is . . . no."

"Now come, Mrs. Burton. You've decided to put up with this and it's pretty swell of you, so come ahead. What was Bowen here for?"

"He was asking a favor. That's all I know."

"A financial favor?"

"I suppose so, yes."

"Did he get it?"

"No. But this has no connection . . . no more of this."

"Okay. When did Bowen leave?"

"Soon after I arrived, I should say a quarter past six. Perhaps twenty after; it was about ten minutes before Dora came, and she was punctual at six-thirty."

"You don't say so." I looked at her. "You mean Dora Chapin."

"Yes."

"She came to do your hair."

"Yes."

"I'll be damned.—Excuse me. Nero Wolfe doesn't permit me to swear in front of ladies. And Dora Chapin got here at six-thirty. Well. When did she leave?"

"It always takes her three-quarters of an hour, so she left at a quarter past seven." She paused to calculate. "Yes, that would be right. A few minutes later, perhaps. I figured that I had fifteen minutes to finish dressing."

"So Dora Chapin left here at seven-twenty and Paul Chapin arrived at half past. That's interesting; they almost collided. Who else was here after six o'clock?"

"No one. That's all. My daughter left around half past six, a little before Dora came. Of course I don't understand—what is it, Alice?"

A door had opened behind me, and I turned to see. It was the woman, the old friend. She said:

"Nick Cabot is on the phone—they notified him. He wants to know if you want to talk to him."

Mrs. Burton's dark eyes flashed aside for an instant, at me. I let my head go sideways enough for her to see it. She spoke to her friend, "No, there is nothing to say. I won't talk to anyone. Are you folks finding something to eat?"

"We'll make out. Really, Anne, I think—"

"Please, Alice. Please—"

After a pause the door closed again. I had a grin inside, a little cocky. I said, "You started to say, something you don't understand . . ."

She didn't go on. She sat looking at me with a frown in her eyes but her brow smooth and white. She got up and went to a table, took a cigarette from a box and lit it, and picked up an ash tray. She came back to the couch and sat down and took a couple of whiffs. Then she looked at the cigarette as if wondering where it had come from, and crushed it dead on the tray, and set the tray down. She straightened up and seemed to remember I was looking at her. She spoke suddenly:

"What did you say your name is?"

"Archie Goodwin."

"Thank you. I should know your name. Strange things can happen, can't they? Why did you tell me not to talk to Mr. Cabot?"

"No special reason. Right now I don't want you to be talking to anybody but me."

She nodded. "And I'm doing it. Mr. Goodwin, you're not much over half my age and I never saw you before. You seem to be clever. You realized, I suppose, what the shock of seeing my husband dead, shot dead, has done to me. It has shaken things loose. I am doing something very remarkable, for me. I don't usually talk, below the surface. I never have, since childhood, except with two people. My husband, my dear husband, and Paul Chapin. But we aren't talking about my husband, there's nothing to say about him. He's dead. He is dead . . . I shall have to tell myself many times . . . he is dead. He wants to go on living in me, or I want him to. I think—this is what I am really saying—I think I would want Paul to.—Oh, it's impossible!" She jerked herself up, and her hands got clasped again. "It's absurd to try to talk about this— even to a stranger—and with Lorrie dead—absurd . . ."

I said, "Maybe it's absurd not to. Let it crack open once, spill it out."

She shook her head. "There's nothing to crack open. There's no reason why I should want to talk about it, but I do. Otherwise why should I let you question me? I saw farther inside myself this evening than I have ever seen before. It wasn't when I saw my husband dead, it wasn't when I stood alone in my room, looking at a picture of him, trying to realize he was dead. It was sitting here with that police inspector, with him telling me that a plea of guilty is not accepted in first degree murder, and that I would have to talk with a representative of the District Attorney, and would have to testify in court so that Paul Chapin can be convicted and punished. I don't want him punished. My husband is dead, isn't that enough? And if I don't want him punished, what is it I want to hold onto? Is it pity? I have never pitied him. I have been pretty insolent with life, but not insolent enough to pity Paul Chapin. You told me that he has a box filled with my gloves and stockings which Dora stole for him, and that Nero Wolfe said it holds his soul. Perhaps my soul has been put away in a box too, and I didn't even know it . . ."

She got up, abruptly. The ash tray slid off the

couch to the floor. She stooped over, and with deliberate fingers that showed no sign of trembling picked up the burnt match stick and the cigarette and put them on the tray. I didn't move to help her. She went to the table with the tray and then came back to the couch and sat down again. She said:

"I have always disliked Paul Chapin. Once, when I was eighteen years old, I promised to marry him. When I learned of his accident, that he was crippled for life, I was delighted because I wouldn't have to keep my promise. I didn't know that then but I realized it later. At no time have I pitied him. I claim no originality in that, I think no woman has ever pitied him, only men. Women do not like him—even those who have been briefly fascinated by him. I dislike him intensely. I have thought about this; I have had occasion to analyze it; it is his deformity that is intolerable. Not his physical deformity. The deformity of his nervous system, of his brain. You have heard of feminine cunning, but you don't understand it as Paul does, for he has it himself. It is a hateful quality in a man. Women have been fascinated by it, but the two or three who surrendered to it—I not among them, not even at eighteen—got only contempt for a reward.

"He married Dora Ritter. She's a woman?"

"Oh yes, Dora's a woman. But she is consecrated to a denial of her womanhood. I am fond of her, I understand her. She knows what beauty is, and she sees herself. That forced her, long ago, to the denial, and her strength of will has maintained it. Paul understood her too. He married her to show his contempt for me; he told me so. He could risk it with Dora because she might be relied upon never to embarrass him with the only demand that he would find humiliating. And as for Dora—she hates him, but she would die for him. Fiercely and secretly, against her denial, she longed for the dignity of marriage, and it was a miracle of luck that Paul offered it under the only circumstances that could make it acceptable to her. Oh, they understand each other!"

I said, "She hates him, and she married him."

"Yes. Dora could do that."

"I'm surprised she was here today. I understood she had a bad accident Wednesday morning. I saw her. She seems to have some character."

"It could be called that. Dora is insane. Legally, I suppose not, but nevertheless she is insane. Paul has told her so many times. She tells me about it, in the same tone she uses for the weather. There are two things she can't bear the thought of: that any woman should suspect her of being capable of tenderness, or that any man should regard her as a woman at all. Her character comes from her indifference to everything else, except Paul Chapin."

"She bragged to Nero Wolfe that she was married."

"Of course. It removes her from the field.—Oh, it is impossible to laugh at her, and you can't pity her any more than you can Paul. A monkey might as well pity me because I haven't got a tail."

I said, "You were talking about your soul."

"Was I? Yes. To you, Mr. Goodwin. I could not speak about it to my friend, Alice—I tried but nothing came. Wasn't I saying that I don't want Paul Chapin punished? Perhaps that's wrong, perhaps I do want him punished, but not crudely by killing him. What have I in my mind? What is in my heart? God knows. But I started to answer your questions when you said something—something about his punishment—"

I nodded. "I said he shouldn't get more than is

coming to him. Of course to you it looks open and shut, and apparently it looks the same way to the cops. You heard shots and ran to the foyer and there it was, a live man and a dead man and a gun. And of course Inspector Cramer has already got the other fixings, for instance the motive all dressed up and its shoes shined, not to mention a willingness to even up with Chapin for certain inconveniences he has been put to. But as Nero Wolfe says, a nurse that pushes the perambulator in the park without putting the baby in it has missed the point. Maybe if I look around I'll find the baby. For example, Dora Chapin left here at seven-twenty. Chapin arrived at seven-thirty, ten minutes later. What if she waited in the hall outside and came back in with him? Or if she couldn't do that because the maid let him in, he could have opened the door for her while the maid was gone to tell Dr. Burton. She could have snatched the gun from Burton's pocket and done the shooting and beat it before you could get there. That might explain the light being out; she might have flipped the switch before she opened the outer door so if anyone happened to be passing in the outside hall they couldn't see in. You say she hates Chapin. Maybe to him it was entirely unexpected, he had no idea what she was up to—"

She was shaking her head. "I don't believe that. It's possible, but I don't believe it."

"You say she's crazy."

"No. As far as Dora could like any man, she liked Lorrie. She wouldn't do that."

"Not to make a reservation for Chapin in the electric chair?"

Mrs. Burton looked at me, and a little shudder ran over her. She said, "That's no better . . . than the other. That's horrible."

"Of course it's horrible. Whatever we pull out of this bag, it won't be a pleasant surprise for anyone concerned, except maybe Chapin. I ought to mention another possibility. Dr. Burton shot himself. He turned the light out so Chapin couldn't see what he was doing in time to let out a yell that might have given it away. That's horrible too, but it's quite possible."

That didn't seem to discompose her as much as my first guess. She merely said, calmly, "No, Mr. Goodwin. It might be barely conceivable that Lorrie wanted . . . had some reason to kill himself without my knowing it, but that he would try to put the guilt on Paul . . . on anyone . . . No, that isn't even possible."

"Okay. You said it yourself a while ago, Mrs. Burton; strange things can happen. But as far as that's concerned, anyone at all might have done it—anyone who could get into that foyer and who knew Chapin was there and that Dr. Burton would come.—By the way, what about the maid that's out this evening? Does she have a key? What's she like?"

"Yes, she has a key. She is fifty-six years old, has been with us nine years, and calls herself the housekeeper. You would waste time asking about her."

"I could still be curious about her key."

"She will have it when she comes in the morning. You may see her then if you wish."

"Thanks. Now the other maid. Could I see her now?"

She got up and went to the table and pushed a button, and took another cigarette and lit it. I noticed that with her back turned you could have taken her for twenty, except for the coil of hair. But she was slumping a little; as she stood her shoulders sagged.

She pulled them up again and turned and came back to the couch, as the inner door opened and the whole outfit appeared: cook, maid, friend Alice, daughter and boy friend. The cook was carrying a tray. Mrs. Burton said:

"Thank you, Henny, not now. Don't try it again, please don't, I really couldn't swallow. And the rest of you . . . if you don't mind . . . we wish to see Rose a few minutes. Just Rose."

"But, mother, really—"

"No, dear. Please, just a few minutes. Johnny, this is very nice of you. I appreciate it very much. Come here, Rose."

The kid blushed. "Aw, don't mention it, Mrs. Burton."

They faded back through the door. The maid came and stood in front of us and tried some swallowing which didn't seem to work. Her face looked quite peculiar because it intended to be sympathetic but she was too shocked and scared, and it would have been fairly peculiar at any time with its broad flat nose and plucked eyebrows. Mrs. Burton told her I wanted to ask her some questions, and she looked at me as if she had been informed that I was going to sell her down the river. Then she stared at the pad on my knee and looked even worse. I said:

"Rose. I know exactly what's in your mind. You're thinking that the other man wrote down your answers to his questions and now I'm going to do the same, and then we'll compare them and if they're not alike we'll take you to the top of the Empire State Building and throw you off. Forget that silly stuff. Come on, forget it.—By the way." I turned to Mrs. Burton: "Does Dora Chapin have a key to the apartment?"

"No."

"Okay. Rose, did you go to the door when Dora Chapin came this evening?"

"Yes, sir."

"You let her in and she was alone."

"Yes, sir."

"When she left did you let her out?"

"No, sir. I never do. Mrs. Kurtz don't either. She just went."

"Where were you when she went?"

"I was in the dining-room. I was there a long while. We weren't serving dinner, and I was dusting the glasses in there."

"Then I suppose you didn't let Mr. Bowen out either. That was the man—"

"Yes, sir, I know Mr. Bowen. No, I didn't let him out, but that was a long time before."

"I know. All right, you let nobody out. Let's get back to in. You answered the door when Mr. Chapin came."

"Yes, sir."

"Was he alone?"

"Yes, sir."

"You opened the door and he came in and you shut the door again."

"Yes, sir."

"Now see if you can remember this. It doesn't matter much if you can't, but maybe you can. What did Mr. Chapin say to you?"

She looked at me, and aside at Mrs. Burton, and down at the floor. At first I thought maybe she was trying to fix up a fake for an answer, then I saw that she was just bewildered at the terrible complexity of the problem I had confronted her with by asking her a question that couldn't be answered *yes* or *no*. I said, "Come on, Rose. You know, Mr. Chapin came in, and you took his hat and coat, and he said—"

She looked up. "I didn't take his hat and coat. He kept his coat on, and his gloves. He said to tell Dr. Burton he was there."

"Did he stand there by the door or did he walk to a chair to sit down?"

"I don't know. I think he would sit down. I think he came along behind me but he came slow and I came back in to tell Dr. Burton."

"Was the light turned on in the foyer when you left there?"

"Yes, sir. Of course."

"After you told Dr. Burton, where did you go?"

"I went back to the dining-room."

"Where was the cook?"

"In the kitchen. She was there all the time."

"Where was Mrs. Burton?"

"She was in her room dressing.—Wasn't you, madam?"

I grinned. "Sure she was. I'm just getting all of you placed. Did Dr. Burton go to the foyer right away?"

She nodded. "Well . . . maybe not right away. He went pretty soon. I was in the dining-room and heard him go by the door."

"Okay." I got up from my chair. "Now I'm going to ask you to do something. I suppose I shouldn't tell you it's important, but it is. You go to the dining-room and start taking down the glasses, or whatever you were doing after you told Dr. Burton. I'll walk past the dining-room door and on to the foyer. Was Dr. Burton going fast or slow?"

She shook her head and her lip began to quiver. "He was just going."

"All right, I'll just go. You hear me go by, and you decide when enough time has passed for the first shot to go off. When the time has come for the first shot, you yell *Now* loud enough for me to hear you in the foyer. Do you understand? First you'd better tell—"

I stopped on account of her lip. It was getting into high. I snapped at her, "Come on out of that. Take a look at Mrs. Burton and learn how to behave yourself. You're doing this for her. Come on now."

She clamped her lips together and held them that way while she swallowed twice. Then she opened them to say:

"The shots all came together."

"All right, say they did. You yell *Now* when the time comes. First you'd better go and tell the people inside that you're going to yell or they'll be running out here—"

Mrs. Burton interposed, "I'll tell them. Rose, take Mr. Goodwin to the study and show him how to go."

She was quite a person, that Mrs. Burton. I was getting so I liked her. Maybe her soul was put away in a box somewhere, but other items of her insides, meaning guts, were all where they ought to be. If I was the kind that collected things I wouldn't have minded having one of her gloves myself.

Rose and I went out. Apparently she avoided the bedrooms by taking me around by a side hall, for we entered the study direct from that. She showed me how to go, by another door, and left me there. I looked around; books, leather chairs, radio, smoke stands, and a flat-top desk by a window. There was the drawer, of course, where the gat had been kept. I went over to it and pulled it open and shut it again. Then I went out by the other door and followed directions. I struck a medium pace, past the dining-room door, across the central hall, through a big room and from that through the drawing-room; got my eye on my watch, opened the door into the foyer, went in and closed it—

It was a good thing the folks had been warned, for Rose yelling *Now* so I could hear it sounded even to me, away off in the foyer, like the last scream of doom. I went back in faster than I had come for fear she might try it again. She had beat it back to the room where Mrs. Burton was. When I entered she was standing by the couch with her face white as a sheet, looking seasick. Mrs. Burton was reaching up to pat her arm. I went over and sat down.

I said, "I almost didn't get there. Two seconds at the most. Of course she rushed it, but it shows it must have been quick.—Okay, Rose. I won't ask you to do any more yelling. You're a good brave girl. Just a couple more questions. When you heard the shots you ran to the foyer with Mrs. Burton. Is that right?"

"Yes, sir."

"What did you see when you got there?"

"I didn't see anything. It was dark."

"What did you hear?"

"I heard something on the floor and then I heard Mr. Chapin saying Mrs. Burton's name and then the light went on and I saw him."

"What was he doing?"

"He was trying to get up."

"Did he have a gun in his hand?"

"No, sir. I'm sure he didn't because he had his hands on the floor getting up."

"And then you saw Dr. Burton."

"Yes, sir." She swallowed. "I saw him after Mrs. Burton went to him."

"What did you do then?"

"Well . . . I stood there I guess . . . then Mrs. Burton told me to go for Dr. Foster and I ran out and

ran downstairs and they told me Dr. Foster had just
left and I went to the elevator—"

"Okay, hold it."

I looked back over my notes. Mrs. Burton was
patting Rose's arm again and Rose was looking at her
with her lip ready to sag. My watch said five minutes
till eleven; I had been in that room nearly two hours.
There was one thing I hadn't gone into at all, but it
might not be needed and in any event it could wait. I
had got enough to sleep on. But as I flipped the pages
of my pad there was another point that occurred to me
which I thought ought to be attended to. I put the pad
and pencil in my pocket and looked at Mrs. Burton:

"That's all for Rose. It's all for me too, except if you
would just tell Rose—"

She looked up at the maid and nodded at her.
"You'd better go to bed, Rose. Good night."

"Oh, Mrs. Burton—"

"All right now. You heard Mr. Goodwin say you're
a brave girl. Go and get some sleep."

The maid gave me a look, not any too friendly,
looked again at her mistress, and turned and went. As
soon as the door had closed behind her I got up from
my chair.

I said, "I'm going, but there's one more thing. I've
got to ask a favor of you. You'll have to take my word
for it that Nero Wolfe's interest in this business is the
same as yours. I'll tell you that straight. You don't
want Paul Chapin to burn in the electric chair for
killing your husband, and neither does he. I don't
know what his next move will be, that's up to him, but
it's likely he'll need some kind of standing. For instance, if he wants to ask Inspector Cramer to let him
see the gun he'll have to give a better reason than idle
curiosity. I can't quite see Paul Chapin engaging him,

but how about you? If we could say we were acting on commission from you it would make things simple. Of course there wouldn't be any fee, even if we did something you wanted done. If you want me to I'll put that in writing."

I looked at her. Her head was still up, but the signs of a flop were in her eyes and at the corners of her mouth. I said to her, "I'm going, I won't stay and bark at you about this, just say yes or no. If you don't lie down somewhere and relax, let it go ahead and bust, you'll be doing another kind of relaxing. What about it?"

She shook her head. I thought she was saying no, to me, but then she spoke—though this didn't sound as if it was directed at me any more than the headshake: "I loved my husband, Mr. Goodwin. Oh yes, I loved him. I sometimes disapproved of things he did. He disapproved of things I did, more often—though he seldom said so. He would disapprove of what I am doing now—I think he would. He would say, let fate do her job. He would say that as he so often said it—gallantly—and about Paul Chapin too. He is dead . . . Oh yes, he is dead . . . but let him live enough to say that now, and let me live enough to say what I always said, I will not keep my hand from any job if I think it's mine. He would not want me to make any new concessions to him, dead." She rose to her feet, abruptly, and abruptly added, "And even if he wanted me to I doubt if I could. Good night, Mr. Goodwin." She held out her hand.

I took it. I said, "Maybe I get you, but I like plain words. Nero Wolfe can say he is acting in your behalf, is that it?"

She nodded. I turned and left the room.

In the foyer I took a glance around as I got my hat

and coat from the table and put them on. I took the black bag from the closet. When I opened the door I gave the lock an inspection and saw it was the usual variety in houses of that class, the kind where you can press a button countersunk in the edge of the door to free the cylinder. I tried it and it worked. I heard a noise in the hall and stepped out and shut the door behind me. There sitting in a chair, twisting the hide on his neck to see who had been monkeying with the door but not bothering to get up, was the snoop Cramer had left to protect the family from annoyance as I had suspected he would.

I started pulling on my gloves. I said to him friendly and brisk, "Thank you, my man. I assure you we appreciate this," and went on to the elevator.

# Chapter 18

At two o'clock that night—Sunday morning—I sat at my desk, in the office, and yawned. Wolfe, behind his own desk, was looking at a schedule I had typed out for him, keeping a carbon for myself, during one of the intervals in my report when he had called time out to do a little arranging in his mind. The schedule looked like this:

6:05    Mrs. Burton arrives home. Present in apartment: Burton, daughter, Bowen, maid, cook.
6:20    Bowen leaves.
6:25    Daughter leaves.
6:30    Dora Chapin arrives.
7:20    Dora leaves.
7:30    Paul Chapin arrives.
7:33    Burton is shot.
7:50    Fred Durkin phones.

I looked at my carbon and yawned. Fritz had kept some squirrel stew hot for me, and it had long since been put away, with a couple of rye highballs because the black sauce Fritz used for squirrel made milk taste like stale olive juice. After I had imparted a few of the

prominent details without saying how I had got hold of
them, Wolfe had explained to Hibbard that it is the
same with detectives as with magicians, their primary
and constant concern is to preserve the air of mystery
which is attached to their profession, and Hibbard had
gone up to bed. The development that had arrived
over the telephone while he was taking his bath had
changed his world. He had eaten no dinner to speak of,
though the need to chaperon the gold leaf on his teeth
had departed. He had insisted on phoning fifty or sixty
people, beginning with his niece, and had been restrained only by some tall talk about his word of
honor. In fact, that question seemed not entirely
closed, for Wolfe had had Fritz cut the wire of the
telephone which was in Hibbard's room. Now he was
up there, maybe asleep, maybe doping out a psychological detour around words of honor. I had gone on
and given Wolfe the story, every crumb I had, and
there had been discussions.

I threw the carbon onto the desk and did some
more yawning. Finally Wolfe said:

"You understand, Archie. I think it would be
possible for us to go ahead without assuming the
drudgery of discovering the murderer of Dr. Burton.
I would indeed regard that as obvious, if only men
could be depended upon to base their decisions on
reason. Alas, there are only three or four of us in the
world, and even we will bear watching. And our weak
spot is that we are committed not to refer our success
to a fact, we must refer it to the vote of our group of
clients. We must not only make things happen, we
must make our clients vote that they have happened.
That arrangement was unavoidable. It makes it necessary for us to learn who killed Dr. Burton, so that if

the vote cannot be sufficiently swayed by reason it can
be bullied by melodrama. You see that."

I said, "I'm sleepy. When I have to wait until
nearly midnight for my dinner and then it's squirrel
stew . . ."

Wolfe nodded. "Yes, I know. Under those circumstances I would be no better than a maniac.—Another
thing. The worst aspect of this Burton development,
from our standpoint, is what it does to the person of
Mr. Chapin. He cannot come here to get his box—or
for anything else. It will be necessary to make arrangements through Mr. Morley, and go to see him.
What jail will they keep him in?"

"I suppose, Centre Street. There are three or four
places they could stick him, but the Tombs is the most
likely."

Wolfe sighed. "That abominable clatter. It's more
than two miles, nearer three I suppose. The last time
I left this house was early in September, for the
privilege of dining at the same table with Albert
Einstein, and coming home it rained. You remember
that."

"Yeah. Will I ever forget it. There was such a
downpour the pavements were damp."

"You deride me. Confound it . . . ah well. I will
not make a virtue of necessity, but neither will I
whimper under its lash. Since there is no such thing as
bail for a man charged with murder, and since I must
have a conversation with Mr. Chapin, there is no
escaping an expedition to Centre Street. Not, however, until we know who killed Dr. Burton."

"And not forgetting that before the night's out the
cripple may empty the bag for Cramer by confessing
that he did it."

"Archie." Wolfe wiggled a finger at me. "If you

persist . . . but no. King Canute tried that. I only say again, nonsense. Have I not made it clear to you? It is the fashion to say anything is possible. The truth is, very few things are possible, pitiably few. That Mr. Chapin killed Dr. Burton is not among them. We are engaged on a project. It is futile to ask you to exclude from your brain all the fallacies which creep, familiar worms, through its chambers, but I do expect you not to let them interfere with our necessary operations. It is late, past two o'clock, time for bed. I have outlined your activities for tomorrow—today. I have explained what may be done, and what may not. Good night, sleep well."

I stood up and yawned. I was too sleepy to be sore, so it was automatic that I said, "Okay, boss." I went upstairs to bed.

Sunday morning I slept late. I had been given three chores for that day, and the first one on the list probably wouldn't be practical at any early hour, so twice when I woke up to glance at the clock I burrowed in again. I finally tumbled out around nine-thirty and got the body rinsed off and the face scraped. When I found myself whistling as I buttoned my shirt I stopped to seek the source of all the gaiety, and discovered I probably felt satisfied because Paul Chapin was behind bars and couldn't see the sunshine which I was seeing on the front of the houses across the street. I stopped whistling. That was no way to feel about a guy when I was supposed to be fighting for his freedom.

It was Sunday morning in November, and I knew what had happened when I had called down to Fritz that I was out of the bathtub: he had lined a casserole with butter, put in it six tablespoons of cream, three fresh eggs, four Lambert sausages, salt, pepper, paprika and chives, and conveyed it to the oven. But before I went to the kitchen I stopped in the office. Andrew Hibbard was there with the morning paper. He said that he hadn't been able to sleep much, that he had had breakfast, and that he wished to God he had some of his own clothes. I told him that Wolfe was up on the top floor with the orchids and that he would be welcome up there if he cared to see them. He decided to go. I went to the phone and called up Centre Street and was told that Inspector Cramer hadn't shown up yet and they weren't sure when he would. So I went to the kitchen and took my time with the casserole and accessories. Of course the murder of Dr. Burton was front page in both papers. I read the pieces through and enjoyed them very much.

Then I went to the garage and got the roadster and moseyed downtown.

Cramer was in his office when I got there, and didn't keep me waiting. He was smoking a big cigar and looked contented. I sat down and listened to him discussing with a couple of dicks the best way to persuade some Harlem citizen to quit his anatomy experiments on the skulls of drugstore cashiers, and when they went I looked at him and grinned. He didn't grin back. He whirled his chair around to face me and asked me what I wanted. I told him I didn't want anything, I just wanted to thank him for letting me squat on the sidelines up at Doc Burton's last night.

He said, "Yeah. You were gone when I came out. Did it bore you?"

"It did. I couldn't find any clue."

"No." But still he didn't grin. "This case is one of those mean babies where nothing seems to fit. All we've got is the murderer and the gun and two witnesses. Now what do you want?"

I told him, "I want lots of things. You've got it, inspector. Okay. You can afford to be generous, and George Pratt ought to hand you two grand, half of what you saved him. I'd like to know if you found any fingerprints on the gun. I'd like to know if Chapin has explained why he planned it so amateur, with him a professional. But what I'd really like is to have a little talk with Chapin. If you could arrange that for me—"

Cramer was grinning. He said, "I wouldn't mind having a talk with Chapin myself."

"Well, I'd be glad to put in a word for you."

He pulled on his cigar, and then took it out and got brisk. "I'll tell you, Goodwin. I'd just as soon sit and chin with you, but the fact is it's Sunday and I'm busy. So take this down. First, even if I passed you in to Chapin you wouldn't get anywhere. That cripple is part mule. I spent four hours on him last night, and I swear to God he wouldn't even tell me how old he is. He is not talking, and he won't talk to anyone except his wife. He says he don't want a lawyer, or rather he don't say anything when we ask him who he wants. His wife has seen him twice, and they won't say anything that anyone can hear. You know I've had a little experience greasing tongues, but he stops them all."

"Yeah. Did you try pinching him, just between you and me?"

He shook his head. "Haven't touched him. But to go on. After what Nero Wolfe said on the phone last night—I suppose you heard that talk—I had an idea you'd be wanting to see him. And I've decided nothing doing. Even if he was talking a blue streak, not a chance. Considering how we got him, I don't see why you're interested anyhow. Hell, can't Wolfe take the short end once in his life?—Now wait a minute. You don't need to remind me Wolfe has always been better than square with me and there's one or two things I owe him. I'll hand him a favor when I've got one the right size. But no matter how tight I've got this cripple sewed up, I'm going to play safe with him."

"Okay. It just means extra trouble. Wolfe will have to arrange it at the D.A.'s office."

"Let him. If he does, I won't butt in. As far as I'm concerned, the only two people that get to see Chapin are his wife and his lawyer, and he's got no lawyer and if you ask me not much wife.—Listen, now that you've asked me a favor and I've turned you down, how about doing one for me? Tell me what you want to see him for? Huh?"

I grinned. "You'd be surprised. I have to ask him what he wants us to do with what is left of Andrew Hibbard until he gets a chance to tend to it."

Cramer stared at me. He snorted. "You wouldn't kid me."

"I wouldn't dream of it. Of course if he's not talking he probably wouldn't tell me, but I might find a way to turn him on. Look here, inspector, there must be some human quality in you somewhere. Today's my birthday. Let me see him."

"Not a chance."

I got up. "How straight is it that he's not talking?"

"That's on the level. We can't get a peep."

I told him much obliged for all his many kindnesses, and left.

I got in the roadster and headed north. I wasn't downcast. I hadn't made any history, but I hadn't expected to. Remembering the mask that Paul Chapin had been using for a face as I saw him sitting in the Burton foyer the night before, I wasn't surprised that Cramer hadn't found him much of a conversationalist, and I wouldn't have expected to hear anything even if I had got to see him.

At Fourteenth Street I parked and went to a cigar store and phoned Wolfe. I told him, "Right again. They have to ask his wife whether he prefers white or dark meat, because he won't even tell them that. He's not interested in a lawyer. Cramer wouldn't let me see him."

Wolfe said, "Excellent. Proceed to Mrs. Burton."

I went back to the roadster and rolled on uptown.

When they telephoned from the lobby to the Burton apartment to say that Mr. Goodwin was there, I was hoping she hadn't got a new slant on this and that during the night. As Wolfe had said once, you can depend on a woman for anything except constancy. But she had stayed put; I was nodded to the elevator. Upstairs I was taken into the same room as the night before by a maid I hadn't seen—the housekeeper, Mrs. Kurtz, I surmised. She looked hostile and determined enough to make me contented that I didn't need to question her about a key or anything else.

Mrs. Burton sat in a chair by a window. She looked pale. If people had been with her she had sent them away. I told her I wouldn't sit down, I only had a few questions Nero Wolfe had given me. I read the first one from my pad:

"Did Paul Chapin say anything whatever to you last night besides what you have already told me, and if so, what?"

She said, "No. Nothing."

"Inspector Cramer showed you the gun that your husband was shot with. How sure are you that it was your husband's, the one he kept in the drawer of his desk?"

She said, "Quite sure. His initials were on it, it was a gift from a friend."

"During the fifty minutes that Dora Chapin was in the apartment last evening, was there any time when she went, or could have gone, to the study, and if so was there anyone else in the study at that time?"

She said, "No." Then the frown came into her eyes. "But wait—yes, there was. Soon after she came I sent her to the study for a book. I suppose there was no one there. My husband was in his room dressing."

"This next one is the last. Do you know if Mr. Bowen was at any time alone in the study?"

She said, "Yes, he was. My husband came to my room to ask me a question."

I put the pad in my pocket, and said to her, "You might tell me what the question was."

"No, Mr. Goodwin. I think not."

"It might be important. This isn't for publication."

Her eyes frowned again, but the hesitation was brief. "Very well. He asked me if I cared enough for Estelle Bowen—Mr. Bowen's wife—to make a considerable sacrifice for her. I said no."

"Did he tell you what he meant?"

"No."

"All right. That's all. You haven't slept any."

"No."

Ordinarily I've got as much to say as there's time for, but on that occasion no more observations suggested themselves. I told her thank you, and she nodded without moving her head, which sounds unlikely but I swear that's what she did, and I beat it. As I went out through the foyer I paused for another glance at one or two details, such as the location of the light switch by the double door.

On my way downtown I phoned Wolfe again. I told

him what I had gathered from Mrs. Burton, and he told me that he and Andrew Hibbard were playing cribbage.

It was twenty minutes past noon when I got to Perry Street. It was deserted for Sunday. Sidewalks empty, only a couple of cars parked in the whole block, and a taxi in front of the entrance to 203. I let the roadster slide to the curb opposite, and got out. I had noted the number on the taxi's license plate and had seen the driver on his seat. I stepped across to the sidewalk and went alongside; his head was tilted over against the frame and his eyes were closed. I put a foot on the running-board and leaned in and said:

"Good morning, Mr. Scott."

He came to with a start and looked at me. He blinked. "Oh," he said, "it's little Nero Wolfe."

I nodded. "Names don't bother me, but mine happens to be Archie Goodwin. How's tips?"

"My dear fellow." He made noises, and spat out to the left, to the pavement. "Tips is copious. When was it I saw you, Wednesday? Only four days ago. You keeping busy?"

"I'm managing." I leaned in a little further. "Look here, Pitney Scott. I wasn't looking for you, but I'm glad I found you. When Nero Wolfe heard how you recognized Andrew Hibbard over a week ago, but didn't claim the five grand reward when it was offered, he said you have an admirable sense of humor. Knowing how easy it is to find excuses for a friendly feeling for five grand, I'd say something different, but Wolfe meant well, he's just eccentric. Seeing you here, it just occurred to me that you ought to know that your friend Hibbard is at present a guest up at our house. I took him there yesterday in time for dinner. If it's all the same to you, he'd like to stay under cover for another couple of days, till we get this whole thing straightened out. If you should happen to turn mercenary, you won't lose anything by keeping your sense of humor."

He grunted. "So. You got Andy. And you only need a couple of days to straighten it all out. I thought *all* detectives were dumb."

"Sure, we are. I'm so dumb I don't even know whether it was you that took Dora Chapin up to Ninetieth Street last evening and brought her back again. I was just going to ask you."

"All right, ask me. Then I'll say it wasn't." He made noises and spat again—another futile attack on the imaginary obstruction in the throat of a man with a constant craving for a drink. He looked at me and went on, "You know, brother—if you will pardon the argot, I'm sore at you for spotting Andy, but I admire you for it too because it was halfway smart. And anyway, Lorrie Burton was a pretty good guy. With him dead, and Mr. Paul Chapin in jail, the fun's gone. It's not funny any more, even to me, and Nero Wolfe's right about my sense of humor. It is admirable. I'm a character. I'm sardonic." He spat again. "But to hell with it. I didn't drive Mrs. Chapin to Burton's last night because she went in her own coupé."

"Oh. She drives herself."

"Sure. In the summertime she and her husband go to the country on picnics. Now that was funny, for instance, and I don't suppose they'll ever do that again. I don't know why she's using me today, unless it's because she doesn't want to park it in front of the Tombs—there she comes now."

I got off the running-board and back a step. Dora Chapin had come out of the 203 entrance and was headed for the taxi. She had on another coat and another furpiece, but the face was the same, and so were the little gray eyes. She was carrying an oblong package about the size of a shoebox, and I supposed that was dainties for her husband's Sunday dinner. She didn't seem to have noticed me, let alone recognize me; then she stopped with one foot on the running-board and turned the eyes straight at me, and for the first time I saw an expression in them that I could give a name to, and it wasn't fondness. You could call it an inviting expression if you went on to describe what she was inviting me to. I stepped into it anyway. I said:

"Mrs. Chapin. Could I ride with you? I'd like to tell you—"

She climbed inside and slammed the door to. Pitney Scott stepped on the starter, put the gear in, and started to roll. I stood and watched the taxi go, not very jubilant, because it was her I had come down there to see.

I walked to the corner and phoned Wolfe I wouldn't be home to lunch, which I didn't mind much because the eggs and cream and sausages I had shipped on at ten o'clock were still undecided what to do about it; bought a *Times* and went to the roadster and made myself comfortable. Unless she had some kind of pull that Inspector Cramer didn't know about, they wouldn't let her stay very long at the Tombs.

At that I had to wait close to an hour and a half. It was nearly two o'clock, and I was thinking of hitting up the delicatessen where Fred Durkin had been a tenant for most of the week, when I looked up for the eightieth time at the sound of a car and saw the taxi slowing down. I had decided what to do. With all that animosity in Dora's eyes I calculated it wouldn't pay to try to join her downstairs and go up with her; I would wait till she was inside and then persuade Pitney Scott to take me up. With him along she might let me in. But again I didn't get the break. Instead of stopping at the entrance Scott rolled down a few yards, and then they both got out and both went in. I stared at them and did a little cussing, and decided not to do any more waiting. I got out and entered 203 for the first and last time, and went to the elevator and said fifth floor. The man looked at me with the usual mild and weary suspicion but didn't bother with questions. I got out at the fifth and rang the bell at 5C.

I can't very well pretend to be proud of what happened that afternoon at Paul Chapin's apartment. I pulled a boner, no doubt of that, and it wasn't my fault that it didn't have a result that ended a good deal more than the Chapin case, but the opinion you have of it depends entirely on how you use it. I can't honestly agree that it was quite as dumb as one or two subsequent remarks of Wolfe's might seem to indicate. Anyway, this is how it happened.

Dora Chapin came to the door and opened it, and I got my foot inside the sill. She asked me what I wanted, and I said I had something to ask Pitney Scott. She said he would be down in half an hour and I could wait downstairs, and started to shut the door, and got it as far as my foot. I said:

"Listen, Mrs. Chapin. I want to ask you something too. You think I'm against your husband, but I'm not, I'm for him. That's on the level. He hasn't got many friends left, and anyway it won't hurt you to listen to me. I've got something to say. I could say it to the police instead of you, but take it from me you wouldn't like that nearly as well. Let me in. Pitney Scott's here."

She threw the door wide open and said, "Come in."

Maybe the shift in her welcome should have made me suspicious, but it didn't. It merely made me think I had scared her, and also made me add a few chips to the stack I was betting that if her husband hadn't croaked Dr. Burton, she had. I went in and shut the door behind me, and followed her across the hall, and through a sitting-room and dining-room and into the kitchen. The rooms were big and well furnished and looked prosperous; and sitting in the kitchen at an enamel-top table was Pitney Scott, consuming a hunk of brown fried chicken. There was a platter of it with four or five pieces left. I said to Dora Chapin:

"Maybe we can go in front and leave Mr. Scott to enjoy himself."

She nodded at a chair and pointed to the chicken: "There's plenty." She turned to Scott: "I'll fix you a drink."

He shook his head, and chewed and swallowed. "I've been off for ten days now, Mrs. Chapin. It wouldn't be funny, take my word for it. When the coffee's ready I'd appreciate that.—Come on—you said Goodwin, didn't you?—come on and help me. Mrs. Chapin says she has dined."

I was hungry and the chicken looked good, I admit that, but the psychology of it was that it looked like I ought to join in. Not to mention the salad, which had green peppers in it. I got into the chair and Scott passed the platter. Dora Chapin had gone to the stove to turn the fire down under the percolator. There was still a lot of bandage at the back of her neck, and it looked unattractive where her hair had been shaved off. She was bigger than I had realized in the office that day, fairly hefty. She went into the dining-room for something, and I got more intimate with the chicken after the first couple of bites and started a

conversation with Scott. After a while Dora Chapin
came back, with coffee cups and a bowl of sugar.

Of course it was in the coffee, she probably put it
right in the pot since she didn't drink any, but I didn't
notice a taste. It was strong but it tasted all right.
However, she must have put in all the sleeping tablets
and a few other things she could get hold of, for God
knows it was potent. I began to feel it when I was
reaching to hand Scott a cigarette, and at the same
time I saw the look on his face. He was a few seconds
ahead of me. Dora Chapin was out of the room again.
Scott looked at the door she had gone through, and
tried to get up out of his chair, but couldn't make it.
That was the last I really remember, him trying to get
out of his chair, but I must have done one or two
things after that, because when I came out of it I was
in the dining-room, halfway across to the door which
led to the sitting-room and the hall.

When I came out of it, it was dark. That was the
first thing I knew, and for a while it was all I knew,
because I couldn't move and I was fighting to get my
eyes really open. I could see, off to my right, at a great
distance it seemed, two large oblongs of dim light, and
I concentrated on deciding what they were. It came
with a burst that they were windows, and it was dark
in the room where I was, and the street was lit. Then
I concentrated on what room I was in.

Things came back but all in a jumble. I still didn't
know where I was, though I was splitting my head
fighting for it. I rolled over on the floor and my hand
landed on something metal, sharp, and I shrunk from
it; I pulled myself to my knees and began to crawl. I
bumped into a table and a chair or two, and finally into
the wall. I crawled around the wall with my shoulder
against it, detouring for furniture, stopping every

couple of feet to feel it, and at last I felt a door. I tried to stand up, but couldn't make it, and compromised by feeling above me. I found the switch and pushed on it, and the light went on. I crawled over to where there was some stuff on the floor, stretching the muscles in my brow and temples to keep my eyes open, and saw that the metal thing that had startled me was my ring of keys. My wallet was there too, and my pad and pencil, pocketknife, fountain pen, handkerchief— things from my pockets.

I got hold of a chair and pulled myself to my feet, but I couldn't navigate. I tried, and fell down. I looked around for a telephone, but there wasn't any, so I crawled to the sitting-room and found the light switch by the door and turned it on. The phone was on a stand by the further wall. It looked so far away that the desire to lie down and give it up made me want to yell to show I wouldn't do that, but I couldn't yell. I finally got to the stand and sat down on the floor against it and reached up for the phone and got the receiver off and shoved it against my ear, and heard a man's voice, very faint. I said the number of Wolfe's phone and heard him say he couldn't hear me, so then I yelled it and that way got enough steam behind it. After a while I heard another voice and I yelled:

"I want Nero Wolfe!"

The other voice mumbled and I said to talk louder, and asked who it was, and got it into my bean that it was Fritz. I told him to get Wolfe on, and he said Wolfe wasn't there, and I said he was crazy, and he mumbled a lot of stuff and I told him to say it again louder and slower. "I said, Archie, Mr. Wolfe is not here. He went to look for you. Somebody came to get him, and he told me he was going for you. Archie, where are you? Mr. Wolfe said—"

I was having a hard time holding the phone, and it dropped to the floor, the whole works, and my head fell into my hands with my eyes closed, and I suppose what I was doing you would call crying.

# Chapter 19

I haven't the slightest idea how long I sat there on the floor with my head laying in my hands trying to force myself out of it enough to pick up the telephone again. It may have been a minute and it may have been an hour. The trouble was that I should have been concentrating on the phone, and it kept sweeping over me that Wolfe was gone. I couldn't get my head out of my hands. Finally I heard a noise. It kept on and got louder, and at last it seeped into me that someone seemed to be trying to knock the door down. I grabbed the top of the telephone stand and pulled myself up, and decided I could keep my feet if I didn't let go of the wall, so I followed it around to the door where the noise was. I got my hands on it and turned the lock and the knob, and it flew open and down I went again. The two guys that came in walked on me and then stood and looked at me, and I heard remarks about full to the gills and leaving the receiver off the hook.

By that time I could talk better. I said I don't know what, enough so that one of them beat it for a doctor, and the other one helped me get up and steered me to the kitchen. He turned the light on. Scott had slewed

off of his chair and curled up on the floor. My chair was
turned over on its side. I felt cold air and the guy said
something about the window, and I looked at it and
saw the glass was shattered with a big hole in it. I
never did learn what it was I had thrown through the
window, maybe the plate of chicken; anyway it hadn't
aroused enough curiosity down below to do any good.
The guy stooped over Scott and shook him, but he was
dead to the world. By working the wall again, and
furniture, I got back to the dining-room and sat on the
floor and began collecting my things and putting them
in my pockets. I got worried because I thought
something was missing and I couldn't figure out what
it was, and then I realized it was the leather case
Wolfe had given me, with pistols on one side and
orchids on the other, that I carried my police and fire
cards in. And by God I started to cry again. I was
doing that when the other guy came back with the
doctor. I was crying, and trying to push my knuckles
into my temples hard enough to get my brains working on why Dora Chapin had fed me a knockout so she
could frisk me and then took nothing but that leather
case.

I had a fight with the doctor. He insisted that
before he could give me anything he'd have to know
just what it was I had inside of me, and he went to the
bathroom to investigate bottles and boxes and I went
after him with the idea of plugging him. I was beginning to have thoughts and they were starting to bust
in my head. I got nearly to the bathroom when I forgot
all about the doctor because I suddenly remembered
that there had been something peculiar about Scott
curled up on the floor, and I turned around and started
for the kitchen. I was getting overconfident and fell
down again, but I picked myself up and went on. I

looked at Scott and saw what it was: he was in his shirt-sleeves. His gray taxi-driver's jacket was gone. I was trying to decide why that was important when the doctor came in with a glass of brown stuff in his hand. He said something and handed me the glass and watched me drink it, and then went over and knelt down by Scott.

The stuff tasted bitter. I put the empty glass on the table and got hold of the guy who had gone for the doctor—by this time I recognized him as the elevator man—and told him to go downstairs and switch the Chapin phone in, and then go outside and see if Scott's taxi was at the curb. Then I made it through the dining-room again into the sitting-room and got into a chair by the telephone stand. I got the operator, and gave her the number.

Fritz answered. I said, "This is Archie. What was it you told me a while ago about Mr. Wolfe?"

"Why . . . Mr. Wolfe is gone." I could hear him better, and I could tell he was trying not to let his voice shake. "He told me he was going to get you, and that he suspected you of trying to coerce him into raising your pay. He went—"

"Wait a minute, Fritz. Talk slow. What time is it? My watch says a quarter to seven."

"Yes. That's right. Mr. Wolfe has been gone nearly four hours. Archie, where are you?"

"To hell with where I am. What happened? Someone came for him?"

"Yes. I went to the door, and a man handed me an envelope."

"Was it a taxi-driver?"

"Yes, I think so. I took the envelope to Mr. Wolfe, and pretty soon he came to the kitchen and told me he was going. Mr. Hibbard helped him into his coat, the brown one with the big collar, and I got his hat and stick and gloves—"

"Did you see the taxi?"

"Yes, I went out with Mr. Wolfe and opened the door of the cab for him. Archie, for God's sake, tell me what I can do—"

"You can't do anything. Let me talk to Mr. Hibbard."

"But Archie—I am so disturbed—"

"So am I. Hold the fort, Fritz, and sit tight. Put Hibbard on."

I waited, and before long heard Hibbard's hello. I said to him:

"This is Archie Goodwin, Mr. Hibbard. Now listen, I can't talk much. When Nero Wolfe gets home again we want to be able to tell him that you've kept your word. You promised him to stay dead until Monday evening. Understand?"

Hibbard sounded irritated. "Of course I understand, Mr. Goodwin, but it seems to me—"

"For God's sake forget how it seems to you. Either you keep your word or you don't."

"Well . . . I do."

"That's fine. Tell Fritz I'll call again as soon as I have anything to say."

I hung up. The brown stuff the doctor had given me seemed to be working, but not to much advantage; my head was pounding like the hammers of hell. The elevator man had come back and was standing there. I looked at him and he said Scott's taxi was gone. I got hold of the phone again and called Spring 7-3100.

Cramer wasn't in his office and they couldn't find him around. I got my wallet out of my pocket and with some care managed to find my lists of telephone numbers, and called Cramer's home. At first they said he wasn't there, but I persuaded them to change their minds, and finally he came to the phone. I didn't know a cop's voice could ever sound so welcome to me. I told him where I was and what had happened to me, and said I was trying to remember what it was he had said that morning about doing a favor for Nero Wolfe. He said whatever it was he had meant it. I told him:

"Okay, now's your chance. That crazy Chapin bitch has stole a taxi and she's got Nero Wolfe in it taking him somewhere. I don't know where and I wouldn't know even if my head was working. She got him four hours ago and she's had time to get to Albany or anywhere else.—No matter how she got him, I'll settle for that some other day. Listen, inspector, for God's sake. Send out a general for a brown taxi, a Stuyvesant, MO 29-6342. Got it down? Say it back.— Will you put the radios on it? Will you send it to Westchester and Long Island and Jersey? Listen, the dope I was cooking up was that it was her that croaked Doc Burton. By God, if I ever get my hands on her— What? I'm not excited.—Okay. Okay, inspector, thanks."

I hung up. Someone had come in and was standing there, and I looked up and saw it was a flatfoot wearing a silly grin, directed at me. He asked me something and I told him to take his shoes off to rest his brains. He made me some kind of a reply that was intended to be smart, and I laid my head down on the top of the telephone stand to get the range, and banged it up and down a few times on the wood, but it didn't seem to do any good. The elevator man said something to the cop and he went towards the kitchen.

I got up and went to open a window and damn near fell out. The cold air was like ice. The way I felt I was sure of two things: first, that if my head went on like that much longer it would blow up, and second, that Wolfe was dead. It seemed obvious that after that

woman once got him into that taxi there was nothing
for her to do with him but kill him. I stood looking out
onto Perry Street, trying to hold my head together,
and I had a feeling that all of New York was there in
front of me, between me and the house fronts I could
see across the street—the Battery, the river fronts,
Central Park, Flatbush, Harlem, Park Avenue, all of
it—and Wolfe was there somewhere and I didn't know
where. Something occurred to me, and I held on to the
window jamb and leaned out enough so I could see
below. There was the roadster, where I had parked it,
its fender shining with the reflection from a street
light. I had an idea that if I could get down there and
get it started I could drive it all right.

I decided to do that, but before I moved away from
the window I thought I ought to decide where to go.
One man in one roadster, even if he had a head on him
that would work, wouldn't get far looking for that taxi.
It was absolutely hopeless. But I had a notion that
there was something important I could do, somewhere
important I could go, if only I could figure out where
it was. All of a sudden it came to me that where I
wanted to go was home. I wanted to see Fritz, and the
office, and go over the house and see for myself that
Wolfe wasn't there, look at things . . .

I didn't hesitate. I let go of the window jamb and
started across the room, and just as I got to the hall
the telephone rang. I could walk a little better. I went
back to the telephone stand and picked up the receiver
and said hello. A voice said:

"Chelsea-two three-nine-two-four? Please give me
Mr. Chapin's apartment."

I nearly dropped the receiver, and I went stiff. I
said, "Who is this?" The voice said:

"This is someone who wishes to be connected with Mr. Chapin's apartment. Didn't I make that clear?"

I let the phone down and pressed it against one of my ribs for a moment, not wanting to make a fool of myself. Then I put it up to my mouth again: "Excuse me for asking who it is. It sounded like Nero Wolfe. Where are you?"

"Ah! Archie. After what Mrs. Chapin has told me, I scarcely expected to find you operating an apartment house switchboard. I am much relieved. How are you feeling?"

"Swell. Wonderful. How are you?"

"Fairly comfortable. Mrs. Chapin drives staccato, and the jolting of that infernal taxicab . . . ah well. Archie. I am standing, and I dislike to talk on the telephone while standing. Also I would dislike very much to enter that taxicab again. If it is practical, get the sedan and come for me. I am at the Bronx River Inn, near the Woodlawn railroad station. You know where that is?"

"I know. I'll be there."

"No great hurry. I am fairly comfortable."

"Okay."

The click of his ringing off was in my ear. I hung up and sat down.

I was damn good and sore. Certainly not at Wolfe, not even at myself, just sore. Sore because I had phoned Cramer an SOS, sore because Wolfe was to hell and gone up beyond the end of the Grand Concourse and I didn't really know what shape he was in, sore because it was up to me to get there and there was no doubt at all about the shape I was in. I felt my eyes closing and jerked my head up. I decided that the next time I saw Dora Chapin, no matter when or where, I would take my pocketknife and cut her head off, completely loose from the rest of her. I thought of going to the kitchen and asking the doctor for another shot of the brown stuff, but didn't see how it could do me any good.

I picked up the phone and called the garage, on Tenth Avenue, and told them to fill the sedan with gas and put it at the curb. Then I got up and proceeded to make myself scarce. I would rather have done almost anything than try walking again, except go back to crawling. I made it to the hall, and opened the door, and on out to the elevator. There I was faced by two new troubles: the elevator was right there, the door standing wide open, and I didn't have my hat and coat. I didn't want to go back to the kitchen for the elevator man because in the first place it was too far, and secondly if the flatfoot found out I was leaving he would probably want to detain me for information and there was no telling how I would act if he tried it. I did go back to the hall, having left the door open. I got my hat and coat and returned to the elevator, inside, and somehow got the door closed, and pulled the lever, hitting down by luck. It started down and I leaned against the wall.

I thought I was releasing the lever about the right time, but the first thing I knew the elevator hit bottom like a ton of brick and shook me loose from the wall. I picked myself up and opened the door and saw there was a dark hall about two feet above my level. I climbed out and got myself up. It was the basement. I turned right, which seemed to be correct, and for a change it was. I came to a door and went through, and through a gate, and there I was outdoors with nothing between me and the sidewalk but a flight of concrete steps. I negotiated them, and crossed the street and found the roadster and got in.

I don't believe yet that I drove that car from Perry Street to Thirty-sixth, to the garage. I might possibly have done it by caroms, bouncing back from the buildings first on one side of the street and then on the other, but the trouble with that theory is that next day the roadster didn't have a scratch on it. If anyone is keeping a miracle score, chalk one up for me. I got there, but I stopped out in front, deciding not to try for the door. I blew my horn and Steve came out. I described my condition in round figures and told him I hoped there was someone there he could leave in charge of the joint, because he had to get in the sedan and drive me to the Bronx. He asked if I wanted a drink and I snarled at him. He grinned and went inside, and I transferred to the sedan, standing at the curb. Pretty soon he came back with an overcoat on, and got in and shoved off. I told him where to go and let my head fall back in the corner against the cushion, but I didn't dare to let my eyes shut. I stretched them open and kept on stretching them every time I blinked. My window was down and the cold air slapped me, and it seemed we were going a million miles a minute in a swift sweeping circle and it was hard to keep up with my breathing.

Steve said, "Here we are, mister."

I grunted and lifted my head up and stretched my eyes again. We had stopped. There it was, Bronx River Inn, just across the sidewalk. I had a feeling it had come to us instead of us to it. Steve asked, "Can you navigate?"

"Sure." I set my jaw again, and opened the door and climbed out. Then after crossing the sidewalk I tried to walk through a lattice, and set my jaw some more and detoured. I crossed the porch, with cold bare tables around and no one there, and opened the door and went inside to the main room. There some of the tables had cloths on them and a few customers were scattered here and there. The customer I was looking for was at a table in the far corner, and I approached it. There sat Nero Wolfe, all of him, on a chair which would have been economical for either half. His brown greatcoat covered another chair, beside him, and across the table from him I saw the bandages on the back of Dora Chapin's neck. She was facing him, with her rear to me. I walked over there.

Wolfe nodded at me. "Good evening, Archie. I am relieved again. It occurred to me after I phoned you that you were probably in no condition to pilot a car through this confounded labyrinth. I am greatly relieved.—You have met Mrs. Chapin.—Sit down. You don't look as if standing was very enjoyable."

He lifted his glass of beer and took a couple of swallows. I saw the remains of some kind of a mess on his plate, but Dora Chapin had cleaned hers up. I moved his hat and stick off a chair and sat down on it. He asked me if I wanted a glass of milk and I shook my head. He said:

"I confess it is a trifle mortifying, to set out to rescue you and end by requesting you to succor me, but if that is Mr. Scott's taxicab he should get new springs for it. If you get me home intact—and no doubt you will—that will not be your only triumph for this day. By putting me in touch with Mrs. Chapin in unconventional circumstances, though it seems inadvertently, you have brought us to the solution of our problem. I tell you that at once because I know it will be welcome news. Mrs. Chapin has been kind enough to accept my assurances—"

That was the last word I heard. The only other thing I remembered was that a tight wire which had been stretched between my temples, holding them together, suddenly parted with a twang. Wolfe told me afterwards that when I folded up my head hit the edge of the table with a loud thud before he could catch me.

# Chapter 20

Monday morning when I woke up I was still in bed. That sounds as if I meant something else, but I don't. When I got enough awake to realize where I was I had a feeling that I had gone to bed sometime during Lent and here it was Christmas. Then I saw Doc Vollmer standing there beside me.

I grinned at him. "Hello, doc. You got a job here as house physician?"

He grinned back. "I just stopped in to see how it went with what I pumped into you last night. Apparently—"

"What? Oh. Yeah. Good God." It struck me that the room seemed full of light. "What time is it?"

"Quarter to twelve."

"No!" I twisted to see the clock. "Holy murder!" I jerked myself upright, and someone jabbed a thousand ice-picks into my skull. "Whoa, Bill." I put my hands up to it and tried moving it slowly. I said to Vollmer, "What's this I've got here, my head?"

He laughed. "It'll be all right."

"Yeah. You're not saying when. Wowie! Is Mr. Wolfe down in the office?"

He nodded. "I spoke to him on the way up."

"And it's noon." I slid to my feet. "Look out, I might run into you." I started for the bathroom.

I began soaping up, and he came to the bathroom door and said he had left instructions with Fritz for my breakfast. I told him I didn't want instructions, I wanted ham and eggs. He laughed again, and beat it. I was glad to hear him laugh, because it seemed likely that if there really were ice-picks sticking in my head he, being a doctor, would be taking them out instead of laughing at me.

I made it as snappy as I could with my dizziness, cleansing the form and assuming the day's draperies, and went downstairs in pretty good style but hanging onto the banister.

Wolfe, in his chair, looked up and said good morning and asked me how I felt. I told him I felt like twin colts and went to my desk. He said:

"But, Archie. Seriously. Should you be up?"

"Yeah. Not only should I be up, I should have been up. You know how it is, I'm a man of action."

His cheeks unfolded. "And I, of course, am supersedentary. A comical interchange of roles, that you rode home last evening from the Bronx River Inn, a matter of ten miles or more, with your head on my lap all the way."

I nodded. "Very comical. I told you a long while ago, Mr. Wolfe, that you pay me half for the chores I do and half for listening to you brag."

"So you did. And if I did not then remark, I do so now—but no. We can pursue these amenities another time, now there is business. Could you take some notes, and break your fast with our lunch?—Good. I spoke on the telephone this morning with Mr. Morley, and with the District Attorney himself. It has been arranged that I shall see Mr. Chapin at the Tombs at

two-thirty this afternoon. You will remember that on
Saturday evening I was beginning to dictate to you
the confession of Paul Chapin when we were interrupted by news from Fred Durkin which caused a
postponement. If you will turn to that page we can go
on. I'll have to have it by two o'clock."

So as it turned out I not only didn't get to tie into
the ham and eggs I had yearned for, I didn't even eat
lunch with Wolfe and Hibbard. The dictating wasn't
done until nearly one, and I had the typing to do. But
by that time the emptiness inside had got to be a
vacuum, or whatever it may be that is emptier than
emptiness, and I had Fritz bring some hot egg sandwiches and milk and coffee to my desk. I wanted this
typed just right, this document that Paul Chapin was
to sign, and with my head not inclined to see the
importance of things like spelling and punctuation I
had to take my time and concentrate. Also, I wasted
three minutes phoning the garage to tell them to bring
the sedan around, for I supposed of course I would
take Wolfe in it; but they said they already had
instructions from Wolfe, and that the instructions
included a driver. I thought maybe I ought to be sore
about that, but decided not to.

Wolfe ate a quick lunch, for him. When he came
into the office at a quarter to two I barely had the
thing finished and was getting the three copies clipped
into brown folders. He took them and put them in his
pocket and told me to take my notebook and started on
the instructions for my afternoon. He explained that
he had asked for a driver from the garage because I
would be busy with other things. He also explained
that on account of the possibility of visitors he had
procured from Hibbard a promise that he would spend

the entire afternoon in his room, until dinner time. Hibbard had gone there from the lunch-table.

Fritz came to the door and said the car was there, and Wolfe told him he would be ready in a few minutes.

What gave me a new idea of the dimensions of Wolfe's nerve was the disclosure that a good part of the arrangements had been completed for a meeting of the League of the White Feather, in the office that evening at nine o'clock. Before he had seen Chapin at all! Of course I didn't know what Dora might have told him, except a couple of details that had been included in the confession, but it wasn't Dora that was supposed to sign on the dotted line, it was her little crippled husband with the light-colored eyes; and that was a job I was glad Wolfe hadn't bestowed on me, even if it did mean his sashaying out of the house twice in two days, which was an all-time record. But he had gone ahead and telephoned Boston and Philadelphia and Washington, and six or eight of them in New York, after we got home Sunday evening and from his room early that morning, and the meeting was on. My immediate job was to get in touch with the others, by phone if possible, and ensure as full an attendance as we could get.

He gave me another one more immediate, just before he left. He told me to go and see Mrs. Burton at once, and dictated two questions to ask her. I suggested the phone, and he said no, it would be better if I saw the daughter and the maids also. Fritz was standing there holding his coat. Wolfe said:

"And I was almost forgetting that our guests will be thirsty. Fritz, put the coat down and come here, and we shall see what we need.—Archie, if you don't mind you had better start, you should be back by three.—Let us see, Fritz. I noticed last week that Mr. Cabot prefers Aylmer's soda—"

I beat it. I walked to the garage for the roadster, and the sharp air glistened in my lungs. After I got the roadster out into the light I looked it over and couldn't find a scratch on it, and it was then I reflected on miracles. I got back in and headed uptown.

I was worried about Wolfe. It looked to me like he was rushing things beyond reason. It was true that Andrew Hibbard's parole was up that evening, but probably he could have been persuaded to extend it, and besides it certainly wasn't vital to produce him at the meeting as a stunt. But it was like Wolfe not to wait until the confession was actually in the bag. That sort of gesture, thumbing his nose at luck, was a part of him, and maybe an important part; there were lots of things about Wolfe I didn't pretend to know. Anyhow, there was no law against worrying, and it didn't make my head feel any better to reflect on the outcome of the meeting that evening if Paul Chapin stayed mule. So that was what I reflected on, all the way to Ninetieth Street.

Wolfe had said that both of the questions I was to ask Mrs. Burton were quite important. The first was simple: *Did Dr. Burton telephone Paul Chapin between 6:50 and 7:00 o'clock Saturday evening and ask him to come to see him?*

The second was more complicated: *At 6:30 Saturday evening a pair of gray gloves was lying on the table in the Burton foyer, near the end towards the double doors. Were the gloves removed between then and 7:20 by anyone in the apartment?*

I got a break. Everybody was home. The house-keeper had me wait in the drawing-room and Mrs. Burton came to me there. She looked sick, I thought, and had on a gray dress that made her look sicker, but the spine was still doing its stuff. The first question took about nine seconds; the answer was no, definitely. Dr. Burton had done no telephoning after 6:30 Saturday evening. The second question required more time. Mrs. Kurtz was out of it, since she hadn't been there. The daughter, having left before 6:30, seemed out of it too, but I asked Mrs. Burton to call her in anyhow, to make sure. She came, and said she had left no gloves on the foyer table and had seen none there. Mrs. Burton herself had not been in the foyer between the time she returned home and around six, and 7:33 when the sound of the shots had taken her there on the run. She said she had left no gloves on that table, and certainly had removed none. She sent for Rose. Rose came, and I asked her if she had removed a pair of gloves from the foyer table between 6:30 and 7:20 Saturday evening.

Rose looked at Mrs. Burton instead of me. She hesitated, and then she spoke: "No, ma'am, I didn't take the gloves. But Mrs. Chapin—"

She stopped. I said, "You saw some gloves there."

"Yes, sir."

"When?"

"When I went to let Mrs. Chapin in."

"Did Mrs. Chapin take them?"

"No, sir. That's when I noticed them, when she picked them up. She picked them up and then put them down again."

"You didn't go back later and get them?"

"No, sir, I didn't."

That settled that. I thanked Mrs. Burton, and left. I wanted to tell her that before tomorrow noon we would have definite news for her that might help a little, but I thought Wolfe had already done enough discounting for the firm and I'd better let it ride.

It was after three when I got back to the office, and I got busy on the phone. There were eight names left for me, that Wolfe hadn't been able to get. He had told me the line to take, that we were prepared to mail our bills to our clients, the signers of the memorandum, but that before doing so we would like to explain to them in a body and receive their approval. Which again spoke fairly well for Wolfe's nerve, inasmuch as our clients knew damn well that it was the cops who had grabbed Chapin for Burton's murder and that we had had about as much to do with it as the lions in front of the library. But I agreed that it was a good line, since the object was to get them to the office.

I was doing pretty well with my eight, having hooked five of them in a little over half an hour, when, at a quarter to four, while I was looking in the book for the number of the Players' Club, on the trail of Roland Erskine, the phone rang. I answered, and it was Wolfe. As soon as I heard his voice I thought to myself, uh-huh, here we go, the party's up the flue. But it didn't appear that that was the idea. He said to me:

"Archie? What luck at Mrs. Burton's?"

"All negatives. Burton didn't phone, and nobody took any gloves."

"But perhaps the maid saw them?"

"Oh, you knew that too. She did. She saw Mrs. Chapin pick them up and put them down again."

"Excellent. I am telephoning because I have just made a promise and I wish to redeem it without delay. Take Mr. Chapin's box from the cabinet, wrap it carefully, and convey it to his apartment and deliver it to Mrs. Chapin. I shall probably be at home by your return."

"Okay. You got any news?"

"Nothing startling."

"I wouldn't expect anything startling. Let's try a plain straightforward question. Did you get the confession signed or didn't you?"

"I did."

"It's really signed?"

"It is. But I forgot to say: before you wrap Mr. Chapin's box take out a pair of gloves, gray leather, and keep them. Please get the box to Mrs. Chapin at once."

"Okay."

I hung up. The fat devil had put it over. I had no idea what items of ammunition he had procured from Dora Chapin, and of course he had the advantage that Chapin was already in the Tombs with a first degree murder charge glued on him, but even so I handed it to him. I would say that that cripple was the hardest guy to deal with I had ever run across, except the perfume salesman up in New Rochelle who used to drown kittens in the bathtub and one day got hold of his wife by mistake. I would have loved to see Wolfe inserting the needle in him.

Wolfe had said without delay, so I let the last three victims wait. I wrapped the box up and drove down to Perry Street with it, removing a pair of gloves first in accordance with instructions and putting them in a drawer of my desk. I parked across the street from 203 and got out. I had decided on the proper technique for that delivery. I went across to where the elevator man was standing inside the entrance and said to him:

"Take this package up to Mrs. Chapin on the fifth

floor. Then come back here and I'll give you a quarter."

He took the package and said, "The cop was sore as a boil yesterday when he found you'd gone. How're you feeling?"

"Magnificent. Run ahead, mister."

He went, and came back, and I gave him a quarter. I asked him, "Did I break anything on your vertical buggy? The lever wouldn't work."

He grinned about a sixteenth of an inch. "I'll bet it wouldn't. Naw, you didn't break it."

So I kept Wolfe's promise for him and got the package delivered without running any unnecessary risk of being invited in for tea, and all it cost me was two bits, which was cheap enough.

Wolfe returned before I got back home. I knew that in the hall, seeing his hat and coat there. Since it was after four o'clock he would of course be upstairs with the plants, but all of his traipsing around had me nervous, and before going to the office I went up the three flights. I had hardly seen the orchids for more than brief glances for nearly a week. Wolfe was in the tropical room, going down the line looking for aphids, and from the expression on his face I knew he had found some. I stood there, and pretty soon he turned and looked at me as if I was either an aphid myself or had them all over me. There was no use attempting any conversation. I beat it downstairs to resume at the telephone.

I only got two of the remaining three, couldn't find Roland Erskine anywhere. As it was, we had done pretty good. A telegram had come from Boston saying that Collard and Gaines would be there, and Mollison was coming down from New Haven. I suspected that

Wolfe would have handled the long distance babies himself even if I hadn't been in bed.

Wolfe didn't come to the office directly from the plant-rooms at six o'clock as usual. Apparently he had stopped in his room, for when he appeared around six-thirty he was lugging a stack of books and I saw they were Paul Chapin's novels. He put them on his desk and sat down and rang for beer.

I told him Mrs. Chapin had the box, and read him the notes of my afternoon call on Mrs. Burton. He gave me some instructions for the evening, which I made notes of because he liked to have everything down, and then he got playful. He made a lot of random remarks and I took them like a gentleman, and then because it was getting on towards dinner I observed that it was about time I got acquainted with the mystery of the pair of gloves on the foyer table. To my surprise he agreed with me.

He said: "That was the contribution of Mrs. Chapin. She furnished other information too, but nothing as interesting as that. She arrived at the Burton apartment, as you know, at six-thirty. The maid called Rose let her in. As she passed through the foyer she saw a pair of gloves on the table, and she stopped to pick them up. She says she intended to take them in to Mrs. Burton, but it would not be charitable to surmise that she had in mind starting a new treasure box for her husband; and that it is supported by the reasons she gives for returning the gloves to the table. She gives two reasons: that the maid had turned and was looking at her, and that the gloves seemed a little heavier than any she had known Mrs. Burton to wear. At any rate, she left them there. But when she went through the foyer, alone, on the way out, she thought to look at them again to satisfy herself whether they were Mrs. Burton's or not. The gloves were gone. She even looked around for them. They were gone."

"I see. And that proves she didn't croak Burton."

"It does. And it identifies the murderer. If it should turn out that factual corroboration is needed of Mrs. Chapin's innocence, which seems unlikely, it can be established that at half past seven she was receiving a summons from a policeman at Park Avenue and Fiftieth Street for passing a red light. Not to mention the probability that the hallman and doorman saw her leaving the building before the event occurred. But none of that should be needed."

"Uh-huh. I suppose you got her confidence by giving her some orchids."

"No. But as a matter of fact, I promised her some. Make a note of that for tomorrow. I got her confidence by telling her the truth, that the conviction of her husband for murder would cost me many thousands of dollars. You see, what happened—what time is it?— Good. She was convinced, as was Chapin himself, that I was responsible for his predicament. Not knowing the nature of my agreement with his friends, he thought I had framed him. Having seen me, he could not of course suppose that I myself had performed the acrobatics in the foyer. Do you know who did that? You. Yes, indeed, you did the killing, I merely devised it. Mrs. Chapin, believing that, seized an opportunity. With you and Pitney Scott fast asleep, she went through your pockets, took his cap and jacket, sat down and wrote a note, and drove the taxicab here. She handed the envelope to Fritz at the door and returned to the cab. The note was brief and quite clear, I can quote it verbatim: *Archie Goodwin will be dead in two hours unless you get in my taxi and go where I drive you.* And it was signed with her name, Dora Chapin. Admirably forthright. What persuaded me that some sort of action was called for was the presence in the envelope of the leather case you had seemed to like."

He paused for a glass of beer. I grunted, and thought I ought to say something, but all I could think of was, "Yeah, I liked it. And you've still got it."

He nodded, and resumed. "The only aspect of the episode that was really distressing came from Mrs. Chapin's romantic idea of what constitutes a remote and secluded spot. Since I was committed to follow her, a bush in a corner of Central Park would have done her just as well, but that infernal female ass bounced that cab far beyond the limits of the city. I learned subsequently that she had in mind an isolated wood somewhere on the edge of Long Island Sound where she and her husband had gone last summer to have a picnic. It became unendurable. I lowered the glass between us and shouted at the back of her ear that if she did not stop within three minutes I would call for help at every passing car and every visible human being. I convinced her. She turned into a byroad and soon stopped under a clump of trees.

"This will amuse you. She had a weapon. A kitchen knife!—By the way, that carving she exhibited to us last Wednesday was done on her own initiative; her husband disapproved. At that time the game was still on of establishing Mr. Chapin in the minds of his friends as a dangerous and murderous fellow, without involving him in any demonstrable guilt. He already suspected that I might uncover him, and his wife's bloody neck was a red herring, though her own idea.—Well. She could not very well have expected to kill me with a knife, since none could be long enough to reach a vital spot; I suppose no gun was available, or perhaps she mistrusts them as I do. Perhaps she meant merely to hack me into acquiescence; and of course she had in reserve my anxiety as to the peril of your situation. At all events, her purpose was to force me to reveal the skulduggery by which her husband had been entrapped. I was to write it. She had pen and paper with her. That attention to detail endeared her to me."

"Yeah. And?"

He drank beer. "Nothing much. You know my fondness for talking. It was an excellent opportunity. She was calm from the outset. She and I have much in common—for instance, our dislike of perturbation. It would have been instructive to see her using the knife on the back of her neck that day, I would wager she did it much as one trims a chop. After I had explained the situation to her, we discussed it. The moment arrived when it seemed pointless to continue our conference in that cold, dark forbidding spot, and besides, I had learned what had happened to you. She seemed so uncertain as to what she had used to flavor your coffee that I thought it best to reach a telephone with as little delay as possible.—Ah! Mr. Hibbard, I trust the long afternoon has been fairly tolerable."

Hibbard walked in, looking a little groggy, still wearing my brown necktie. Behind him came Fritz, to announce dinner.

# Chapter 21

They piled in early. By nine o'clock ten of them had already arrived, checked off on my list, and I was doing the honors. Four of them I hadn't seen before: Collard and Gaines from Boston, Irving from Philadelphia and Professor Mollison of Yale. Mike Ayers, stony sober on arrival, helped me get drinks around. At nine sharp Leopold Elkus joined the throng. I had no idea what Wolfe had told him to get him there; anyway there he was, and what he wanted to drink was a glass of port, and I restrained an impulse to tell him there was no nitroglycerin in it. He recognized me and acted gracious. Some more came, among them Augustus Farrell, who had phoned on Saturday that he was back from Philadelphia and had landed the commission for Mr. Allenby's library. Wolfe, surmising that what he was really phoning about was the twenty bucks due him for Wednesday's work, had had me mail him a check.

They didn't seem as subdued as they had a week before. They took to the drinks with more gusto, and gathered in groups and talked, and two or three of them even came up to me and got impatient. Collard, the Boston textile man who owned the cliff that Judge

Harrison had fallen off of, told me he hoped to see the last act of the opera, and I said I was sorry but I myself had had to give up that hope long ago. I overheard Elkus telling Ferdinand Bowen that it appeared likely that Nero Wolfe was in an advanced stage of megalomania, and tried to get Bowen's reply but missed it.

There were fifteen of them present at a quarter past nine, which was the time Wolfe had told me he would make his entrance.

It was a good entrance all right. He did it in perfect style. I was watching for him, not to miss it. He came in, three paces in, and stood there, until they had all turned to look at him and the talking had stopped. He inclined his head and used his resonance: "Good evening, gentleman." Then he faced the door and nodded at Fritz, who was standing on the threshold. Fritz moved aside, and Andrew Hibbard walked in.

That started the first uproar. Pratt and Mike Ayers were the quickest to react. They both yelled "Andy!" and jumped for him. Others followed. They encircled him, shouted at him, grabbed his hands and pounded him on the back. They had him hemmed in so that I couldn't see any of him, to observe what kind of psychology he was taking it with. It was easy to imagine, hearing them and looking at them, that they really liked Andy Hibbard. Maybe even Drummond and Bowen liked him; you've got to take the bitter along with the sweet.

Wolfe had eluded the stampede. He had got to his desk and lowered himself into his chair, and Fritz had brought him beer. I looked at him, and was glad I did, for it wasn't often he felt like winking at me and I wouldn't have wanted to miss it. He returned my look and gave me the wink, and I grinned at him. Then he drank some beer.

The commotion went on a while longer. Mike Ayers came over to Wolfe's desk and said something which I couldn't hear on account of the noise, and Wolfe nodded and replied something. Mike Ayers went back and began shooing them into chairs, and Cabot and Farrell helped him. They subsided. Pratt took Hibbard by the arm and steered him to one of the big armchairs, and then sat down next to him and took out his handkerchief and wiped his eyes.

Wolfe started the ball rolling. He sat pretty straight, his forearms on the arms of his chair, his chin down, his eyes open on them.

"Gentlemen. Thank you for coming here this evening. Even if we should later come to disagreement, I am sure we are in accord as to the felicitous nature of our preamble. We are all glad that Mr. Hibbard is with us. Mr. Goodwin and I are gratified that we were able to play the Stanley to his Livingstone. As to the particular dark continent that Mr. Hibbard chose to explore, and the method of our finding him, those details must wait for another occasion, since we have more pressing business. I believe it is enough at present to say that Mr. Hibbard's disappearance was a venture on his own account, a sally in search of education. That is correct, Mr. Hibbard?"

They all looked at Hibbard. He nodded. "That's correct."

Wolfe took some papers from his drawer, spread them out, and picked one up. "I have here, gentlemen, a copy of the memorandum of our agreement. One of my undertakings herein was to remove from you all apprehension and expectation of injury from the person or persons responsible for the disappearance of Andrew Hibbard. I take it that that has been accomplished? You have no fear of Mr. Hibbard himself?—Good. Then that much is done." He paused to look them over, face by face, and went on. "For the rest, it will be necessary to read you a document." He put the memorandum down and picked up another paper, sheets clipped to a brown paper jacket. "This, gentlemen, is dated November twelfth, which is today. It is signed with the name of Paul Chapin. At the top it is headed, CONFESSION OF PAUL CHAPIN REGARDING THE DEATHS OF WILLIAM R. HARRISON AND EUGENE DREYER AND THE WRITING AND DISPATCHING OF CERTAIN INFORMATIVE AND THREATENING VERSES. It reads as follows—"

Cabot the lawyer butted in. He would. He interrupted: "Mr. Wolfe. Of course this is interesting, but in view of what has happened do you think it's necessary?"

"Quite." Wolfe didn't look up. "If you will permit me:

> "I, Paul Chapin, of 203 Perry Street, New York City, hereby confess that I was in no way concerned in the death of Judge William R. Harrison. To the best of my knowledge and belief his death was accidental.
>
> I further confess that I was in no way concerned in the death of Eugene Dreyer. To the best of my knowledge and belief he committed suicide.
>
> I further confess—"

There was an explosive snort from Mike Ayers, and mutterings from some of the others. Julius Adler's mild sarcastic voice took the air: "This is drivel. Chapin has maintained throughout—"

Wolfe stopped him, and all of them. "Gentlemen! Please. I ask your indulgence. If you will withhold comments until the end."

Drummond squeaked, "Let him finish," and I made a mental note to give him an extra drink. Wolfe continued:

> "I further confess that the verses received by certain persons on three separate occasions were composed, typed and mailed by me. They were intended to convey by inference the information that I had killed Harrison, Dreyer and Hibbard, and that it was my purpose to kill others. They were typed on the typewriter in the alcove of the smoking-room at the Harvard Club, a fact which was discovered by Nero Wolfe. That ends my confession. The rest is explanation, which I offer at Nero Wolfe's request.
>
> The idea of the verses, which came to me after Harrison's death, was at first only one of the fantasies which occupy a mind accustomed to invention. I composed them. They were good, at least for one purpose, and I decided to send them. I devised details as to paper, envelopes and typing which would leave no possibility to proving that they had been sent by me. They worked admirably, beyond my expectations.
>
> Three months later the death of Dreyer, and the circumstances under which it occurred, offered another opportunity which of course was irresistible. This was more risky than the first, since I had been present at the gallery

*that afternoon, but careful consideration convinced me that there was no real danger. I typed the second verses, and sent them. They were even more successful than the first ones. I need not try to describe the satisfaction it gave me to fill with trepidation and terror the insolent breasts which for so many years had bulged their pity at me. They had called themselves the League of Atonement—Oh yes, I knew that. Now at last atonement had in fact begun.*

*I supplemented the effect of the verses verbally, with certain of my friends, whenever a safe opportunity offered, and this was more fertile with Andrew Hibbard than with anyone else. It ended by his becoming so terrified that he ran away. I do not know where he is; it is quite possible that he killed himself. As soon as I learned of his disappearance I decided to take advantage of it. Of course if he reappeared the game was up, but I had not supposed that I could continue the business indefinitely, and this was too good a chance to be missed. I sent the third verses. The result was nothing short of magnificent, indeed it proved to be too magnificent. I had never heard of Nero Wolfe. I went to his office that evening for the pleasure of seeing my friends, and to look at Wolfe. I saw that he was acute and intuitive, and that my diversion was probably at an end. An attempt was made by my wife to impress Wolfe, but it failed.*

*There are other points that might be touched upon, but I believe none of them require explanation. I would like to mention, though, that*

*my testimony on the witness-stand regarding
my reason for writing my novel* Devil Take the
Hindmost, *was in my opinion a superlative bit
of finesse, and Nero Wolfe agrees with me.*

*I will add that I am not responsible for the
literary quality of this document. It was written by Nero Wolfe.*

> *Paul Chapin.*"

Wolfe finished, dropped the confession on the
table, and leaned back. "Now, gentlemen. If you wish
to comment."

There were mumblings. Ferdinand Bowen, the
stockbroker, spoke up: "It seems to me Adler has
commented for all of us. Drivel."

Wolfe nodded. "I can understand that viewpoint.
In fact, I suppose that under the circumstances it is
inevitable. But let me expound my own viewpoint. My
position is that I have met my obligations under the
memorandum and that the payments are due."

"My dear sir!" It was Nicholas Cabot. "Preposterous."

"I think not. What I undertook to do was to remove
your fear of Paul Chapin. That's what it amounts to,
with the facts we now have. Well: as for Andrew
Hibbard, here he is. As for the deaths of Harrison and
Dreyer, it should have been obvious to all of you, from
the beginning, that Chapin had nothing to do with
them. You had known him all his mature life. I had
merely read his books; but I was aware last Monday
evening, when you gentlemen were here, that Chapin
could not possibly commit a premeditated murder, and
not even an impromptu one unless suddenly de-
mented. And you, Mr. Hibbard, a psychologist! Have

you read Chapin's books? Why are they so concerned with murder and the delight of it? Why does every page have its hymn to violence and the brute beauty of vehement action? Or, to change heroes, why did Nietzsche say, *Thou goest to woman, forget not thy whip*? Because he had not the temerity to touch a woman with the tip of a goose-feather. The truth is that Paul Chapin did murder Harrison and Dreyer, and all of you. He has murdered you, and will doubtless do so again, in his books. Let him, gentlemen, and go on breathing.

"No. Harrison and Dreyer and Hibbard are out of it. Consult the memorandum. There remains only the matter of the warnings. Chapin admits he sent them, and tells you how and why and where. The trilogy is done. There will be no sequels, and even if there were I should not suppose they would alarm you. If he should desire to use the same typewriter again he would have to come to this office for it, for it rests there on Mr. Goodwin's desk."

They all looked, and I moved out of the way so they could see it. Wolfe drank beer, and wiped his lips. He resumed:

"I know, of course, where the trouble lies. Paul Chapin is in the Tombs charged with the murder of Dr. Burton. If that had not happened, if Dr. Burton were here with us this evening alive and well, I have no doubt that all of you would acquiesce in my position. I have done the work I was engaged for. But as it is, you are confused; and what confuses you is this, that whereas you formerly had no security at all against Paul Chapin's injurious designs, you now have more than you need. I offer you the security I undertook to get for you, but you are no longer interested in it because you already have something just as good:

namely, that Chapin is going to be electrocuted and can no longer murder you even in books.—Mr. Cabot, I ask you as a lawyer, is that exposition of the situation correct? What do you think of it?"

"I think . . ." Cabot pursed his lips, and after a moment went on, "I think it is remarkably ingenious rubbish."

Wolfe nodded. "I would expect you to. I take it, gentlemen, that Mr. Cabot's opinion is approximately unanimous. Yes?—So it becomes necessary for me to introduce a new consideration. This: that Chapin did not kill Dr. Burton, that I can establish his innocence, and that if tried he will be acquitted."

That started the second uproar. It began as a muttering of incredulity and astonishment; it was Leopold Elkus that put the noise in it. He jumped out of his chair and ran around Wolfe's desk to get at him and grabbed his hand and began pumping it. He seemed to be excited; he was yelling at Wolfe something about justice and gratitude and how great and grand Wolfe was; I didn't hear anything about megalomania. The others, busy with their own remarks, didn't pay any attention to him. Mike Ayers, roaring with laughter, got up and went to the table for a drink. I got up too, thinking I might have to go and haul Elkus off of Wolfe, but he finally trotted back to the others, gesticulating and still talking. Wolfe lifted his hand at them:

"Gentlemen! If you please. I seem to have startled you. Similarly, I suppose, the police and the District Attorney will be startled, though they should not be. You of course expect me to support my statement with evidence, but if I do that I must ask you for more impartiality than I observe at the moment on most of your faces. You cannot be at the same time juridical and partisan, at least not with any pretense at competence.

"I offer these items. First, at a few minutes before seven on Saturday evening Paul Chapin answered the telephone in his apartment. It was Dr. Burton, who asked Chapin to come to see him immediately. A little later Chapin left to go to Ninetieth Street, arriving there at seven-thirty. But there was something wrong with that telephone call, namely, that Dr. Burton never made it. For that we have the word of his wife, who says that her husband telephoned no one around that time Saturday. It seems likely, therefore, that there was somewhere a third person who was taking upon himself the functions of fate.—I know, Mr. Adler. And I think I perceive, Mr. Bowen, that your face carries a similar expression. You would ask if I am gullible enough to believe Mr. Chapin. I am not gullible, but I believe him. He told his wife of the telephone call, and she told me; and there is the switchboard operator at the Chapin apartment house.

"Item two. Consider the details of what is supposed to have happened in the Burton foyer. Dr. Burton took the pistol from his desk and went to the foyer. Chapin, there waiting for him, took the pistol from him, shot him four times, turned out the light, threw the pistol on the floor and then got down on his hands and knees to look for it in the dark. What a picture! According to the story of Mrs. Burton and of the maid, Dr. Burton had been in the foyer not more than six seconds, possibly less, when the shots were fired. Burton was a good-sized man, and powerful. Chapin is small and is handicapped by a major deformity; he cannot even walk without support. Well . . . I am going to count six seconds for you. One . . . two . . . three . . . four . . . five . . .

six. That was six seconds. In that space of time, or less, the crippled Chapin is supposed to have got the gun from Burton's pocket, God knows how, shot him, dropped the gun, hobbled to the switch to turn off the light, and hobbled back to the table to fall to the floor. In your juridical capacity, gentlemen, what do you think of that?"

Leopold Elkus stood up. His black eyes were not floating back into his head now; he was using them for glaring. He let the bunch have the glare, right and left, saying loudly and clearly, "Anyone who ever believed that is no better than a cretin." He looked at Wolfe. "I shall have apologies for you, sir, when this kindergarten is over." He sat down.

"Thank you, Dr. Elkus.—Item three, for what conceivable reason did Chapin turn out the light? I shall not take your time by listing conjectures only to have you reject them as I have done. Make your own when you have leisure for it, if it amuses you. I only say, the actions even of a murderer should be in some degree explicable, and to believe that Chapin shot Burton and then hobbled to the wall to turn out the light is to believe nonsense. I doubt if any of you believe that. Do you?"

They looked at one another as if, having no opinions of their own, they would like to borrow one. Two or three shook their heads. George Pratt spoke up, "I'll tell you what I believe, Wolfe. I believe we hired you to get Paul Chapin into trouble, not out of it." Drummond giggled and Mike Ayers laughed. Nicholas Cabot demanded:

"What does Chapin have to say? Did he shoot or didn't he? Did he turn out the light or didn't he? What does he say happened during those six seconds?"

Wolfe shook his head and his cheeks unfolded a

little. "Oh no, Mr. Cabot. It is possible that Mr. Chapin will have to tell his story on the witness-stand in his own defense. You can hardly expect me to disclose it in advance to those who may consider themselves his enemies."

"What the hell, no one would believe him anyway." It was Ferdinand Bowen relieving himself. "He'd cook up a tale, of course."

Wolfe turned his eyes on Bowen, and I had mine there too. I was curious to see if he would take it. I didn't think he would, but he did; he kept his gaze steady back at Wolfe.

Wolfe sighed. "Well, gentlemen, I have presented my case. I could offer further points for your consideration: for instance, the likelihood that if Chapin intended to kill Dr. Burton as soon as he set eyes on him he would have gone provided with a weapon. Also, Chapin's constitutional incapacity for any form of violent action, which I discovered through his novels, and which all of you must be acquainted with as a fact. And in addition, there are items of evidence which I cannot divulge to you now, out of fairness to him, but which will certainly be used should he come to trial. Surely, surely I have offered enough to show you that if your minds have been cleared of any fear of injury from Paul Chapin, it is not because a policeman found him sitting in Dr. Burton's foyer, stunned by an event he could not have foreseen; it is because I have laid bare the purely literary nature of his attempt at vengeance. The question is this, have I satisfactorily performed my undertaking? I think I have. But it is you who are to decide it, by vote. I ask you to vote yes.—Archie. If you will please call the names."

They began to talk. Bowen muttered to his neighbor, Gaines of Boston, "Pretty slick, he's a damn fool if he thinks we'll fall for it." Elkus glared at him. I caught a few other observations. Cabot said to Wolfe, "I shall vote no. In case Chapin does get an acquittal, and evidence is presented—"

Wolfe nodded at him. "I am aware, Mr. Cabot, that this vote is not the last dingdong of doom. As you shall see, if I lose." He nodded at me, and I started the roll call. On the list I was using they were alphabetical.

"Julius Adler."

"No. I would like to say—"

Wolfe cut him off. "The no is sufficient. Proceed, Archie."

"Michael Ayers."

"Yes!" He made it emphatic. I thought, good for him, with two weeks' wages up.

"Ferdinand Bowen."

"No."

"Edwin Robert Byron."

"Yes." That evened it up.

"Nicholas Cabot."

"No."

"Fillmore Collard."

"Yes." Wowie. Nine thousand berries. I paused because I had to look at him.

"Alexander Drummond."

"No." Sure, the damn canary.

"Leopold Elkus."

"Yes!" And it was even again, four and four.

"Augustus Farrell."

"Yes."

"Theodore Gaines."

"No."

"L. M. Irving."

"No."

"Arthur Kommers."

"No." Three out-of-town babies, three noes in a row, and I hoped Wolfe was proud of his long-distance phoning.

"Sidney Lang."

"Yes."

"Archibald Mollison."

"Yes."

It was even again, seven and seven, and just one more to go, but I knew what it would be before I called it. It was George Pratt, the Tammany bird who had tried to get Inspector Cramer worried about his four grand. I said it:

"George R. Pratt."

"No."

I counted them over to make sure, and turned to Wolfe: "Seven yeses and eight noes."

He didn't look at me. They all began talking. Wolfe had rung for another bottle of beer, and now he opened it, poured a glass, watched the foam go down in front of him, but he didn't look at it. He drank some more beer, and wiped his lips with his usual care. Then he leaned back and shut his eyes. They were all talking, and two or three of them directed questions or remarks at him, but he kept his eyes closed and paid no attention. Leopold Elkus walked to the desk and stood and looked at him a minute, and then went back again. They were getting louder, and the arguments were warming up.

Finally Wolfe came to. He opened his eyes, and saw that a fresh bottle of beer had arrived, which I had attended to, and opened it and drank some. Then he picked up a paperweight and rapped on the desk. They looked around, but went on talking. He rapped again, and they began to quiet down.

He spoke. "Gentlemen. I must again ask your indulgence—"

But Cabot was feeling his oats. He broke in, snappy: "We have voted. According to the memorandum, that settles it."

Wolfe got snappy too. "It settles that vote, sir. It does not settle the destiny of the human race. If you wish to leave us, of course you may, but we would still have a quorum without you.—Good. I have two appeals to make. First, to those eight who voted no. Please heed me. I appeal to each and all of you—you understand, to each one of you—to change your vote to yes. I have a specific reason to hope that one of you will decide to change. Well, gentlemen? I shall give you one minute."

They shook their heads. One or two spoke, but mostly they were silent, gazing at Wolfe. There had been a new tone in his voice. He had taken out his watch and kept his eyes on it. At the end of the minute he returned it to his pocket and looked up.

He sighed. "Then I must proceed to my second appeal. This time, Mr. Bowen, it is to you alone. I ask you to vote yes. You of course know why. Will you vote yes?"

They all looked at the stockbroker. Including me. He was still taking it, but not so good. He damn near stuttered, shooting it back at Wolfe. I would say he did just fair with it: "Certainly not. Why should I?" His mouth stayed open; he thought he would talk some more, and then he thought he wouldn't.

Wolfe sighed again. "Mr. Bowen, you are a simpleton.—Gentlemen, I would like to explain briefly why I have not done sooner what I am going to do now. There were two reasons: because I am not fond of interfering in affairs that are not my concern, and because it would be expensive for me. To be exact, it will cost me twelve hundred dollars, the amount of Mr. Bowen's payment under the memorandum. Besides that, as I have said, it was none of my business. If any person is suspected of having committed a crime, and if I am offered a sufficient sum of money to catch him up, I will do it. That is my business. I understand that there are individuals who will undertake to apprehend wrongdoers, especially murderers, without being paid for it. They do it, I presume, for amusement, which is not astonishing when you consider what odd diversions have been sought by various members of our race. I myself have other means of escaping boredom, but this is the only one I have developed of avoiding penury. I will hunt anyone down if you pay me enough. But no one has offered to pay me for discovering the murderer of Dr. Burton. By exposing him and delivering him to justice I shall lose twelve hundred dollars, but I shall ensure the collection of a larger sum.—Now. Mr. Farrell, would you mind moving to another chair? If you please. And you, Archie, take the seat Mr. Farrell is vacating, next to Mr. Bowen."

I moved. My eye hadn't left Bowen since Wolfe had asked him to vote yes, and now all eyes were on him. Nobody was saying a word. The stockbroker was up against it. By skating all around him with inference and insinuation but not directly accusing him, and prolonging it, Wolfe had him plenty perplexed. The others staring at him didn't help him any. I suppose he was trying to decide whether it was time for him to jump up and begin resenting things. He didn't glance at me as I sat down by him; he was looking at Wolfe.

Wolfe was on the phone. He kept his usual tempo, taking his time, though he had to try three numbers before he reached the man he wanted. He finally got him. Nobody on the chairs moved by a hair while he was talking.

"Inspector Cramer? This is Nero Wolfe. That's right. Good evening, sir.—Inspector, I would like you to do me a favor. I have guests in my office, and no leisure at present for long explanations. I believe you know how much reliance may be placed in any positive statement I may make. Well. Will you send a man to my office—perhaps two would be better—for the murderer of Dr. Loring A. Burton? I have him here.— No. No, indeed. I beg you, explanations can come later.—Of course, proof; what good is certainty without proof.—By all means, if you wish to come yourself. Certainly."

He pushed the phone back, and Bowen jumped up. His knees were trembling, and so were his little lady-hands, which I was watching to see that he didn't make a pass. I took advantage of his being up to feel his rear for a gun; and my hands on him startled him. He forgot what he was going to say to Wolfe and turned on me, and by God he hauled off and kicked me on the shin. I got up and grabbed him and pushed him back into his chair and observed to him:

"You try another friendly gesture like that and I'll paste you one."

Drummond, who had been sitting next to Bowen, on the other side, moved away. Several others got up. Wolfe said:

"Sit down, gentlemen.—I beg you, there is no occasion for turmoil.—Archie, if you will kindly bring Mr. Bowen closer; I would like to see him better while talking to him. If it is necessary to prod him, you may do so."

I stood up and told the stockbroker to find his feet.

He didn't move and he didn't look up; his hands were in his lap twisting in a knot and there were various colors distributed over his face and neck and I was surprised not to see any yellow. I said, "Get a move on or I'll move you." From behind me I heard George Pratt's voice:

"You don't have to prove you're tough. Look at the poor devil."

"Yeah?" I didn't turn because I didn't care to take my eyes off of Bowen. "Was it your shin he kicked? Speak when you're spoken to."

I grabbed Bowen's collar and jerked him up, and he came. I admit he was pitiful. He stood for a second trying to look around at them, and he tried to keep the quaver out of his voice: "Fellows. You understand why . . . if I don't say anything now to . . . to this ridiculous . . ."

He couldn't finish it anyhow, so I hauled him away. I put a chair up and sat him in it, then I perched on the edge of Wolfe's desk so as to face him. Two or three of the bunch got to their feet and approached us. Wolfe turned to face the stockbroker:

"Mr. Bowen. It gives me no pleasure to prolong your discomfiture in the presence of your friends, but in any event we must wait until the police arrive to take you away. Just now you used the word ridiculous; may I borrow it from you? You are the most ridiculous murderer I have ever met. I do not know you well enough to be able to say whether it was through vast stupidity or extraordinary insouciance; however that may be, you planned the most hazardous of all crimes as if you were devising a harmless parlor game.

"I am not merely taunting you; I am depriving you of your last tatters of hope and courage in order to break you down. You stole a large sum from Dr.

Burton through his account with your firm. I know
nothing of the mechanism of your theft; that will be
uncovered when the District Attorney examines your
books. You found that Dr. Burton had discovered the
theft, or suspected it, and on Saturday you went to his
apartment to appeal to him, but already you had
arranged an alternative in case the appeal failed. You
were with Burton in his study. He went to his wife's
room to ask her if she cared enough for Estelle Bowen
to make a big sacrifice for her, and his wife said no.
Burton returned to the study and you got your answer; but during his absence you had got his automatic
pistol from the drawer of his desk and put it in your
pocket. Since you were his close friend, you had
probably known for a long time that he kept a gun
there; if not, you heard him in this room a week ago
tonight telling all of us that on the occasion of Paul
Chapin's last visit to him he had got the gun from the
drawer before he went to see Chapin in the foyer.
Would you like a drink?"

Bowen made no reply or movement. Mike Ayers
went to the table and got a shot of rye and came over
with it and offered it to him, but Bowen paid no
attention. Mike Ayers shrugged his shoulders and
drank it himself. Wolfe was going on:

"Soon you left, at twenty minutes past six. No one
went to the foyer with you; or if Burton did go, you
pushed the button on the edge of the door as you went
out, so it would not lock, and in a moment re-entered.
At all events, you were alone in the foyer and the
Burtons thought you had gone. You listened. Hearing
no one, you went to the telephone. You had your
gloves in your hand, and not to be encumbered with
them while phoning, you laid them on the table. But
before your call had gone through you were inter-

rupted by the sound of someone approaching in the
drawing-room. Alarmed, you ran for the concealment
which you had already decided on: the curtained closet
next to the light switch and the double doors. You got
behind the curtain in time, before Miss Burton, the
daughter of the house, came through, leaving the
apartment.

"You realized that you had left your gloves lying on
the table, and that concerned you, for you would need
them to keep fingerprints from the gun—and, by the
way, did it occur to you that the phone would show
prints? Or did you wipe them off? No matter. But you
did not at once dash out for the gloves, for you needed
a little time to collect yourself after the alarm that the
daughter had given you. You waited, and probably
congratulated yourself that you did, for almost at once
you heard the double door opening again, and footsteps, and the opening of the entrance door. It was
Dora Chapin, arriving to do Mrs. Burton's hair.

"Mr. Paul Chapin was out Saturday afternoon and
did not return until rather late. This morning on the
telephone, the switchboard operator at 203 Perry
Street told me that there was a phone call for Mr.
Chapin some fifteen or twenty minutes before he
arrived home. So it seems likely that about six-forty
you emerged from your hiding place, got the gloves,
and tried the phone again, but there was no answer
from the Chapin apartment. You returned to the
closet, and fifteen minutes later tried again. Of course
you did not know that the last phone call of yours, at
about five minutes to seven, happened to coincide with
Mr. Chapin's entrance into the hall of 203 Perry
Street; the switchboard operator called to him, and he
answered that call at the switchboard itself, so the
operator heard it. Apparently you imitated Dr. Bur-

ton's voice with some success, for Mr. Chapin was deceived. He went upstairs to his apartment for a few minutes, and then came down to take a cab to Ninetieth Street.

"After phoning Chapin you returned again to the closet and waited there, with an accelerated pulse, I presume, and an emergency demand on your supply of adrenaline. Indeed, you seem practically to have exhausted the latter. I imagine that it seemed quite a while before Chapin arrived, and you were surprised to find that it had been only thirty-five minutes since your phone call. At all events, he came, was admitted by the maid, and sat down. In your closet, you kept your ears keen to learn if he took a chair that would turn his back to you; you had your gloves on, and the gun in your right hand ready for action. Still you strained your ears, to hear the approach of Dr. Burton. You heard his steps crossing the drawing-room, and the instant the sound came of his hand on the doorknob, you moved. Here, I confess, you showed efficiency and accuracy. Your left arm shot out past the edge of the curtain, your fingers found the light switch and pushed it, and the foyer was in darkness except for the dim light that wandered through the door from the drawing-room after Dr. Burton had opened it. With the light off, you jumped from the closet, found Chapin in his chair, and shoved him off onto the floor—not difficult with a cripple, was it, Mr. Bowen? By that time Dr. Burton had approached the commotion and was quite close when you shot him, and there was enough light from the drawing-room door for you to tell where his middle was. You pulled the trigger and held it for four shots, then threw the gun to the floor—and made your exit, after closing the double door. In the hall you ran to the stairs, and ran down them. There were only four flights, and one more to the basement, and a short stretch of hall to the service entrance. You calculated that even if you encountered someone, there would be no great danger in it, for the guilt of Paul Chapin would be so obvious that no questions would be asked of anyone outside of the apartment.

"Now, Mr. Bowen, you made many mistakes, but none so idiotic as your sole reliance on Chapin's obvious guilt, for that one was the father of all the others. Why in the name of heaven didn't you turn on the light again as you went out? And why didn't you wait until Chapin and Burton had talked a minute or two before you acted? You could have done just as well. Another inexcusable thing was your carelessness in leaving the gloves on the table. I know; you were so sure that they would be sure of Chapin that you thought nothing else mattered. You were worse than a tyro, you were a donkey. I tell you this, sir, your exposure is a credit to no one, least of all to me. Pfui!"

Wolfe stopped, abruptly, and turned to ring for Fritz, for beer. Bowen's fingers had been twisting in and out, but now they had stopped that and were locked together. He was shaking all over, just sitting in his chair shaking, with no nerve left, no savvy, no nothing; he was nothing but a gob of scared meat.

Leopold Elkus came up and stood three feet from Bowen and stood staring at him; I had a feeling that he had a notion to cut him open and see what was inside. Mike Ayers appeared with another drink, but this time it wasn't for Bowen, he held it out to me and I took it and drank it. Andrew Hibbard went to my desk and got the telephone and gave the operator the number of his home. Drummond was squeaking something to George Pratt. Nicholas Cabot passed around

Bowen's chair, went up to Wolfe and said to him in a tone not low enough for me not to hear:

"I'm going, Mr. Wolfe. I have an appointment. I want to say, there's no reason why you shouldn't get that twelve hundred dollars from Bowen. It's a legal obligation. If you'd like me to handle the collection I'd be glad to do it and expect no fee. Let me know."

That lawyer was tough.

# Chapter 22

Three days later, Thursday around noon, we had a caller. I had just got back from taking a vast and voluminous deposit to the bank, and was sitting at my desk bending my thoughts towards a little relaxation in the shape of an afternoon movie. Wolfe was in his chair, leaning back with his eyes shut, still and silent as a mountain, probably considering the adequacy of the plans for lunch.

Fritz came to the door and said: "A man to see you, sir. Mr. Paul Chapin."

Wolfe opened his eyes to a slit, and nodded. I whirled my chair around, and stood up.

The cripple hobbled in. It was a bright day outside, and the strong light from the windows gave me a better look at him than I had ever had. I saw that his eyes weren't quite as light-colored as I had thought; they were about the shade of dull aluminum; and his skin wasn't dead pale, it was more like bleached leather, it looked tough. He gave me only half a glance as he thumped across to Wolfe's desk. I moved a chair around for him.

"Good morning, Mr. Chapin." Wolfe nearly opened his eyes. "You won't be seated? I beg you . . .

thanks. It gives me genuine discomfort to see people stand. Allow me to congratulate you on your appearance. If I had spent three days in the Tombs prison, as you did, I would be nothing but a wraith, a tattered remnant. How were the meals? I presume, unspeakable?"

The cripple lifted his shoulders, and dropped them. He didn't appear to be settling down for a chat; he had lowered himself onto the edge of the chair I had placed for him, and perched there with his stick upright in front and both his hands resting on the crook. His aluminum eyes had the same amount of expression in them that aluminum usually has. He said:

"I sit for courtesy. To relieve you of discomfort. For a moment only. I came for the pair of gloves which you removed from my box."

"Ah!" Wolfe's eyes opened the rest of the way. "So your blessings are numbered. Indeed!"

Chapin nodded. "Luckily. May I have them?"

"Another disappointment." Wolfe sighed. "I was thinking you had taken the trouble to call to convey your gratitude for my saving you from the electric chair. You are, of course, grateful?"

Chapin's lips twisted. "I am as grateful as you would expect me to be. So we needn't waste time on that. May I have the gloves?"

"You may.—Archie, if you please. To me."

I got the gloves from a drawer of my desk and handed them across to Wolfe. He came forward in his chair to place them in front of him on his own desk, one neatly on top of the other, and to smooth them out. Chapin's gaze was fastened on the gloves. Wolfe leaned back and sighed again.

"You know, Mr. Chapin, I never got to use them. I retained them, from your box, to demonstrate a point

Monday evening by showing how nearly they fitted Mr. Bowen, thus explaining how Dora Chapin—your wife—could mistake Mr. Bowen's gloves for a pair of Mrs. Burton's; but since he wilted like a Dendrobium with root-rot there was no occasion for it. Now"— Wolfe wiggled a finger—"I don't expect you to believe this, but it is nevertheless true that I halfway suspected that your knowledge of the contents of your box was intimate enough to make you aware of the absence of any fraction of the inventory; so I did not return these. I kept them. I wanted to see you."

Paul Chapin, saying nothing, took a hand from his walking-stick and reached out for the gloves. Wolfe shook his head and pulled them back a little. The cripple tossed his head up.

"Just a morsel of patience, Mr. Chapin. I wanted to see you because I had an apology to make. I am hoping that you will accept it."

"I came for my gloves. You may keep the apology."

"But, my dear sir!" Wolfe wiggled a finger again. "Permit me at least to describe my offense. I wish to apologize for forging your name."

Chapin lifted his brows. Wolfe turned to me:

"A copy of the confession, Archie."

I went to the safe and got it and gave it to him. He unfolded it and handed it across to the cripple. I sat down and grinned at Wolfe, but he pretended not to notice; he leaned back with his eyes half closed, laced his fingers at his belly, and sighed.

Chapin read the confession twice. He first glanced at it indifferently and ran through it rapidly, then took a squint at Wolfe, twisted his lips a little, and read the confession all over again, not nearly so fast.

He tossed it over to the desk. "Fantastic," he

declared. "Set down that way, prosaically, baldly, it sounds fantastic. Doesn't it?"

Wolfe nodded. "It struck me, Mr. Chapin, that you went to a great deal of trouble for a pitifully meager result. Of course, you understand that I required this document for the impression it would make on your friends, and knowing the impossibility of persuading you to sign it for me, I was compelled to write your name myself. That is what I wish to apologize for. Here are your gloves, sir. I take it that my apology is accepted."

The cripple took the gloves, felt them, put them in his inside breast pocket, grabbed the arms of his chair and raised himself. He stood leaning on his stick.

"You knew I wouldn't sign such a document? How did you know that?"

"Because I had read your books. I had seen you. I was acquainted with your—let us say, your indomitable spirit."

"You have another name for it?"

"Many. Your appalling infantile contumacy. It got you a crippled leg. It got you a wife. It very nearly got you two thousand volts of electricity."

Chapin smiled. "So you read my books. Read the next one. I'm putting you in it—a leading character."

"Naturally." Wolfe opened his eyes. "And of course I die violently. I warn you, Mr. Chapin, I resent that. I actively resent it. I have a deep repugnance for violence in all its forms. I would go to any length in an effort to persuade you—"

He was talking to no one; or at least, merely to the back of a cripple who was hobbling to the door.

At the threshold Chapin turned for a moment, long enough for us to see him smile and hear him say: "You will die, sir, in the most abhorrent manner conceivable to an appalling infantile imagination. I promise you."

He went.

Wolfe leaned back and shut his eyes. I sat down. Later I could permit myself a grin at the thought of the awful fate in store for Nero Wolfe, but for that moment I had my mind back on Monday afternoon, examining details of various events. I remembered that when I had left to call on Mrs. Burton Wolfe had been there discussing soda water with Fritz, and when I returned he had gone, and so had the sedan. But not to the Tombs to see Paul Chapin. He had never left the house. The sedan had gone to the garage, and Wolfe to his room, with his coat and hat and stick and gloves, to drink beer in his easy chair. And at a quarter to four it was from his room that he had telephoned me to take the box to Mrs. Chapin, to give him a chance to fake a return. Of course Fritz had been in on it, so he had fooled me too. And Hibbard shooed off to the third floor for the afternoon . . .

They had made a monkey of *me* all right.

I said to Wolfe: "I had intended to go to a movie after lunch, but now I can't. I've got work ahead. I've got to figure out certain suggestions to make to Paul Chapin for his next book. My head is full of ideas."

"Indeed," Wolfe's bulk came forward to permit him to ring for beer. "Archie." He nodded at me gravely. "Your head full of ideas? Even my death by violence is not too high a price for so rare and happy a phenomenon as that."

# The World of
# Rex Stout

Now, for the first time ever, enjoy a peek into the life of Nero Wolfe's creator, Rex Stout, courtesy of the Stout estate. Pulled from Rex Stout's own archives, here is rarely seen, never-before-published memorabilia. Each title in the Rex Stout Library will offer an exclusive look into the life of the man who gave Nero Wolfe life.

### The League of Frightened Men

Nero Wolfe goes Hollywood! A movie poster from 1937, featuring Walter Connelly as the famous Nero Wolfe.

The continuing adventures of Nero Wolfe. From the week of November 26, 1956, this comic strip picks up where the panel in *Fer-de-lance* ended.

# THE LEAGUE OF F

A COLUMBIA PICTU

Copyrighted by Columbia Pictures Corp., New York, N. Y., 1937.

# ...IGHTENED MEN

## WALTER CONNOLLY
### AS THE FAMOUS DETECTIVE, NERO WOLFE

LIONEL STANDER · EDUARDO CIANNELLI · IRENE HERVEY

This advertising is the property of Columbia Pictures Corporation and is leased pursuant to an agreement for use only in connection with the exhibition of the above motion picture and prohibiting its sub-lease or resale.

U.S.A.

# REX STOUT'S
# NERO WOLFE

A grand master of the form, Rex Stout is one of America's greatest mystery writers and Nero Wolfe, his literary creation, is one of the greatest fictional detectives of all time. Together, Stout and Wolfe have entertained—and puzzled—millions of mystery fans around the world.

## THE REX STOUT LIBRARY

An ongoing program dedicated to making available the complete set of Nero Wolfe mysteries, these special collector's editions will feature new introductions by today's best writers and never-before-published memorabilia from the life of Rex Stout.

❏ THE LEAGUE OF FRIGHTENED MEN, Introduction by
   Robert Goldsborough
   25933-4   $4.99/$5.99 in Canada
❏ FER-DE-LANCE, Introduction by Loren D. Estleman
   27819-3   $4.99/$5.99 in Canada
❏ THE RUBBER BAND, Introduction by Nelson DeMille
   25550-9   $4.99/$5.99 in Canada
❏ THE RED BOX, Introduction by  Carolyn G. Hart
   24919-3   $4.99/$5.99 in Canada
❏ WHERE THERE'S A WILL, Introduction by Dean R. Koontz
   29591-8   $4.99/$5.99 in Canada

Available at  your local bookstore or use this page to order.
Send to:   Bantam Books, Dept. BD 17
            2451 S. Wolf Road
            Des Plaines, IL  60018
Please send me the items I have checked above.  I am enclosing
$_____ (please add $2.50 to cover postage and handling). Send
check or money order, no cash or C.O.D.'s, please.

Mr./Ms._____

Address_____

City/State_____Zip_____
Please allow four to six weeks for delivery.
Prices and availability subject to change without notice.      BD 17 2/92

# Rex Stout's
# Nero Wolfe is back!

Robert Goldsborough has brilliantly re-created the sedentary supersleuth and his loyal sidekick, Archie Goodwin. Even the most devout Nero Wolfe fans are brimming with enthusiasm.

"A half dozen other writers have attempted it, but Goldsborough's is the only one that feels authentic, the only one able to get into Rex's psyche. If I hadn't known otherwise, I might have been fooled into thinking this was the genuine Stout myself."— **John McAleer, Stout's official biographer and the editor of** *The Stout Journal*

"I report with glee that Nero lives through the brilliant writing of Robert Goldsborough...I double-dare you to put it down. Triple-dare you."—**Larry King,** *USA Today*

"A smashing success...Nero and Archie are back to stay, and that's cause for dancing in the streets."—*The Chicago Sun-Times*

"Mr. Goldsborough has all of the late writer's stylistic mannerisms down pat...And Wolfe is as insufferably omniscient as ever."—*The New York Times*

❑ **THE BLOODIED IVY**      27816-9  $4.99/$5.99 in Canada
❑ **DEATH ON DEADLINE**   27024-9  $4.95/$5.95 in Canada
❑ **FADE TO BLACK**          29264-1  $4.99/$5.99 in Canada
❑ **THE LAST COINCIDENCE** 28616-1  $4.50/$5.50 in Canada
❑ **MURDER IN E MINOR**   27938-6  $3.95/$4.95 in Canada

Available at your local bookstore or use this page to order.

Send to:   Bantam Books, Dept. MC 20
            2451 S. Wolf Road
            Des Plaines, IL  60018

Please send me the items I have checked above.  I am enclosing $_____ (please add $2.50 to cover postage and handling). Send check or money order, no cash or C.O.D.'s, please.

Mr./Ms._____

Address_____

City/State_____Zip_____

Please allow four to six weeks for delivery.

Prices and availability subject to change without notice.     MC 20 2/92

# If you haven't already
## heard the good news...
# Nero Wolfe

is back in all his sedentary, gourmandizing glory.

### Thanks to **Robert Goldsborough**,
"Nero Wolfe has never been in better form."
—*Alfred Hitchcock's Mystery Magazine*

---

And now you can catch your favorite orchid-loving, overweight detective and his faithful, enterprising assistant, Archie Goodwin, on audiocassette.

☐ **THE BLOODIED IVY**, Robert Goldsborough
45141-3 $14.95/$16.95 in Canada. 180 minutes

☐ **FADE TO BLACK**, Robert Goldsborough
45247-9 $14.95/$17.95 in Canada. 180 minutes

☐ **THE LAST COINCIDENCE**, Robert Goldsborough
45182-0 $14.95/$16.95 in Canada. 180 minutes

---

Available at your local bookstore or use this page to order.
Send to:  Bantam Books, Dept. NW 2
           2451 S. Wolf Road
           Des Plaines, IL 60018
Please send me the items I have checked above.  I am enclosing $_____ (please add $2.50 to cover postage and handling). Send check or money order, no cash or C.O.D.'s, please.

Mr./Ms._____

Address_____

City/State_____Zip_____
Please allow four to six weeks for delivery.
Prices and availability subject to change without notice.   NW 2 2/92

Where Can YOU Get Murder, Mystery, Mayhem
And Enjoyment Altogether?

# THE AGATHA CHRISTIE MYSTERY COLLECTION!

Enjoy **AND THEN THERE WERE NONE** as your introductory novel in The Agatha Christie Mystery Collection. Sample this novel for 15 days—RISK FREE! If you aren't satisfied, return it and owe nothing. Keep **AND THEN THERE WERE NONE** and pay just $12.95 plus s&h (and sales tax in NY & Canada). You will then receive a new volume about once a month with the same RISK-FREE privilege!

FREE! **THE NEW BEDSIDE, BATHTUB & ARMCHAIR COMPANION TO AGATHA CHRISTIE** (a $12.95 value!!!) is yours to keep FREE, just for previewing the first novel. You'll enjoy this 362-page guide to Christie's World of Mystery.

EXCLUSIVE VALUE! These Collector's editions, bound in Sussex blue simulated leather, are not sold in any bookstores!

Remember, there is no minimum number of books to buy, and you may cancel at any time!

— — — — — — — — — — — — — — — — — — — — — — — — —

YES! Please send me AND THEN THERE WERE NONE to examine for 15 days RISK-FREE along with my FREE gift. I agree to the terms above.
Send to:  **THE AGATHA CHRISTIE COLLECTION**
          **P.O. Box 972**
          **Hicksville, NY 11802-0972**

Mr/Ms._____

Address_____

City/State_____ Zip_____
Orders subject to approval.  Prices subject to change.
Outside U.S., prices slightly higher.        41640    ACBBB